F
MIL

Miller, Linda Lael.

Knights.

$22.00

DATE			

KNIGHTS

Books by Linda Lael Miller

Knights
Pirates
Princess Annie
The Legacy
Taming Charlotte
Yankee Wife
Daniel's Bride
Caroline and the Raider
Emma and the Outlaw
Lily and the Major
My Darling Melissa
Angelfire
Moonfire
Wanton Angel
Lauralee
Memory's Embrace
Corbin's Fancy
Willow
Banner O'Brien
Desire and Destiny
Fletcher's Woman

Published by POCKET BOOKS

Linda Lael
Miller
KNIGHTS

POCKET BOOKS
New York   London   Toronto   Sydney   Tokyo   Singapore

POCKET BOOKS, a division of Simon & Schuster Inc. 1230 Avenue of the Americas, New York, NY 10020

Copyright © 1996 by Linda Lael Miller

Miller, Linda Lael.
    Knights / by Linda Lael Miller.
       p.   cm.
    ISBN 0-671-52850-5
    1. Knights and knighthood—Fiction. I. Title.
PS3563.I4173K58   1996
813'.54—dc20   95-38163
                                                                      CIP

First Pocket Books hardcover printing May 1996

10 9 8 7 6 5 4 3 2 1

POCKET and colophon are registered trademarks of Simon & Schuster Inc.

Printed in the U.S.A.

For my mother,
Hazel Bleecker Lael,
with love and gratitude for a
thousand stories and snickerdoodles,
among other things.
This one is all yours, Mom.
I love you.

Prologue

Not so long ago, and not so far away....

There was magic in this place. Not the pretend stuff, either, but the real thing.

The child Megan stood a little apart from her boarding school classmates, forgetting her loneliness for the moment as she clasped the magnificent doll in her arms and gazed in fascination at a gap in one of the abbey walls. No one else seemed to notice that the space was shimmering with specks of blue and gold and silver, and abuzz with an odd, silent music all its own.

As she looked on, the rusted iron bars of a gate shaped themselves out of nothing. Behind her, the other students chattered, pleased to pass a sunny spring afternoon outside the high, thick walls of Briarbrook School, oblivious to everything but this brief escape from their studies.

Megan took a step nearer to the gate, inexplicably drawn, though she supposed she should have been frightened. Her hold tightened on the doll as she advanced.

Just then, a fairy-tale princess appeared on the other side of the gate, smiling and beckoning. She was beautiful, in a gown of sapphire blue, with golden hair trailing down over her shoulders and past her waist. Her skin was very white, her eyes the same vivid color as her clothes.

"Megan," the lady said, in a sweet voice that reminded the child of the wind chimes on the neighbors' back porch, far away in America.

Five on her last birthday and wise beyond her years, partly because she was an only child and partly because she was very bright, Megan Saunders knew better than to speak to strangers. She glanced back, seeking permission or rebuke from one of her teachers, but as usual no one was paying any attention to her. Sometimes, she actually thought she was invisible.

Holding her doll, all she really owned except for her uniforms and books and a box full of playclothes left from her old life in America, she took another step toward the gate.

The lady crouched, her long dress pooling around her, her white hands grasping the bars loosely, for balance. She spoke again, but her words sounded strange, like another language, and Megan frowned in confusion.

"I mustn't speak to people I don't know," Megan said, addressing the doll in her arms, rather than the princess. It was not a toy, really, but an exquisite model of Queen Elizabeth I, of England, who was sometimes called Gloriana. Or so the saleslady in the toy department at Harrods had said when Megan's parents had bought it for her, as if to say they were sorry for leaving her.

Though they hadn't been, of course. They could hardly wait to get rid of Megan and go their separate ways, and they'd made no secret of it.

They were getting a divorce, her mommy and daddy, and they'd signed papers in the headmistress's office, before going away. According to one of the older girls at Briarbrook School, Megan was an orphan now, because Mommy had gone back to America forever—Erica Fairfield Saunders was the sole heiress to a large fortune and liked to play—and Daddy, a native Englishman who preferred to be called Jordan, even by his own daughter, didn't want to be "tied down." He had his career in the London theater to think about.

He also had a large chunk of Erica's inheritance.

Somewhere, too, there was money set aside for Megan, not that she cared. She was, after all, only five years old.

Raised in lavish neglect, Megan did not particularly miss

either Erica or Jordan, but she knew that other girls and boys were loved, even cherished, by their mothers and fathers, and she yearned to be like those children. To belong somewhere.

"Don't be afraid," the lady said, and Megan was somewhat startled to realize that she'd understood.

"I'm all right," she replied, puzzled but still not afraid. "How do you know my name?"

"By a kind of magic," came the answer, which Megan readily accepted. She had spent a lot of time alone, before coming to England, and she'd gotten very good at imagining things. Princesses and princes, castles and dragons were among her favorites.

"What is your name?" Megan demanded.

"Elaina," was the reply. The gate creaked on unoiled hinges as she opened it, but the sound wasn't spooky at all.

Megan looked back to see if anyone was watching, and no one was. She held out the doll for the lady Elaina's inspection. "This is Gloriana," she said.

The gateway widened. "Lovely," said Elaina, in a wonderfully gentle voice, warm as a hug.

"There are five Megans in my class at Briarwood," the child confided, close enough now that she could touch the lady if she wanted, see the weave in her splendid dress and the texture of her flowing hair. "I think that's too many, don't you?"

Elaina frowned, as though working something through. "Perhaps we ought to call you Gloriana instead," she decided. She stepped back, and Megan, more than willing to be Gloriana, passed over the threshold.

"I like that much better," the little girl said solemnly. A deep quietness had settled over the grounds, and turning, she saw the other schoolchildren as if through a dense, silent rain. They looked like ghosts, gradually fading from shadow to vapor to nothing at all.

"Do you want to go back to them, Gloriana? Back to that other world?" asked Elaina, lowering herself again, to look into her eyes. "The choice is entirely yours. You needn't stay here, if that isn't what you want."

Gloriana. It was wonderful to be called by that name.

She thought of her lonely cot in the dormitory, her tat-

tered books, and the desk in her schoolroom. Her parents
had probably forgotten all about her by now; they'd been so
anxious to get their divorce and get on with their lives. They
hadn't kissed her good-bye or promised to visit or even told
her to be a good girl.

She still cried every night, when all the lights were out,
though she knew it was silly.

"Could I live in a castle and ride a pretty pony like a
princess in a story, and marry a prince when I grow up?"
she asked.

Elaina's smile warmed her all the way through. "You shall
definitely live in a castle and have a pony—and, well, if not
a prince, might you not accept a very nice baron for a husband? You needn't decide today, since it will be many years
before you'll make a proper wife."

Gloriana nodded, looked back through the gate, and saw
with relief that the other children had not reappeared, nor
had the world they inhabited. Now there was nothing to be
seen but cobblestones and flowers, the gate and the high
abbey wall.

"I'm very hungry," Gloriana said solemnly. She'd left her
lunch, packed by the school cafeteria, aboard the bus. None
of that seemed real now; it was all blessedly far away, on
the other side of the rainbow.

"Then you must come with me," Lady Elaina replied
sweetly, offering her hand.

Gloriana accepted. "Are you a fairy godmother?" she inquired, as they walked along a narrow path weaving its way
out of the courtyard and through a maze of high stone walls.

"No," Elaina said, "definitely not."

"But you did magic." For just a moment, Megan was back,
troublesome and too smart for her own good.

"No, dear," the lady argued cheerfully, hoisting the little
girl up to stand upon a bench so that she might look straight
into her eyes. "It is you who worked a spell, not I." She
frowned, assessing Megan/Gloriana's field trip garb of jeans,
T-shirt, and sneakers. "We must do something about those
garments before anyone sees you."

"What's wrong with them?" Gloriana asked, puzzled.
Usually, the students at Briarwood wore uniforms, and to
put on regular clothes was a rare treat.

4

"None of them have been invented yet," Elaina said thoughtfully. "There will be enough questions as it is, with you just appearing out of nowhere—"

Gloriana felt a lump form in her throat and swallowed painfully. "Maybe I'll be too much trouble," she whispered. She was used to being in the way, a problem to be dealt with. She remembered how her mommy and daddy had screamed at each other, and thrown things, and referred to her as "*your* kid," as though neither wanted to admit that she beloned to them.

Elaina embraced her suddenly, almost squashing the doll between them, and when she drew back, there were tears in her eyes. "Of course you won't be any trouble at all," she said earnestly, after a few sniffles. "You are the answer to a thousand prayers. Now—come along, child. There are things we must do. . . ."

Chapter

I

Dane St. Gregory, fifth baron of Kenbrook, raised one gloved hand in a gesture of weary command. At his back, the remains of his private army came to a clattering, snuffling, and decidedly graceless halt. His charger, Peleus, an agile, muscular beast with a hide as black as the deepest fold of Lucifer's heart, planted wide hooves on the stony soil of the ridge and, nickering, tossed his massive head. Dane had bought the animal just a fortnight ago, at a horse fair in Flanders, and he'd spent a great many deniers in the process—so many that the purchase had all but emptied his purse.

The expense was well justified in Kenbrook's mind, for such sturdy mounts, full of stamina and thus ideal for fighting, were rare in England. He had only to breed the stallion to the best mares at Hadleigh, and over time, the enterprise would yield a herd of such steeds. The profits, he knew, would be substantial.

Dane drew a long breath and released it slowly, fixing his attention on the landscape. Far below, the lake glittered pale green, like a misshapen jewel, capturing the late summer afternoon sunlight, sending it dancing over a windswept surface in glimmering shards. Hadleigh Castle, that grim and

ancient fortress, boasting three baileys and twice as many
towers, loomed upon the southern shore. At the base of its
drawbridge, which spanned an empty moat, but still within
the outermost walls, huddled the small, shoddy village, also
called Hadleigh. It was a community of huts and hovels,
with sheep and swine and chickens choking the narrow
lanes, but there was an inn with a tavern and a humble
church boasting one stained-glass window—a modest depic-
tion of St. George slaying the dragon.

The grand house of Cyrus the wool merchant stood a little
apart from the others, a sturdy structure of red brick, with
a tiled roof, gardens, and a small courtyard. Doubtless, Dane
assured himself, his child-bride, Gloriana, would be eager
to return to that gracious haven. Neither Hadleigh Castle
nor Kenbrook Manor were half so hospitable, despite their
august histories and their many rooms.

Dane shifted uneasily, aching in all his old wounds. The
merchant would be furious on hearing the news he bore,
and not without cause.

He set his jaw and leaned forward, resting one forearm on
the pommel of his saddle and surveying the pleasant vista
spread before him. The marriage to Gloriana was meaningless—the chit had been a mere seven years of age when
their vows were said, after all, and he a callow lad of sixteen.
Neither of them had even been present for the ceremony;
the little girl had stayed in London Town, attended by her
doting mother, while Dane himself had already set sail for
the Continent, there to learn the lucrative soldiering trade.
The match was loveless on both sides, he reasoned, quite
unlike the one he meant to make with Mariette, and therefore, Gloriana had no cause for heartbreak. Indeed, she
might well be overjoyed to find herself free of him.

The idea, for all its vast convenience, was somehow
unsettling.

He let his gaze sweep beyond the village gates, and there,
of course, was the crumbling abbey, just a quarter mile along
the rutted road that curved around the lake like the languid
arm of a lover. The lane disappeared into a dense forest of
oak and emerged, at length, before the gates of Kenbrook
Manor.

Dane smiled. Built on the site of a Roman fortress and

boasting one squat tower, that forbidding pile of stones had been in steady decline for centuries. The roof had collapsed here and there, and in winter, icy winds swept the passageways, extinguishing lamps and torches. There were ghosts prowling about, it was said, truculent ones lacking all charms and graces. On occasion, the wolves got in and made a den of the place.

For all its shortcomings, the manor was Dane's by right, and he had always loved it. He would set about making the place habitable, and by the time he was free to take Mariette to wife, Kenbrook would be restored to its original glory. Dane meant to sire sons within its walls and raise the lads to be knights, stout fighting men to take up the cause of justice and make a father proud. He hoped for daughters, as well, pretty, accomplished girls who might make fortuitous marriages.

With a sigh, he turned to look down into the exquisite face of the young woman beside him. Resplendent upon her small dapple-gray palfrey, fresh and unruffled despite several grueling days on the roads and the turbulent crossing from Normandy before that, Mariette de Troyes favored him with a sweet, demure smile. Then she lowered her eyes, lashes fluttering.

Dane's heart swelled with pride and an emotion he reckoned to be pure adulation. "Look, Mariette," he bid her quietly, pointing toward Kenbrook Manor. "There stands our home."

Mariette adjusted her elaborate headdress, a pristine wimplelike affair that hid her hair, her crowning glory, from everyone except her servingwoman and Dane himself. Although he had not been intimate with Mariette—she was gently bred and had passed her tender years in a French nunnery—he *had* caught illicit glimpses of those lush ebony tresses on occasion. One day soon, when His Holiness had granted the proper decree, thus dissolving the sham marriage to Gloriana, it would be Dane's privilege to see and touch that splendid mane of silk, to run his fingers through it and bury his face in its fragrant softness, night and morning.

"It seems a place of sorrow," Mariette ventured to say, in a timid voice.

One thought having led to another, Dane had become so intent upon the various prerogatives of a husband that, for a moment, he didn't know what she was talking about. Following her gaze—her eyes were a soft shade of hazel—he saw that she was surveying the hall.

He felt the vaguest twinge of disappointment, far down in his belly, and disregarded the sensation immediately. "Yes," he said, rather solemnly, thinking of his unborn sons, forgetting for the moment that a score of men were rallied behind him with their ears cocked. "There has been much grief at Kenbrook over the centuries, but that time is now past. We shall fill the place to its beams with children, Mariette—our sons and daughters."

The blush in her cheek made a fetching contrast to the snowy white cloth of her headdress.

Dane took her reaction for maidenly virtue and wheeled his glistening charger about, that he might face his men. They were grinning now, a gap-toothed lot, covered in grime from the tops of their shaggy heads to the soles of their soft leather boots and smelling worse than their horses. Dane felt heat climb his neck, but he gave no other indication that he regretted speaking of personal matters within their hearing.

"A welcome awaits you at Hadleigh Castle," he told them, in a voice raised to carry. "Avail yourselves of it, but mind your manners. My brother is master there, but the rules of the company still hold, and you flout them at your peril."

The men nodded in accord and, at a signal from Dane, wheeled their mounts round and plunged—whooping at the prospects of ale and women—down the steep trail that joined the castle road below. Only one man lingered. Dane's friend, a red-haired Welshman called Maxen, was the best swordsman in the company, but for himself, and he wisely held his tongue.

Maxen and Mariette's servingwoman, Fabrienne, brought up the rear of the small procession, while Dane and his future bride led the way.

Gloriana rode astride the small, spotted horse Gareth had given her at Easter, bent low over the animal's back, her copper-gold hair a wild, tangled banner in the gentle breeze. Her kirtle, dark blue and richly embroidered at collar and cuff, was smudged and hiked halfway up her calves, revealing her bare, dirty feet. She laughed as Edward, her young brother-in-law and closest friend, drew up beside her on his own mount, a dun-colored gelding called Odin.

"God's blood, Gloriana," the boy shouted, "will you pull up?"

There was an agitated expression in Edward's pale blue eyes that went beyond the loss of yet another race, on yet another summer afternoon. Concerned, Gloriana drew back on the bridle and brought her lathered pony from a gallop to a trot and then to a walk.

"What is it?"

Edward shoved a hand through his mane of shaggy brown hair and then pointed toward the hill rising beyond Hadleigh Castle. "Look," he said, tight-lipped.

Gloriana did so, and saw a gaggle of men descending the trail on horseback, their gleeful shouts little more than a pulsing echo in the fragrant air, because of the distance. "Visitors," she said, turning her curious gaze back to Edward. His eyes were slightly narrowed, and his freckles stood out on his pale skin in complicated constellations. "How grand. They've come to pay you honor and celebrate your splendid achievement. Perhaps they will have tales to tell."

Edward stood in the stirrups of his saddle, which had belonged to both his elder brothers in turn before coming down to him. Gloriana had bought him a lovely new one at the summer fair, and it was hidden away in her chamber. Two days hence, when Edward and several other young men were to be knighted, she would present it to him as her gift. Now sixteen, he had worked toward his goal from the age of eight, and Gloriana, knowing the true measure of his accomplishment, was proud of him.

"Not visitors," he said, when some moments had passed, in a quiet and somehow odd voice. "Do you not see their colors? Green and white. These are Kenbrook's men, Glory—your husband has returned."

Gloriana's heart fluttered, for she had heard stirring tales of her mate's exploits for years; even troubadours sang of his bravery, his chivalry, his strength of heart and mien.

She resisted an urge to smooth her hair and straighten her torn and rumpled garments. She had long dreamed of Kenbrook's homecoming, of course, and in her imaginings she was always clad in an immaculate gown of malachite-green velvet, wearing a circlet of gilded oak leaves in her hair and delicately embroidered slippers upon her feet. Her present state of grooming was sadly at variance with the fantasy, and a little cry of dismay bubbled into her throat and swelled there as she shaded her eyes and peered at the oncoming party.

Dane St. Gregory rode well behind his rowdy army, his pale hair, a legacy of some Norse ancestor, gleaming brighter than burnished gold in the sunlight. There was about him an air of dignity and power and danger that gave weight to the many legends of his prowess.

With another exclamation, Gloriana spurred her patient mount off the road, skirting the gaping village gates for the orchard of apple tress that grew along the ancient wall. With Edward galloping behind her, shouting in annoyance, she rode hard for the postern leading into the garden behind her father's brick house.

It was hers now, she thought with a pang of grief as, ignoring Edward's bellowed protests, she bent from the mare's back to work the stubborn iron latch and push the gate open. A great many things were Gloriana's, for Cyrus the wool merchant and his wife, Edwenna, had perished a twelve-month before, when a fever swept through London Town. Their legacy was extensive.

Edward caught up just as she was urging the pony through the narrow passage.

"Blast it," he fumed, "this gate should have been sealed *years* ago. Suppose our enemies were to learn of it!"

"They would surely pass through," Gloriana said, in a tone full of dark and dire portent, "and skewer us all with their swords!" Leaving Edward to close the postern, she crossed the overgrown garden where she had played so happily as a little girl, when she and Edwenna were down from London Town, and hurried through the village proper. As she mounted the drawbridge, the first of Kenbrook's men were arriving at the inn, abandoning their horses in the dooryard and brawling among themselves as they made for that establishment, where passable wine and ale could be had.

"No control over his own men," grumbled Edward, who had caught up with Gloriana by then. "That's Dane for you."

Intent on a bath and fresh clothing, Gloriana ignored the comment and galloped past smiling guards into the third and outermost bailey. At last, at last, Kenbrook was home. Gloriana, now twenty, had begun to fear, secretly of course, that she would be too old to bear children by the time her husband returned from his travels. She'd had nightmares in which she was a shriveled crone, grown over with warts like a garden taken by weeds, when Dane St. Gregory finally came back to England to claim his bride.

Her heart hammering with a mingling of panic and glorious anticipation, Gloriana crossed the middle and innermost baileys and was off her horse and running toward a side entrance to Hadleigh Castle in almost the same motion. She streaked across the great hall—the stone floor was bare of rushes and servants were sweeping and scrubbing—and along the broad passage leading to her private quarters, a sumptuous apartment that had once belonged to Lady Elaina, the absent mistress of the household.

Along the way, Gloriana collided with Gareth, her elder brother-in-law and master of Hadleigh Castle, for his private chambers lay in that direction. He laughed and grasped her upper arms to steady her.

"Does the devil pursue you?" he teased. "You flee as if he does."

"Dane has come back!" Gloriana sputtered. Beyond, Edward could be heard, bursting into the great hall. There was a clatter, and one of the servants berated him good-naturedly for overturning her scrubbing pail. "I can't let Lord Kenbrook see me like this!"

Gareth's blue eyes twinkled. He resembled Dane in some ways, even though he was almost twenty years older and neither so tall nor so broad in the shoulders, and his hair, while thick and fair, had darkened to a butternut color. "Dane has come home at last? A surfeit of good news. No doubt my brother is hungry for the sight of his bride—as well he should be after so much time has passed. My guess is, he will not care overmuch if said wife looks rather more like a wood nymph than a baroness."

Gloriana pulled free of Gareth's grasp, with a murmured

and quite incoherent apology, and fled down the passage and into her own apartments. There, she flung herself into the process of hasty transformation.

In the courtyard of Hadleigh Castle, Dane dismounted and then helped Mariette down from her horse. His hands nearly spanned her waist, and it seemed that she weighed no more than the goose he'd bought at Christmas as a gift for his men. For a moment it troubled him that she was so small; even stout women ofttimes perished while giving birth to a child; the last Lady Hadleigh had died whilst bearing Edward. What chance had a creature as fragile as Mariette, when St. Gregory sons were known for their great size?

It seemed, just briefly, that a cloud passed over the sun, blotting out its light.

Dane spoke to Fabrienne, in French, but his gaze still rested upon Mariette's face, with its translucent, milk-white flesh and delicate bones. "Take your mistress inside," he said. "There, the servants will do your bidding."

Fabrienne, despite her lovely name, was a plain and halting creature, with pale, lashless eyes, protruding teeth, and hair the color of a mouse's pelt. Nevertheless, she was obedient and uncomplaining—for the moment, at least.

"Yes, my lord," she replied, with a slight curtsy. Then she took Mariette's arm and squired her carefully up the stone steps that led to the gallery. Beyond was the great hall.

Lingering in the courtyard, Dane watched the women out of sight, absorbed in thought.

Maxen, still mounted on his squat Welsh pony as he bent to claim the reins of Dane's prized stallion, interrupted. "I do not envy you, my friend," he said. "To put aside a wife for the love of another is an undertaking fraught with danger."

Dane scowled at Maxen, the only man on earth he would have trusted so unhesitatingly with his temperamental horse. "What," he asked, "makes an ugly knave like yourself an authority on the fair and fragile sex?"

Maxen countered Dane's expression with a placid smile. "Experience," he answered, reining his mount toward the second bailey, where the stables were. "I'll see that the stallion is fed and groomed. If you want sympathy later, or balm for scratches and tooth marks, look for me in the tavern."

"Scratches and tooth marks, indeed," Dane muttered, turning his back on the Welshman and starting, with resolve and a certain well-concealed trepidation, for the stone steps. Gloriana would be *happy* to be set at liberty, he promised himself. She was twenty by now, and well past her prime. Such women often welcomed the peace and solace of the convent, where they might read and sew and reflect upon seemly subjects, untroubled by the attentions of a husband.

The great hall was in a state of chaos—the floor had been cleared of rushes and swept. All around, servants knelt, scouring the ancient stone as though to rid it of some deep-settled stain. Clearly, a celebration was planned, but Dane knew he was not to be the guest of honor—he had not announced his return to Hadleigh Castle, having made the decision to come home in some haste.

A youthful, arrogant voice echoed from the musician's gallery, high overhead, causing Dane to pause in mid-stride and look up.

"And so the hero has at last bestowed himself upon us. Pray—will you tarry?"

Resting his hands on his hips, Dane assessed the speaker, a lad of tender years, and recognized Edward by his resemblance to their lost mother. The boy had been a small lad when Dane had seen him last, eager to take up the duties of a squire and forever underfoot. Letting the first comment pass, he addressed his reply to the question. "Yes," he said. "I mean to restore Kenbrook Hall and live there."

Even from that distance, the flush that suffused Edward's patrician features was clearly visible. "With your wife."

"Yes," Dane said. He would ignore his young brother's disdain; boys of that age had contentious humors in their blood and were ofttimes testy and sullen.

"And this mistress you've brought home from the Continent? Where shall she be kept?"

Dane did not reveal his irritation, which was instant and intense. He was damned if he would explain his personal affairs to a stripling calling out impudent questions from a minstrel's perch. "Go and have a swim in the lake, Edward," he counseled evenly. "Perhaps the waters will cool your overheated disposition." With that, Kenbrook dismissed the boy and started for the stairs. Fatigue had settled deep into his bones, like an aching chill, and he required strong ale, food, and an hour of solitude.

Edward said nothing, but by the time Dane had gained the second floor and found his way to his own chambers, the boy was waiting in the passageway, leaning against a wall.

Dane hid a smile and reached for the latch. So, he was tenacious, as well as swift, this young brother of his. That was surely a good omen. "What is it?" Dane inquired, as smoothly as if they had not had an exchange only moments before.

Fresh color surged into Edward's face, and his expression was sulky as he thrust himself away from the wall. He still had a few spots on his face, the marks of tempestuous youth, but he was altogether a fine-looking, stalwart lad, and though willful, he would no doubt make a good soldier. "I will not permit you to humiliate Gloriana this way," he said, after an audible swallow. "She deserves only good things."

"Yes," he said. Dane had no doubt that his erstwhile wife deserved better than him, though whether the improvement would come through entering a convent or taking another husband remained to be seen. Personally, he thought the nunnery an excellent choice.

He pushed the towering door open, and the smells of mice and mildew filled his nose. As he stepped over the threshold, Edward was directly on his heels.

The place was dank and swathed in a musty net of shadows and cobwebs. Evidently, he thought, with a rueful half-smile, his esteemed elder brother, Gareth, had not expected him to return to Hadleigh Castle at all.

"She's been waiting for you, Gloriana has," Edward babbled on, and Dane was glad of the gloom in that vast chamber, for it allowed him time to absorb the implications of what his brother was saying without revealing his reactions. Dane had not been expecting to hear that his wife had looked forward to his arrival—she'd been a mere infant when they were bound to each other and probably didn't even remember him.

He wrenched down one of the tattered tapestries that had been draped over the windows, then another. "Nonsense," he said, as welcome light and fresh air streamed into the

room. Flecks of dust sparkled in the great shafts of sunshine. "My 'wife' has not laid eyes on me more than once
or twice in all her days, and that from a distance. God's
teeth, will you look at my bed? It appears to have been a
nest for every rat in the realm."

Edward had calmed down a bit, but anger still emanated
from him like heat from a brazier. He'd hoisted himself
onto the broad sill of one of the windows, his knees drawn
up. "I will spare you the obvious retort," the boy said.

"Thank you," Dane replied, yanking down the last of the
tapestries. "I suppose it would be a waste of my time to ask
you to go and fetch a handful of servants to put this place
to rights?"

Surprisingly, Edward levered himself down from the sill,
making a royal ceremony of dusting off his leggings and
tunic. "Not at all," he answered. "I shall be happy to take
my leave of you, my lord." Green and tender stalk though
he was, he crossed the room with the dignity of a much
older man, and then he paused in the doorway. "Be gentle
in your dealings with Gloriana," he warned in parting. "You
are my brother, blood of my blood and flesh of my flesh, but
if you do milady injury of any sort, I shall see you dead
for it."

With that, Edward went out.

Dane stood in the center of that time-ravaged room, staring after Edward. He was not afraid of his younger brother
or any other mortal soul, and he certainly intended to deal
kindly and justly with the current Lady Kenbrook, but he
had been forced to take note of something important. Edward was not the boy he remembered, but a man, and one
to be reckoned with.

He smiled, then crossed the room to his bed, pulled off
the feather ticking, no doubt infested with fleas as well as
mice, and flung it aside. Exhausted, he stretched out on the
rope netting beneath and sank into the brief and vigilant but
profound sleep of a soldier.

There was a tiny courtyard off Gloriana's chamber, with
an arbor of yellow roses on one side and a stone bench on
the other. By her order—and she did feel a little guilty,
since the servants were so frightfully busy—her tub was car-

ried outside and set beneath the canopy of flowers. Warm water was brought, and Gloriana herself added lavender before shedding her clothes and stepping into the bath.

As she soaked, dreaming of her reunion with her husband, a breeze caressed the courtyard and a rainfall of golden petals descended in a scented cloud. They covered the surface of the water, like a blanket of gossamer velvet, and Gloriana told herself this was a good omen, a blessing from the Fates. This night, she would go to Kenbrook's chambers as his wife, and he would find her pleasing.

Gloriana dozed despite her excitement, lulled by the buzzing of the bees and the comforting clamor of daily life at Hadleigh Castle, a mingling of many sounds—birds chirping, horses neighing, shouts and the clanking of swords as the men-at-arms practiced their art, servants going about their business and calling out to each other.

The water was cold when Gloriana awakened; perhaps that was why her senses were instantly and acutely attuned, rather than languorous from what must have been a long nap. She knew almost before opening her eyes that she was not alone in the courtyard.

He was sitting on the stone bench, watching her, his broad shoulders slightly stooped, his hands loosely clasped and dangling between his knees. His fair hair gleamed in the changing light, and his eyes, troubled, were a fierce Nordic blue. They were, she thought as something sharp and warm pierced her heart, the eyes of a Viking.

"My lord," she said shyly, with an inclination of her head. Her hair was wet through, clammy against her cheeks and her neck.

She swallowed hard. Over the years of their marriage, she had rehearsed this meeting a hundred times, nay a thousand, but now, when it mattered, all the pretty words had fled. In her imaginings, Kenbrook had been the grandest of men, full of valor, handsome beyond bearing, strong as the proud warhorse he managed so easily. And her imaginings paled before the vital reality of the man himself.

The girlish adulation she had always felt for him was quite real, however, and now it had doubled and redoubled just since she had opened her eyes and found him there, watching her.

"You are Gloriana?" he asked, almost as if he hoped she would say she was someone else. His voice sounded hoarse, and he looked quite stunned, perhaps even feverish as he studied her.

"Yes, my lord," she said meekly.

"We must talk." There was no anger in the way he spoke, but she sensed reluctance in him and a sort of troubled resolution. Lord Kenbrook cleared his throat. "Not while you are in a state of near nakedness, of course."

Gloriana flushed with a combination of indignation and despair. Some men, she thought, would be pleased to come upon their wives in such a condition. No doubt he found her wanting, and it was unfair of him to judge her so swiftly. He had not seen her dressed in green, after all, with her hair brushed and braided through with ribbon. "We did not expect you, my lord," she said moderately. "If you had written, or sent a courier, preparations might have been made."

He had continued to stare at her, and she had the very clear impression that he hadn't heard a word she'd said. "You are not at all as I thought you would be," he remarked.

Gloriana was stung, but she made herself smile, and that dispelled some of the terrible nervousness that had heretofore tangled her tongue and scattered her thoughts. "I see," she murmured.

Dane made no move to rise from the bench. "You do not see," he said with some impatience and, to Gloriana's way of thinking, rather presumptuously. "You are twenty years of age—an old woman by anyone's reckoning. I did not think to find you so—fetching."

He'd struck close to the bone with that first comment, but he'd also called her "fetching." Gloriana was both injured and exultant.

"How very generous of you," she said, for she tended toward sauciness and had never entirely curtailed that quality. "To pronounce me fit to look upon, I mean."

Dane's golden eyebrows drew together in a frown. He stood but did not move toward Gloriana, who still huddled, shivering, in her tub. "You are also somewhat impudent," he said, with an air of distraction, as though cataloging the characteristics of a temperamental horse. "No doubt, Gareth has allowed you to do whatever you pleased while I was away—my brother has ever been indulgent, with women, with children, with servants." He paused, and a muscle flexed in his jaw. "I only hope it is not too late to render you suitable for the proper purposes of God and man," he finished.

Then, turning on one heel, Dane St. Gregory, fifth baron of Kenbrook and first husband of Gloriana St. Gregory, strode into the bedchamber. Moments later, the outer door slammed.

"I hate him," Gloriana marveled. She sank beneath the water but, with no hope of drowning, finally rose above it again. Methodically, trembling with the chill of an English afternoon fading to evening, she washed her hair, scrubbed the rest of her body, and climbed out of her bath. After a cursory toweling with a bit of rough cloth reserved for the purpose, she took her chemise, a sturdy garment made of undyed muslin, from the bush where she'd left it and wrenched it on over her head.

She was seated on the bench, where Dane had been, combing the tangles out of her hair and cursing under her breath with every tug, when Edward came out of her room and into the courtyard. He carried a clean kirtle of the palest blue, which he tossed to her, and then leaned with one foot braced against the end of the bench while she put on the gown.

"Come, Gloriana," he said, taking out a small knife and undertaking to clean his fingernails with its point, "you'll do better to dry your hair by the fire. You could be taken by a fever if you catch a chill."

Gloriana did not move. She was not fragile like other people; sickness had passed her over more times than she could count. Still, for all her physical strength, she wasn't impervious to emotion, and she teetered on the brink of tears.

"Glory?" Edward persisted.

"I'm all right," she said, somewhat snappishly, combing with a vengeance now and refusing to meet his gaze. She would not let him see her weep, though he had ever been her friend; her pride was bruised and she was too vulnerable.

Edward came and crouched before her, looking up into her face, robbing her of the last vestige of privacy. "Why do you lie?" he asked. At the same time, he reached out and took her hand, the one that had wielded the comb, and held it still. "Have the servants been carrying tales? By God, I'll have them flogged, every one, if they've uttered a word to cause you hurt."

A sense of dread came over Gloriana, like a wintry shadow thrown across her spirit. "What is there to carry tales about?" she asked, in a small voice, bracing herself for the answer. She had known all was not right, of course, by her husband's greeting, but there was clearly more to the matter.

Much more.

"Tell me, Edward," she whispered when he hesitated.

He closed his eyes for a moment, then raised himself up far enough to take a seat beside her on the bench. He held both her hands in his, stroking the knuckles with his thumbs. "I suppose it will be kinder, if you hear the news from me," he said. The pain in his face was genuine. "It's not as if such things don't happen, as if other men don't—"

Gloriana squeezed his fingers hard.

"Dane's brought his mistress home from the Continent," Edward said, forcing the words out in a reluctant rush.

Gloriana felt the color drain from her face; rage followed shock, and she rose to her feet, only to be pulled back down by Edward. It was true that other men kept mistresses, and even sired children with them, but Gloriana's view of marriage was not conventional. She'd seen the warm relationship between her father, Cyrus, and her mother, the gentle Edwenna, and the noble union shared by Gareth and his beloved Elaina. She wanted that kind of dedication, that kind of love, for herself and Dane, and she would settle for nothing less.

"Oh, Edward," she whispered, and sagged against him, her sodden hair tumbling over his tunic. "Whatever shall I do?"

He kissed her temple, her oldest and dearest friend, the boy she thought of as her brother, and wrapped his arms around her. "The solution is simple," he said tenderly. "You shall divorce the rogue and marry me."

Chapter

2

*O*ne of the massive doors of Gareth's study stood ajar, a sure sign that Lord Hadleigh expected a visit. Dane was still ruffled from his encounter with Gloriana when he stepped over the threshold.

Gareth, apparently unaware of his brother's presence, stood at one of the windows with both hands braced upon the sill, gazing toward the abbey. His thoughts could have been no plainer if they'd been written in letters of fire—even now, then, Gareth pined for his fey Elaina.

"Is she still with the nuns?" Dane asked. He spoke quietly, but his voice came out sounding rough.

His brother's broad, sturdy shoulders stiffened almost imperceptibly, as if in response to a cudgel blow, and he turned at last to face Kenbrook.

"She is no better," he said with a nod, and though he smiled, both his words and his eyes brimmed with sorrow. "But no worse. We must be thankful for whatever blessings heaven deigns to grant us."

Dane crossed the room and stood before his brother. For a long moment, the two men simply looked at each other in silence, thinking their own thoughts and sharing no part of them.

Gareth, a score older than Dane, had been a second father to him and to Edward, since their sire had been a knight, in service to the King, and thus kept himself far from Hadleigh Castle most of the time. Their father had fallen in a skirmish with the Irish when Edward was still learning to walk, and sadly, his heirs had not missed him overmuch, for he had been a stranger to them.

"It is good to have you home again," Gareth said at last, and cleared his throat. He reached out to lay a hand on Dane's shoulder. "You look well and, God be thanked, whole. Tell me—have you looked upon your wife? I dare say our Gloriana has fulfilled every promise of loveliness and virtue."

Dane had hoped the subject of Gloriana would not come up quite so quickly. He was still reeling from the sight of the woman reclining beneath a layer of yellow rose petals, presumably naked. He had expected something very different—a shriveled female, someone barren and bitter, and perhaps toothless, with wrinkles and streaks of gray in her hair.

But Gloriana was beautiful, breathtakingly so. And where she was concerned, Kenbrook's thoughts, usually so well marshaled, were ajumble. "Yes," he muttered, averting his eyes. He had seen so little of her, but he could imagine the rest only too vividly.

Finally, he managed a pained smile and touched his brother's arm. "Sit down, Gareth," he said. "There are matters we must discuss."

Frowning slightly, Gareth took a seat behind the large, unornamented oak table that served as his desk. Dane perched on a high stool nearby, catching one foot in the lowest rung as he had always done.

"I do hope," Gareth said gravely, "that you are not about to tell me you cannot stay in England. You are sorely needed here, Dane." He gestured in the direction of the hall, rising beyond the shining waters of the lake. "Kenbrook is falling into ruin, the roads are choked with bandits, and our troubles with Merrymont continue. Without your help, I fear we shall soon have naught but chaos."

Merrymont was a neighboring baron, and the enmity between his household and Hadleigh's went back for generations. Dane doubted that anyone remembered what had caused the original disagreement, but enough had happened since to ensure ongoing hostilities. "I intend to stay," he said.

Gareth heaved a sigh of relief. "Good tidings, indeed," he replied, settling back in his hard chair and assessing Dane again, very thoughtfully. "What is it, then? Say what you must, brother—we have rejoicing to do, what with your return and Edward's impending knighthood—and when you've made your speech, we'll both join your rowdy men at the tavern." He paused, and a sparkle glinted in his eyes. "Unless you want to spend the remains of the day with Gloriana, of course."

Dane swore under his breath. "No," he said wearily, shoving splayed fingers through his hair. "But we must speak of my wife, 'tis true." He paused, in misery, and then blurted, "I wish to annul the marriage to Gloriana."

The color drained from Gareth's face, and he seemed coiled in his chair, like a beast about to spring. "On what grounds?" he rasped. "By God, Dane, if you dare to impugn the lady's morals—"

Dane felt a throbbing in the side of his neck, along with a sensation of rising heat. "I do not," he interrupted sharply. "How could I, when I have not laid eyes on her in three and ten years? And that is exactly my point—Gloriana and I are strangers. We have no love for each other, as you and Elaina have, and I shall not spend whatever is left of my life with a woman I neither know nor care about. I wish to marry another."

An awful silence fell, during which Gareth remained in his chair, though Dane had the distinct impression that his brother was barely restraining himself from violence. Finally, Lord Hadleigh spoke.

"You are a knight," he said. "Where is your honor?"

The word struck Dane in the belly and quivered there like the point of a lance, even though he'd long since worked that question through for himself. "Where is the honor in sharing a house with one woman and loving another?" he asked. "Tell me, Gareth—shall I do either lady credit by making one a mistress and forcing the other to wear the meaningless mantle of 'wife'?"

At last, Gareth hoisted himself from his chair, and though he kept a careful distance, Dane noted that his brother's hands were curled into loose fists. "You are a fool," Gareth said. "No other kind of man would spurn such a one as Gloriana."

"If you are so taken with the lady," Dane suggested evenly, moving off the stool, "then marry her yourself."

Gareth turned away. "Damn your eyes, Dane, you know that is impossible."

"What I know," Dane pressed, though gently, "is that your wife is moonstruck, now weeping, now laughing, now wandering off into the countryside like a witless child. I know that she has never given you a single heir. Elaina would be none the wiser, Gareth, if you put her aside and took another wife. Or have her requirements changed since I went away? Does Elaina ask more of you these days than occasional visits and pretty trinkets?"

Gareth was a long time in facing his brother again, and when he did, there were tears glistening in his eyes. "I love Elaina," he said simply, fiercely. "What glib remedy have you to offer for *that*, Kenbrook?"

Dane met Gareth's gaze directly, though he wanted to do otherwise. He had known, after all, that the interview would be difficult, and he had steeled himself for it.

"None," he replied coolly. "I, too, am fond of Elaina. She was ever kind to me, and I would defend her against any foe—you must know that. But her mind is unstable, Gareth. It wouldn't matter to her if you kept a harem, as long as you continued to visit her at the abbey as you've always done."

Gareth sighed. "On this subject, I fear we shall never agree," he said.

"Will you tell me, then, that you have not been with a woman since Elaina's confinement began?" Dane put the question gently, but he spoke with a brother's frankness and with every expectation of an answer.

"Would that I were so noble," Gareth said, his countenance grim. There was a ewer of wine on the corner of his table, along with a half-dozen wooden cups. He poured two portions and handed one to Dane.

Kenbrook took a sip and winced. It was crude and vinegary stuff, after what he'd sampled in France and Italy. "You speak as one who repents of sin," he said to Gareth. "I am your brother, not your confessor. I make no judgments and dispense no penance."

A semblance of a smile played on Gareth's mouth, and the wine, bad as it was, had restored some of his color. "How is it," he asked wryly, "that we speak of my marriage, when it is your own that is imperiled?"

"Gloriana will be happier without me," Dane said.

Gareth made a *harumph* sound and looked thoughtful as he refilled his wine cup. "She may kill you, thus ending the dilemma for both of you."

Dane chuckled and reached for the ewer. The wine was no better than before, but with each draft, the taste bothered him less and less. The tension in his belly and between his shoulder blades began to ease.

"She'll thank me, the fair Gloriana, for my wisdom and foresight," he said with restored confidence. "If not today, then tomorrow."

Gareth arched one eyebrow, and his expression was skeptical. "Just what do you intend to *do* with Gloriana?"

"There are two choices," Dane replied. "I can send her to a nunnery or marry her off to someone else." He paused, frowning. "I don't care much for that idea, though—getting Gloriana another husband, I mean. Can't be sure he'd be good to her. But if she became a nun—"

Gareth laughed outright. "Gloriana?" he marveled. "You have been away too long, brother, and you know little of the ways of women." He held up one hand when Dane started to protest this last, and effectively silenced him. By then, Gareth's mirth had subsided to a glimmer in his eyes. "I do not speak of charming the creatures, Dane—I have no doubt that you are an accomplished womanizer. However, it would seem to me that your understanding of how they *think,* these daughters of Eve, is in woeful error. And there is still the matter of the dowry."

Dane narrowed his eyes. "The dowry?"

Gareth leaned against the windowsill, his still-muscular arms folded. "Have you forgotten, Dane? We were given gold when the marriage contract was made, a great deal of it. Gloriana is rich in her own right—she inherited considerable land, jewels, the house in the village, and several properties in London. Perhaps you are ready to part with your wife's legacy, but that still leaves the question of the gold. It has gone, Dane, and long since—we spent it, on debts and soldiers, bribes and taxes. If you spurn Gloriana, we must return every penny, in full measure, with interest."

Dane sat on the stool again. Gloriana's fortune was not a consideration and had never been, but the dowry was something else. No honorable man squandered a woman's bride-price and then put her aside, even when she had other means, both financial and physical, of attracting another husband. The money had to be repaid, and that might take years.

Gareth came to stand beside Dane, and slapped him on the shoulder. "There's no sense in worrying about it now," he said. "You have come home, after too long an absence. Tomorrow, our young brother becomes a knight. There will be time enough later to undo this coil and set matters aright."

At length, Dane let out a rough sigh and then nodded. "To the tavern," he said.

Gareth grinned and headed for the door. After only a moment's hesitation, Dane followed.

Alone in her chamber, Gloriana considered her situation. She had refused Edward's marriage proposal gently, reminding him that, for all Lord Kenbrook's obvious shortcomings, the man was her legal husband and that she, like everyone else in Christendom, was allowed but one spouse at a time. She did *not* say that she could never offer him any greater love than that which a sister held for a brother.

Edward had sighed and planted a tender kiss on Gloriana's forehead. Then, without another word, he had left her.

Now, more than an hour later, she was fully dressed, in a gown of apple-green wool, and her heavy, waist-length tresses, though quite damp, were neatly combed. Her scalp still stung a little from working out the snarls, but that was nothing compared to the smarting in her heart. Kenbrook had brought a mistress to Hadleigh Castle—it was unbelievable. Had her indignation not been greater than her pain, Gloriana might have thrown herself down on the bed and wept. As it was, fury sustained her.

It wasn't as though she were naive, Gloriana insisted silently, turning away from the large oval of polished silver that served as her mirror. Men did take mistresses—her foster father, Cyrus, had been a devoted husband to Edwenna, and yet the servants at the London house had whispered about a woman in Flanders. Her own brother-in-law, Gareth St. Gregory, who was, by Gloriana's reckoning, among the finest men in England, adored his poor Elaina, would see her want for nothing, in fact. For all his devotion, though, Gareth kept a lover, a dark-haired Irish beauty called Annabel, in a cottage beside the lake.

It was wrong, Gloriana reflected, for a man or a woman to break their wedding vows, but the reality was that good people went astray sometimes, for a thousand different reasons. She had never thought, even in her most sentimental moments, that Dane would keep himself chaste while he traveled the world, waiting for a seven-year-old bride to grow up. All Gloriana had truly expected of her husband was a chance to prove herself a spirited, attentive, and entertaining wife, and now she had been denied that opportunity, out of hand.

It was unfair treatment, that's what it was, Gloriana raged to herself, opening the largest of her three chests and surveying the wimples and headdresses inside. No proper woman went about with her hair uncovered, according to conventional standards, but Gloriana found veils cumbersome and wore them as seldom as possible. Biting her lip, she slammed the chest lid down on the whole array and walked resolutely to the door.

Supper was about to be served, and she was hungry.

Fresh rushes had been laid in the great hall, and Gloriana caught the distinctive scents of lavender and sage, dittany and mint and rue, scattered on the damp stone floor. Oil lamps, suspended from the crossbeams overhead by lengths of iron chain, glowed with costly light, and the long table, lined with guests and men-at-arms, was scoured pale. Trenchers of roast venison, capon, and rabbit were interspersed with bowls of boiled turnips and beets. On the dais was another, smaller table, where Gareth normally dined—along with Elaina, during her rare, brief visits to the castle. The steward, a Scot called Hamilton Eigg, had a place there, too, as did

Cradoc, the friar, and any honored guest. Edward also generally sat with his eldest brother, and so did Gloriana.

For the moment, only Eigg and Cradoc were in evidence,
but Gareth often came late to the table and tonight Kenbrook would surely be in his company. While Gloriana had
no objection to dining in the company of her husband, she
wasn't quite ready to break bread with his mistress.

Gloriana was standing in the middle of the great hall,
wondering whether to stay or flee, when Edward came up
beside her, caught her elbow in his hand, and guided her
toward the steps of the dais.

"Have no fear," he whispered, for he was good at divining
her thoughts. "My brothers are in the village, quaffing ale,
and are not likely to join us. The woman has a headache,
I'm told, and will keep to her room—which, it may console
you to learn, is some distance from Kenbrook's chambers."

For tonight, at least, Gloriana thought with despairing relief, she was to be spared a public introduction to her husband's lover. The reprieve was temporary, of course, but she
was grateful all the same. "I don't suppose you've managed
to find out her name," she whispered back as they stepped
together onto the dais.

"She is called Mariette," Edward answered.

Eigg and the priest rose out of deference to Gloriana, and
she offered a faltering smile and joined them on the bench.

"You have forgotten your headdress, Lady Kenbrook,"
Cradoc pointed out mildly, between spoonfuls of savory stew.
The friar was a pleasant middle-aged man with silver in his
tonsured hair and a long, crooked scar beneath his right eye.

Gloriana lowered her head to murmur a quick prayer and,
using the point of her knife, helped herself to a steaming
turnip and a slice of venison. She seldom thought of the
Time Before, in that place Edwenna said she had only imagined, but at odd moments she remembered things. Just
then, she recalled a pronged implement, called a fork, and
longed for one.

"She didn't forget," Eigg commented wryly, tearing a
hunk of brown bread from the loaf. He was younger than
Cradoc by a decade, a handsome man with dark hair and
eyes and a good head for figures. "Her ladyship, it would
seem, is wont to defy religious convention."

Normally, Gloriana did not mind the steward's teasing and even took a harmless pleasure in it. That evening, however, she was on the prickly side. "You'll get me burned for a heretic if you keep up that kind of talk," she said, in a stiff tone. "May I remind you, sir, that I attend mass every morning, as faithfully as anyone else?"

"If it's sin that intrigues you," Edward put in, bending to look around Gloriana to Eigg, "look to the lady's husband."

Eigg wiped his trencher methodically with his portion of bread, while Cradoc snatched a roast pigeon from a tray borne by a passing servant.

"And now," said the priest, chewing, "we shall suffer a discourse on virtue—from none other than Edward St. Gregory, who has done more penance than any lad between here and London."

Out of the corner of her eye, Gloriana saw Edward's color rise, and she allowed herself a smile. It was true that Edward had an uncommon gift for mischief, and no one knew that better than the friar, who had tutored them both, in their turns.

Before the youngest St. Gregory could offer a retort, there was a stir at the entrance to the hall, and Gloriana forgot her fleeting amusement.

It seemed that Gareth had come to supper after all, and Dane was beside him.

Gloriana started to rise, her first instinct being an unworthy desire to escape, but even as she changed her mind, Eigg grasped her wrist to prevent her from bolting.

"Things will be too easy for his lordship if you go," he said quietly, in a tone pitched to reach Gloriana's ears and no other's. "Stay, Lady Kenbrook, for it is your right to dine at this table."

Gloriana watched her husband stride through the hall, flushed with drink, a comradely arm around his elder brother's shoulders. They were surrounded by members of Kenbrook's seedy army, all of them bellowing a discordant version of some bawdy tavern song, and the men at the lower table joined the singing.

Gareth's hounds, waiting placidly beneath the trestle for table scraps, wriggled out from under and scattered, whining, in all directions. This phenomenon produced a swell of raucous laughter, for these were hunting dogs who had faced wild boars and dodged the spiked antlers of cornered stags.

Gloriana sat stiffly, her chin raised and her shoulders straight, watching her husband's approach. When Kenbrook drew closer, she saw that he was not so drunk as she had thought, but the knowledge was cold comfort. His eyes, blue as a stormy northern sea, were bright with merry defiance and a certain mockery.

Her hand tightened around the wooden wine goblet she shared with Edward, but she overcame the urge to fling it at her husband's head. As Dane mounted the dais and came to stand behind her, Gloriana forced her fingers to go limp, to lie flat on the tabletop.

She felt the warmth of his body against her back, even though they weren't touching, and a strange, powerful sensation surged through her, wicked and primitive. His breath brushed her neck as he bent to speak quietly into her ear, and goose bumps raced down her arms and chest, hardening her nipples where they pressed against her chemise and fostering an ache in her most personal parts.

"Go at once," Kenbrook commented evenly, "and cover your hair."

Gloriana turned on the hard bench and looked up into his face. Although he smelled of ale, his eyes were clear and he had not slurred his words. She opened her mouth to speak and then closed it again, but not because she was afraid of this stranger she had wed. She simply had no wish to provide an evening's entertainment for everyone else in the great hall.

Edward initiated a protest, but before he'd stammered out more than a few words, one of Dane's battle-hardened hands moved from Gloriana's shoulder, where it had come to rest lightly, to the boy's. It was plain by Edward's indrawn breath and pale cheeks that Dane's hold was less than gentle.

"Hold your tongue, pup," Kenbrook warned. "I will not suffer your interference."

Gloriana felt her temper slipping. "Unhand him," she hissed. "Now."

Dane chuckled and released his brother, and Gloriana imagined the bruise Edward would surely have by morning. And all because he had sought to defend her.

Slowly, and with the regal dignity she had spent years perfecting, Gloriana rose from the bench. Cheeks burning, she nonetheless offered a slight nod to Kenbrook, that being the closest thing to the accustomed curtsy she could manage at the moment, and swept past him, holding her skirts, to descend the steps of the dais.

Instead of taking a seat beside Gareth, Kenbrook followed Gloriana into the passageway outside the great hall, there to catch her elbow in a grasp so gentle that she barely felt it and, at the same time, so firm that she couldn't have escaped. Seeing no point in wasting energy only to make a fool of herself, Gloriana did not attempt to break free.

She glared up at Dane, wishing she had never learned to love him, and waited in silence.

In the light of the torches burning in the passage, Kenbrook looked more like a Viking than ever. He seemed impossibly tall, and his body exuded heat and strength. Gloriana did not need to touch him to know he would feel like a statue clothed in flesh, and his eyes, as he stared down at her in seeming consternation, were cold.

A flood of unseemly warmth rushed through her.

"Will you be returning to the great hall?" The question was odd, and there was no expression at all in Kenbrook's voice when he uttered it. "After you've covered your hair, I mean?"

"No, my lord," Gloriana said, staring pointedly at his hand until he released her. He need never know that he'd set her senses aflame, just by touching her. "I find the company most tedious, and in any case, I have no intention of covering my hair."

For a long moment, Kenbrook was silent, and plainly stunned, as though she had struck him with the flat side of a broadsword. Evidently insubordination, even in so mild a form, was almost incomprehensible to him. Or perhaps he was simply stupid.

Gloriana knew better, of course. He was known to be brilliant, especially in matters involving strategy, but she was angry enough, hurt enough, to indulge herself in purposeful misconception for a few moments.

When he spoke, his voice was calm, even pleasant. Gloriana sensed that, while Dane was not the sort to harm a woman physically, he was dangerous all the same, for he could break her heart in a thousand different ways. Her body throbbed with dark, primal desires she could not begin to define.

"As long as you are my wife, Gloriana," he said, "you will obey me."

She was tired, and Kenbrook's homecoming, however enlightening, had been a bitter disappointment. All her pretty dreams were melting away, like spring snow, and she had exhausted her store of restraint by holding her tongue in the great hall. "If you are not bound by our sacred vows, my lord," Gloriana replied, "neither am I."

"Exactly what do you mean by that?"

"I think you know," she said.

"Mariette." The name was followed by a weighted sigh.

"Your mistress," Gloriana said, in a tone of tremulous triumph. What she felt, of course, was something quite different.

"Mariette is not my mistress," Kenbrook hissed, resting his hands on his lean hips now. The light of the torches glimmered in his hair and in the beginnings of a golden beard. "I assure you, my association with the mademoiselle has been of the purest nature."

Gloriana fought back the sudden tears burning behind her eyes and aching in her throat. If she wept before this man now, she would never forgive herself. "You might have given me a chance to please you," she said, "before you brought her here to take my place."

"You do not understand—"

"I'm afraid I do," Gloriana went on. "Now, I should like to retire to my chambers and rest. This has been a most trying day."

"Yes," Kenbrook agreed, after a long and rather thunderous silence, thrusting a hand through his hair. "Yes, you're right, it has. We'll speak tomorrow."

Gloriana bit her lower lip and nodded. There were things she wanted to say to her husband, questions she wanted to ask, but this was not the time. She must rest, bring her emotions under control, sort through the shards of her hopes and try to reassemble them into something new.

"In Elaina's solar, after mass," he elaborated, and she

thought she heard a note of sorrow in his voice. Laughter echoed from the great hall, and the sound was harsh and somehow foreign.

Hadleigh Castle had been Gloriana's home since she was twelve years old, and she'd been happy there. She had never doubted, until her husband returned to claim her, that she belonged within those ancient, sturdy walls. Now she wondered if there was any place for her in all the world and looked forward to the morrow, not with anticipation, but with disquiet.

Gloriana's handmaiden, Judith, had already come and gone when she reached her bedchamber. A tallow had been lit, though it was not completely dark outside, this being a summer's night, and the covers were turned back on the bed. A basin of fresh water waited on a crude washstand beneath an ornate crucifix that had been Edwenna's most treasured possession.

Gloriana longed now for her foster mother's counsel and consolation, as she had many other times since the fever had taken that good woman, as well as her husband, to realms unknown. Friar Cradoc believed that Edwenna and Cyrus were together in heaven, for they had both been devout and paradise was the eventual destination of all who kept the commandments of the Church—after a short visit to purgatory, perhaps, where penance could be served and the last stains of sin might be eradicated.

Gently, Gloriana touched the pierced feet of the small wooden Christ. She hated to think of sweet Edwenna or of Cyrus, for that matter, spending so much as a moment in purgatory, a terrible place almost as frightening as hell itself. Gloriana had not known her foster father well, for he had been away so much, but Edwenna had been unfailingly kind and devoted herself to the avoidance of sin. Surely even a jealous and wrathful God would not wish to punish such a woman.

Bowing her head, Gloriana murmured a quick but heartfelt prayer for the souls of Edwenna and Cyrus, then splashed her face at the basin and pulled her woolen gown off over her head. After folding the garment carefully and placing it in the proper chest, she blew out the candle and climbed into bed in her chemise. There, beneath the covers, as she had been assiduously taught, Gloriana wriggled out of her undergarment. It seemed cumbersome to go to so much trouble to be decent when one was all alone in a room anyway, but she performed the ritual nonetheless, because modesty required it.

Lying in the gathering darkness, Gloriana finally allowed herself to weep. She had looked forward to this night for so long, expecting to be held by her husband, and cherished, and finally deflowered. She had even dared to hope she and Kenbrook might conceive a child right away. Instead, she was alone, while Dane's true love slumbered beneath the same roof, and there was naught to look forward to but an ominous interview in Lady Hadleigh's solar after morning mass.

Although she thought she would lie sleepless until the morning came, Gloriana drifted off within moments and found herself in the grip of a dream that had not visited her in a long time.

Purgatory, perhaps she was in purgatory, for this was a loud, busy place where everything moved too fast and people wore strange garments and spoke in a tongue Gloriana could not understand, even though it was familiar to her. In the dream, she was not Gloriana St. Gregory, a woman grown, but a child called Megan.

She carried a beautiful doll in her arms and wandered, lost and alone, through the ruins of an old abbey, searching for someone who did not particularly want to be found. She watched as a gate took shape in a crumbling wall, almost remembering.

Strange words came from her lips, and she knew what they meant only by the desolation in her heart. *They don't want me.*

She awakened suddenly, thrusting herself up and out of the dream, gasping for breath, her slender but sturdy body damp with perspiration.

Gloriana lay trembling in her bed, remembering at last. Once, she had chattered incessantly about the Other Place, and even written about it, believing it to be real. The Lady Elaina and eventually Edwenna, as well, had cautioned her not to share the tales with anyone else. Over time, Gloriana had put away her writings and gradually faced the fact that she'd only imagined the adventure. Often, years passed without her thinking, even once, of that land she'd created in her mind, but then an image or a word would pop into her mind or she'd dream about it, as she had this night.

She snuggled down in her thick feather mattress and closed her eyes, determined to sleep, but her bladder wanted emptying. Resigned, she reached for her chemise and, with a dutiful sigh, pulled it on over her head before slipping out from under the covers. Gloriana did not know which she hated more, the chamber pot beneath her bed or the noxious privies at the end of the passage, which emptied into a special conduit beneath the castle.

A memory came to her, if something that had never happened could be called by such a name, of a clean and glistening device made for personal convenience, and she yearned for that luxury. In the meanwhile, she contented herself with the chamber pot and, after washing her hands in the basin, climbed back into bed and went through the whole rite of removing her chemise all over again.

After much tossing and turning, Gloriana finally slept, and this time her rest was untroubled. At cock's crow she rose and dressed hastily in the chilly dawn. Her gown was simple brown wool, and she donned a cloak as well, for warmth and for the hood that would hide her hair. This was done out of deference to God, and not her husband, for it would be blasphemous to appear in church without a proper covering.

The mysterious Mariette must have been ill for, unlike everyone else in the vast household, she did not appear at mass that morning. Dane arrived soon after Gloriana did, flanked by both Edward and Gareth, and slipped into the pew beside his wife. She noted, in a sidelong look, that there was a grim set to his jaw and a certain pallor to his skin. If Kenbrook had slept at all the night before, he had not rested well.

Gloriana shifted uneasily on the pew, for plainly his lordship was not looking forward to the forthcoming conference in Elaina's solar any more than she was.

Chapter

3

$\mathcal{M}$embers of the household smiled and nodded as Gloriana and Dane left the church together after morning mass. Whatever rumors might be circulating, the occupants of Hadleigh Castle were obviously pleased to see husband and wife walking side by side. No doubt they failed to notice, as Gloriana could not *help* doing, that Dane's hand was pressed to the small of her back, propelling her along.

He inclined his head to those who called a greeting to him but did not speak, being intent on his business—whatever that was. They mounted an outside staircase, at the top of which was a door opening onto Elaina's deserted solar.

Like most of the great keep, the chamber had been swept and aired and laid with herbs and fresh rushes in preparation for tomorrow's ceremonies of knighthood. Gloriana thought fleetingly that here this was odd, since by Gareth's own order the room was practically sacrosanct—a dusty shrine to his lost-though-living wife.

Something like pain moved in Dane's face as he surveyed the place, but the interlude was as brief as the brush of a butterfly's wing. In less than a moment, it was over and he had set Gloriana before him, his hard, swordsman's hands resting gently on her upper arms. He started to speak and then fell silent again, plainly exasperated by his own reluctance.

"You want to speak to me about the woman," Gloriana said. There were tremors in her heart, but somehow she managed to keep her outer countenance still. Or so she hoped.

Dane allowed his hands to slide slowly down Gloriana's arms. Again it struck her that, while he was a strong man, capable of great violence if the tales his soldiers were telling were true, he cradled her elbows in his palms with care. He sighed.

"How easy this all seemed when I was yet far from this place," he said.

Gloriana, aware that he neither wanted nor expected comment, offered none. She waited, gazing up at him with what her body had hidden showing vividly in her eyes. She was oddly injured by his tenderness, full of strange, fearful and bittersweet feelings, which meant, of course, that giving him up would be all the more difficult.

He led her to a bench carved with unicorns, maidens, birds, and flowers, and sat her down beside him. He held her hand, unthinkingly interweaving his fingers with hers. "I have brought Mariette from France," Dane said, at long last, "with the thought of marrying her."

Gloriana swallowed hard. She was not given to guile nor mummery, and the reverberations of her shattering heart had finally reached the surface. "But you are my husband," she whispered, stricken.

Dane averted his gaze, then forced himself, visibly, to look at her again. "Gloriana," he said softly, hoarsely, "surely you can see that ours was never a marriage of love, but a contract."

She blinked. It was a new notion, this idea of marrying for love. When there was tender sentiment before the wedding, it was only a happy accident—no, love grew moment by moment, day by day, as a couple came to know and appreciate each other. She, Gloriana, had never been given a *chance* to have that, and fury filled her at the injustice of it.

"My father," she said coolly, smoothing the skirts of her kirtle, "believed you to be a man of integrity who would honor his agreements."

Dane flinched a little, to show he had felt the barb, and then smiled. "Do you want a husband, lovely Gloriana, who desires another?"

Gloriana pulled her fingers from his and stood, causing the mantle to fall from her hair. She did not trouble herself to replace it. "No," she said fiercely, in a whisper that seemed to echo through the vast solar. "No, I do not." She had turned her back on him, in a desperate effort to hide some of her turmoil, and she felt him standing close behind her.

To his credit, he did not venture to touch her. "It won't be so bad," Dane reassured her quietly. "There are fine convents all over England, where a woman of your gifts might pass her days pleasantly—"

Gloriana spun on him. "Convents?" she repeated, disbelieving. "You think to put me into a nunnery as if I were mad, like Elaina, or an adulteress?"

Dane stood his ground, his arms folded. He was, after all, a fighting man, Gloriana reminded herself, more content in conflict than in peace. The faintest hint of temper flashed in his glacial eyes. "You make it sound as though I would cast you into gaol. Convents are not such terrible places. Mariette herself was raised and educated in one—"

"Then let *her* go and spend her days weaving and praying and stitching—I, sir, shall not!"

"You are my responsibility, if not my true wife, and you will be properly looked after, whether you wish it so or not!"

An angry laugh escaped Gloriana, and she waved both arms in wild exclamation. "Your *responsibility,* am I? Well, I'm something more than that, as it happens—I am a flesh-and-blood woman, with a heart that beats and lungs that draw air, and I shall not be trundled off to the convent for the convenience of your conscience. I have gold, I have houses of my own, here and in London Town. I require no 'help' from you!"

Dane closed his eyes for a moment, and Gloriana knew he was struggling to control himself. Care for him though she did, that being her private and eternal curse, she wished just then that the top of his head would blow off. "You will not live alone," he decreed, when he spoke at long last, his voice low and even and somehow dangerous.

"I wouldn't be alone," Gloriana replied, with stubborn reasoning. "I should have my servants to attend me."

"That is not the same," Dane said carefully. "A woman cannot be left unprotected, unsupervised—"

Gloriana muttered a word she might have learned in that other life, the one she dreamed about so rarely, the one Edwenna had warned her not to speak of except in her prayers. "Widows," she pointed out, "live in just such a situation, all over England, perhaps all over the world."

"You are not a widow."

"Pray, do not compound my tribulations by reminding me, good sir," Gloriana replied sweetly, with a little curtsy. "I shall instead bear the name of harlot, a woman spurned for no other reason than the fecklessness of her husband and shuttled off to a convent the way a lazy servant might use his toe to nudge a dead mouse under the rushes of the great-room floor."

Even in that dim light, Gloriana saw Dane go pale and then vividly red. "You would be named harlot," he said, breathing the words in the way dragons breathed fire, "only if you persisted upon this foolish and fanciful course you would set for yourself. Fortunately, you will be spared this mistake, and taken in hand!"

For Gloriana, the interview was over. Leaving her mantle in a pool at Dane's feet, she moved, hem and slippers rustling, over the fresh rushes toward the outside door. In its latticed light, she turned to look back at her husband. "You are without honor," she said, in dulcet tones, "and have no honest claim to knighthood. You may go straight to hell, for all I care, and roast there on a spit."

With those rash words, which probably endangered her own soul, Gloriana left Elaina's solar and fled gracefully down the outer stairway.

Dane stood alone in the room where, as a green and besotted boy, he had once sat at his sister-in-law's feet, listening as she played the harp or sang merry songs or told marvelous stories of wizardry. How he had loved those tales of hers—full of magic and mischief they'd been—and he remembered them now, not word for word, but dream for dream. He felt a compelling need to be near Elaina, though of course he knew that, in her madness, she could not lend him comfort as of old. Stories would not help him now, nor songs and harps.

He encountered Edward, who had no doubt been lying in wait, at the bottom of the courtyard stairs. The boy was peeling a pear with a thin-bladed knife, and Dane wondered, forcing back a smile, if the stripling fancied himself a fearsome figure.

"Hello, Edward," Dane said. "I go to pay respects to the lady Elaina. Will you join me?"

Edward looked surprised, though whether it was the invitation that had caught him off guard or Dane's patent refusal to explain his encounter with Gloriana in the solar, Dane could not guess. Nor, in point of fact, did he care.

"Elaina?" Edward echoed, as though he had yet to hear the name. "But she's mad."

Dane was already striding in the direction of the second bailey and the stables therein when he replied. "Perhaps," he allowed. "Or perhaps our sister-by-marriage is merely wiser than all the rest of us."

"But she sees things that aren't there," Edward scrambled to point out, taking two strides for every one of Dane's, "and they say she hears voices."

Dane shrugged and kept walking. "Mayhap it is we who are blind, and deaf," he said. He spoke thoughtfully this time, wondering if those terms did not apply to him in some ways, at least where Gloriana was concerned. "In any event," Dane went on, shaking off a sense of mild dismay, "I have no fear of the gentle Elaina."

Within the stables, Dane found Peleus and saddled the great stallion himself, as he generally did. The beast was headstrong and had trampled more than one hapless groom in the brief time Dane had owned him. Edward, who had apparently elected to make the short ride to the abbey along with him, led a respectable gelding out into the sunlit yard. Dane recognized the worn saddle and smiled slightly.

"I would speak of Gloriana," Edward said, as they rode slowly through the outer bailey toward the gates, which stood open despite Gareth's alleged problems with Merrymont.

"And I would not," Dane answered, as the hooves of their

horses clattered over the ancient timbers of the drawbridge. "Soon you shall be made a knight, Edward. Let us talk of that instead."

The road that curved beyond the empty moat was lined with oak tress, and their leaves made pleasant, moving patterns of light and shadow. Despite his dilemma, a quiet joy burned within Dane's bosom, the knowledge that he was home.

"I will be a mercenary," Edward said. "Like you. Perhaps I will go and fight the Turk."

Horrific images rose before Dane's eyes, like specters, things he had seen done by and to the much-fabled Turk, but he forced them back behind the mental walls he had erected to contain them. He'd had much practice, since he'd gone soldiering, at putting such memories aside. "It is your life," he said simply, "to do with as you will." He saw Gloriana's face in his mind, wearing an ironic expression that said the same was true of her.

"Would you do it again?" Edward asked. "Leave Kenbrook Hall, I mean, and England to fight for gold?"

Leather creaked as Dane turned in the saddle to assess his young brother anew. "When I have worked out the answer to that question for myself," he said, "I will share it with you. War is not a sport, Edward, like the scraps you have with other boys who fancy themselves knights, nor is it a game, like chess. No, it is a grim and ugly business, the making of war, and I am weary of it."

"You are old," Edward said, as though that fact dispensed with all else.

Dane laughed, then recalled that he had thought the same thing about Gloriana, that she would be a crone, with withered skin and bad teeth, if she had teeth at all. What a naive fool he'd been, for all his traveling and fighting, no wiser, in some ways, than Edward. "Yes," he replied, knowing no argument would serve, in the circumstances. "I am old, and fit for nothing but lying on my belly before the fire, like an aged dog with too many hunts behind him."

Edward was silent for a time, which was a mercy, to Dane's mind. A soldier, a commander of men, Dane was not used to idle talk, and he did not relish it. He was beginning to hope they would gain the abbey gates without exchanging another word when the lad spoke again.

"I would court Gloriana," he said, with a note of glumness in his youthful voice. "She is beautiful and kind, full of spirit and joy. She is quick-minded, in the bargain."

"Does the lady return your sentiments?" Dane asked. The high abbey gates were shut, and he bent from Peleus's gleaming ebony back to grasp the latchstring. Another sign, he thought, of either carelessness or a zealot's belief in peace that admittance could be gained so easily.

"Gloriana believes herself to be devoted to you," Edward answered, with a directness Dane could not fail to admire. "She will get over that, as time passes."

Dane recalled the lady's admonition that he go "to hell . . . and roast there on a spit," and smiled sadly as he rode through the open gateway. She'd gone a long way, had the lady Gloriana, toward putting her "devotion" behind her. Why did that cause him sorrow, he wondered? Surely it was the best that could be hoped for, that Gloriana should cease caring for him and resign herself to a quiet life in the seclusion and safety of an abbey such as the one he and Edward entered now.

The abbess, Sister Margaret, swept into the small courtyard, clad, as were all the members of her order, in a plain gray kirtle and wimple. She beamed at the sight of Dane, and the motion sent wrinkles spreading gently over her face, like cracks in brittle ice.

"So," she said, as Dane dismounted. "What we have heard is true—you have come home to Hadleigh Castle at last."

Dane raised his eyes to the gloomy hulk in the distance. "I have indeed come home," he answered, "but to Kenbrook Hall. I will reside there, once I have attended to a few difficult matters."

Edward uttered a small, disdainful grunt, but offered no other comment.

"How fares the lady Elaina?" Dane asked. Sister Margaret had given him her hand, and he had squeezed it slightly, for their affection for each other was great.

Sister Margaret sighed and turned to lead the way across the crumbling stones of the courtyard. The abbey, like Kenbrook Hall, was old, with a history that reached far back into the mists of history, beyond the things that had been recorded on scrolls and pages of parchment and into the realm of legend. "She claims to have truck with the fairies," the abbess answered, "and it's certainly true that Lady Hadleigh seems to grow younger, while the rest of us age. I think, now and then, that her fancies are not fancies at all, that she not only knows the little people but is somehow one of them and privy to their most cherished secrets."

"Perhaps you have attended our brother's wife too long," Edward observed.

Dane gave the lad a withering look over his shoulder, and Edward was suitably chagrined, though the effect would probably wear off all too soon.

Elaina sat, bathed in sunshine, in a corner of a small courtyard. Her face was raised to the light, a small smile played upon her mouth, and her eyes were closed. Her hair gleamed like burnished gold, and her kirtle, made of some gossamer fabric, moved softly in the breeze and seemed, in its own way, as alive as the grass or the birds or the fluttering green leaves of the oak trees.

She opened her eyes and gazed upon her visitors without surprise. Her countenance was placid and serene, and Dane thought, as she got up and glided toward them, *If Elaina is mad, then so am I.*

"Dane," Elaina said, and stood on tiptoe to kiss his cheek. "You've grown since I saw you last. And there are no scars— at least, not visible ones. I suppose that is good."

"Milady," Dane replied, by way of greeting, and would have bowed if she had not gripped his shoulders and prevented him. She searched his face and saw the tears he would not permit to come to his eyes.

"My Dane," she said, with affection, "you grieve for me, but you shouldn't. I am the happiest of women." Elaina turned briefly to Edward, who stood beside the abbess and the open gate, looking as though he would bolt. "Go, Edward," she said. "You are uncomfortable here." It was not a complaint, this last, but a simple statement.

The boy left the courtyard willingly, and the abbess followed, closing the metal gate behind her.

Dane embraced his sister-in-law and planted a brotherly

kiss on her forehead. Her hair and clothing smelled pleas-antly, as Gloriana's did, of summer herbs and fresh air and oil smoke. "Why do you stay in this place?" he asked. "You are no more mad than any of the rest of us."

Elaina turned away at this and hugged herself, as if struck by a chill. "This is my lot, and I am content with it, for the most part." She lowered her lovely head briefly, bowed by some secret grief, and then rallied, turning to face him again with shining eyes. "How did you find my husband? Is he hearty?"

"Gareth is well. He misses you, as do we all."

"Yes," Elaina answered thoughtfully. "I suppose he does, though he has his Irish mistress, you know—the lady Annabel."

Dane opened his mouth, but before he could utter some foolish platitude, Elaina came to him and silenced him with the light touch of her fingertips.

"Hush," she said. "Do not court damnation by speaking lies. I cannot begrudge Gareth his poor comforts—he was always kind to me, though I have been no sort of wife to him. Do you think she will ever bear him a child?"

"I cannot predict the future," he answered gently, "but I think not. Such women profit by their barrenness, and surely know how to maintain the advantage."

"It makes me sad to think that Gareth may never have children," Elaina confessed, and again she seemed to hear some silent piper, some tune just beyond the ken of Dane's ears. "He would make a fine father."

Dane nodded. "Gareth has been a good brother to Edward and me, as near a thing to a father as we've had."

Elaina returned to the bench where she had been sitting when Dane first entered the little courtyard with Edward and Sister Margaret. She folded her hands in her lap and looked as pure and peaceful, sitting there, as an angel in-dulging in a daydream. "I had despaired of you, Dane," she said, just when he thought she'd forgotten his presence en-tirely. "I wondered if you would ever return and be a hus-band to your lovely Gloriana."

"You know her, then." It was all Dane could say in that moment.

"Of course I know her," Elaina scolded, laughing, and she

was herself again, her old self, when she met his eyes. "Gloriana has lived in or near Hadleigh Castle since she was twelve, after all. How old was she when she became your bride, Dane?"

"Seven," Dane admitted. "It's barbaric, this marrying of children to children. I will not countenance such a thing when I have sons and daughters of my own."

Elaina arched an eyebrow and smiled. "Beware of rash vows, Kenbrook," she warned, in a teasing tone. "Fate is tempted by words like 'never' and 'always' and invariably seeks to make a mockery of whoever uses them. Anyway, in this case the match was a good one, made in higher kingdoms than our own."

Dane sat beside her, uttering a heavy sigh as he did so. "I believe I love another woman," he said. Even that morning, before prayers, he would have said he loved Mariette without qualification, but now he wasn't so sure. He had been seared, however much he wished it weren't so, by Gloriana's peculiar fire. He had never expected such beauty, such spirit, such exquisite nobility.

"Goose," Elaina said. "Gloriana is your destiny, and you are hers. I knew it when she first stepped through that gate, just there." She pointed, and Dane saw an ordinary portal and was reminded of why his sister-in-law lived in the abbey, rather than at Hadleigh Castle with her husband. "Do you know what lies on the other side of that gate, Dane?"

He shook his head, deeply saddened. "No, sweet."

"Another world," Elaina replied. She was very pale, and he saw fragile blue veins pulsing beneath the soft flesh of her temple. "It is a passageway into the world ours will one day become. And there are other gates, other thresholds and corridors, that lead to still other—"

Dane had taken her hand; he raised it to his lips and kissed the knuckles lightly. *"Shh,"* he whispered, heartsick. "You grow weary, Elaina. I have tired you, and you must rest."

She nodded. "Yes," she said, and tears pooled in her lashes as she rose from the bench and pulled free of Dane's grasp. "Yes, I must lie down. I can hear it, you see." Elaina raised both hands to her ears, as if to shut out some dread-

ful din. "Such a wretched, hurried place, full of carts without horses to pull them, moving fast and trumpeting to each
other, like a thousand stags in a thousand forests—"

Dane prayed she would leave the courtyard, before he
broke down and wept for her. "I will come again," he promised, for it was all he had to offer. Though he had bought
splendid gifts for Elaina, they were in his chamber at Hadleigh Castle, for he had not thought to fetch them before
leaving his brother's keep.

"Send Gloriana to me on the morrow," Elaina pleaded,
hesitating at the gate he and Edward and the abbess had
used, as wraithlike and fragile as a child. "I must see her."

At his nod of acquiescence, which she waited to see, she
vanished.

Dane lingered a few moments, recovering himself, and
then strode into the larger courtyard, where he found Edward and the abbess, waiting with the horses. There was no
sign of Elaina, for she had no doubt retreated to the chapel
or her cell.

Dane took a coin from the leather bag tied to his belt and
pressed it into the abbess's callused palm, shutting her bony
fingers around it. He did not ask Sister Margaret to look
after Elaina, for that would have been an insult, since everyone knew she was devoted and made every effort on Lady
Hadleigh's behalf. Instead, Dane simply mounted Peleus
and reined the great, impatient animal toward the outer
gate.

"What did you expect to gain by visiting Elaina?" Edward
asked when they were away from the abbey and the drawbridge was in plain sight, just ahead.

It was an intuitive question, and Dane had no sensible
offer to give. "I am fond of the lady," he said evenly. "As you
should be, since she was as near a mother as you ever had."

Edward's youthful, tumultuous skin was flushed. "It is
said that Elaina is a witch, that she casts spells. She made
the swine die one year, and another—"

"Swill!" Dane interrupted furiously. "What ignorant, superstitious dolt dared utter such a claim?"

The boy subsided, but he did so ungraciously. "Do you
think I'd tell you, Kenbrook?" he asked. "And see you cut
out their tongues with your dagger?"

Dane tipped back his head and gave a raw burst of laughter. There was no mirth in the sound and no mercy in Dane himself. "That I would do," he said, and sobered. "Have a care, Edward. There are those who would burn Elaina for her foibles and think it a service to the Almighty. Be vigilant, if you care for our lady sister at all, and put a stop to such talk whenever you hear it."

Edward swallowed hard, and then he nodded.

No other words passed between the two brothers as they rode side by side over the drawbridge, passing through the outer bailey and dismounting at the stables. Edward left his gelding to the care of a groom, while Dane, troubled, attended to Peleus himself.

Gloriana knelt in the attic of the house that had been her father's and was now hers, staring at the contents of the last trunk, the one in the farthest, dustiest corner. Edwenna had taken great care to hide the truth about her adopted daughter.

The first item Gloriana removed was wrapped in porous cloth, and even before she unwound the bandagelike covering, she knew the doll would be inside. The elegant model of a queen yet to be born, with its bright Tudor hair and pale skin, its jeweled dress and tiny slippers.

"Elizabeth I," Gloriana whispered. She who would come to the throne in the sixteenth century and reign over a turbulent England for a great many years. She whose nickname Gloriana had taken for her own.

Gloriana closed her eyes and swayed slightly, there in the stifling, dusty heat of the attic. Carefully, with trembling hands, she laid the costly doll aside and took another bundle from the trunk. Trousers—jeans, she'd called them, in that other incarnation. A small garment—a T-shirt, she remembered—cut to fit a child. Shoes, hard-soled and yet flexible.

Studying these items, Gloriana felt exultation, followed by a surge of nausea. With a combination of tenderness and fear, she tucked them all back in the trunk and closed the lid quickly. She did not begin to understand what had happened to her, all those years ago, but she knew that Edwenna had been wise in hiding them. The people of Hadleigh Village would surely deem her a witch if they saw these strange belongings.

Although Gloriana had never seen anyone burned or hanged for having dealings with the devil, she knew such things were not uncommon. Staring at the trunk, her grubby hands knotted together in her lap, Gloriana racked her brain. A part of her wanted to destroy everything, to burn the whole house to the ground if that was what it took, but another part cherished these odd possessions. They were, after all, her last link with Megan, the child she had been, and the faraway world that had spawned her.

She swallowed and leaned forward, like a supplicant before the altar of God, her forehead pressed to the filthy lid of the trunk. If only there were somebody she could go to, somebody who would give her counsel and comfort. But she dared trust no one—not Edward, her closest friend, not Gareth, generous as he was, and especially not Kenbrook, her erstwhile husband. He wanted to be rid of her in order to take the Frenchwoman to wife and might even betray her in order to be free.

Gloriana's breath was quick and shallow, and she began to feel light-headed, as if she would swoon. No, she told herself, clutching her stomach with both hands now, like a poison victim, and rocking back and forth on her knees. No, Dane would never permit her to be burned as a witch. But he might well put her away in a convent, as Gareth had banished Elaina to the abbey; it would salve Kenbrook's conscience if he could say his first wife was mad. He'd be granted an annulment, no doubt, and no one would blame him for marrying again.

Gloriana rose shakily to her feet, smoothing her kirtle with fitful motions of her hands, though it was hopelessly crumpled and much soiled. She drew a deep breath and straightened her shoulders. Perhaps, she reflected, feeling sick, she really was a witch, an unwitting tool of Lucifer. The thought made her shudder, for although Gloriana was rebellious, daydreaming during mass and often falling asleep in vespers, refusing to cover her hair except when she was actually inside the church, there was no evil in her.

She must get rid of the items inside the chest at the first viable opportunity and never speak of what she remembered.

She crossed the attic floor and stooped to pass through the tiny doorway, which opened onto a step and narrow staircase, every step hewn from solid oak. Trailing dirty fingers along the wall, she made her way down to the second floor and then the first. The familiar furniture gave her comfort; she could almost make herself believe that Edwenna would come bustling around a corner, full of kindly purpose, and make everything all right.

Gloriana sat down on the bottommost step and propped her chin in her hands. She had not been attempting to manipulate Kenbrook earlier, in the solar, when she'd told him she would live in her own house and manage her personal affairs herself. Nor had she been making an empty threat. Pride would not allow her to live under the same roof with Dane St. Gregory while he courted and wooed another woman.

An angry tear streaked down Gloriana's smudged cheek, and she struck it away with a quick dash of her hand. That was one decision made—all well and good. But the fact remained that she loved Kenbrook with the whole of her heart and the full range of her soul. Every instinct urged her to fight for him and for the children who would never be born if he threw her away.

The front door opened, its huge iron hinges creaking, and Gloriana gazed, with some vexation and no little surprise, upon the very one she'd been thinking about, her husband.

She quelled an urge to touch her hair and arrange her skirts. "What do you want?" she demanded, looking him up and down.

He sighed and thrust a hand through his gilt hair. "You are an unholy mess," he said, ignoring her question, which had been, in her opinion, a reasonable one. "What have you been doing?"

Gloriana thought of the doll, the odd clothing, the shoes of which the thirteenth century knew no like. "I hardly think I need explain," she said. "This is my house, after all, and what I do within these walls is my own concern."

Dane leaned against the heavy wooden door, which was quite tall and some four inches thick, and sighed again. His arms, as was his habit, were folded across his chest. "I will not debate that point with you," he told her, not unkindly.

"Not now, at least. You are plainly upset, and the fault is mine. I truly regret any sorrow I might have caused you."

Gloriana waited in silence. Whatever remorse Kenbrook might feel, he wasn't going to say he'd changed his mind about annulling their marriage. She knew that by the expression on his face.

"In time," he said, "you will understand."

Gloriana suppressed an unseemly impulse to spit upon his boots, which were well within range. "I understand now," she replied, without raising her voice or even blushing. "You are a scoundrel, a liar, and a cheat. I shall be glad to see the back of you."

Dane shook his head and pushed away from the door with a sleek, easy grace that did unreasonable things to Gloriana's heart. "I am all those things," he agreed, "and more."

It took the passion out of her rage, what Kenbrook said, and Gloriana was annoyed. "Please go away," she said.

He came closer, curving his long fingers around the top of the newel post, looking down at Gloriana through lashes too thick to belong to a man. "I saw the lady Elaina today," he said, as if she had not just ordered him out of her house. "She wishes you to visit her, on the morrow."

As quickly as that, Gloriana's mood was transformed. "Is she well?" she asked softly.

Dane did not reply but there was no need of it anyway, for the answer showed plainly in his face.

Chapter

4

*V*espers, conducted in the chapel by Friar Cradoc, made a formal end to the Sabbath day. Gloriana attended, wearing a fresh kirtle the color of lilacs and a white wimple that fitted tightly around her face. Her heart was not prayerful as she sat, barely able to keep from fidgeting, in the customary pew, for there were too many other matters on her mind.

Dane was always a part of her thoughts, and of course Elaina, who wanted a visit from her on the morrow. Then, like a thorn in a festering wound, there was the Frenchwoman, Mariette de Troyes, who sat circumspectly in the back of the chapel with her maid and the red-haired man called Maxen. Mariette was beautiful, in a fragile, ethereal sort of way but, Gloriana thought uncharitably, too frail by half to hold her own with a man like Kenbrook.

Perhaps out of diplomacy, though Gloriana was reluctant to credit the man with the sensitivity such an act would require, her husband had taken a seat at the front of the small, ancient church. Gareth sat at his right side, and Edward at his left.

Friar Cradoc, perhaps with St. Paul's injunction to pray without ceasing in mind, alternately droned and thundered his way through unending litanies of mortification, adoration, gratitude, and, finally, supplication.

A festive supper would follow the service, the first of many events planned to celebrate the knighthood of Edward and the seven other young men who had trained with him. No doubt Mademoiselle de Troyes would be installed at the head table, Gloriana reflected miserably. Perhaps she would even be bold enough to sit beside Dane as if she were already his wife.

Color suffused Gloriana's face at the prospect of such a humiliation, and although she had been ravenously hungry only moments before, having missed the midday meal, her stomach felt sour.

Then the service was over, and Gareth, being the liege lord of nearly everyone present, was first to rise and make his way down the center aisle, striding without pause toward the doors. Dane, who was behind him, stopped beside Gloriana's pew and gazed down at her with a mingling of amusement and vexed curiosity in his eyes.

She longed to wrench off her headdress and fling it in his face, lest he be pleased with her in even that small way. Another part of her yearned shamelessly for his approval.

He extended his hand to her, and she hesitated. The chapel by then was already empty, except for them, for people were hungry and eager to begin the merrymaking.

With unaccustomed awkwardness, Gloriana rose and glanced back toward the place where Mariette had sat, between her maid and the Welshman. "I will not sit at your left hand," she said with tremulous certainly, "while your mistress holds court at your right."

Dane let his hand fall to his side. "Surely you cannot think I would disgrace you in such a way—or Mariette."

"On the contrary," Gloriana replied evenly, and without particular rancor, "I cannot think why you would hesitate." She eased past him, into the aisle, moving briskly toward the exit, and was not surprised when he kept pace with her.

The dusk was redolent with the perfumes of summer— the vital, reedy scent of the nearby lake, the woodsy smell of the forest, the acrid fragrance of smoke, wooing the wayfarer home to safety and supper. Torches blazed, setting the courtyard alight, and carts bearing a mummers' troupe rattled noisily over the cobblestones.

Gloriana felt an odd twinge of something very like nostalgia, a fear that at any moment she might be snatched from these people, this time, this place, never to return. As dangerous as it was, as dirty and backward, this simple world was her home, and she loved it.

"Do you think me such a brute?" Dane asked, after pondering her accusation for several moments, effectively jarring her out of her unhappy ponderings. "Can you possibly believe I designed this coil on purpose, with the intention of causing you hurt?"

She stopped and stared up at him, at the same time wrenching the hateful wimple off her head. She saw Dane's eyes widen momentarily as her hair spilled to freedom in the torchlight, and did not trouble herself to wonder what he was thinking. In truth, she did not care. "Yes, Kenbrook," she said, "I think you are indeed a brute, and other things besides. I would never credit you with *planning* the injury you've done me—your failing, sir, is not malice, but unheeding selfishness. You have considered your own desires in the matter and little else."

She made to walk away from him, but he stopped her, taking that now-familiar hold on her arm, one neither tender nor harsh. The glow of the torches danced eerily over his patrician features, and Gloriana was reminded that he was a warrior, said to be fearless and utterly without mercy on the battlefield.

"Then you will be glad to be free of me," he said, with quiet logic.

A lump formed in Gloriana's throat, fair choking her, and humiliating tears stung her eyes. "I have wasted my life, waiting for you," she answered, in a gasping whisper. There were others in the courtyard, after all, and their conversation should have been a private one. "I could have had a home where I might be mistress, a husband who loved me, a child or two. You have robbed me of all those things. Now you expect to cloister me, like some troublesome possession you will neither keep near at hand nor truly discard. As I said today in the house where I shall go to live as soon as Edward's been knighted, you may join your friend, the devil, in the fires of hell."

His fingers loosened, like the hand of a wounded man releasing the handle of his sword, and Gloriana swept away, leaving him in the center of the courtyard. Before entering the great hall, she slipped into the shadows and, using the insides of her wrists, dashed the tears from her cheeks. Then, after drawing a deep, sustaining breath, she marched into the light and clamor of the hall, where seasoned knights, some Gareth's men, some under Dane's command, lined the long tables. Serving wenches moved among them with trays and pitchers, dodging pinches and swats even as they invited them. A juggler in a colorful costume plied his trade before the dais, keeping seven golden balls aloft while he danced to the spritely tune falling in a merry shower of notes from the minstrels' gallery.

Mariette de Troyes was indeed seated at Gareth's table, nibbling delicately at a drumstick from a guinea fowl while the Scotsman, Eigg, regaled her with some intricate story, his telling full of gesticulations and punctuated with somewhat foolish laughter. The empty seat beside the young Frenchwoman was Kenbrook's usual place; Gloriana's own was further down the table, beside Edward.

While most everyone was engaged in eating or talking or listening to the pleasant music, she felt more than one pair of eyes studying her, assessing her every expression and movement. She lifted her chin and walked boldly forward, mounting the dais steps, nodding to Edward and to Gareth as she passed them. Instead of sitting beside her young brother-in-law, who was obviously waiting for her, Gloriana settled herself at Mariette's side.

Eigg's animated discourse fell off into silence, as did much of the raucous chatter on the floor of the hall. Even the music from the gallery seemed to recede, but that, Gloriana thought, might have been her imagination. The blood was thrumming in her ears, fit to render her deaf.

Mariette turned to her, and Gloriana saw surprise in the exquisitely beautiful face. The emotion was quickly subdued, however, and the girl spoke in polite, tentative French.

"My English is poor," she said. "Perhaps you will be tolerant."

Gloriana liked her rival instantly, a fact that only made matters more difficult. Mariette reminded her of the crocuses that broke through the snow when spring was still only a distant hope, flourished, and then were gone. "And I have only a little French," Gloriana replied. "Just enough, I think, to cause you to laugh at me."

Mariette's smile was brilliant and short-lived, like the crocuses. "I shall not laugh. I am in want of a friend, after all."

Others might have taken that last remark for presumption, under the circumstances, but Gloriana received it with warmth. The girl was far from home, in a strange country, and of a timid countenance, clearly anxious and frightened. To spurn her offer of friendship would be cruel, to blame her for invoking Kenbrook's lust, unfair. "You have found one in me," said the baroness to her ascribed successor.

There was a stir at the far end of the hall, and Gloriana saw, through her lashes, that Dane had entered and was even now striding between the long tables toward the dais. His gaze was fixed on Gloriana's face, and she saw a grim fury in him that made her breath catch—not from fear, but something more complex and made partly of pleasure.

"Our husband approaches," Gloriana said to her companion.

Mariette giggled, a fretful sound, rather than a frivolous one, then pressed slender, fluttering fingers to her lips. "He is terrifying, is he not?" the girl whispered.

Gloriana supposed that, in his own way, Dane *was* a frightening man. For herself, she felt no impulse to flee. "Kenbrook has been too long on the battlefield," she confided, in her bumbling French. "He has forgotten his manners, if he ever had any in the first place."

"He did not," commented Gareth, who had come to stand behind Mariette and Gloriana. "He has ever been a barbarian and a tyrant, my brother."

Gloriana felt Gareth's hand come to rest, very lightly, upon her shoulder.

"Come, Gloriana," he said. "The music is jolly and I would dance to it."

Others had left the table, Gloriana saw, to step to the tune. "I have not yet taken my supper," she said, for she could be stubborn. When she was still at her lessons, Friar Cradoc had oft made her say extra prayers in consequence of this flaw, in the hope that God would expunge it from her nature.

So far, He had not and, although the good friar might

have been surprised by this oversight on the part of the Almighty, Gloriana wasn't. She reasoned that God had other, more pressing concerns than the failings of one maiden.

"As your guardian and the master of this keep," Gareth said pleasantly, his fingers tightening on her shoulder as Dane stormed nearer, "I command you to obey me."

Gloriana sighed with all the force of a player upon a stage and rose from the bench. "I would not consider defying you," she said in a tart whisper, smiling all the while.

"A wise philosophy," Gareth replied. Gloriana was barely on her feet before he'd gripped her arm and half-dragged her down off the dais, through the rushes, and into the midst of the revelers. Dane watched them for a few moments, as if considering whether or not to push through the crowd in pursuit. Then, after approaching the dais to speak to Mariette, he sat down at one of the lower tables to break bread with his men.

One of the mummers approached, silently, and offered Gloriana a mask, a garish and tragic face with a handle. She took it, chagrined that in spite of her efforts to present a cheerful façade, her misery showed so plainly.

She curtsied and held the mask to her face, gracefully following Gareth's steps as he guided her. "I hate him," she said.

"I don't blame you," Gareth answered smoothly. He had always been a reasonable and perceptive man. "I am told that you intend to move into your father's house in the village and live alone there, except for your servingwoman."

"I shall leave the castle immediately following Edward's ceremony," she confirmed.

Gareth had maneuvered her out of the hall and into a cool passageway, dimly lit by smoking oil lamps suspended from iron brackets set into the walls. Gloriana lowered the mask and sank onto a bench. She was exhausted, not from the dancing, but from the effort of maintaining her dignity. Ever since Dane had returned, she had been as fragile as the shell of a sparrow's egg.

Bracing one foot against the bench upon which Gloriana sat, Gareth regarded her in silence for some moments. Then he sighed, and for the first time ever, she noticed that he was aging. "You must see reason," he said, at some length. "It is neither prudent nor fitting for a young woman to set up household alone. Not when she has kinsmen to care for her."

Gloriana set the mask aside with a thump. "Nevertheless," she said, "I intend to do it. I have gold—I can hire my own men-at-arms, if I wish to, and make them protect me. As for propriety—I simply don't care about that."

"Who, then, shall protect you from your bodyguards?" Gareth inquired. "Gloriana, as strong and brilliant as you are, you are a woman." He gestured with one hand in the direction of the hall, where noise erupted even then, in scattered and boisterous bursts. "Do you hear those brutes in there, lining my tables? Half of them have no better manners than my hounds. They would never obey you. Indeed, they would themselves present a very real danger." He paused again while Gloriana digested his unsettling words, then went on. "I swore to your father that I would preserve your reputation and your virtue in the event that your husband failed in those duties. I shall keep my word, Gloriana— I always do. And if you try to impede me in this aim, I will take appropriate steps."

Gloriana's hands became fists among the folds of her kirtle. "Your promise was just while I was yet a child," she said, as calmly as she could. She loved Gareth, after all; he had ever been kind and generous. "Now I am a woman. I have lands and a fortune to command. I may go where I wish and do what I want."

"Where do you get these ideas?" Gareth muttered, his abundant patience wearing thin at last.

Gloriana thought of that other world, the one she had left behind when she was just five years old, and supposed that was the answer to Gareth's question. She did not say so, of course. "You are no different than your brother," she accused. "Kenbrook would send me to a nunnery, lest I prick his conscience by my presence, and you—*you*, Gareth, who have ever been my friend—hint that you will make me a prisoner if I do not obey your dictates."

Gareth had the good grace to look ashamed, but only for an instant. A moment later, he was flushed with righteous conviction. He did not need to say that any number of intractable women had lived out their lives in tower chambers, watching the seasons change from their narrow windows and never touching the earth again until they were buried.

When at last he broke the protracted silence that stretched between them, he spoke with the voice of a stranger. "I love you as if you were my sister—nay, my own daughter—but you will pay heed to my wishes, Gloriana St. Gregory, or live to regret your lapse."

She rose, with what dignity she could manage, to face the lord of Hadleigh Castle and all the lands, excepting those of Kenbrook of course, for miles around. Not trusting herself to speak, Gloriana executed a deep, mocking curtsy, then turned on her heel and hurried back into the hall.

Mariette was leaving, accompanied by her maid, as Gloriana entered. Dane stood in the center of a knot of rowdy men, engaged in a drinking contest with the Welshman and a ruddy-faced Hamilton Eigg. All around them, men and wenches alike perched on benches and tabletops, watching, cheering on one contender and then another.

Gloriana was patently digusted and sought Edward, only to find him making his way through the throng to reach his brother's side. Only Friar Cradoc was still on the dais when Gloriana climbed the steps, seeking a better view. Edward, she thought virtuously, would put an end to this indecorous nonsense. He was, after all, nearly a knight.

"A sad spectacle," commented the friar from his solitary place at the family table. "Sin has come to Hadleigh Castle, milady."

Gloriana hadn't the heart to tell her teacher and priest that sin had taken up residence sometime previously. "Don't worry," she counseled distractedly. "Edward will put a finish to this."

Edward had at last reached the heart of the melee. There, he spoke to Dane and was answered with a booming gust of laughter, a slap on the back that nearly sent him sprawling, and a mug filled to overflowing with what appeared to be stout. To Gloriana's stunned disbelief, Edward raised the tankard to his lips, tilted back his head, and drank until the great hall rocked with the other men's shouts of encouragement. The foremost of these, of course, was Gloriana's own untried husband, the now-drunken Dane St. Gregory, fifth baron of Kenbrook.

"They have corrupted Edward!" Gloriana burst out, gathering her skirts to plunge into the mob and set matters aright.

The friar had risen from his bench while she was watching Edward's descent into dishonor, and he stopped Gloriana by linking his arm through hers. She would have stumbled if the priest hadn't taken a firmer hold.

"There is naught you can do, child," Cradoc told her in the quiet voice that had guided her through Latin and French, mathematics and archery, Greek history and the basics of herbal medicine. "Go to your chambers, if you would please your aged tutor, and remain there until the bells summon you to morning mass."

Gloriana opened her mouth, then closed it again. Dane's mug was refilled from the sloshing tip of a pewter pitcher, along with Edward's and Master Eigg's. She had engaged in enough battles for one day and had already learned that there was no reasoning with Kenbrook or his elder brother, Lord Hadleigh. Edward, in his youthful foolery, was already beyond help, for that night, at least.

For a long moment, Gloriana simply stood there on the dais, watching as the contest of idiots went on. Only when Dane felt her gaze and raised his tankard to her in an impudent toast did she remove herself from the hall.

Judith was waiting in the bedchamber. She had lighted the lamps, turned back the covers, and poured tepid water into a basin. After helping Gloriana out of her gown, the young girl bobbed her head.

"May I go now, milady?"

Although Gloriana had offered the girl a couch upon which to sleep, she insisted on returning to the kitchen, where she, like many of the other household servants, slept on a pallet in front of the fire.

"Stay a moment, please," said Gloriana, sitting before her mirror and taking up the ivory comb Edwenna had bought for her long ago in London Town. "I have a question to ask."

"Yes, milady?" Judith chirped, sounding somewhat worried and bobbing again.

"If I were to leave Hadleigh Castle and live in my father's house in the village, would you go along and attend me?"

Judith fidgeted, shifting from one foot to the other. Her

kirtle, though clean, was made of roughly woven wool, and her straggly brown hair fell, unbound, to her waist. "Leave Hadleigh Castle, milady? But they'd never let you do that, not without Lord Kenbrook, and he's got a house of his own, hasn't he?"

"I am going," Gloriana said purposefully. "Without Lord Kenbrook or his permission."

Judith paled visibly in the flickering glow of the fire and murmured some pagan exclamation before saying, "But, milady, you can't go leaving his lordship's keep just because that's what you want to do!"

"Very well," Gloriana replied, with a sniff. "Never mind. You may stay here, Judith, and sleep with the hounds and the other servants in the kitchen. Of course in my house, you would have had a room of your own, with a bed you needn't have shared—"

The girl's eyes went wide. "A lot of good that would be," she blurted out, "when Lord Kenbrook comes to drag us back here by our hair!"

Gloriana sighed. "I should put an arrow through Kenbrook's heart if he tried such a thing."

Judith's eyes grew larger still. "They'd hang you by the neck, lady or no, if you did such as that."

"Oh, for heaven's sake, Judith," Gloriana snapped, at the end of her patience. "I was not speaking literally. I was merely trying to make a point. Will you go with me or not?"

Judith considered, swallowing visibly and scratching once or twice. "I'll go if you wish it, milady. But you watch—we'll both be tossed into the abbey till the end of our days when this is over, just like Lady Hadleigh."

The prospect sent a shiver tripping down Gloriana's spine. Elaina seemed suited to convent life, but Gloriana knew she herself would feel like a captive and go mad for the want of freedom. "Lord Hadleigh is a just man," she said, but with less conviction than she might have felt before her interview with Gareth in the passage outside the great hall. "He will never punish you for obeying my wishes."

Judith nodded, said "Yes, milady" again, and scurried out. The thick door of the chamber thundered shut behind her.

Gloriana, hair trailing, clad only in her chemise, crossed

the room to pull down the latch, Then, after washing and kneeling beside her bed for one last, hasty prayer, she climbed beneath the covers. The ritual squirming scramble to remove her shift followed, and then she settled into the feather ticking to sleep.

The carousing in the great hall was clearly audible, even from that distance, and as Gloriana lay listening, her eyes burned with tears she refused to shed. She'd done enough weeping on Kenbrook's account, and if she perished in the effort, she would not cry for him again. He simply wasn't worth it.

Except that she believed she was beginning to love him. Despite her own formidable will and the dictates of common sense, she felt her separation from Dane as an amputation.

It isn't supposed to be this way, she cried inwardly.

A tap sounded at her chamber door, and was repeated.

Edward, no doubt, too drunk to stand. He'd be sorry in the morning, she thought with satisfaction, when faced with the rigors of the day. "Go away," Gloriana called.

"Please," replied a small, frightened voice, in faltering English. "Let me in, mademoiselle, for I am terrible afraid."

Mariette.

Gloriana sprang from the bed, pulled her chemise back on, and went to the door. The latch stuck, but she raised it and admitted the woman her husband had chosen as his bride.

Mariette was weeping, and she shivered in her thin, lace-trimmed kirtle. A gossamer nightcap glimmered on her dark hair. "I do not like this place," she said. "There is much noise and I am sore frightened!"

Gloriana, who had once hoped to hate this woman, found herself eager to lend comfort instead. She led Mariette to the bench facing the fire and seated her there, then fetched a bedcovering to wrap around the slender, trembling shoulders.

"I want to go home," Mariette snuffled, when she had ceased her disconsolate wailing.

Gloriana sat beside her and put an arm around her shoulders. *"Shh,"* she said, as gently as a doting mother comforting a fretful child, struggling to remember her French. Unfortunately, her command of that poetic language had never been more than inadequate. "You will be married soon. Then you will be happy."

Mariette summoned up a moist smile. "Yes," she said, laboring to respond in English. The smile trembled, then fell away. "But for me to be happy, you must suffer, and this I hate to know. You have been much kind to me."

Gloriana sighed gently. "I shall go on being your friend, Mariette, no matter what." *Unless I find myself imprisoned in one of the towers or shut away in a nunnery,* she added silently.

Mariette's hazel eyes were large and limpid with tears. "I thought you would be old. With warts and wrinkles. Kenbrook, he told me this. I am full of amazing when I see you."

Gloriana smiled and gave Mariette a small, reassuring squeeze. "And I am full of amazing when I see you," she answered honestly. Dane had told the truth about one thing, at least—Mariette was not his mistress. Any woman so timid and fragile had to be innocent as well.

Mariette uttered a gulping sob. "My heart is handsome, when I look to Kenbrook. But I see too that you care for him. I will go home to France, with Fabrienne."

There, however awkwardly stated, was the dreadful truth. Mariette loved Dane, perhaps as passionately as did Gloriana herself, but she was willing to step aside, to return alone to her own country.

Gloriana was touched, but she shook her head. "No," she replied. "It is you Dane loves, you he wishes to have for his wife, not me. I had thought to fight for him, but now—well, I realize I can't force him to care for me."

"Poor Gloriana," Mariette said, her lovely eyes brimming again as she patted Gloriana's hand. "Your heart, has he been broken?"

Gloriana did not wish to discuss the subject of broken hearts. Not then, at least, with darkness gathered close around them and matters looking so bleak. "Tell me how you met Kenbrook," she said, genuinely interested.

Mariette's expressions changed from moment to moment, each one clearly reflecting the corresponding emotion. "I am in the market one day, with Fabrienne. He is there." She smiled and sighed dreamily. "He is strong and handsome." A frown replaced the smile, and fear flickered in her wonderful eyes. "Bandits come to make stealing. One of them take me onto his horse." A shudder moved through her delicate frame. "Fabrienne, she scream. There is fighting. Kenbrook, he make sparks with his sword." Another smile, this one beatific. "I am saved."

It was a stirring story, and Gloriana had been able to imagine it in vivid detail: the colorful awnings on the merchants' booths, the bright cloth, the squawking chickens and warbling doves in their crates, the chilling ring of metal striking metal. She could hardly blame Mariette for falling in love with her rescuer; any woman would have under such dramatic circumstances.

Gloriana smiled. "I am glad. That he saved you, I mean."

Mariette stood, the bedcovering still draped around her. "You are kind," she said. "I will sleep now, if you do not hate me."

Gloriana followed Mariette to the door. "I could never hate you," she said. Her life might have been easier if that hadn't been true. They said good night, and Mariette stepped into the passage, where Fabrienne was pacing, muttering Gallic complaints. She immediately claimed her charge and squired her back to her own chamber.

Gloriana had not expected to sleep, and she was right. She dozed a few times, tossed fitfully, and was wide awake long before the cock's crow signaled the coming of dawn. Hastily, she washed and dressed and slipped out of her chamber, slinking along shadowy passages and avoiding the main corridors, until she reached a side door, long since forgotten by everyone but her, and passed through it.

The chapel bells pealed, summoning all and sundry to mass and prayers, and Gloriana felt more than a little guilt at evading her Christian duty, but she walked steadily in the opposite direction. Dawn turned the blossoms in the apple orchard to pink and apricot as she passed between the whispering trees on her way to one of the side gates. Presently, she was outside the castle wall and walking along a rutted woodland track toward the abbey.

Morning prayers were over by the time Gloriana reached the convent wall and tapped briskly at a wooden gate. A pair of eyes assessed her through the small, grilled window, and then the portal swung open wide. The nun who had admitted Gloriana was, nevertheless, disapproving.

"It is not mete for her ladyship to traverse these woods

alone," the woman scolded. "There are outlaws aboard these days, and wolves too. And boars."

Gloriana replied with a meek nod. "I was very careful," she lied. In truth, she had not once thought of wild animals or robbers, for her mind had been filled with Dane. Still, wolves and boars and outlaws were very real dangers, and she should have brought along a bow to protect herself. "Is the lady Elaina about?"

"She is at her prayers," said the sister, closing the gate with a smart slam and fitting the strong latch in place. "As you should be, milady, at this, the Lord's hour."

Gloriana wisely refrained from pointing out that the good sister herself had not been at prayer. The abbey's main chapel was some distance from the gate by which Gloriana had entered. "May I wait for her? She sent word to Hadleigh Castle, yesterday, that she would see me."

The nun sighed. "I suppose," she said, pointing toward the small courtyard where Elaina spent most of her time in spring and summer and well into autumn. "Take a seat there, by the fountain, and bide until her ladyship's wont to join you."

"Thank you," Gloriana said, and made a face at the good sister's back.

The wait was not a long one. Elaina arrived, as soundlessly as a shade, the way she always did, but she was thinner, and there were shadows under her eyes. She took Gloriana's hands in hers as Gloriana rose to kiss both her cheeks.

"I have been away too long," Gloriana said, full of sorrow.

Elaina smiled. "Nonsense. Dane is home, and you must attend him."

Gloriana averted her eyes as the two women sat down on the cool marble bench, their hands still clasped. "Attend him? He has spurned me. He wants another."

"He is a fool, and does not know what he wants," Elaina said fondly. But then her hands tightened almost painfully on Gloriana's, and there was an urgent note in her voice when she went on. "You must not allow Dane to take another wife and put you away, Gloriana. The results will be tragic for all of us."

Gloriana felt a shadow fall across her heart. Everyone knew that Elaina was mad, but her affliction had brought with it a number of strange gifts, one of which was an ability to foretell the future with uncanny accuracy. "What can I do?" she whispered. "He doesn't want me."

Elaina's hand trembled as she reached up and smoothed Gloriana's wild hair back from her face. "Great difficulties and terrible dangers lie ahead," the madwoman said in a calm yet urgent voice. "But you have the heart of a lioness, my bold Gloriana. Follow where it leads you, even into the very flames of hell, for heaven lies beyond and you can reach it by no other path."

"I don't understand," Gloriana protested.

Elaina stood. "Follow," she said tenderly, and would add not another word.

Chapter

5

*W*hen Gloriana returned to Hadleigh Castle, riding a small gray mule borrowed from the abbess and entering through the main gate, she saw that a tattered pavilion had been erected in the outer bailey, beside the mock battlefield where Gareth's men-at-arms commonly polished their fighting skills. A platform had been raised, upon which trumpeters would stand, in full livery of the Hadleigh red and gold. A quintain, a dummy in full armor meant to serve as a target, swayed from the crossbar of a high post in the center of the field.

Today, Gloriana thought with some sorrow, marked the official end of Edward's boyhood. After the dubbing, scheduled to take place in the keep's inner courtyard after a festive breakfast in the great hall, Edward would be a soldier and vulnerable to all the attendant perils of his profession.

She proceeded into the second bailey, stopping at the stables to surrender the mule to a groom and give orders that the animal be returned to the abbey forthwith.

Gloriana paused in the chapel to offer a quick prayer of apology for having missed the morning mass. Then, after stopping beside a fountain to splash her face with cool water, she entered the great hall.

Edward and his fellow aspirants were seated at a special table, set parallel with the base of the dais. They all wore the customary white silk garments, shirts and breeches and tunics, with colorful cloaks over these.

Gloriana caught Edward's eye—his face clearly showed the effects of last evening's drinking contest with Dane and the sleepless vigil in the chapel that had followed—and smiled her encouragement. Aspiring members of the order of chivalry were required to watch and pray throughout the night that preceded their dubbing, that their souls might be prepared and purified for the solemn oath they would make in the morning.

Edward's answering smile was wan, but full of pride and quiet affection.

Only after that exchange did Gloriana trouble to raise her eyes to the dais and scan it for Dane. He was there, of course, resplendent in his green and white tunic, seated be-side Gareth. Mariette was not present, a fact which at once concerned Gloriana and caused her to feel relief. She had not wanted to give up her place on the dais on this day of all days, but she would have done so before sharing the table with both Kenbrook and his future bride.

After tendering a deep curtsy to Gareth, who was regard-ing her with a thoughtful frown, Gloriana climbed the dais steps and took her place beside her husband—the man Elaina had enjoined her to win for herself, at all costs.

She had not entirely decided that he was worth the effort.

Kenbrook rose as she seated herself and offered the slightest bow of his leonine head. "At last," he said, and while his smile was charming, his voice was acidic. "Where have you been?"

Gloriana sat down and helped herself to crusty brown bread and a wedge of yellow cheese, both of which were arrayed in abundance on great wooden platters. "The lady Elaina wished to see me," she answered, with exaggerated politeness, never meeting his gaze. "Since you delivered the summons yourself, only yesterday afternoon, and since the lady is my dearest friend in all the world but for Edward, you might have de-duced as much and never troubled to ask the question."

"You left the keep alone." Dane spoke in a flat, expres-sionless tone.

"Of course," Gloriana replied. "Everyone was too busy to escort me, after all. Edward was having his ceremonial bath, and then there was the special mass, which even the lowliest of the servants attended. Who should I have asked to ride with me to the abbey?"

"You might have waited," Dane pointed out, obviously struggling to keep his temper. "I am sure that when the Lady Elaina asked for your attendance, she did not expect you to arrive, unescorted and unchurched, before the cock had ceased his crowing!"

Gloriana ate hungrily of the delicious cheese before replying sweetly, "Nevertheless, I have been to the abbey and returned in safety, riding Sister Margaret's little donkey."

Dane reached for his wine, drank deeply, and set the tankard down with a resounding thump. Out of the corner of her eye, Gloriana saw both Father Cradoc and Master Eigg lean forward over their trenchers to stare. "You are incorrigible," Kenbrook said evenly.

Gloriana smiled brilliantly. "How fortunate that I am not your problem," she replied, meeting his gaze at last. "Were I you, I should turn my thoughts to the lovely Mariette, who is fragile and quite terrified of this uncivilized country of ours and all its unruly occupants."

To Gloriana's great satisfaction, a rush of color surged up Kenbrook's neck and simmered at his jawline. "She told you this?"

"Yes," Gloriana said, spearing another bit of cheese with the point of her knife. "We are friends. She is quite aggrieved at spoiling my marriage—it seems she expected me to have warts and wrinkles—and wants very much to return to France. I begged her to remain here, of course. The sooner we have severed the bonds of our unholy matrimony, the sooner I may go about making a life for myself."

Dane took another swallow of wine, an audible gulp this time, which might have meant she'd gotten under his skin— or merely that he was thirsty. A night of ale-swilling and carousing undoubtedly made for a parched tongue, as well as a headache and a roiling stomach. Gloriana hoped so, for St. Gregory's sake.

"We have already discussed the matter of your 'life.' Pray,

spare yourself the trouble of making one, as a suitable voca-
tion will be provided for you."

Gloriana's smile was angelic, beatific, blinding—she
meant it to be so. "The devil take you," she said adoringly.
"And all your pompous plans for tucking me away in some
genteel and luxurious prison."

Kenbrook gave a long and ragged sigh. "I truly think you
are my punishment for forgotten sins," he said.

"Mayhap," Gloriana agreed cheerfully. "I'm not surprised
that they've slipped your mind—your misdeeds, I mean—
for their number is surely beyond counting, like the stars in
the heavens."

"It is a happy thing for you, milady," Kenbrook said,
beaming upon the hallful of happy breakfasters as he spoke,
"that I do not believe in raising my hand to a woman. Oh,
to absent my own principles just long enough to take you
across my knee and whack some sense into you."

"While that may be where you keep what sense you have
been blessed with," Gloriana countered, "my own resides in
my head and heart." She sighed in a deep and worldly fashion. "Alas, I confess that I suffer from a similar scruple to
yours, my lord. Were murder not a mortal sin, I should put
an arrow through your treacherous heart and dance for joy
before all Creation."

Gareth, who had apparently been listening to the conversation from its inception, interceded at last. "Stop this spar-
ring at once, or I swear I shall have you both clapped in
irons and carted off to the dungeons, leaving the rest of us
in peace."

Dane started to protest, but Gloriana, who remembered
that she loved Kenbrook, touched his arm to prevent him.
Beneath the green-and-white-checked silk of his sleeve, his
muscles felt like tempered steel.

"This is Edward's day," she said quietly. "I would not
spoil it with our discord."

Dane hesitated, and she thought she saw pain in his eyes
as he regarded her, along with barely suppressed annoyance.
"Nor would I," he agreed. "Shall we call a truce, Lady
Kenbrook?"

She nodded, her mouth curved into a smile. "Until the
morrow," she said.

Kenbrook laughed and raised his wine goblet. "Until the morrow," he replied.

"How fleeting," Gareth remarked dryly, "is this sweet harmony."

Neither Gloriana nor Dane offered a comment.

Once the friends and family of Edward and his fellow aspirants had taken their breakfast, a trumpet sounded from the courtyard. Dane rose and offered his arm to Gloriana, who took it in a suitably meek and docile manner.

Just the touch of her fingers on the swell of his forearm sent unsettling tremors through his muscles and along his bones. Kenbrook wanted, at one and the same time, to thrust her away from him and to draw her close. The thought of bedding her, assiduously avoided these many years since their sham of a wedding, thundered in his mind and lay like a molten weight in his groin.

Dane was many things, but he was not a liar. From the moment he had seen Gloriana that first day, reclining in her tub, blanketed in yellow rose petals, he had desired her with an ardor no amount of reason or bad English wine could assuage. The night before, after Edward and the others had staggered off to the chapel to keep the required vigil, Dane had taken himself to the lake's edge, there to swim naked in moon-dappled waters. Even the chill had not relieved him—only one thing could do that.

He watched Gloriana out of the corner of his eye as he escorted her with some ceremony from the great hall and into the sunny courtyard, with its fluttering banners of every color. Gloriana was pure, Dane reminded himself, for all her saucy tongue and improper ideas, and he did not intend to despoil her—no matter what her attractions.

The decision was not entirely noble, for if Dane bedded this fiery woman, their marriage could not rightly be broken, and a divorce would become necessary. The little chit might even be trying to entice him, despise him though she surely did, just to ruin his plans and delay her own consignment to a nunnery.

Grimly, Dane set his mind to ignoring his virgin wife. His body was considerably less obliging; it knew Gloriana's slen-

der, agile frame for a perfect counterpart, and ached, in the
most primitive of ways, to join itself with her.

Fortunately, the celebratory nature of the day offered no
little distraction, for even as Dane and Gloriana took their
places in the courtyard, standing side by side, trumpets
blared over the tunes of minstrels wandering through the
crowd. With Gareth and Friar Cradoc, the fathers, uncles, or
brothers of Edward's fellow novices mounted the improvised
dais with appropriate pomp and decorum.

Although his relationship with Edward was prickly, Dane
felt a rush of pride fit to bring water to his eyes. He quelled
the response before it could do him dishonor and watched
his young brother lower himself to one knee, along with the
other lads, his head bowed for the friar's prayer. The minstrels fell silent, and the onlookers folded their hands reverently and pondered the ground.

In a ringing voice, Cradoc enjoined the God of heaven to
look with favor and mercy upon these brave soldiers of the
Cross, to purify them, to sustain their valor through every
trial, and finally to grant them a holy peace when at last
they lay down their swords to await the Resurrection. After
adding a plea for a good harvest, the priest ended his discourse with God, and the young soldiers on the platform
raised their eyes to him, but did not rise from their positions
of ceremonial humility.

"Do you swear loyalty to your God and your liege lord?"
the holy man asked of each novice in turn, in a thunderous
yet somehow tender voice.

Dane felt his heart constrict, thinking of the perils these
brave and hopeful boys would face once they went soldiering.
Even the graphic and often bawdy tales of the old soldiers
now tending Gareth's horses, guarding the gates, and walking the parapets could not prepare the lads for the singular
sorrows and glories that lay ahead of them. The varied faces
of war, sometimes beautiful, sometimes hideous, and very
often merely tedious, were unfathomable to anyone who had
not looked upon them personally.

"I swear," Edward vowed in a clear and solemn voice in
his turn, "to uphold the laws of God, honor the will of my
lord brother, Hadleigh, and preserve my honor until the moment of my death and beyond."

Gareth was holding a ceremonial sword, a family heirloom said to have a piece of St. Andrew's heel bone sealed within its hilt. He stepped forward, touching Edward's left shoulder with the gleaming blade, then his right. "I dub thee Sir Edward St. Gregory, knight of the realm and brave servant of Christ."

In a swift, sidelong glance of Gloriana, Dane saw a tear shining on her cheek.

Edward kept his head down, as was required of him, and did not speak.

One by one, the other lads were dubbed by the male heads of their own families with other swords, no doubt containing other relics. The fathers, brothers, and uncles were, every one, vassals and knights in Gareth's own service.

The boys rose gracefully to their feet, their youthful faces flushed with the knowledge of their new and hard-won status. Most had been training for this day from the age of seven or eight, first serving as squires to an elder knight, then learning to ride and to fight tirelessly with lance and sword and mace. The course of preparation was a long and arduous one, involving many bruises and broken bones, and none but the most doggedly persistent of the lads saw the ordeal through to its finish.

There was still the ritual called the buffet to be performed, and Dane, feeling Gloriana tense beside him, waited in silence.

Edward stood before his eldest brother, looking lithe and small-boned in his white silk garments, his head high and his gaze level with Gareth's. Without revealing a hint of reluctance, although Dane knew Hadleigh felt exactly that, the master of the keep drew back his hand and struck Edward such a blow that, despite the boy's effort to withstand it, he reeled. Blood streamed from his nostrils and trickled from one corner of his mouth, the droplets staining his otherwise pristine tunic.

Righting himself, Edward stood proudly before his brother and his lord, and a cheer of jubilation and pride rose from the crowd.

"Beasts," Gloriana muttered.

"Must I explain," Dane retorted pleasantly, "that the buffet is a necessary part of the rites, designed to assure that the knight remembers his oath?"

"You just did," Gloriana pointed out. "And I still think it is brutal and barbaric."

Dane did not respond. These lads, he knew, would suffer far worse than a hard cuff from a man of their own blood.

After Edward, each of the other boys was struck in just the same way, not by Gareth, but by the man who had dubbed the boy and heard his promise to serve honorably. Gloriana stood by staunchly through it all, although Dane could tell she wanted to turn her head, and he knew a certain admiration for her courage. Few women were blessed with the kind of mettle he sensed in her.

The formal part of the ceremony was now ended, with great shouts of joy that seemed to reverberate from the keep's ancient walls. The trumpets declaimed, dazzling in the sunshine, and the minstrels played their lutes and lyres and pipes again, and out of the merry cacophony came a strangely harmonious refrain.

Edward, having wiped his bruised face on the sleeve of his shirt, searched the gathering from the platform. When his gaze found Gloriana and his face lit up, Dane felt the sting of brief but venomous envy. Kenbrook slipped an arm around his bride's waist and dug his fingers into her rib cage when she made to pull away.

When Edward reached them, however, Gloriana sprang forward and flung her arms around the lad's neck, and he embraced her in an unsuitably familiar fashion, whirling her round and round as they laughed together. Dane ground his back teeth and reminded himself that he didn't intend to keep the chit anyway and that Edward had earned a bit of female adulation.

"I have a gift for you," Gloriana said, beaming up into Edward's face, which was incandescent with joy and pride. "I've been saving it since the summer fair, and it was so hard not to tell you!"

"Show me," Edward said, still holding her hand, and he finally glanced at Dane.

Kenbrook offered him quiet congratulations. Later, perhaps after supper, he would give Edward the jewel-handled dagger and leather scabbard he had bought for him in Italy. Gareth would present the boy with a horse, lance, and armor later, in another far less formal ceremony on the tilting grounds.

Edward murmured his thanks for his brother's good wishes—he and Dane had made a beginning at mending their differences the night before—but he did not resist when Gloriana pulled him away. Though younger than Gloriana, Kenbrook thought as they rushed off to examine whatever gift she meant to offer, Edward would make a suitable husband for her. He had no lands of his own, of course, and no fortune, but Gloriana was rich enough for both of them. Although tenderness was not normally a consideration in such cases, Edward plainly worshipped the little troublemaker and would no doubt trade his very soul to bed her.

Dane could not think why he balked at the idea of handing Gloriana over, along with the exquisite dagger. All he knew was that he would have died first. No, his original plan had been the best one: Gloriana was bound for the nunnery, where she would be safe and comfortable . . .

And untouched by a lover's hands.

Muttering a curse, Dane thrust his fingers through his hair and searched the throng for Gareth. Before he could take a step toward his brother, however, someone grasped his shirtsleeve.

"Monsieur?"

It was Fabrienne, Mariette's maid. Dane waited out a flash of irritation and then met the plain woman's accusing gaze. They had never been friends, but neither were they enemies. That would have required an effort they were not willing to make.

"How fares your gentle mistress?" Dane asked, as worry for Mariette replaced his impatience.

"She is well enough, my lord," Fabrienne replied, in careful, deliberate French. Although Dane was fluent, and she knew it, she generally addressed him with haughty precision, as though speaking to a dog or an idiot. "Though you neglect her sorely."

Kenbrook wasn't about to explain the obvious: that this day belonged to Edward and the other newly minted knights. He had inivited Mariette to attend the festivities as an honored guest, and she had batted her lashes demurely and refused.

It troubled him, that timidity of hers.

"What do you want?" he asked bluntly.

Fabrienne smiled. "Some tribute for Mademoiselle, to show your regard for her. A trinket, a ribbon—a penny, perhaps?"

Dane had neither trinkets nor ribbons, neither being a normal part of his personal accoutrements, but he opened his purse and took out the requested coin. Fabrienne snatched it from his palm, eyes glittering, and dropped it into a pouch suspended from her girdle.

Kenbrook offered a mocking bow; both of them knew Mariette would never see the penny. He had bought a brief interlude of peace, and while he wouldn't miss the coin, he resented the necessity of paying it. The first thing he would do once he and Mariette were married—well, *practically* the first thing—was send Fabrienne back to France.

"My lady Mariette may wish to join us on the tilting ground," he said.

Fabrienne made a contemptuous sound and trundled away toward the castle.

"What a noisome creature," Gareth commented, startling Dane, who had not been aware of his approach. "Why did you pay her? What hold does she have on you?"

Dane turned to his brother, annoyed with him and, at the same time, unaccountably glad of his company. "I vow, you are wont to gossip, in your old age," he replied, with a slap to Gareth's shoulder and a bright grin. "I paid her to go away and leave me alone—a bargain at twice the price—she has no hold on me."

Gareth nodded then said, "Where is your first wife?"

Dane held his grin steady, although it was difficult. "The lady Gloriana has gone traipsing off somewhere, in Edward's company. And I didn't even have to pay her. Is Elaina here today, Gareth, or did you bring your mistress instead?"

"God's blood," Gareth rasped, reddening again and wiping his brow with a linen kerchief, "but you are an insolent cur. Elaina has no desire to watch the titling, and so will join us for vespers and supper. And Annabel, as if you deserved to know, is far too discreet to attend me in public. She offers quite another kind of solace."

Kenbrook was reminded of his own desperate straits, where the sort of "solace" Gareth spoke of was concerned, and felt a grinding ache in his groin. Gloriana was his wife, but he could not bed her. Nor would he turn to Mariette, for it was not his practice to deflower virgins without marrying them first.

It would be easy enough to find a willing woman—several had already offered their services, in fact—but he'd lost his taste for wenching. Two females were quite troublesome enough, without throwing a servant or a whore from the village tavern into the mix.

"I am envious," Dane confessed, and received a wolfish grin for his trouble. "Tell me, wise brother, how you manage to bed one woman when you so plainly worship another?"

The grin faded, replaced by a shadow of pain that caused Dane to regret his glib words. "There comes a time," Gareth said, in a low and somewhat wistful voice, "when the loneliness becomes intolerable."

"I'm sorry," Dane said, and he meant it. "I had no right."

The grin was back. "I shall have a pint of ale for your penance," Gareth said, and slapped Dane hard on the back. "Nay, two. Edward did passing well last night at keeping up with you and that hollow-legged Welshman, did he not?"

"He did indeed," Dane agreed, with a laugh. "I will join you shortly."

Gareth nodded, and Dane watched as his brother set out toward the outer bailey, joining a brilliantly colorful stream of chattering celebrants.

"Do you like it?" Gloriana asked as Edward ran his hand over the sleek leather seat of the saddle she had given him. They were in her small, private courtyard, and the air was heavy with the perfume of the yellow roses that grew in profusion over the arbor.

His eyes glistened as he looked at her. "Oh, Glory—it is the finest saddle any man has ever owned."

"Any *knight,*" Gloriana corrected, for even though she feared for Edward, she was also fiercely proud of him. She knew better than anyone how true was his heart, how noble his soul. "You will have a steed after today, and armor, and a fine sword and shield and lance. But what shall become of poor Odin?"

Edward smiled at the mention of his dun-colored gelding, the horse of his boyhood, as beloved as his favorite hound.

"He'll carry nothing heavier than my squire after this day, and dine henceforth on sweet grass," the boy-turned-man replied, hoisting the saddle from the bench, where Gloriana had set it. A blush brightened his cheeks. "Thank you, Glory."

Gloriana bit her lower lip. She wanted to weep, so poignant and sweet was her affection for him. "You are most welcome, Sir Edward," she answered, with a little curtsy. "Come—you must claim your sword and lance and prove that you are an able knight. You will be careful, won't you?"

He was standing very close. Reverently, he kissed her forehead. "If I should slay dragons and drive back the Turk and perform great feats of valor, like Artos, the warrior king," he said, "would you find cause then to love me?"

She looked up at him, wishing she possessed the power to change her own heart and care, in the way of women and men, for Edward instead of his brother. "I shall always love you, you know that," she said, and felt the tickle of a tear streaking down her cheek.

Edward sighed. "In the same way you love Gareth."

Gloriana bit her lower lip, then nodded. "Yes."

He touched her cheek, brushing the tear away with the side of his thumb. "I am bound by honor to warn you, here and now, Lady Gloriana. It is not in me to give up gracefully. I yearn to possess you, soul and body, and that will never change."

"It *will* change," Gloriana insisted. "Someday, very soon, you'll meet a fetching maiden—"

"It is more likely," Edward interrupted dolefully, "that a suitable marriage will be arranged for me." He offered a flimsy and faintly bitter smile.

"Perhaps," Gloriana agreed. "Whatever happens, you mustn't waste your fine heart pining for me."

He had taken her hand, and he raised it to his mouth and brushed the knuckles lightly with his lips.

"If you kiss her," Dane's voice interceded coolly from the gate, which had moved silently upon its hinges, "I shall run you through where you stand, brother or no brother."

Gloriana stepped back from Edward and instantly regretted the impulse. After all, she had done nothing wrong and had no just cause to feel guilty.

Edward assessed his brother with a frown, but did not release his hold on Gloriana's hand. "Make up your mind, Kenbrook," he said. "Which woman will you protect?"

Gloriana suppressed an urge to hush her friend; Edward's dubbing had apparently conferred more upon him than the right to be called Sir. He had changed, in some fundamental way, in what amounted to a twinkling.

"Let her go," Dane commanded.

Edward seemed unruffled, as before, and in no hurry to comply. Gloriana, however, took a strange chill at her husband's words and pulled her hand free.

"I asked you a question," Edward said to his brother.

"And I will not answer it," Dane replied. "Gareth awaits, with your steed and your armor and your sword. Go, Sir Edward, and show all the whores and maidens and serving girls that you have at last become a man."

Edward went pale, but not with fear. The stains on his shirt from the obligatory buffet he'd suffered at Gareth's hand seemed more vivid than before. He took a step toward Dane, and Gloriana caught his arm and held fast with all her strength.

Her gaze, however, was fixed on Kenbrook, and she could not have hidden her fury even if she'd tried. "We have a truce, you and I," she said, to the tall Viking in the gateway. "As of tomorrow morning, however, I shall tell you exactly what I think of you."

Kenbrook threw back his head and laughed, which served to heighten Gloriana's rage and caused Edward to tear himself free of her grasp. Instead of pouncing on his brother, who was older, bigger, and much more experienced in the ways of battle, Edward rolled his shoulders beneath the blood-spattered tunic and drew a deep breath. He seemed to grow taller, deeper of chest, and broader of back before Gloriana's very eyes.

"Mayhap, I must prove to you, as well as to the 'whores and maidens and serving girls,' as you so coarsely put it, that I am indeed a man."

Time seemed to stop for a moment, but maybe it was only Gloriana's heart. The silence was awful, a pulsing void shutting out every other sound. If Edward challenged Kenbrook to a contest of arms, there could be only one outcome, and

Gloriana would have died to prevent that. Although she did not love the youngest St. Gregory brother in the fashion he desired, her regard for him was rooted in her very soul. She cast a pleading look at Dane.

"No," Dane said at last, meeting his young brother's blazing stare. "You don't need to prove anything to me, Edward, least of all that. I will not apologize for objecting to your handling of my wife, but I do concede that you are right on one account: I must choose between Mariette and Gloriana or forfeit my honor."

There was nothing for Edward to say. He had, in many respects, prevailed in the encounter. For Gloriana's part, she was still reeling from Kenbrook's statement. She had not thought there was a choice to be made—his commitment to Mariette had seemed unshakable. For all that he drove her insane with his arrogance and his commands, she felt a stir of hope so sweet that she raised her hand to her heart, that place where her fondest dreams were stored.

Sir Edward, whose colleagues and admirers awaited him on the tilting field, hoisted his newly acquired saddle from the bench and looked back at Gloriana over one shoulder. He did not need to speak to ask if she wanted to stay, for one quality of their friendship was a means of communication that required no words. He simply raised an eyebrow.

"I'll be along in a few minutes," she said.

Dane stepped back to allow Edward to pass through the gate and into the hedge-lined walkway that led back to the main courtyard. "I do believe he would have fought me with any weapon I cared to name," he reflected, turning back to Gloriana.

She had taken a seat on the marble bench, having had one too many surprises in the last little while. "I should never have forgiven you," Gloriana said.

"Do you love him?"

"Wildly," Gloriana said with a smile. She had, after all, sworn to a truce. "But not in the way you mean."

"I sometimes think he would be better suited to Mariette than I am," Kenbrook confessed, again catching Gloriana off guard. Her delight was tempered by the distinct possibility that her husband was not warming toward her, but merely being fickle—not to mention possessive.

"You may be right," Gloriana said carefully, lowering her eyes to hide her unseemly feelings.

Kenbrook stood now at the end of the bench, one foot braced against it, forearms resting lightly on his raised knee. Gloriana felt his grin as surely as she felt the sunlight and the breeze from the lake, and was not in the least surprised when she looked up and saw it.

"I had not thought to hear those words from your lips, milady," he teased.

Gloriana stood, disturbed by Kenbrook's nearness in a way she did not clearly understand. "Is there something you wish to say to me?" she asked, keeping her distance. "While I do not relish the prospect of watching Edward and his friends ride at each other with lances raised, I am expected to attend. No doubt the barbaric festivities will begin at any moment, if they haven't already commenced."

Kenbrook reached out and pulled the gate closed when she would have dashed through the opening, and Gloriana found herself pressed against it, effectively caged by her husband's arms. "Yes," he said. "There is something I wish to say to you, Lady Kenbrook. You are to kiss no other man but me."

His mouth was a fraction of an inch from Gloriana's, and her whole body trembled in anticipation of contact. "That is an unreasonable mandate," she protested, but shakily. "I shall not agree, unless you make the same promise."

Kenbrook's chuckle was like a caress, and her lips seemed to swell beneath it. "Very well," he said. "I promise I shall not kiss another man." In the next instant, he was taking her mouth, gently at first, and then with a thoroughness that weakened her knees. Her heart was like imprisoned thunder in her bosom, her groin ached, and her breasts grew full and heavy.

And still he mastered her, with his lips and his tongue, burning his image into her very soul.

Gloriana sagged against the courtyard gate when it was over, struggling to breathe.

Kenbrook stared down at her in apparent consternation and traced the outline of her flushed face with the tip of one finger. "God help me," he said, in a hoarse undertone, "for I am surely cursed."

Chapter

6

*T*hroughout that long and eventful afternoon of games and mock battles—during which all who were present sweated, spectators and knights ranged upon the tilting field alike—Gareth's glance did oft find his prodigal brother, Dane, and the beauty ever at his side. Gloriana seemed changed, as though she were only now her true self and had held her splendor in check throughout preceding years, awaiting Kenbrook's triumphal return.

They seemed to be in uncommon accord, these two, now absorbed in the many and varied contests of the field, now talking earnestly as though there were no one else but they two in all of Creation. It was Gareth's fondest hope that they would reconcile and go forward with their marriage—indeed, it was vital.

Alas, Hadleigh was a pragmatic man, and he was certain the armistice was a temporary one, inspired by the grandeur and high emotion of the day. Once they had all gone back to their ordinary lives, with the French girl Mariette there to complicate matters, Gloriana and Dane would surely find themselves once again at odds.

After the last trumpet had signaled the end of the afternoon's final game, Gareth plucked his kerchief from inside his tunic and blotted his wet, gritty face. For all the vast affection he bore them both, his reasons for wanting peace between Gloriana and Dane were not altogether sentimental. If Kenbrook denied the marriage, the hefty percentage of profits from Gloriana's father's still-thriving trade company would be forfeit. Lands and estates and cargo-bearing ships would revert to Gloriana's sole control, with the guidance of her managers and agents, of course, and the holdings of both Hadleigh and Kenbrook would then perish.

Gareth swabbed the back of his neck and murmured a mild curse. He could not allow such a thing to happen. He must take drastic action, however much he hated to interfere between his much-beloved ward, Gloriana, and his brother.

With a gesture, Gareth summoned the most trusted of his men-at-arms and, in a low voice, gave the necessary orders.

The knights had raised clouds of dust in their valiant displays of skill upon the field, and Gloriana's person, like that of everyone else's, was covered with the grit. Before evening prayers, when Edward and the others would dedicate their shiny new swords to the service of God, before the supper and merriments to follow, she meant to slip into her chamber to wash and change her gown.

Dane, who had been attentive throughout the afternoon and made the whole thing bearable with his commentary, escorted her as far as the great hall. Things had altered between them since that kiss against the courtyard gate, but Gloriana was afraid to put too much store by a few hours of happiness. There was still Mariette, after all, and the looming prospect of a lifetime spent behind cloister walls.

Kenbrook waylaid Gloriana when she would have parted from him and cupped her grimy face in his hand. "Your hair," he said. "You won't cover it, once the chapel service has ended?"

Gloriana felt warm color fill her cheeks, while something else pooled in her heart, and shook her head. "No, my lord," she answered, without mockery.

Satisfied, he released her, and she turned and hurried away.

Judith had brought a hip bath to her room, and Gloriana

stepped gratefully into the now-tepid water, washing herself from head to foot before climbing out again. She was seated on her bench in the little courtyard, brushing the dust from her hair, when the servingwoman dragged the tub out and emptied it near the wall.

The summer's eve proved balmy, and the merry notes of the minstrels rode light upon the breeze.

"I was that proud of Master Edward," Judith confessed. She herself was filthy with the dust of the field, for all except the kitchen servants, who were busy preparing that night's grand supper, had been permitted to watch the games. "He's found an admirer, you know, in that French girl your husband brought home."

Gloriana felt a twinge of guilt because she had not missed Mariette during the day's festivities. "However would you know such a thing, Judith? The poor girl has kept to her room practically since she arrived at Hadleigh Castle."

Judith nodded, eager to impart her bit of privileged information. "Aye, milady, you speak true. But there is a balcony off the lady's chamber, and she saw all she could of the dubbing from there."

Despite her liking for Mariette, which was sincere, Gloriana was nonetheless irritated. "Mademoiselle was probably watching Kenbrook, not his brother," she scoffed, rising to go back into her chamber and put on a becoming green kirtle.

For all the weight of the hip bath, even empty, Judith hurried after her. "Oh, no, milady. Her eyes were on Sir Edward and no other. My own sister Mag was kept in to help look after the girl, for that annoying Fabrienne had a headache. Mag was there through it all."

It was quite true that Edward cut a dashing figure, especially now that he was a knight, and it should not have surprised Gloriana to learn that Mariette found him attractive—such fancies ofttimes struck suddenly.

Still, the news *did* surprise her.

Kenbrook, Gloriana reminded herself, was not the only handsome and desirable man in the world. She smiled, humming softly, as she dressed. Now, if only Edward would take notice of the delicate French flower . . .

"Might I take my leave now, milady?" Judith chimed,

shattering Gloriana's pleasant speculations. "We're to have a fete of our own, this night, the servants are."

"Go," Gloriana commanded, with another smile.

Alone, she wound her hair into a tidy plait, woven through with green and gold ribbons purchased at the summer fair. After coiling the braid at her nape of her neck, she added a mantle of apple green. The bells summoning all and sundry to the eventide prayers began to peal as she was inspecting her countenance in the silver mirror.

The chapel was of course filled, with Edward and his chivalrous companions lining a special bench at the foot of the altar, resplendent in their new livery of scarlet and gold. In the first pew sat Gareth, with the lady Elaina at his side, and Dane, who was alone and watchful. Servants jammed the rear of the church, where Gloriana hesitated until Kenbrook's gaze, sweeping the congregation, found her at last.

His sudden smile was all the invitation Gloriana required. She walked up the rush-covered aisle to take her place beside her husband. Dane, too, had had a washing and exchanged his dusty garments for a shirt, tunic, and drawers of modest gray and brown woolens.

Before seating herself, Gloriana bent to kiss the Lady Elaina's papery cheek. Gareth seemed preoccupied and greeted his ward with a quick nod before looking away. Edward turned upon his seat of honor and favored Gloriana with a blazing smile.

She felt Dane stiffen slightly as she took her place beside him.

"Brazen pup," he muttered.

Gloriana suppressed a smile. "Be kind," she admonished her bristling husband. "This is, after all, the house of God." she assessed the plain but commodious chapel with new eyes. "Our marriage took place here, did it not?"

"I suppose so," Kenbrook answered, with benign disinterest. "I was halfway to Italy when my proxy uttered the fateful vows, and you, I believe, were a mere snippet, far away in London Town."

She remembered, suddenly, coming to this chapel with Edwenna for the first time, praying no one would ever learn the secret they shared with Lady Elaina—that Gloriana had once been called Megan. She had come from another world, the neglected daughter of wealthy, spoiled parents, one American, one English.

"Gloriana?" Dane's voice, roughened by worry, snatched her from the current of recollections that had threatened to drown her. "Are you all right? God's breath, you look as though you haven't a drop of blood in you!"

Gloriana felt warm and light-headed, as though she might swoon. She who had never fainted in all her life, even after falling out of a tree one summer afternoon and breaking her arm. Had that happened here, in England, or in that country, as yet uncharted, that lay far beyond the sea?

"Gloriana," Dane insisted.

She'd been in the Saunderses' spacious backyard, had heard wind chimes, soft on the breeze, just before tumbling out of the apple tree . . .

"I'm fine," she whispered, shaken, as Friar Cradoc took his place behind the altar for the beginning of vespers. Despite her protestations, memories buffeted her without mercy, memories she had managed to evade, stifle, and smother for most of her life.

She had broken her arm in America.

She had come to London, not by ship, but aboard a great, noisy craft called an airplane. They'd had seats in the first-class section, and her parents had gulped down cocktails the whole way and argued in hushed voices. They'd been planning to divorce, and the source of their contention had been Megan herself. Each wanted the other to raise "the kid," but they could not agree, and so they were taking her to England, where she would be put into a special school and forgotten.

Gloriana closed her eyes as a wave of sorrow swept over her.

Dane put his arm around her waist and spoke quietly, while the good friar prayed one of his eloquent, booming prayers. "What is it?" Kenbrook asked.

If only she could tell him, Gloriana thought, recovering her composure by valiant effort. That was the worst part of remembering, worse even than knowing that her own mother and father hadn't wanted her. She dared not confide in Dane or anyone else, for fear of being pronounced mad.

Perhaps she was.

But no, she had the clothes, the little shoes, the doll, all tucked away in the trunk in the attic of her house in the village. They were solid proof that that other world had existed, though she could not risk showing the items to anyone. Even Cyrus, her adoptive father, had never been told the full story. He'd believed Gloriana to be a foundling, as Edwenna had claimed she was, raised until the age of five inside a convent. An indulgent husband, for all his rumored exploits of romance on the Continent, Cyrus had accepted Gloriana as his own simply because Edwenna had desired it so.

To Gloriana's recollection, the merchant had never asked questions, and he had treated her with a cool but steady affection her real father had never even pretended to feel. A dowry had been set aside, plans and agreements had been made, documents had been signed. Gloriana had become Cyrus's sole heir, and Edwenna had raised her to know naught but love and warmth, joy and safety.

She would be eternally grateful, she thought now, seated beside Dane, that fate had intervened, and brought her to her rightful place.

Tears stood in Gloriana's eyes as the priest recited the mass in Latin and then offered yet another prayer. One by one, the fledgling knights rose, as bidden, to lay their swords upon the altar and swear their fealty to the cause of Christ.

Edward was the last to do so, and colored light from St. George's window streamed down upon him as he knelt like the others and offered his vows. Then, rising, he did not sheath his blade and sit, as the others had, but instead stepped down from the altar dais and stood facing Gloriana.

His gaze straying neither to left nor right, he lowered himself to one knee and laid the gleaming sword at Gloriana's feet. "You I shall serve and defend," he said gravely, "putting none before you but the Savior Himself."

There was a thrumming silence, followed by a burst of excited chatter. Beside Gloriana, Dane was ominously quiet, and neither Gareth nor Elaina offered comment.

Gloriana leaned forward, cupping Edward's translucent face between her hands, and kissed his forehead. Flushed, he took up his sword, having sworn a public oath by his actions, slipped the sleek blade into its scabbard, and returned to his place among the other knights.

The service ended, and Gareth was the first to rise, as always, and take his leave. The lady Elaina, beautiful in a blue gown and veil, was on his arm. After them went Friar Cradoc, and then the eight knights in their splendid, unbloodied livery. Edward hesitated, as if to speak, then thought better of the idea and left the church.

Dane put Gloriana's arm through its own and squired her down the aisle and out into the main courtyard. Torches burned brightly all around, and there were mummers and acrobats and jesters plying their trades, eager to make merry. The delicious smells of roasting venison, eel pies, and other delicacies teased the noses and stomachs of the hungry celebrants. Supper was to be taken outdoors, from booths and tables, as at a fair.

Tonight there would be dancing in the courtyard, along with games and gifts and entertainments on a scale generally reserved for Easter and the twelve days of Christmas. Gloriana had, with Edward, looked forward to the fun for many months. Now her emotions were in turmoil, and she did not know whether to go or stay, speak or hold her peace.

Kenbrook, who had not spoken a word since Edward's declaration in the chapel, seated Gloriana on the rim of the central fountain and left her, returning a few minutes later with an eel pie and a tankard of wine. She took them gratefully, and ate with as much delicacy as she could manage, under the circumstances, while Kenbrook sat beside her.

"He is quite a showman, my young brother," Dane said, and Gloriana could discern no rancor in his tone or manner.

Gloriana was beginning to feel stronger, now that she'd had a few bites of the delicious pie and a steadying sip or two of the wine. "I pray you, do not lose patience with him," she said quietly. Merrymaking was all around, affording them an odd sort of privacy. "Edward is young, and newly knighted, and his head is full of tales of damsels and dragons, kings and wizards. He will tire, one day, of the game."

"Perhaps," Dane agreed hoarsely, watching Gloriana, his own food untouched and apparently forgotten in his hand. "But it is not uncommon for a man to love one woman all his days. It may be so for Edward, in his obvious regard for you."

"I truly hope not," Gloriana said, her heart aching as she recalled Edward's magnificent gesture in the chapel and the look on his face as he made his vow to her.

"Can you never return his affection?"

At another time, the question might have made Gloriana impatient or even angry. As it was, however, she felt only a certain poignant sorrow. "I have told you the truth of the matter," she said. "I cannot love Edward in the way he wishes, though I would if I had the choice."

The Viking-blue eyes, softer now, searched hers. Torch-light gilded the fair hair. "Because you love another," he said.

"Unwisely so," Gloriana replied, and knew she had said too much and been too frank.

Kenbrook touched her lower lip with one finger, sending shivers of desire through her with even that innocent contact. "Tonight," he decreed, with a smile, "we shall dance and make merry, and speak only of things that do not matter. We have the morrow to make war."

Gloriana laughed, although she felt uncommonly weary and broken inside. The thought haunted her that, if she had once been wrenched from the world of airplanes and cocktails and easy divorces, she might be taken from this one, in the same way.

"We shall have peace," she said to Dane, "at least until the morrow."

Lady Elaina, standing beside her husband and already tiring, longing for the solace of her small, spare cell at the nunnery, watched as Dane and Gloriana danced, in the midst of many others, beneath the flickering glow of the torches. "You are right," she said quietly, to Gareth, who had just confided his plan. "The night seems magical, with the music and the mummers capering everywhere, but they are proud, stubborn people, Dane and Gloriana, and it won't be long before they're arguing again."

"It seems rash, what I am about to do," Gareth confided. "Even desperate."

Elaina patted his arm. "The situation calls for uncommon

measures, my husband. And the results, should your efforts fail, will be dire indeed." She sighed and let her temple rest a moment against the outer bulge of his shoulder. Once she had delighted in Gareth's steely muscles and eager lust, but since the dark sickness had come upon her, bringing melancholy in its wake, she'd been content to leave such matters to his Irish mistress. "I am weary," she said. "Perhaps one or two of your men-at-arms would see me home to the abbey?"

Gareth flung her a look laden with pain and unflagging affection. " 'Home,' Elaina?" he asked. "What of Hadleigh Castle? Will you never return?"

Elaina regarded him in silence for several moments, her heart breaking. She could not begin to explain the things she had learned by virtue of her sufferings and the brief periods of elation that punctuated them. She could not say what she knew of Gloriana and the world beyond a certain gate in the abbey, and of the singular fates that awaited all of them.

"No, my beloved," she said softly. "I am lost to you. Do not mourn me."

Tears glistened in his eyes. "You ask the impossible," Gareth replied, but he did not press her further. He never did. Later, when the night's bitter work was done, he would undoubtedly turn to the Irish woman, Annabel, seeking the solace she herself could not give. Elaina conferred a private blessing upon them both.

Gareth carried her on his own horse to the abbey gates, which opened at their approach. Once, she thought sadly, she and her husband had ridden just this way, but for very different reasons. In those long-ago days, Gareth would have taken her to some private place in the woods and made love to her, on a bed of soft grass, until they were both spent from their sweet exertions.

Elaina laid a hand to Gareth's face before he could dismount and help her down. The abbess waited in the gateway, holding a lamp and gazing toward the ruin that was Kenbrook Hall.

"My beloved," Elaina whispered, and kissed her husband's mouth with love but not passion. "Godspeed."

With that, she slid out of his grasp to land lightly on the

ground, for she had been an able horsewoman in her day and a part of her remembered.

Gareth sat watching in silence as the abbess led Elaina through the gate, and locked it. Elaina wept soundlessly as she walked, for all the hurt she had caused and for all she had lost.

Sister Margaret was still distracted. "It is the oddest thing," she mused as they crossed the dark courtyard, the glow of the lamp spilling before them. "I could swear I saw a light in one of the towers at Kenbrook Hall."

Elaina held her tongue, for there were some things she would not utter even to a friend and adviser. Beyond the abbey wall, she heard the hoofbeats of Gareth's horse as he rode away at last. He could not know that a part of Elaina's very soul rode with him and would be his companion throughout eternity.

Edward avoided Gloriana throughout the evening, although he cast the occasional look of yearning in her direction, and she was grateful. She could not marry him, that fact remained unaltered, but not for all of this world and all of that other one would she cause him pain.

Eventually, the men began to trail off toward the village tavern, led by the eight new knights, and the mummers and jesters melted into the night. The torches were burning low when Gloriana slipped away from Dane—to bid him good night would put a formal end to their truce—and made her way through the dark gardens toward her own courtyard.

It never occurred to her to be afraid, for she had had the run of Hadleigh Castle since she was a child, and no one had ever dared to bother her. That night, however, as she was passing a tall hedge, there came a rustling sound behind her.

She thought it was Edward, playing a trick, or Dane, looking to start tomorrow's war early, and turned, her hands on her hips, to peer impatiently into the gloom. "Whoever you are, go away immediately," she commanded.

It was then that an arm closed around her middle from behind and a hand closed over her mouth.

"Do not be a-feared, milady," whispered a familiar voice

that she did not quite recognize. "By my soul, no one is going to hurt you."

Gloriana was not reassured, and she kicked and struggled, but all to no avail. Her attacker had the strength and bulk of an ox, and if he chose to break his own vow and do her injury, she could do naught to stop him.

She renewed her efforts, for Gloriana was not one to do nothing, even when there was no hope of success. Her assailant cursed fondly and held her fast, and others came out of the hedges and shadows, men she could not see clearly enough to recognize, to aid in her capture. She was, in a matter of moments, gagged, blindfolded, and bound hand and foot.

Gloriana's mind was completely alert throughout the incident, awaiting any miraculous chance for escape, silently calling to Dane, to Edward, to Gareth—to anyone who would listen—for rescue. She was put into a cart, not roughly but with something very like tenderness, and then covered in straw. The stuff tickled and pricked and made it difficult to breathe.

Gloriana's agitation was growing, and she worked to remain calm. She must think. Was this a prank, some rite of initiation, perpetrated by Edward and his fellow knights? But no, that couldn't be. Edward would never allow such a cruelty, let alone participate.

Provided Edward knew what was happening in the first place, of course.

A shiver moved down Gloriana's spine as she recalled some of the dreadful tales she had heard the servants exchange in the great hall late at night, by the light of winter fires. Her captor might be Merrymont, the awful enemy of the St. Gregorys, or a bandit, who would sell her, like spoils, to be carried far from England in the hold of a ship, destined to meet her end in the Sultan's harem.

By force of will, Gloriana stemmed that train of thought. The cart was lumbering over rough ground, which meant it was not passing through the main courtyard, the baileys, or the village, toward the drawbridge. No, they were traveling around the edge of the lake; she could hear the soft whisper of the water and, though barely, discern its pleasant scent through the smothering straw. All that lay in that direction was Kenbrook Hall.

Gloriana would have sat straight up in the cart if she hadn't been so securely bound. Kenbrook Hall, the official home of Dane St. Gregory, fifth baron of Kenbrook! She should have guessed, she thought bitterly, that all Kenbrook's attentions, from the kiss by her courtyard gate to the last dance of the evening, had been part of a grand ruse. She had expected hostilities to resume in the morning, but he had been cunning and contrived to deal with her in his own way.

Fury nearly overwhelmed her.

Kenbrook would pay. By the heel bone of St. Andrew himself, sealed inside Gareth's ceremonial sword, by every angel in heaven and every demon in hell, Gloriana swore to take vengeance.

The journey to the deserted ruin seemed to take hours, and perhaps it did, for Kenbrook's men were surely too clever to draw attention to themselves by making any sort of haste. It was full dark and a cloud had swallowed the moon when they rattled into a courtyard and Gloriana was, at last, lifted out of her nest of straw and relieved of her blindfold.

She still could not recognize the men who had taken her, but that didn't matter, she knew who they were. No doubt these paid soldiers of Kenbrook's were enjoying this night's dark exercise.

Gloriana was carried like a child through a courtyard littered with fallen stones, into the keep itself, and up a familiar set of stairs. She and Edward had played here, after she came to live at Hadleigh Castle. He'd been Arthur, while she was his lady, Guinevere.

She took some small comfort from the memory and did not resist her captors. This was not an act of surrender, however, but merely the careful conservation of her strength. To escape Kenbrook and whatever plans he had made to dispose of her, she would need all her wits.

After they had mounted more stairs and still more after that, a pair of great doors opened before them, squealing on their iron hinges, and Gloriana blinked. The chamber ahead was aglow with light.

"Set her down gently, you brute, or I'll have you whipped until you can't stand upright!" The terse command all but stopped Gloriana's heart, for the voice was not Kenbrook's at all, but Gareth's.

Gloriana stared wide-eyed at her brother-in-law as she was placed, like the most fragile and precious of icons, upon a chair. Because she was still gagged, she could not speak to him, and that was just as well. The words that came to her mind were not worthy to pass a lady's lips.

"Leave us," Gareth said, and began to pace back and forth at the edge of the lamplight. The room had seemed so blazingly bright only moments before, but now it was nearly dark.

The men-at-arms went out.

"As God is my witness," Gareth said, in a gruff tone, "you will not be harmed. I do this because I had no choice." He came to her and removed the gag gently, and then took away the bonds on her hands and feet.

She was too numb to flee, too stunned to scream or even ask for an explanation. She had worked up an ire for Kenbrook and did not know what to do when faced, instead, with Gareth. Her guardian. Her protector. Her brother, for all practical intents and purposes.

Her betrayer.

He left the circle of light and returned, momentarily, with a cup of wine.

Gloriana took it with a trembling hand and drank.

"Why?" she whispered, at long last. She was trembling and utterly exhausted, but she was no longer afraid.

"You are to be kept here, for a time," Gareth said gently, drawing up a short stool and sitting down. "Only for a short interval, Gloriana," he hastened to add, when she made to protest. "You will lack for nothing, I promise."

"Except my freedom," Gloriana said. A tear zigzagged down her cheek.

Gareth looked as though he might cry too, which was an amazing thing, for this man was not weak. Even his sworn foe, Merrymont, would have vouchsafed that much. "I cannot explain," he said raggedly. "There is a reason, a good one, and you must trust me, Gloriana. I beg you for that, and nothing else."

"How can I trust you, after what you've done?"

He sighed and rose from his stool, but his gaze was locked with hers. "I believe you do, in spite of everything. Because you know, somewhere inside, that you have no more loyal friend in all the earth than Gareth St. Gregory."

It was true, though Gloriana wouldn't have admitted it. And she still had her misgivings, and a grudge that was growing bigger by the moment. "Just wait," she said, "until Lady Elaina hears of this."

"Lady Elaina helped to plan it," Gareth answered. Then, unbelievably, he crossed the broad room, so much of which lay in darkness, his spurs jingling. His rap could be heard at the doors and then the protest of the hinges as one was opened for him. "Good night, Gloriana," he said, and he was gone, leaving her sealed within her prison cell.

Gloriana sat for a long time, while the lamp burned low, recovering the strength in her aching arms and legs and trying to deal with the knowledge that two of the people she trusted most had conspired to kidnap and imprison her. Even worse, no explanations were forthcoming—she was, it seemed, expected to endure the ordeal, and trust her tormenters.

Once she'd finished her wine and rested, Gloriana picked up the lamp and began to explore the room. It was vast, fully a third the size of the great hall at Hadleigh, and there was a window for each of the four directions, open to the night air.

Gloriana leaned out of the northern one and saw Hadleigh Castle in the distance and the sparkling waters of the lake. She set the lamp on the broad sill and cupped her hands around her mouth.

"Help!" she yelled, although she knew it was useless.

No one would hear, and if by chance the breeze carried her cry to the ear of a passerby, that man or woman would think her a spirit, haunting the ancient hall, and flee in terror. Her one hope was that Edward, finding her missing in the morning, might think to look in this place where they had shared so many happy, innocent hours.

Considerable time had gone by when Gloriana heard a stir on the stairway outside the chamber.

"God's blood," someone muttered, "he's heavy as a plow horse."

"Have a care you don't hurt him," scolded another voice.

"This from the very one who brought a stone down on the poor man's head!" retorted a third party.

Gloriana stood just beyond the inward swing of the great door and bolted through the space the moment it opened, only to be caught up from the floor, with her feet still running, and carried back inside. Two other men dragged their unconscious burden, none other than Kenbrook, over the threshold and dropped him carelessly on his face.

Gloriana got free of the man who had stopped her from escaping and went to Kenbrook's side, kneeling on the cold stone floor. His spun-gold hair was blackened and matted with blood.

"Dane?" she whispered, afraid for him in a way that she had never been for herself.

"He'll be fit tomorrow," said one of Gareth's men from the shadows. And then they were gone, locking the doors resolutely behind them.

Gloriana touched her husband's shoulder. "Dane," she said again.

He groaned. "My head," he said, quite unnecessarily, making an attempt to rise and failing.

"Just lie there for a moment," Gloriana commanded, scrambling to her feet and taking up the lamp, which she'd left on the table earlier. "I'll get some water and a cloth."

She had seen these items in her explorations, along with food, wine, firewood, manuscripts, a chess set with ivory and onyx men, and, perhaps most telling of Gareth's intentions, one large bed.

Having ignored her instruction to lie still, Kenbrook was sitting up when she returned, though he had not managed to gain his feet. "What the devil—?"

Gloriana knelt behind him and began cleaning the wound on the back of his head. "You've come home to Kenbrook Hall, my lord," she said dryly, "and the devil had nothing to do with it."

Chapter
7

"If the devil has not brought us here," Dane asked, drawing in a sharp breath or two as Gloriana, kneeling behind him, dabbed at his head wound with a damp cloth, "who has?"

Gloriana had had a little time to get used to the idea, and though she was angry with Gareth and certainly longed to escape, she hesitated to make him out a complete villain. She was still considering how best to reply to Kenbrook's question when he came up with an answer on his own.

"God's blood," Dane muttered, brushing away Gloriana's hand and levering himself, with no little difficulty, to his feet. "It was that fatheaded brother of mine—who else would dare to hold me captive in my own keep?"

Gloriana rose, too, and set the cloth and bowl aside on the table. "Why would he do such a monstrous thing to either of us?" she asked, baffled. "I have known naught but kindness from Hadleigh, and yet—"

Dane swayed unsteadily and righted himself by grasping the back of a crude wooden chair. "I'll have his teeth for this. I'll have his ears and the hairs on his—"

Gloriana waited, and was disappointed when Kenbrook did not deliver the rest of the oath. "I can only conclude," she observed, after a hopeful interlude, "that Gareth wants us to kill each other."

Dane laughed mirthlessly and dropped onto the chair with a barely muffled groan. "Kill each other?" he repeated, with a touch of mockery in his voice. "Think, Gloriana. Use the brain Friar Cradoc and the others have trained so assiduously, lo these many years. Hadleigh would have us mate, like a pair of rabbits shut up in a hutch, and thus render our marriage binding."

Gloriana was grateful for the shadows, for she wanted to smile and dared not let Kenbrook see. She might not approve of Gareth's high-handed methods, but she could not fault his ultimate design. Since the kiss by the courtyard gate, she had known that she felt more than admiration for her husband, more than common esteem.

"Oh," she said, standing just outside the reach of the lamp's glow.

"Is that all you can say? You've been kidnapped! And not because Gareth thinks the two of us make an exemplary pair, either. No, Gloriana—it is your dowry Gareth wishes to protect. A good portion of it came to him, and I'll wager he'd be destitute if his share was revoked."

Gloriana was stricken. She had known the terms of the agreement, of course, known there was a great deal of gold being invested and reinvested in her name. She had always thought Gareth's affection for her was real, however, and she was crushed to see him in this new and very disturbing light. "No," she whispered, even though she knew Kenbrook was right.

Her husband went ruthlessly on. "As your guardian, Hadleigh has had access to a percentage of the profits and would always have had, provided you were married to me. Or if you became my widow. Only if you and I parted company would the pact be nullified."

Gloriana put a hand over her mouth and turned away.

"Surely you knew the arrangement your father made?"

"I knew," Gloriana confirmed, barely able to get the words out. She was alone in the world, except for Edward, just as Megan had been alone. Her place in the St. Gregory family had been no more than a pretty illusion, false as a mummer's trick.

The chair scraped as Dane rose to his feet, and she felt him draw near. His hands came to rest of her trembling shoulders. His voice was gruff. "Gloriana—"

She was weeping—she who had vowed never to shed another tear in the presence of Kenbrook. "Leave me alone," she managed to say.

Kenbrook turned her around, instead, and pulled her close against his chest in an awkward but hearteningly earnest manner. "I was too blunt," he said. "I'm sorry. Gareth's affections for you are quite genuine, I assure you, if that's what brought on this torrent of tears. Even if there were no trading company spewing gold, he would want us together for all of time and eternity—and scheme to make it so."

Gloriana rested her head against his chest. The longing to tell Dane her secret was frighteningly strong, but she knew she did not dare to speak the words. "What will we do?"

Dane smoothed her hair, which had come loose from its plait during her struggles, and was prickly with straw from the cart she'd ridden in. "There is no escaping from this tower," he said. "We must accept that and hope Gareth will come to his senses. Or—"

Gloriana tensed, her breath catching in her throat, and drew back to look up at him with widened eyes. She didn't make a sound, couldn't have.

"Or," Dane went grimly on, "we could consummate our marriage, in which case Gareth would certainly release us." He read her expression then, though not with complete accuracy, as his next words proved. "Fear not, fair maiden," he added, with a crooked grin. "I am not such a brute as to ravish an unwilling woman."

Gloriana felt bone-melting heat surge from the apex of her thighs into every limb and digit. "How would Gareth know whether or not we had—you had—?" She paused, struggling to recover her dignity. "Why couldn't we just lie?"

Kenbrook sighed. "He would demand proof," he said gently.

Gloriana was horrified. "Proof?"

"The sheet from yonder bed," Dane explained.

She closed her eyes. "That is barbaric."

"We are fortunate," he replied, "that my brother has not required us to admit witnesses. That is a common custom in marriages where titles, gold, or property are at stake."

He was right, Gloriana knew, for she had heard of similar things. Highborn women, for instance, were often required to bear their children before a gathering of officials, lest one babe be exchanged for another, thus subverting the birthright of the proper heir.

"Gareth would keep us here, truly, until—?"

"I think so," Kenbrook replied, sounding resigned as well as irritated. And the blow to his head had been a sharp one; he was pale, and his clothes were bloodied. "Having gone to such dangerous lengths to achieve his ends, I seriously doubt that he would relent now."

"Perhaps Edward will learn what has happened and mount a rescue."

Kenbrook was actually rude enough to laugh at that suggestion. "Sir Edward might well try to save us—or more particularly *you*—that much I'll grant. But Gareth is a seasoned fighter, and he will have no trouble putting down the faltering advances of a novice."

Gloriana pressed the fingertips of both hands to her temples. "I could not bear it, were Edward to be injured or killed on my account."

"Edward will thrive, milady," Kenbrook assured her, with a smile in his voice. "By no account would Gareth ever raise a sword to the lad, or allow his men to do so. Now, lie down, I bid you, and take your rest. You are quite safe with me."

She nodded; there was no sense in sitting up through what little remained of the night, pacing and bemoaning her situation. Perhaps things would appear more hopeful under the light of the morning sun.

"We shall share the bed," Gloriana said, with forlorn magnanimity. "I cannot ask you to sleep on the floor or upright in a chair."

Kenbrook grinned. "I had not thought to sleep anywhere, milady, but beside you."

Gloriana interlaced her fingers and bit her lower lip. She had dreamed a maiden's dreams for years, awaiting her husband's return, longing to understand, at last, the mysteries of love. She was by nature a passionate and sensual person.

Now, suddenly, even with Kenbrook's promise of chastity, she felt exceedingly shy about lying down beside him.

"I usually pray before I sleep," she said, and immediately felt silly.

Kenbrooke's grin broadened, and he spread his hands. "Please," he said. "Do not endanger your immortal soul on my account."

Gloriana glanced at him uncertainly, then went to the bed and knelt beside it. She prayed silently, beseeching the Virgin to grant her discretion, wisdom, and especially virtue. Then she drew back the heavy velvet coverlet, kicked off her slippers, and lay down, fully clothed, on the sheet beneath.

Kenbrook, seating himself with a heavy sigh on the opposite side, made a great and complicated business of taking off his boots, stretching his arms with a huge expulsion of breath, and, finally, stretching out. Gloriana lay rigid as a corpse, her eyes open wide even though her lids seemed weighted with weariness. Her body pulsed with the need of sleep—and with a maiden bride's eager, reluctant need to end her suspense.

Dane moved beneath the covers, causing the rope springs to sway dizzyingly, and though there was a considerable distance between them, due to the size of the bed, Gloriana was quite conscious of the fact that he was removing his breeches and shirt.

"Sleep, Gloriana," he commanded, though he could not possibly have seen her in that thick, moonless gloom and gauged her alarm by her expression. "If I am to have you, it will happen in the broad light of day. Lovemaking is an art, not a science, and when I caress a woman, I like to watch her responses."

Gloriana's blood ran scalding hot at the suggestion, but not because she was angry. She should not have spoken, but she did. "I have heard that women weep," she confided, in a troubled whisper.

Dane sighed. "Should I succumb to your undeniable charms and my brother's devious plot, you shall not weep, at least not for sorrow. You have my bond on that."

Gloriana's cheeks throbbed with heat. Perhaps, she thought, it was the all-encompassing darkness that gave her license to be so bold. "What—what would my part be in the matter?"

Kenbrook gave a low, husky burst of laughter, and she felt him turn onto his side. *Is he naked?* she wondered. If only she dared to extend her arm and touch him.

"Your part," he answered, in his own good time, "would be to receive me."

She imagined that and felt light-headed. There was a warm, inexorable ache in that place shaped to take him inside her. "Does—wouldn't it hurt?"

He reached out, found her braid, and gave it a little tug. "There can be pain the first time," he said quietly. His tone contained no trace of mockery or amusement, and Gloriana was grateful. "I would, of course, prepare you well beforehand, and that process can be very pleasurable indeed."

Gloriana was silent for a long time. Then, softly, she said, "I am so curious."

"Are you asking me to pleasure you, Gloriana?"

She swallowed. "Would you? If I *were* asking, I mean?"

He laughed. "Oh, yes. Gareth shall not have his wish tonight, but I am more than willing to introduce you to certain parts of the ritual."

Gloriana was trembling. Either the Virgin had not heard her prayers, or she was a worse sinner than she'd ever dreamed. "I believe I should like to learn," she said.

"Get up, then," Dane said, "and take off that infernal dress. A woman's body is an exquisite instrument, made to release the most beautiful music of all, but a minstrel must touch the strings of his lyre in order to play it."

A delicious shiver went through Gloriana, and she did as she was instructed, rising and slowly removing her kirtle and chemise. Dane, whom she had expected to lie waiting upon the bed, arose instead and lit other lamps from the one that had been left burning on the table, until the whole chamber was aglow.

Gloriana stood as if paralyzed beside the bed, utterly naked. "I had not thought of the lamps," she whispered.

"I would see you," Kenbrook said evenly, utterly bare himself except for a pair of trunks, "and thus know if my touch brings you the gratification I shall attempt to give."

She grasped the ornately carved bedpost, in order to steady herself.

"Come here," Dane said.

Gloriana hesitated only a moment or two, then moved slowly toward him, into the center of the light. He assessed her untried body in a long, appreciative glance.

"You are uncommonly beautiful," he told her in a hoarse voice.

She remembered the kiss and all it had awakened in her. Had it not been for that, she might not have wanted him so much. "You will not take me?"

Dane shook his head. "No," he answered. "But I shall give you all you want of pleasure, short of that."

"It is not fair," Gloriana heard herself saying, "that I am exposed while you are covered."

With a complete lack of self-consciousness, Dane loosed the ties of his trunks, and they opened and slipped to the stone floor. He stepped out of them, his manhood rising hard and high against his belly.

Gloriana caught her breath. "I do not see how I could—how I could manage," she said.

Dane chuckled again and approached, laying his hands lightly upon her proud shoulders. "You needn't worry about that," he replied. "When and if the time ever comes, you will accommodate me very nicely. Nature, you see, has anticipated that particular event."

She wanted, suddenly, to flee, and yet she would not have denied herself, even if it meant owning all that lay in the four directions. "Will you kiss me?"

"Undoubtedly," Kenbrook said. He was looking, not at her mouth, but at her small, firm breasts, with their eager, jutting tips. He raised his hands slowly and cupped them in his palms, as he might hold the most fragile of treasures.

Gloriana drew in her breath, for she had never imagined the elation so simple a caress could bring.

"Only the beginning," Kenbrook said, chafing the nipples with his rough thumbs and then his palms.

A deep shudder moved through Gloriana, and with a soft cry, she tilted her head back and closed her eyes, surrendering to the amazing, fiery joy Kenbrook's touch stirred in her.

He filled his hands with her breasts, possessively but without force, and she thought of the comparison he had made earlier, between a fine instrument of music and a woman's body. Her flesh sang under the deft guidance he gave it, and she began to breathe faster and to make the slightest whimpering sound low in her throat.

Kenbrook bent his head and found her mouth with his own, stroking and fondling her all the while, and Gloriana did not open her eyes or make an effort to return his kiss. She was too dazed, too distracted by the unfamiliar sensations he was awakening in her.

He kissed her lightly at first, and then very deeply, holding her by the hips now. Her breasts, wanting something he had not given them, were pressed against his chest and further stimulated by the whorls of hair and the hardness of his flesh. Instinct made her grasp at his shoulders and try to pull him closer—onto her.

Into her.

Dane kissed her muscles to the consistency of warm candle wax, then held her at arm's length. He murmured some nonsensical plea to the old gods and then, bending his head to suck her nipple into his mouth, introduced her to an ecstasy so keen that she cried out and entangled her hands in his hair.

Gloriana arched her back, that he might have better access to her breast—surely it was a brazen act, but she didn't care. From the time her body had begun to change, she had awaited this communion, and now that it was finally, finally upon her, she gave herself up to every nuance of his lovemaking. Her flesh burned, her hair was damp at the scalp, the surface of her skin slippery with the heat.

He turned to her other breast and devoured that, and when he'd satisfied himself, he caught her head between his hands and kissed her again, this time with a hunger that inflamed her even further.

"Now," Kenbrook rasped, tearing his mouth from hers.

Gloriana expected him to take her to the bed, but instead he drew the chair he'd sat in earlier into the middle of the floor and led her to it. He set her hand on its back, for balance, and lifted one of her feet to the seat.

Nothing in all her maidenly imaginings could have prepared her for what happened then. Kenbrook knelt before her and stroked her inner thighs with his swordsman's hands, and she looked down on him and waited, holding her breath.

When he parted her and took her into his mouth, she sobbed with joy and urged him closer with her free hand. The rising tension, the exaltation, the promise of violent, all-encompassing satisfaction, caused her to rock against him, as though riding his tongue. Dane alternately teased and consumed her, and steadied her with his hands, still suckling, when the tumult began.

Gloriana was flung, as if by a catapult, to a place where she could see the backs of the stars, and Dane gave her no chance to retreat from the experience. When it was over, at last, she fell forward over his shoulder, boneless and only half conscious, and he carried her to the bed and laid her gently down.

She raised her arms to him, for his need of release was plain even to her innocent eyes, but Kenbrook shook his head.

"No, Gloriana," he said. "Not tonight."

Perhaps not ever. The words lay unspoken between them.

Gloriana was just beginning to breathe normally. She was flushed from head to foot and glistening with perspiration, and her heart still raced like a deer pursued over uncertain ground by wolves. Without speaking, she reached out, caught hold of his hand, and brought it to rest on her belly.

With a groanlike sound, barely audible, Kenbrook was again on his knees. His hand moved downward, to cup the place he had just mastered so thoroughly, and Gloriana tensed with renewed desire. Having known the splendor once, she wanted it again.

Kenbrook knew that, of course, without asking, and plunged one of his fingers deep inside her.

Gloriana raised both hands to her head, like a woman in the throes of madness, and moaned.

Dane bent over her and kissed her mouth, her breasts, her belly, all the while stroking her internally in a way that at once soothed and excited her. A delicious interval of growing fever had passed when he found a special, secret place inside her, one he had apparently been searching for.

Gloriana cried out and hurled her hips high off the bed.

Once again, the stars seemed to fall away behind her, as if she had worn them for a robe that was now shed, fragment by glittering fragment. Having driven her outside the boundaries of her own mind, Kenbrook patiently guided her back, stroking her thighs, whispering comforting words, soothing her in her wondrous delirium.

By the time Gloriana could assemble her thoughts into coherent patterns again, her husband had raised himself from the floor, gone round to extinguish all but one lamp, and found his way back to the bed. He'd stubbed his toe and cursed several times in the process, but did not speak a word when he lay down.

"Dane?"

There was a great shifting of weight while he settled himself for slumber. *"Hmm?"* he asked.

"What about you?" she asked.

His exclamation, though she didn't make out the actual term, was another oath. "Go to sleep, Gloriana," he said.

She indulged in a long, contented sigh. "Oh, I shall sleep, without question. But I am still concerned about you."

"Don't be." Dane did not sound at all friendly, given the intimacy of the acts he had performed upon her eager body. "I've been a soldier fully half my life, and I have undergone far greater hardships than any this day has wrought."

Gloriana gazed upward, into the darkness. The chamber's ceiling was not visible. "I am sorry, Dane," she murmured. "I thought only of my own desires. It did not occur to me that you would suffer."

Kenbrook swore again and rolled over, setting the rope springs to swaying again. "There are times," he said, "when honor is a wretched burden. Nonetheless, where you are concerned, Lady Gloriana, it must be served. Now, if you have even the faintest shadow of mercy in your soul, cease tormenting me with reminders of what might have been and *go to sleep!*"

Except for the things she had learned that very night, Gloriana was still innocent. Instinct told her, however, that she could seduce Dane simply by lying close to him, perhaps touching and kissing him.

Integrity prevented her from employing such tactics. Without her express permission, Dane would not have shown her the pleasure she had known. For obvious reasons, reasons that bruised Gloriana's heart, Kenbrook did not want to consummate their marriage, and she must respect his wishes. His body was his own to give or withhold, as Gloriana's was hers alone.

"Good night, then," she said. "And thank you."

He let out a loud, somewhat angry moan.

"What did I say that was wrong?" Gloriana asked, somewhat wounded.

Kenbrook did not answer, but hurled himself from the bed and began stumbling about in the gloom, evidently searching for his clothing, muttering as he stomped and bumped about.

Gloriana suppressed a strange urge to laugh and put it down to hysteria. There was, after all, nothing funny about their situation. They were prisoners, and there was no guessing how long they might be shut up together.

"What are you doing?" she asked, when she could trust herself to speak. Tears seemed more imminent now than laughter, but she would dive from one of the tower windows before she wept for him again.

Dane did not reply, but she heard a stopper being drawn from a ewer and guessed that he had found the wine. She sighed, settled in deep, and closed her eyes.

Sometime in the wee hours, Kenbrook returned to the bed and flung himself down, fully clothed, to sleep as soundly as a dead man.

Gloriana sat upright in bed the following morning, covers pulled to her chin, watching sunlight pouring in from another set of windows high overhead, filling the tower like some golden liquid. The chamber was not the grim, forbidding place she had thought, but more like a well-furnished solar. Extensive efforts had been made to make the room habitable.

There were braziers to provide heat and plenty of coals to feed them. Ample supplies of food and water had been laid in, and Gareth—or perhaps it had been Elaina—had even thought to send along a trunkful of kirtles and tunics and chemises. Fresh rushes covered the floor, and there were no cobwebs within reach of a broom.

Kenbrook sprawled beside Gloriana, on his stomach, his back rising and falling with the deep, even meter of sleep. She bent over and peered at the wound on the back of his head, which looked fairly good, all things considered, then rose and crept over to peer behind an intricately painted screen.

As she had hoped, the screen concealed a chamber pot. She was dressed and washing her hands and face at the basin, near the bed, when Kenbrook stirred at last and then hoisted himself onto one elbow.

"It wasn't a nightmare after all," he said in a tone of immense disappointment.

"No," Gloriana answered, blotting her face dry with a bit of undyed linen provided for the purpose. She was embarrassed, remembering the way she'd carried on the night before while Kenbrook dallied with her and then denied himself rather than make a promise, with his body, that he did not want to keep. "Plainly," she said, with what dignity she could manage, "our truce is ended."

Kenbrook sat up with exaggerated effort, one hand pressed to the back of his head. "Do not try my patience, woman," he warned. "I am not a man who is at his best at this hour of the morning."

Bells chimed, pure and silvery, from the other side of the lake. "We're missing mass," Gloriana observed, sticking to plain subjects, lest she say something incendiary.

"That," Kenbrook said, heaving himself to his feet at long last, "is a great pity." He moved unsteadily to the food stores on the other side of the room and examined the crocks and baskets until he found a loaf of bread and a bit of cheese. "Let us meditate upon the trials of Joseph, robbed of his many-colored coat and flung into a pit by his wretched brothers."

Gloriana rolled her eyes. She was trying to be civil, but if Kenbrook was going to go about comparing himself to people from Holy Writ, she would not be able to hold her tongue for long.

Kenbrook went, with his bread and cheese, to the northern window, which overlooked the lake and presented an imposing view of Hadleigh Castle. "Damn you, Gareth," he bellowed, at the top of his lungs, his voice echoing. "Damn you to hell!"

"A fine thing to go shouting over the countryside," Gloriana said huffily, helping herself to a ration of food and sitting down at the table, like a civilized person. "It's no use hoping someone will hear you, you know, and come to the rescue. Everyone believes Kenbrook Hall is haunted, and you'll be taken for a spirit." She could not resist a little sting. "An evil one, at that."

Dane turned from the window, bearing a dark expression. One would not have believed he was the same man who had loved her so patiently, so passionately, only a few hours before. "They'll have to come back to bring us food and water, unless they mean us to perish of starvation and thirst," he said. "When they do, we'll overpower them. God's blood, when I get my hands on Gareth, he'll wish he'd died in infancy!"

Gloriana ate with precise motions designed to keep her temper in check. "You are overly optimistic, sir," she said, in tones equally measured. "As strong as you may fancy yourself to be, you surely cannot hope to prevail against half a dozen of Gareth's best men."

Kenbrook scraped back a chair, turned it round, and sat astraddle it. His eyes, as he glared at Gloriana, were narrowed and full of blue fire, while his hair only looked more wonderful for being in disarray. "You liked me better last night, methinks," he said. "Called my name, over and over, you did, and if Gareth's men were posted in the hall, they're sure to think their purpose has already been served."

"Stop," Gloriana said, and the word was half a plea, half a command.

He took a bite of cheese, chewed ponderously, and finally swallowed. "It was that very chair, wasn't it," he went on, in a relentless undertone, "where you stood with one foot up, while I—"

"Yes!" Gloriana cried, red from her knees to the roots of her hair. "Yes, damn you, it was this chair! Why do you torture me?"

Kenbrook's magnificent face softened. "An apt question," he conceded. "Perhaps I should put you through your paces again, good wife, thus rendering you mild and sweet-spirited. At least, until you catch your breath and can harangue me once more."

Gloriana lowered her eyes, mortified that a part of her wanted to submit to him, even then. "I confess," she said shakily, "that I have never known such feelings as you made in me. I would remind you, however, that my body is my temple and my own to command. Husband or none, you have no rights to it."

Dane was silent until she looked up and met his gaze. He had speared a piece of bread on the point of his knife, and although he put the morsel into his mouth in the most ordinary way, something about the gesture made Gloriana squirm on her chair.

"I suppose it is inevitable," he said, "that we shall mate. Gareth has judged me well—I cannot endure many nights like the one just past, without breaking."

"You would force me?"

He cut off another chunk of bread and once again ate from the knife. "I would not be required to force you, Gloriana," he said with pointed indulgence, after a lengthy silence designed, surely, to nettle her. "You are a hot-blooded little thing, and I could make you want me without laying a hand to you."

Gloriana, who feared he was right, was infuriated by his arrogant presumption all the same. "You are not so charming, sir, as you seem to think."

Kenbrook merely smiled at this. "Last night was only an introduction to the pleasures of the flesh, you know," he said, and there was a dark sensuality in the languor with which he spoke that entranced Gloriana, almost like a wizard's spell.

She gave herself an inward shake, but she still felt as though her muscles were turning to warm honey. She sat very straight in her chair and looked through Kenbrook as though he were transparent, willing herself not to listen, not to think, not to feel.

Kenbrook began to describe, in slow, vivid words, how he would prepare her, how he would tease her, how he would bring her to the edge of satisfaction and then deny her, beginning the process all over again. He told her what she would say to him in her abandon and what he would say to her, and how he meant to arrange her for his convenience and her delight.

Gloriana shifted on her chair.

Dane went on painting verbal pictures, impossibly erotic scenarios that caused her blood to simmer in her veins and her woman-place to ache. He talked and talked, never raising his voice, never hurrying, until Gloriana was fit to swoon. Her skin felt slick, all over, and she wanted him a hundred, nay a thousand times more, than she had the night before.

She had no way of knowing how much time had passed when Kenbrook said, in that same quiet, untroubled voice, "Come here, Gloriana."

Gloriana stood, fully aware of what she was doing, and moved to Dane's side.

Without speaking again or rising, he used his knife to sever the laces that held the bodice of her gown closed, and the garment fell back over her shoulders. With one tug of Kenbrook's hand, it fell to the floor in a soft pool of fabric, leaving her bare before him except for her thin linen chemise.

He set the knife aside to trace the shadows of her nipples with the tip of one finger, and the expression on his face was not that of a conqueror, but of a reverent pilgrim who has at last reached his place of worship.

"What of this, Gloriana?" he asked, in a throaty voice, bunching the gauzy cloth of her undergarment in his fist. "What would you have me do?"

"Tear it away," she whispered.

Ever the gentleman, Kenbrook complied.

Chapter
8

ad Kenbrook not already been sitting, he knew he
would have been felled, as if by a blow from a broadsword,
at the sight of Gloriana standing before him, naked, in all
her purity and perfection. In that moment, he saw the whole
of his future, as if some seer had conjured it before his eyes,
complete in every detail.

He whispered something insensible, out of his awe, and
at last reached down to the floor and snatched up the chemise he had sundered, at her request, with his hands. He
shoved it at her and said in a hoarse voice, "Cover yourself."

Gloriana pressed the fragile cloth against her breasts, her
eyes great pools of confusion and hurt as she watched him rise
to his feet and move away from her. "What is it?" she asked.

Dane strode across the room, selected a ewer filled with
wine, and poured himself a double portion. The stuff tasted
odd, but then it was English and crude in comparison to the
offerings of France and Italy. "I have had a change of heart,"
he said, turning to face her, the cup in his hand.

It was the greatest understatement he had ever uttered.

A fetching blush rose to pulse in her exquisite face. "Perhaps you sought to humiliate me," she said quietly. "If so,
you certainly succeeded."

Kenbrook swallowed another sip of wine, frowned at the cup, and set it aside. "I have no desire to do anything at this moment except hurl you down onto yonder bed and make you truly mine, once and for all. Since that would hardly be an auspicious beginning, I shall control my animal impulses as long as I am able."

Her wonderful, gem-bright eyes widened. "I don't understand."

"I am certain you do not," Kenbrook assured her, "and who could blame you? I only made the discovery myself a few moments ago, though I suspect the matter has been brewing somewhere in the back of my brain since I returned to Hadleigh and saw you again, grown into the full flower of womanhood."

Gloriana swallowed visibly, and her eyes showed plainly that she was trying not to jump to conclusions. It wrung his heart to see that she cared so much.

Dane took a step toward her, meaning to reassure her, then stumbled. His vision, clear an instant before, underwent a violent shift, and he could see nothing but a blur of shapes and colors. Perhaps, he thought numbly, raising one trembling hand to his head, the wound had been worse than he'd guessed. He took another step and then fell headlong into a spinning darkness.

Gloriana watched in horror as Kenbrook struck the heavy timber floor with his full weight, and was kneeling beside him before she'd consciously decided to move. She said his name, and he responded with a groan but did not open his eyes.

Panicked, Gloriana called to him again and shook him, but he made no answer, nor did he waken. She scrambled to get water and doused his head with the stuff, and still he failed to stir. Finally, she tried to drag him across the floor, hoping to hoist him onto the bed, but his inert frame was so heavy she could not manage even an inch of progress.

Tears burned on her cheeks as she dashed back for a pillow and blanket.

"Dane!" she called, patting his face smartly.

He merely sighed.

Gloriana barely heard the noise at the door at first; then

she realized Gareth had returned and was about to enter. She dashed behind the folding screen and wrenched on a plain brown kirtle, never bothering with a chemise.

"Gareth, hurry!" she shouted. "Something is wrong with Dane!"

The ancient lock turned, and then the door opened, and two of Gareth's biggest men entered, looking cautiously from right to left, obviously expecting an ambush. Their eyes fell on Kenbrook, lying prostrate in the middle of the floor, and one of them actually smiled.

"All's well, your lordship," the man called over his shoulder. "The trick worked, and Lord Kenbrook is having himself a wee rest."

Gloriana stood over Dane, her hands bunched into fists, her whole being suffused with rage. It was the wine, she thought, recalling that her husband had taken a deep draft just before collapsing. They'd drugged a portion of it, with an eye to subduing Kenbrook, that they might enter the prison chamber without fear.

Gareth followed close behind the two giants, who kept watchful eyes on Kenbrook despite his insensate condition. Seeing the look on Gloriana's face and interpreting it accurately, her brother-in-law raised one hand in a bid for silence.

"It will do him no lasting harm," he said, sparing no more than a glance for his brother. He smiled fondly. "You look well, Gloriana. Are you happy here?"

All that kept Gloriana from flinging herself upon her alleged guardian, snarling and scratching like a she-wolf, was the sure knowledge that he would find such an attack merely irritating, perhaps even amusing.

"How did you know that Dane would take your poisoned wine?" she asked. "If I had been the one to drink it, and *he* had kept his wits about him, you would be better off closed up in this room with a field bull than with Kenbrook!"

Gareth sighed. Behind him were servants, huffing and blowing, bringing barrels and a large copper bathtub, among other things. "You hardly drink at all," he replied, "but Dane likes his wine, and I knew he would be ready for the second ewer sooner or later. It was mere good fortune that it happened so quickly."

"I shall never forgive you for this," Gloriana said. There was no inflection in her voice at all, only a cool smoothness.

"On the contrary," Gareth replied, with the utmost gentleness, "I have every reason to believe you not only will forgive me—in good time, of course—but declare your undying gratitude." He crouched beside Dane and touched the pulse at the base of his brother's throat with an almost tender solicitude. Gloriana could not doubt that, however bizarre his means of showing it, Gareth loved Dane in spirit and in truth. "He'll come round in an hour or so, I trust," he mused, and rose again to face Gloriana.

The servants Gareth had brought were all over the chamber it seemed, laying out a meal and fresh garments for both Gloriana and Dane, setting water to heat over a special brazier brought for the purpose. One, a woman Gloriana knew well from the castle, went to the bed and tossed back the rumpled covers.

"Not yet," the chambermaid said, in answer to her lord's unspoken question, which had been asked with a mere raising of his eyebrows.

Gloriana's face burned. "Perhaps," she muttered bitterly, thinking of the conversation she'd had with Dane the night before, "you will require witnesses."

Gareth looked away, ashamed, but when he met Gloriana's gaze again, she saw purpose and resolve blazing in his blue eyes. She realized then that he was as stubborn as the abbess's little gray mule and wondered why she had not seen it before. "Do not try my patience," he snapped. "Nor is it prudent to taunt me with suggestions you would not wish me to enforce!"

She subsided, but only slightly. A new truth was dawning on her in those moments, a soul-shaking surprise that her pride would never allow her to confess, except in her private prayers. She, Gloriana, who treasured her freedom, did not truly wish to leave the tower just yet. She wanted to stay there, alone with Kenbrook, until they'd settled what needed settling, for good or for ill. The outside world held too many disractions.

"What has Edward to say of my disappearance?" she threw out.

Gareth was already turning to leave, but he paused at her question and, with an expression of deep chagrin, replied, "Poor lad. He believes you and Kenbrook have reconciled and gone off to celebrate the resumption of your marriage in the usual way. There'll be no help from that quarter, if that was what you were hoping for. The boy is heartbroken, I confess—but also resilient, as youths always are. He's already set himself, our Edward, to the task of consoling the mademoiselle."

With that, the servants went out, followed by Gareth and, finally, the soldiers. The door was soundly closed and locked behind them.

Gloriana looked round and saw that they had filled the copper tub and set out soap and cloths for drying. She knelt again and shook Dane. "Awake," she told him, in a voice at once stern and kindly. "If you do not, I shall take your bath for myself, and you will have none."

Miraculously, Kenbrook opened his eyes. If it hadn't been for the bewilderment she glimpsed in their blue depths, Gloriana would have suspected him of deliberately feigning unconsciousness all the while Gareth was in the chamber.

"Ah," he said, levering himself onto an elbow, "but I would see you unclothed."

Gloriana smiled, more than passing glad that Dane had come around, and was willing to overlook his impudence. Letting his comment pass, she said in exaggerated tones of sympathy, "You have suffered sorely, my lord, between that lump on your head and your swooning spell."

Kenbrook gained a sitting position, then stood, wavering. "I did not swoon," he said pointedly. "I presume this was some trick of Gareth's—the wine tasted odd, I will say, even for the poor swill that it is."

"You presume aright," Gloriana replied. "You were drugged. I suspect your brother arranged the tampering not so much to subdue you, as I first believed, but to ensure that you would not be harmed in a struggle."

Kenbrook made his unsteady way to the tub and hauled his tunic off over his head before ridding himself of his shirt

and breeches and woolen hose, as well, and stepping into
the water.

Gloriana watched him, unblinking, the whole while, thinking how splendid he was, even though he bore the scars of
fierce battles upon his chest and right thigh. He settled into
the tub with a lusty sigh.

"We were having a conversation just before you collapsed,"
Gloriana reminded him, busying herself at the table, where
a basket full of cakes and other delicacies had been left by
one of the servants.

Kenbrook made a lengthy enterprise of remembering.
"Ah, yes," he said. "You had just offered yourself to me, as
boldly as a tavern wench might do, and I, in my knightly
virtue, had set the whole of the chamber between us, in
order to save you from your own base nature."

"You are past arrogant," Gloriana said, biting into one of
the little honeycakes from the basket, but there was no
venom in her voice.

"Pray, come here and scrub my back, fair Gloriana."

"Scrub your own back," Gloriana replied promptly, sitting
down at the table. For the moment, she was more interested
in the honeycake.

"There was a time," Kenbrook informed her in long-
suffering tones, "when women obeyed their masters. The
world is changing."

Gloriana thought of the airplane that had originally
brought her to England, as the child Megan Saunders.
"Yes," she agreed. "You cannot begin to imagine what lies
ahead."

"And you can?"

She did not respond, for the temptation to tell him her
strange story was perilously strong. She wondered where her
writings were, the bits and scraps of parchment upon which
she had so busily scratched out her memories when she
was yet a child. She supposed Edwenna had destroyed the
scribblings or hidden them, as she had the doll and clothes.
But they had not been in the trunk in the attic of Cyrus's
house, with the other things.

Kenbrook was luxuriating in his tub. If the treated wine
had left him with any ill effects, he hid them well. "There
is something very unusual about you," he said, tilting his

head sideways to consider her. "You are stronger than most women, and bigger. Your skin is good and your teeth are uncommonly sturdy."

"You make me sound like a horse to be sold or traded at the fair," Gloriana commented, without particular concern. She was perishing to know what he'd been about to tell her when the drugged wine had brought him low, but she wasn't about to ask.

He smiled and sank to his chin. "You know I speak truth," he said. "You are different from other women. You get odd ideas—the sort an ordinary female would blush to consider, let alone execute."

"Perhaps I am mad," she suggested, rather blithely, "like the lady Elaina."

"Elaina is not mad," Dane responded, without a hint of reprimand in his voice. "She merely sees and hears more clearly than the rest of us do."

Gloriana sat very still. She might have spoken, might have told him everything she knew and had guessed about herself, but suddenly the room was filled with a strange whirring sound, as though from a swarm of bees. A blue mist rose all round, blotting out the light, obliterating Dane, moving and changing like a gossamer curtain.

She watched in horrified fascination as the tower room changed before her eyes into a strange version of itself. The floor was different, and the walls were hung with brightly colored paintings. People in strange dress moved about, studying the artwork and talking among themselves in that odd, quick language she remembered from earliest childhood. Gloriana was yet seated, but the table had vanished, and she had no sense of the chair beneath her. A very little boy in short pants, a shirt, and shoes like the ones hidden away in the attic of the village house was the only one who seemed to see her.

"Lay-dee," he said, pointing.

Gloriana was terrified that she would be parted from Dane, perhaps forever. She prayed, in frantic silence, to be returned to the thirteenth century, for that was her home.

She did not know how long she remained, suspended, before the vision faded and she was back in the chamber she recognized, with Dane. He was no longer in the tub, but standing beside her, clad only in the tunic he'd discarded earlier. He cupped her chin in his hand and stared deep into her eyes.

"God's blood, Gloriana, what just happened here?" he demanded in a raw whisper. He was understandably pale and visibly shaken.

"I don't know," she managed to reply miserably, after several failed attempts at speech. "What did you see?"

He dragged a chair close and sat upon it, his knees pressing against Gloriana's. "What sort of trick was that?" he countered. His eyes were narrowed, and he was trembling a little, this brave soldier who had faced the Turk. "I swear, Gloriana, there was something more potent than common sleeping powders in that wine. You vanished, even as I was looking at you." Dane caught her hands in his, found them cold, and rubbed them absently, to restore circulation. "Either my wits have deserted me or you are a sorceress, working spells."

Gloriana shivered, for to be accused of performing magic was a deadly matter. Many unfortunates had perished after such a charge was made, and their punishments had been too terrible to think about. "I am not a witch," she whispered desperately. "Please—do not utter such blasphemy again!"

"I saw you disappear," Dane insisted, gripping her shoulders. He wasn't hurting her, but she couldn't have escaped his hold on any account.

She lowered her head. "Surely it was the wine," she said, "and nothing more."

"Look at me," he commanded.

Gloriana's will failed her; she raised her eyes to meet his. "I cannot explain," she said despondently. "For I myself do not understand. I was here, and then I was—I was still in this room, but in another part of time, I think. There were people, but their clothes were odd—"

Kenbrook was plainly dissatisfied with her answer. His stare, full of wonder and confusion, made her feel like some sort of peculiar specimen found on the underside of a moldy leaf. His voice was raspy. "Has this ever happened before?"

"Once," Gloriana confessed, barely able to force the word past her lips. "When I was a little girl."

"Tell me?"

She clasped her hands across her middle and bent slightly forward, not sick, but unable to sit still. She didn't want to tell, could hardly bear to remember. "I was with a group of other children, from Briarwood School. I'd been left there, at the school, I mean, because my mother and father didn't want me. We—we came to see the village, and the castle, and there was a gate—"

Dane drew Gloriana out of her chair and onto his lap. His arms made a circle of safety around her. "Edwenna, not want you?" he scoffed in the tenderest way. Moved by her distress, he smoothed her hair with his hands. "Utter nonsense. She adored you—everyone knew she lived to indulge your every wish."

Gloriana slipped her arms around Kenbrook's neck. "Edwenna," she whispered, as though to bring that good woman back by magic. She turned her head and looked deep into her husband's troubled and bewildered eyes. "Edwenna wasn't truly my mother."

"You were a foundling," Dane said quietly. "I remember that now."

"This is a snarl, and I am caught," Gloriana whispered. "I wish to tell the truth to at least one living person, my lord, but I am so afraid."

"What could be so terrible that you would not tell your husband?" Dane's voice was low and thoughtful, almost coaxing. In attempting to calm her, he had plainly soothed himself as well.

"A husband who wishes to send me to a nunnery that he might marry someone else," Gloriana reminded him. Her heart was thudding so hard she feared she would swoon from it, so fast did her blood rush through her veins.

"I started to explain that earlier, before Gareth's treated wine had its effect. Something has changed for me—I would preserve this marriage. Tell me your dark secret, Gloriana."

She gnawed at her lower lip for a few moments. "You won't believe me," she said. "Not in the beginning, at least. But I can prove some of what I am about to say, once we're free again."

Kenbrook leaned back in the chair, watching her face, and simply waited for her to go on.

Gloriana plunged her fingers into her hair. "But when I show you evidence of my claim, you will name me witch—"

"I could already do that," Dane interrupted reasonably, lowering her hands, holding them between his own. "After all, I saw you vanish into the ether just a few moments past."

She stared at him. "You know what they would do, and I am not evil—I swear I am not!"

"No one is going to hurt you," Kenbrook insisted. "Besides, I have no plans to tell the world what happened here—if for no more admirable reason than that I do not wish to put my own sanity in question."

It was true that Kenbrook would be thought demented if he told her secret to anyone. He might even be accused along with Gloriana of working the devil's will. She must tell him now, she knew that, and yet she could not think how to frame the words of her confession. She turned her thoughts within, engaging them in the problem, and Kenbrook was uncommonly patient and did not prod her.

A long time had passed when she spoke, and even then, she faltered. "Things are not so simple as they seem, and it would appear, too, that time is not a matter of moment following moment, year following year. Creation is—it has many layers, I think, rather like an onion, or the rings inside a tree trunk. Each is separate, in its way, yet still part of the whole."

Kenbrook frowned slightly and nodded for her to continue.

"You and I come from different parts of the tree."

He chuckled and shook his head. "You'll have to make it clearer than that, milady. I am a soldier, not a scholar."

"Imagine history as the trunk of a great oak, with many, many rings," Gloriana said, after a moment or two of hard thought. "Each ring represents a different year."

"Go on."

"I was born in a very distant age," Gloriana said all in a rush, squeezing her eyes shut. "One that has not yet dawned."

"You are saying that you've come to us from some later time." Dane spoke matter-of-factly, without judgment but also without affirmation.

Gloriana stared at him, amazed that he had spoken so calmly, so reasonably. "Yes."

"What year?"

"I was a small child at the time," Gloriana said, watching his face, trying to work out whether he believed her or not. He was clearly fascinated. "I don't remember the year. Maybe I never knew in the first place." She couldn't bear the suspense another moment. "You do believe me, don't you?"

Kenbrook considered her at length. "I am inclined to think you speak the truth," he said at last. "If you can disappear—and I trust the testimony of my eyes and my brain, for I am not a fanciful man—it seems possible that you might also travel through time. Surely, one feat is no stranger than the other."

Gloriana was so relieved that she sagged against him, resting her head upon his shoulder and drawing deep, tremulous breaths. "Thank you," she said.

He stroked her hair. "We will speak of this again, and I shall wish to see this proof you spoke of earlier." His lips brushed her forehead. "I could not stand it if you were lost to me," he said so softly that her heart heard the words more clearly than her ears.

She sat upright again to look into Dane's fierce blue eyes. "It would not be honorable," she reminded him, "to swear your devotion only because you are held captive in a tower and want a pleasant diversion. "

"You are my wife," he said. "I would claim you."

A hot flush suffused Gloriana from toes to scalp. "Now?"

"Only if that is your wish."

She bounded off his lap. It was her wish that their marriage should be real, and that meant consummation. She could not doubt that the experience would be more than pleasant, given the sweetly wicked things he had taught her in the night. So why was she hesitating? Why was her heart pounding, fit to burst through her chest wall?

Dane stood, and the faintest shadow of a smile rested upon his lips. "Perhaps you need time, after all, to accustom yourself to the idea."

Gloriana was pacing, hands clasped, fingers interlocked. "The sun is high," she said, in a whisper. "Besides, someone might be listening at the door." A truly horrid thought struck her. "Or looking through the keyhole!"

After retrieving his trunks from the floor next to the bathtub, Dane crossed the room to the great double doors and hung the garment over the latch, easily obscuring the view. He returned to the table, keeping the width of its surface between them, and purloined a honeycake from the basket. "As for the other part," he said, after taking a bite and relishing it in a way that roused still other unseemly memories of the night before, "you'll simply have to be quiet."

Gloriana raised the fingertips of her right hand to her temple. Things were happening too fast; only minutes ago, some secret veil had been parted, and she had slipped through into another time. She had uttered a truth so long and so well hidden that she'd almost forgotten it herself. Now Kenbrook, who had wanted, just yesterday, to put her aside and take another woman for his wife, wished to bed her after all.

She could not stand still, but moved from one part of the tower room to another in her agitation. Dane watched her, in amused silence, until she wore herself out and slumped down onto a wooden chest.

Kenbrook went to the harp, which stood on the opposite side of the chamber, and strummed the strings, making brief, chaotic music.

"What are you afraid of, Gloriana?" he asked.

She wet her lips nervously. "I fear being used, my lord," she said truthfully, "and then cast aside. I fear that you merely wish to spend the shock of what I have told you— what you have seen—"

He strummed the harp strings again, perfectly composed and patently unhurried. "There is plenty of time for both of us to get used to the idea," he replied. "Gareth, damn his eyes, has seen to that."

Having thus spoken, he found trunks and woolen hose among the garments that had been provided for his captivity and finished dressing. When he came back to the table in the center of the room, he carried a board and chess pieces, also left by their benign jailers.

Gloriana watched from her perch on the chest, feeling silly and incredibly shy and very shaken. "How can you be so calm," she demanded as he prepared the board for play, "when you saw a woman vanish before your eyes?"

"I have seen other strange sights," Kenbrook replied,

without bothering to look up. She had suspected her husband would not be an easy man to surprise, but to witness such a spectacle and be virtually unmoved was incredible. No wonder Dane had a reputation for keeping his head in all manner of situations. "Shades and specters, for instance."

Gloriana gasped, then lowered her voice to a hushed whisper. "You are baiting me, my lord," she accused. "You cannot have seen such things!"

He smiled. "There are more ghosts in this pile of stones," he said, drawing back a chair and inviting her to take it with a grand gesture of one hand, "than all of London. Hadleigh Castle has its share, too."

"There are always shadows and strange sounds in such old places," Gloriana said. She rose, however, and walked slowly toward Kenbrook to take the offered chair. He had given her the jade chess pieces, and she turned the board so as to have the ivory ones.

Kenbrook sat across from her, regarded his inanimate troops, and sighed. "After you," he said.

"Edward used to claim there were Roman soldiers marching these halls," Gloriana told him, advancing a pawn. "He only wanted to scare me, as I suspect you are trying to do."

Her husband moved a corresponding pawn, but only after great deliberation, and she nursed a hope that he might be a passable player. Gareth had never beaten her at the game, nor Edward, nor Cradoc, for all his influence in the spheres of heaven. Eigg, the Scot, had put her king in checkmate once, but that had been five years ago, and he had not managed to best her again.

"If I wanted to frighten you," Dane said reasonably, watching her move with the intensity of a general assessing the strategy of an enemy, "I would wait until nightfall to tell tales of ghosts and goblins. That way, you might seek safety in my arms."

Gloriana made another quick, seemingly impetuous move, but she was well aware of the position and potential use of every piece on the board. "There is much to settle between us, Lord Kenbrook."

He quelled the grin that curved his mouth, but not quickly enough to hide it from Gloriana's sharp gaze. "I disagree, milady. We have made too much of our differences. It is time we considered our common interests."

"Which are?"

"Chess, for one," Kenbrook said, pondering the small, checkered field of battle. He nodded toward the manuscripts stacked on one of the tables, pages enough to provide a year's reading for both of them. "Poetry and history." He raised his eyes, at last, to meet hers. She saw laughter in them and a tender acceptance that pinched her heart. "And pleasure," he finished.

Gloriana dropped her gaze to the board. "I cannot deny what you say," she allowed, taking his bishop. "I am very fond of chess."

Kenbrook laughed. Then, in three moves, he put her king in checkmate.

"Do you love me, Gloriana?" he asked when she was still gasping in disbelief over this swift and utterly unprecedented defeat.

She looked at him steadily. "Yes," she said.

"Do you wish to be my wife, truly, and bear my children?"

"Yes," she said again.

"To do those things, you must lie down with me."

Gloriana regarded him for several moments before answering. "Suppose you find me wanting?"

One side of Kenbrook's impudent mouth tipped upward, in what was almost but not quite a grin. "I have already found you most satisfactory," he said, and held out one hand to her. "You cannot but please me, milady. The question is, shall I please you?"

Gloriana laid her palm across his, felt his fingers close around the fragile bones, and shut her eyes for a breathless moment as he brought her to her feet.

He did not lead her immediately to the bed, as she had both hoped and feared he would do, but instead drew her into his arms and kissed her. It was the sweetest and most tender of contacts, and Gloriana's fears fled as the beginnings of ecstasy spread, rootlike, through her veins.

In the end, it was Gloriana who brought Dane to the marriage bed, wooing him there with her kisses, caressing and leading him with light, fluttering motions of her hands. He removed her gown and chemise, and then his own garments, before laying her down on the mattress.

"So incredibly beautiful," he whispered, and then lay beside her and roused her, with his hands and his mouth and his wicked promises, to a state of fiery, desperate wanting. It was not sudden, this culmination of their desires, for the courting process had begun long since, when first they had kissed in Gloriana's courtyard, and was only now coming to fruition. When he mounted her, she was already writhing in the flames of the desire he had ignited. "This first time—"

She touched his mouth with her fingertips. "I don't care," she told him.

Kenbrook's self-control, so unassailable the night before, suddenly snapped. With a groan from deep in his chest, he entered her in a single unbroken thrust, breaching her maidenhead.

Gloriana felt a brief, powerful sting, but her passion, like Dane's, was all-encompassing. She flung herself upward, welcoming him, and her response was his undoing. He made a guttural, growl-like sound and took her in earnest, quickening his pace, delving deep.

She rose to meet him, thrust for thrust, crying out in joyous, pagan abandon as he drove her higher and higher. She was not subjugated, but glorified, and as she arched beneath Dane, sweetly frantic, Gloriana discovered that womankind was made for the receiving of pleasure, as well as the giving of it. She surrendered, trembling, to the demands of her body, and heard Dane's low, ragged shout of triumph as he joined her in their secret place beyond the stars.

Chapter
9

*W*hen at last their desire had been spent, Gloriana
slept, curled against Dane's side. He was content to simply
lie there, holding her, listening to the deep, even tempo of
her breathing, watching the daylight reach its crest and
then begin to recede back and back across the tower room
floor, like an ebbing tide.

She stirred, in the grasp of some dream, and Dane
soothed her with whispered words. Then, finally calm and
free of distractions, he allowed his very disciplined thoughts
to turn to the marvel he had seen earlier, before their
chess game.

Gloriana had been sitting at the table, nibbling at a honeycake, while he'd reclined in the bath, watching her, men-
tally framing the words to tell her that he had been a fool,
that he wanted her to bear his children. That he might even
love her, though he hadn't been at all sure about that part.
His feelings for Gloriana were new to him, full of tumult and
pathos, darkness and splendor, sunshine and laughter, and
he had yet to make sense of them.

Before he'd been able to declare himself, Gloriana had
disappeared—simply vanished, between one moment and
the next. There was no other way to describe what had hap-

pened, to himself or to anyone else, should he ever be foolish enough to try. What troubled Dane even more than that bit of magic was the fact that Gloriana had not worked it on purpose; she had been snatched away, against her will, by a force neither of them could even begin to understand. Which meant she might again be taken from him, at some unguarded moment.

For how long would Gloriana be lost to him if that happened—an hour, a day? Forever?

Dane shivered, then turned on the overstuffed mattress and, although he did not want to awaken Gloriana, held her a little more tightly. He had never known such intensity of feeling or such fear. To think that all these years she had been growing and blossoming at Hadleigh, a spirited flower, waiting for him, and he, the fool's fool, had deliberately stayed away.

What precious and mysterious stuff time was, more worthy of cherishing than gold or gems—and so much had been wasted.

He raised his head, the better to look at Gloriana. Her face, translucent in slumber, ivory-gold flesh flushed with faint pink from their passion, seemed beautiful beyond bearing. He, who prayed only by rote when forced to attend mass or vespers, offered a silent, eloquent prayer that he might be a worthy husband to this woman, bringing her honor and giving her naught but joy.

As if she'd heard his unuttered plea to heaven, Gloriana's lashes fluttered and she opened her eyes. "I hope we've made a child," she said.

"So do I," he answered gruffly.

"What will you say to Mariette? She has come so far—"

Dane touched Gloriana's nose with a fingertip. "I will say, dear wife, that I am sorry, and offer to send her back to her home in France. With a suitable escort, of course."

Gloriana rested her head on his shoulder. Her hair, a wild tangle of gold-tinged copper, felt like silk against his skin. "It may be that Edward will court her. My handmaiden, Judith, told me that she fancies him." She paused, then looked up at Dane in a parody of guilelessness. "Mariette, I mean."

"I know whom you meant," Dane replied with a grin, giving her a painless pinch on the backside. "Mayhap losing me will not break the mademoiselle's heart after all."

"Mayhap," Gloriana teased, batting her dense lashes.

He raised his eyebrows and tried to look fierce. "Impudence," he accused. "I shall have amends for that, milady."

A fetching blush heightened her color, but the look in her eyes was, beyond doubt, saucy. "How may I appease you, my lord?" she asked, in a voice no less impertinent for its dulcet tones.

For an answer, Dane gripped her by the waist and, moving swiftly, raised her up and set her down again, astraddle his hips. Her glorious eyes widened as she felt his manhood beneath her, swollen to the size of a pillar in a Druid temple and ready to conquer. The tips of her succulent breasts turned hard as brook pebbles.

"Are you contemplating your fate, milady?" Dane asked.

She nodded, biting her lip, and shifted slightly, as if to take him inside her.

Dane was as eager as she, but he knew, if she didn't, that pleasure was heightened by anticipation. He had taken her quickly the first time, and there had been several skirmishes after that, but now he wanted to savor every sensation.

Gloriana cupped her hand under her breast and bent to brush Dane's mouth with the taut nipple.

"Brazen little tart," he said, and punished her with a single lap of his tongue, quickly withdrawn. "Where have you learned such wanton ways?"

She groaned, disappointed, and tried to get him to take her breast. "In your bed, my lord," she answered breathlessly. "Please, Dane—"

"What?" He asked, running his hands from her shoulders to her buttocks, which he weighed and then squeezed between his fingers. " 'Please, Dane'—do what?"

Gloriana had started to squirm a little, and he hoped she couldn't guess what she was doing to him. "You are a wretch."

Dane brought one hand around and spread his fingers over her belly, while his thumb delved between the moist lips of her femininity and found the small, hardened bit of flesh where her passion was centered. Plying that nubbin, he watched with enjoyment as Gloriana arched her back and whimpered, thrusting her wonderful breasts forward, tempting him almost beyond his capacity to endure.

With his free hand, he squeezed one of her nipples lightly, preparing it. "I am waiting, Gloriana," he said, "for you to tell me what you want."

She flung herself forward, with a little cry, burying her face beside his head in the pillow, wriggling moist and hot on the pad of his thumb. *"Ooh*—I would have—I would have you take suckle from my nipples, my lord, and—*oooooh*—I don't know what to call it—to have you inside me—"

Dane found a breast and drew on it hard with his mouth, though he had ceased working her woman-place with his hand, lest she find an early, lesser release before the more acute and enduring one he planned for them both. Gloriana grasped his face in her hands, as if she feared he would break away and withhold the attentions she wanted so feverishly.

In truth, he could not have turned from her, except to scramble for the other breast, because he needed to take, in those moments, as much as she needed to give.

Gloriana reared back when they were both gasping, riding him as he heaved beneath her. But they were still unjoined, and Dane, though near the breaking point, was not willing to surrender so soon. He pushed her backward, onto her heels first and then onto her back, and thrust his face between her legs as he wanted to thrust his manhood. Knees drawn high and wide apart, Gloriana gave a lusty cry of exultation and welcome, and he followed every rise and fall of her hips, every frantic twist and turn.

When Dane sensed that she was ready, he drew back, though she clutched at his head and hair and sobbed in protest. Kneeling between her thighs, he looked down into her face, silently asking permission and at the same time giving warning. Then, arranging her, he found her moist entrance and, after teasing her briefly, eased inside. His need was savage, but Gloriana was tender yet, having been breached for the first time just hours before, and he would not hurt her.

Trembling, her pink-and-gold flesh shimmering with perspiration, Gloriana arched her back to receive him and made a low, keening sound in her throat. Her hair fanned out around her on the bedclothes like an aura of fire, and Dane was stricken by the sight of her, by the sweet torment of possessing her. For a moment he believed his calloused, soldier's heart would truly break, like some fragile trinket bought at the fair.

Gloriana's thighs tightened rhythmically against his hips as he probed her, deeply, slowly, over and over. Her hands were never still upon his back, now caressing, now clawing, now grasping his buttocks, now trying to part his shoulder blades. Pain and pleasure encompassed him, until he could not discern one from the other, and still he moved upon her, in and out, in and out.

Dear God. How long could he bear such ecstasy without perishing of it?

"Dane," Gloriana whispered, as one in a fever. Her fingers trailed down his face, over his chest, making circles around his nipples, playing upon his taut belly as he strained.

She quickened under him and then flexed, her exquisite body like a fine bow drawn taut, and he felt her small, hot muscles constrict where they sheathed him. While she shuddered, gasping his name as though it were a litany to save her from the splendid suffering of climax, Dane erupted inside her with a low sound from deep in his belly, more like the growl of a mating wolf than the moan of a man. He held himself rigid, spilling his seed into her—once, a second time, a third. When she had wrung the last of his essence from him, he collapsed and lay trembling in her arms, his head upon her breasts.

She murmured to him, comforting him in that ironic way of lovers who, having roused the fire in the first place, would douse its blaze and salve the burns as though in recompense.

Dane, for his part, had no trouble putting a name to the tangle of emotions she had wrought in him. He called them love.

Gloriana slept again, holding Dane close, and awakened at twilight, feeling ravenous. With a gentle shake, she roused her beloved and rolled, laughing, from beneath him just when he would have taken a nipple in his mouth. He raised himself onto an elbow and watched her with gleaming eyes as she went naked to the table and began to eat, grabbing up bits of bread and cheese and cake at random.

Dane got up, as lean and graceful as a panther she had heard about once. Or had she actually seen such a creature, long ago, in the unborn future, in that place called America? She had a vague impression of cages, like small dungeons, a great menagerie full of noise and fury.

But Kenbrook was circling her, slowly, wearing a mischievous smile that set her heartbeat racing, and Gloriana forgot the moment of sadness she had known and laughed again as he pounced and snatched the honeycake from her fingers.

After that, they fed each other, playing at first, then performing their own lovers' communion. Dane emptied his tub out a tower window, then heated water for Gloriana, with painstaking patience, over a large brazier. She bathed by candlelight, while Dane explored the strings of the harp with light passes of his fingers, stumbling across the occasional tune.

When Gloriana had washed, and soaked away the virgin's soreness, Dane dried her with a soft cloth, and the sensation of being cared for, attended, and nurtured was so blissful that she was nearly transported by these things alone.

She donned a chemise, which rested whisper-soft against her skin, revealing the shadows of her nipples and the thicket of curls at the joining of her thighs. They ate again, this time with more decorum, and by then the twilight had come. Using a flint, Dane lit the lamps, and they sat upon the great bed, with their backs pressed to the headboard. The master of Kenbrook Hall read aloud, from a script of quaint poetry, to the mistress, who did not hesitate to correct his few mistakes.

When they tired of reading, they played chess, the board perched between them on the feather-stuffed mattress, and Dane did not know victory that night. Finally, he put away the game and doused the lamps.

They made love again, sweetly and slowly, without urgency, and then they slept.

When Gloriana awakened, the tower room was brimming with sunlight and Dane was up and groomed, standing at the northern window, looking out. He wore a green tunic and trunks, hose and soft leather boots, and Gloriana felt a twinge of sorrow, for he looked like a man who expected to travel.

As if he'd sensed her gaze, Dane turned and favored her with a devastatingly brilliant smile. "Arise, my lady," he said, "and make ready. Our captors approach, to confer freedom upon us. Do you suppose an angel told them that we have, at last, sealed the bargain our proxies made so long ago?"

Gloriana could not keep herself from smiling, so engaging was Kenbrook in both form and countenance. "I do not think angels speak of such things," she said, rising and pulling on a chemise and then the brown kirtle she had worn the day before. She would have liked to bathe, but she was oddly self-conscious that morning. Besides, Dane had spotted Gareth and a party of men riding toward the hall, which, coupled with the fact that the marriage had been well and truly consummated, meant their time as intimate captives would soon be at an end.

Dane left the window and came to stand before her, resting his hands on her shoulders. "I must contradict you, milady," he said tenderly, "for angels do surely speak of love. Were it not so, you would not have sworn your passion so fiercely in my arms last night."

Gloriana blinked back tears. For once, they were made of bliss, those tears, and not of sorrow, but still she refused to shed them. "Flatterer," she accused, slipping her arms around his neck. "You call me an angel now, but methinks you had another sort of being in mind before, when we were at odds."

He gave her a lingering, knee-melting kiss. When it was over, he cupped her chin in his hand and smiled into her eyes. "You possess a rare and peculiar grace, milady, in knowing when to be an angel and when to be otherwise."

Far below the castle window, the hooves of horses clatterd on the ancient cobblestones. Soon, the idyll would be over, for to gain one form of liberty, another must be forfeit. "You, by contrast," she retorted shakily, attempting to smile, "are never angelic but always 'otherwise.'"

Dane's blue eyes were bright with merriment and light, but he saw into her heart, however darkly, and narrowed his gaze in concerned speculation. "What troubles you, Gloriana? I see something hiding there, behind that incomparable face."

She sighed. Gareth and his troops were inside the hall now, their words and footsteps were audible on the steep stairs. "When the—" She paused and flushed, though she willed herself not to. "When the proof of our consummation is known and we are let out—"

The clamor was drawing nigh, almost at the door.

"Yes?" Dane prompted, as though they had all the time ever meted out to mankind.

"I wish to know how you will treat me, my lord," Gloriana said, with rising resolve. "Am I to live and work beside you, as your true wife? For I promise you, whatever pretty sentiments I may cherish toward you, I shall flee if you attempt to imprison me."

The lock was turning in the great timber door even as Kenbrook laid both hands to Gloriana's face and brushed the high ridges of her cheekbones with the pads of his thumbs. "You shall be my wife, Gloriana," he promised. "Here, at Kenbrook Hall. And this will be our chamber, while the rest is restored. Our sons and daughters will be conceived here, and born here as well, if that pleases you."

Gloriana blinked. There was a short rap at the door, but that was only a formality. The portal would swing open within a moment. "What of Mariette?"

Dane kissed her forehead, even as the doors creaked open and Gareth's brawny oafs entered, braced for combat. Kenbrook paid them no heed at all. "I shall return her to France, if that is what she wants. If not, she may marry another, such as Maxen, the Welshman, or our own Edward, or enter the abbey. Neither she nor any other will be my mistress, Gloriana—not as long as you love me."

"Accord at last!" boomed Gareth, in delight, from the region of the door. "Be gone, you louts—there is no need here for such as you."

Reluctantly, Dane took his gaze from Gloriana's to find his elder brother. The guards, in obedience to their lord's command, were removing themselves, with many a grumble and backward glance, from the bridal chamber.

"I need not ask, Kenbrook, if you've made the lovely

lady your own," Gareth said, with a mingling of self-congratulation and something else that might have been the mildest envy. "It is plain, from the glow about her and the shine in your own eyes, that the alliance is no longer a sham, but genuine and fruitful, as God meant it to be."

Gloriana slipped her hand into the crook of Kenbrook's elbow, lest he be provoked by this sermon to do violence, but the gesture proved unnecessary.

Kenbrook was indeed in high spirits. "You see rightly, my brother," he said. "Will you take wine to celebrate our good fortune?"

Gareth made a wry face, obviously thinking of the tactic he had used the day before to render his brother temporarily helpless. "Even if I live to walk the earth for ten and ninety years, Kenbrook, I shall never taste any wine of your offering."

Dane raised an eyebrow, one arm resting loosely around Gloriana's waist, holding her against his side. "You do not trust me, my lord?"

"Where all else is concerned, my faith in you is as steadfast and enduring as the walls of this keep. In the matters of your imprisonment and brief incapacitation—however pure we all know my motives to have been—I am not so ingenuous as to think you will fail to seek revenge in like measure. Though we have been apart these many years, after all, it was I who raised you, and I know well the devious workings of your mind."

Gloriana saw an unsettling glint in Kenbrook's eyes, and Gareth surely did as well.

"Take note of your own words," Dane said, and though he spoke mildly, it came to Gloriana that venom is venom, however sweet. "They are wise ones, and true."

An awkward silence followed, then Gareth cleared his throat. "As I said before, it is clear from your aspects that all is well between you." He glanced briefly toward the bed, where the marks of Gloriana's surrender did indeed color the sheets, beneath the tumbled cover. "Therefore, I shall not ask to see the—er—proof."

"You are not only generous," Dane remarked in that same quiet, innately dangerous tone of voice, "but prudent as well.

As it happens, the lady Gloriana and I plan to make our home here. You may leave whenever you wish."

Gareth opened his mouth, then closed it again, like a fish cast up on the bank. Gloriana, too, was surprised, for she'd expected the transition to be a more gradual one.

Red from throat to scalp, Gareth hesitated only a moment, then turned and strode out of the tower room, leaving the great doors agape behind him.

Gloriana watched her brother-in-law go and felt sadness crouching in the back of her heart, behind the new and complicated emotions Dane had awakened in her.

"Pray," Kenbrook said with gentle amusement, "do not mourn so, milady. My brother and I will make our peace in our own way, and in good time, I think. Meanwhile, you need not be estranged from Gareth or anyone in his household." He took her hand. "Now come, Lady Kenbrook, and I will show you parts of this hall you cannot have known before."

Gloriana followed him out of the great circular room into the passage she had last seen as a captive, bound and wriggling. They descended the stairs swiftly and entered the great hall, which was so old that there were no fireplaces, but only pits in the floor and smoke-holes high above, to let in the rain. The place was a ruin, but Gloriana loved it and knew it for her home.

"I used to play here, with Edward," she said as Kenbrook dragged her along. As fast as she moved, as long as her legs were, she could barely keep up with him, and her words came out breathless. "He was Artos—Arthur, the warrior king. And I was Guinevere."

Dane stopped at the head of another set of stairs and turned to look into Gloriana's face. In the deep shadows of the room, she could not make out his expression. His voice, however, was wry, and bore a hint of mischief.

"You have no need of an Arthur now, and I no want of a Guinevere. Theirs was an ill-fated alliance, after all, but ours will stand to the end of time and beyond."

Despite her happiness, which was complete, Gloriana felt a brief chill of apprehension. "Please do not speak so, my lord," she said, with a little shiver. "You mustn't tempt Fate to belie your words."

Kenbrook leaned forward on the stair, his hand still clasping hers, and kissed her lightly. It was a portent, that brief meeting of mouths, of past pleasures to be known again.

"As you wish, milady," Dane said, and drew her on into the bowels of the castle, where she and Edward had never dared to venture even on their boldest quests. The vast chambers, though dank, were not completely in darkness, for light entered from narrow windows beneath the heavy beams supporting the ceiling.

Gloriana caught a whiff of sulfur and heard the vague, lapping chatter of water.

"So, Guinevere," Dane teased, hauling his tunic off over his head. "Arthur did not bring you here. I am pleased."

"What—?" Gloriana faltered in her amazement and stood staring about her.

"They were fond of cleanliness, the Romans, among other things," Dane explained, shedding his trunks, too, and then his leggings.

Gloriana clutched her brown woolen kirtle closed at the front, although it had not been unlaced, and peered after Kenbrook into the shifting of light and shadow.

The peculiar quality of the light struck her then; it danced and shimmered, as if reflected off water.

"This is a Roman bath?" she asked, hardly able to believe in the survival of something so ancient.

"Yes," Dane called from further on, his voice echoing in the vast chambers. "There's a spring—no doubt that's one of the reasons the Legions chose this site for a fortress."

Gloriana followed his voice and the sound of bubbling and splashing, until she came to a vast, square pool, surrounded by statues in various states of ruin. Broken tiles, still bearing traces of paint, edged the bath.

"How could it have survived?" Gloriana marveled, pulling off her kirtle and the chemise beneath it, setting them distractedly aside.

"The spring renews itself," Dane said, holding out an arm glistening with water, "and the Romans built all their edifices, particularly those designed for pleasure, to withstand the centuries. Be careful how you proceed. There are cracks, of course, and the moss makes it slippery."

Steam rose from the bubbling pool, along with the inevitable spoiled-egg smell.

Gloriana made her way toward Dane, cautiously eager and ever practical. "How does it drain?"

Kenbrook rested his hands on her shoulders. The hot, churning water felt wonderful, gently pummeling the muscles of her thighs and buttocks, chest and stomach, easing away the last lingering aches from their lovemaking and soothing the tender places. "There is a conduit system, leading down to the lake," Dane said, his words tingling against the flesh of Gloriana's mouth. It was plain his mind was not on the engineering feats of the Romans.

As he bent his head and kissed her with hungry fervor, Gloriana closed bold fingers around his manhood. A sense of magnificent power filled her, exulted her, as Dane's responding moan rolled over her tongue.

There were no further preliminaries. With a single, powerful motion of his arms, Dane lifted Gloriana out of the water and set her squarely upon his staff, feasting greedily at her breasts as he slid her downward, with excruciating slowness, until she had sheathed him to the hilt.

Instinctively, Gloriana wrapped her legs around his hips and tilted her head back, already convulsing around him in a silent and violent rhythm, the legacy of Eve.

Kenbrook took longer, but when at last he found his ease, his shout of triumph echoed throughout the shadowy chamber.

Gloriana sagged against Kenbrook, her arms around his neck, her legs encircling his pelvis, her head resting on his shoulder. They were still joined as he carried her to the shallow stone steps at the far side of the pool, laid her there, and washed her as tenderly as if she were a goddess lately tumbled from Mt. Olympus and still stunned from the fall.

When the bath had ended, they lay still on steps with edges worn smooth by time, sated and silent, entwined in each other's arms while the warm water lapped around them.

Gloriana dozed, awakened, and dozed again. She could not remember knowing such contentment at any time in her life and might have lain there on those steps until the keep fell to rubble if Kenbrook hadn't made her get up and put on her clothes.

Horses and men were waiting in the courtyard when they

again reached the center hall, with its high, slitlike windows and grim fire pits. Apparently untroubled by the fact that his clothes were clinging to his skin and water still glistened in his hair and on his face and neck, Kenbrook went out to meet them.

Gloriana followed, moments later, after trying in vain to make herself appear dry and unruffled. She feared that the pleasure of her deflowering showed plainly in her face, for the lingering effects burned like a winter flame within her, and she would have hidden until the men went away if the idea hadn't offended her pride. For all that the castle was little more than a ruin, she was the mistress of Kenbrook Hall, and it was her right as well as her duty to take her place at Dane's side.

When she went out, she recognized the red-haired Welshman, though the twenty-odd others were still strangers to her.

Maxen nodded respectfully. "Milady," he said.

She inclined her head in response, but did not speak.

Kenbrook turned to smile down at Gloriana, and she could see that he was pleased. His words further confirmed the fact. "My men have come to take up residence at Kenbrook Hall with us," he said.

Like any hostess, Gloriana was wondering, rather frantically, what she would feed these men and where they would sleep, but in her own way she was as happy as Dane. They were his men-at-arms, and it was right that they should serve him, however decrepit his holdings.

"Find places for your horses," Dane said, "and come in. My wife and I bid you welcome."

While the score of soldiers were setting up household in their own quarters, which were, like the stables, on the far side of the broad courtyard, a caravan of carts appeared on the narrow, winding road leading past the abbey and on to Kenbrook Hall. Gloriana knew they were bringing supplies and servants, and was so pleased that she flung herself into Dane's arms and kissed him soundly before running off to meet the new arrivals.

Judith, walking beside one of the overburdened carts, greeted her with a broad smile. "There you are, milady," she said. "Has he kept you well, the master of Kenbrook Hall?"

Gloriana blushed to recall just how well Kenbrook had "kept" her. "I am fit," she said. "What is all this?"

"Gifts from Lord Hadleigh, milady. And, of course, your own possessions too." The young woman raised her eyes to the hall and gave a slight but eloquent shudder. "The others and me, we'll be sleeping in a pile like kittens, of a night," she confided. " 'Tis a fearsome place, this, full of wailing ghosts."

"Nonsense," Gloriana said. The blame for any "wailing" heard in Kenbrook Hall could not be placed on spirits, she thought wantonly. It was a private observation, of course, and she did not speak of it aloud.

The carts clattered over the courtyard and were unloaded by servants and soldiers, who carried the contents into the castle under Gloriana's direction. Dane, in the meantime, was closeted away somewhere with Maxen, no doubt making plans for the restoration of Kenbrook Hall.

Gloriana had a few plans of her own, and gold to carry them out, but she would speak to her husband later, when they were alone.

By evening, Judith and her dedicated band of helpers had swept the main hall clean of cobwebs and other debris and scattered rushes over the floor. A cooking fire blazed outside the room that would eventually serve as a kitchen, and whole suckling pigs roasted over them, on spits.

Messengers went on horseback to Hadleigh Castle and to the abbey, and by twilight the invited guests were arriving.

Gareth came, and Lady Hadleigh was with him. Edward rode a little distance behind, looking proud and able on his war horse. Mariette, with Fabrienne, trundled along beside him in a cart driven by one of the grooms.

Gloriana braced herself, there in the now-busy courtyard with its flickering torches, for acrimony. She hoped she would not lose Mariette for a friend, but at the same time she felt no remorse for having won back her husband.

Mariette greeted her with a dazzling smile, to her surprise, bounding out of the back of the straw-filled cart and flinging herself into Gloriana's embrace.

"You are happy!" crowed the girl, in French. "I can see this, for your eyes smile, as well as your mouth."

Gloriana laughed, partly in relief, partly in joy, and hugged her friend. "You have forgiven me, then?"

Mariette's lower lip jutted out prettily. "Ah," she said, switching to English. "In these matters of the heart, you have been treacherous." Another dazzling smile lit her face. "I will forgive you, however, because I am noble."

Out of the corner of her eye, Gloriana saw Edward dismount and hold out the reins of his horse to his squire, a boy of seven or eight, who scrambled down off the beast's back to take them. Poor Odin, the dun-colored gelding, had been retired and replaced by this stallion Gareth had provided.

Edward's handsome face was somber and seemed gaunt somehow as he regarded Gloriana in silence. She wanted to weep for him, her Arthur, who had laid his sword so chivalrously at her feet in the chapel the day of his dubbing. While she had never asked for his love, it had wounded her to reject him.

Before Gloriana could speak to him, Dane appeared at her side. He put an arm around her briefly, while nodding at Edward. Then, turning to Mariette, he asked leave to speak with her in private.

Gloriana lingered when Dane and Mariette had gone to stand a little apart. She did not watch them, but focused her attention on Edward instead.

"I am told you have an admirer in the mademoiselle," she said.

Edward did not smile or even glance in Mariette's direction. "Mariette admires all men—in theory, at least. I think she would find the singular realities less appealing. I trust Kenbrook means to ship her back to France?"

Gloriana nodded, studying Kenbrook and Mariette for a moment as they sat talking on the rim of a dry fountain. Their words were inaudible, and as Gloriana watched them, she felt another chill and thought again of the unseen, overlapping worlds, one imposed upon another.

Let me stay, she prayed silently. *Please let me stay here, at Kenbrook Hall, forever and ever, with my husband.*

Chapter

10

There was much feasting in the great chamber and courtyard of Kenbrook Hall, and the night was filled with torchlight and minstrels' music. While Dane laughed with Gareth and half a dozen other men, all of them ranged round one of the fire pits in the keep's main chamber, Gloriana stood next to Elaina, near an inner doorway. Arms linked, heads close together, they spoke in soft but not secretive voices.

"It is wonderful to see this old place coming to life," Elaina said with a smile. There was a new fragility in her, something that weighed upon her spirit. Conversely, her beautiful face had a translucent quality, as though she saw some vision veiled to all others. "Oh, they are *splendid,* Gloriana, your strong, fair-minded sons and your daughters, who so wisely rule the hearts of their husbands."

Gloriana was glad no one else was close enough to hear, for Elaina's remarks were dangerous ones in so superstitious a society. "Do you see them?" Lady Kenbrook asked, very quietly. "My children?"

It did seem that Elaina was watching some grand spectacle, full of color and movement, for her eyes widened and sparkled. Lady Hadleigh, whether despite her madness or because of it, very often saw the future plainly. Much hardship had been averted through the years because of her warnings to Gareth that one crop would be blighted or that a coming winter would be unusually bitter.

"Yes," Elaina said, blinking, as if the scene were fading. She turned, tightening her fingers on Gloriana's arm until they felt like the talons of a falcon. "I saw them."

Gloriana felt a tremulous fear at the stark changes in Elaina's aspect. "What is it?" she whispered, afraid of the answer.

"You must suffer greatly, to be fitted for your destiny," Elaina said, "and so must Dane. But if you falter or fail, Gloriana, if you do not endure and press on in the face of every trial, your children will never be born, never play their vital roles in weaving the future."

Gloriana glanced nervously about and, seeing a small cluster of servant women perhaps a dozen feet away in the shadows of one of the great stone pillars supporting the ceiling, pulled the agitated Elaina away. They slipped out a side passage and found themselves in a moon-washed garden, overlooking Kenbrook Hall's ancient churchyard.

Roman officers slumbered beneath the oldest stones, with their wives and children, and generations of Dane's family were interred there as well. The keep and its lands had come to him through his mother, Aurelia, who rested in an elaborate crypt guarded by marble angels.

"You must tell me what to do," Gloriana pleaded, holding both of Elaina's hands. "I fear being taken away from Dane—"

"You will be separated," Elaina said flatly, firmly. "Then, one day, you will come to a crossroads. Your mind will want to turn one way, your heart, the other. In most cases, a wise woman would take the former course, but you, Gloriana, must have the courage and faith to pursue the second. Yours is the heart of a lioness, and it will lead you aright if you trust it."

Gloriana sagged onto a stone bench erected in antiquity, and battled tears. "I do not wish to leave Dane—I cannot bear being parted from him! We've been apart too long as it is—"

"It is the only way," Elaina said in more gentle tones. "Now, Gloriana—go in and attend to your guests. Welcome

your husband warmly to your bed, and keep your own counsel about all the future holds. Dane has battles of his own
to fight, and knowing that your time together is short will
only weaken him."

"Why?" Gloriana asked, in an agony of sorrow. "Why can
we not simply live out our lives, like other people?"

"Because you are not *like other people,*" Elaina insisted
with a touch of asperity. "From your bloodline and Dane's
will come men and women who have the ears of king after
king. They shall offer wise counsel, your progeny, and the
rulers, however temperamental and impulsive, will heed
them."

The weight of that knowledge was almost enough to crush
Gloriana. "I could bear anything, if only I were close to
Dane," she said.

Elaina stood before the bench and rested one hand on
Gloriana's shoulder. "As steel is tempered by the fire, so
the human spirit is made strong by adversity. Follow the
path that is laid before you, Gloriana. If you do not, the
Kenbrook line will be gone in a few generations, and all of
England will be the poorer for it." With that, she bent,
kissed the top of Gloriana's head, and turned to make her
way back into the keep.

Gloriana lingered, standing at the low wall overlooking
the chapel and the churchyard beyond, pondering Elaina's
words. *The woman is mad,* she reminded herself, a little
desperately. But inside, in the soul of her soul, Gloriana
knew Lady Hadleigh had spoken truly. A difficult time lay
ahead but, if she could manage to endure, lasting happiness
would follow.

She covered her face with both hands, too stricken to
weep. She must go from Dane's house, his heart, his bed,
and there was no knowing when the parting would come or
how long it would last. The prospect was crushing.

"You are overtired," a familiar masculine voice observed
from just behind her. Dane took a gentle hold on her arm.
"Come, Lady Kenbrook. I'll put you to bed."

Gloriana turned to face the man she had loved completely
from a tender age. With a sob, she hurled her arms around
his neck and held on tightly.

"What is it, sweet?" Dane asked, in a gruff voice, lifting

her easily into his arms. "Did Elaina say something to upset you? You mustn't forget that she's moonstruck."

Gloriana rested her head on Dane's shoulder and sniffled once. "I don't wish to talk about Lady Hadleigh or her malady," she said, and that was the first of her sacrifices. In truth, she wanted to pour out the whole story to Dane and beg him to make things different somehow so that they needn't be parted. Because she knew he could do nothing but suffer with the knowledge of what was to come, she held her peace. "My feet ache, and I think you should rub them with oil until I sleep."

Dane laughed as he carried her, avoiding the main hall for a side passage and the stairway that lay beyond. Although it was quite dark, he knew his way, and it struck Gloriana that he must have spent a great deal of time in the keep before he went away to fight the Turk. "You are sorely spoiled, milady," he said. "I shall have to take a firm hand with you, I can see that, or you will surely have me dancing, leashed and collared, like a mummer's monkey."

Gloriana spread her fingers over his chest, felt the strong, steady beat of his heart against her palm. "I will always love you," she told him.

They had gained an upper gallery by then, and he set her on her feet suddenly, gripping her shoulders and looking deep into her eyes. "I heard a dire note in that brief speech, milady. What did it mean?"

She reached up to caress his face with one hand. He was backlit by the fierce silver-white glow of a full moon, but the rest of him was swathed in shadow, and she could not read his expression. "I will care for you until the end of my days, and beyond if that is possible. That is all I was saying."

Dane grasped her chin in his fingers, lifting her face to the light. While he was hidden, her every emotion was surely visible. She prayed he would not see that he had been right, that she was, after a fashion, bidding him farewell.

"I love you, Gloriana," Dane said in a raspy, wondrous whisper. And then he kissed her.

Gloriana responded—she could not help that—but when Dane released her mouth, she asked, "What of Mariette? We have not spoken since you had your talk with her in the courtyard."

Dane took her hand and pulled her along behind him, striding along the gallery as confidently as if it were lit by a thousand candles, instead of intermittent patches of glimmering moonlight. "The mademoiselle is fond, as it happens, of the cloistered life," he answered. "She wishes to join the abbey, under Sister Margaret's care."

"But I thought—I thought she favored Edward—?"

"Edward will be busy fighting these next few years," Dane answered. "He is not ready to be a husband."

They were climbing the stairs that spiraled up and up toward the tower room, and Gloriana, breathless, began to wish her husband were still carrying her. "What do you mean, 'Edward will be busy fighting'?" she huffed. "Is he going away, as you did? I confess I had hopes he would forswear that ambition."

"He will not have to go away to fight," Dane said, stopping again, his fingers tightening almost painfully around Gloriana's. "Merrymont's men have burned one of the outlying villages."

She sagged against the curved stone wall of the tower staircase, for this was news she had not gotten wind of during the evening's merrymaking. "And Gareth and the others are going to take revenge?"

A muscle moved visibly in Kenbrook's jaw, and Gloriana dreaded his next words almost more than the fate that would soon force them apart. "Not only Gareth's men will fight, but mine as well. Such deeds as Merrymont's cannot be tolerated."

Gloriana had to stiffen her knees to keep from sliding right down to the floor. "What will you do, Dane?" she whispered brokenly. "Raid one of his villages? Cause innocent people to suffer, as Merrymont did?"

Dane practically dragged her up the remaining steps and into the tower room. He slammed the great doors shut before turning to Gloriana, who was standing near the table, trembling a little and wide-eyed.

Kenbrook's nostrils flared slightly, and the light from the braziers danced around him, like flames made of shadow. "Do you think me a monster, Gloriana?" he breathed. "Can you believe, for so much as a moment, that I would do such things? For any reason?"

Gloriana swallowed. "War is destructive work," she said with timid conviction. "Fields are trampled, huts burned, farmers and village folk alike are killed and carried off. It matters little, it seems to me, which lord they serve, for they suffer in any event."

"Our quarrel is with Merrymont and his men, and no other," Dane said coldly.

She sighed and sank into a chair at the table. The room, so recently a prison, was now a clean, well-lit chamber. The bed had been prepared, scented water brought for washing, fresh clothing laid out for the morrow.

Gloriana wondered if she would awaken in this room with the dawn or find herself in some other. "I am sorry," she said softly, and she meant it. "I know that you are a just man, and would do no harm to blameless folk."

Dane shed his tunic, but kept on his leggings, trunks, and shirt. Opening a good-sized box on the table nearest the bed, he took out a small vial. When he approached Gloriana, his temper had calmed and his eyes were serene.

He drew up a stool and sat upon it, facing Gloriana, lifting one of her feet into his lap. He made a sensual experience of removing her slipper, and she gasped as he ran his fingers lightly over her high arch.

"I did not actually mean for you to rub my feet, my lord," Gloriana babbled hastily. "I was only talking."

Kenbrook poured glistening golden oil into his palm and set the vial aside. Then, using all his fingers, but especially his thumbs, he began to work the small, tired muscles in the curve of Gloriana's right foot.

She gave a great, languid sigh and settled back in her chair.

"You find this pleasant, milady?" Dane teased.

Gloriana was feeling something very like sexual arousal, only different. This was a thing of the spirit, more than of the body, and profound. "Oh," she breathed with another sigh, even more heartfelt than the first. "It is too wonderful."

His thumbs made circles on the ball of her foot, working the costly, scented oil in deep. "No joy is too fine for you," he said. His voice was low and worked a trance of sorts. Gloriana forgot her ominous conversation with Elaina in the courtyard overlooking the graves of his ancestors, forgot the impending war with Merrymont and his army.

She felt herself melting, slipping down and down on the chair. *"Ummm,"* she said. There was, could be, no evil in the world, no sorrow. It had been a mistake to think so . . .

Kenbrook laughed and lifted her other foot, making Gloriana shiver and open her eyes halfway as he peeled away a second slipper and tossed it aside. "You are as shamelessly sensual as a cat stretching beside a fire," he said. "Whenever you grow intractable in future, I shall simply rub oil into some part of you, thus rendering you pliant again."

Dane's mention of the future was sufficient to jolt Gloriana out of her pleasant stupor, and she felt her heart swell to bursting with love as she looked into her husband's fire-lit face.

"Take me to bed," she pleaded, "and plant your child in me."

He continued to massage her foot. "There is a certain merit in that suggestion," he said hoarsely, "though I think you are already breeding."

Gloriana laid a hand to her abdomen, for the possibility, wondrous as it was, had not occurred to her before that moment. "How could you know?" she whispered, in awe. "Do you see visions, like Lady Elaina?"

Dane chuckled and bent gracefully to kiss her knee before raising his head and smiling into her eyes. "I have no powers but those that love gives me," he said.

She blushed. The powers love gave Kenbrook were considerable, but to say so could only make him more arrogant. "But you seem very certain that I am already carrying your child—"

"A son," Dane speculated. His eyes glittered as he reached for the vial of oil, set Gloriana's foot gently on the floor, and stood. "In truth, I would have preferred a daughter the first time," he said. "I understand they are great comforts to their mothers when the master of the house is away."

Again, Gloriana felt sorrow brush her heart. She set it firmly aside, knowing how precious each moment was. "When did you sire this son by me, my lord?" she asked, a smile quivering on her mouth, as Dane raised her to her feet with one hand.

"This day," he said, with confidence, "in the Roman bath."

Gloriana felt again the heat of the springs, the bubbling caress of the water, the hard thrusts of Kenbrook's manhood, deep inside her. She flushed as her eyes fell on the flask of oil in his hand.

"Are you bringing that to bed with us, my lord?"

"This and something else," Dane replied, and bid her with a tilt of his head to precede him across the chamber.

She went compliantly, dropping her kirtle in a pile at her feet, with the chemise whispering down to join it only moments later.

As the lamps and braziers flickered and spat, feeding on the darkness, Gloriana's cries of pleasure filled the tower. In the fiery midst of her ecstasy, she wondered if the servants, believing the keep to be haunted, would be afraid.

Later, in the small hours, Gloriana awakened from a deep sleep to find herself already in the throes of a powerful climax. While she arched beneath her husband, he kissed the cleft between her breasts and murmured gentle words of adoration.

The morning dawned gray and pink and gold, and when Gloriana opened her eyes, she saw immediately that Dane had already left their chamber. The braziers were lit against the morning chill, however, and there was a honeycake resting on Dane's pillow in the indentation left by his head.

Her body still humming with residual pleasure, Gloriana sat up, reached for the morsel Dane had left for her breakfast, and began to eat. From beyond the lake waters, she heard the tolling of the chapel bells at Hadleigh, summoning all within hearing distance to mass.

Gloriana stretched. Later, she would arrange for a like service to be held in the keep's small sanctuary, but today she felt lazy. Besides, it looked like rain.

It was only when Judith came, breathless from the climb up the tower stairs and bearing a ewer of hot water, that Gloriana recalled what Gareth and Dane and the others had planned for this day. She wriggled into her chemise and ran barefoot to the western window, which should afford a view of the courtyard.

Sure enough, Dane was there, his pale golden hair glistening even in the gloom of the morning, mounted on his fierce black stallion, Peleus. Behind him, wearing their battle colors, his score of soldiers had already aligned themselves into a fighting force.

"No," Gloriana whispered. Her shoulders sagged, and fresh tears threatened.

"Come away, milady," Judith said gently, taking her arm. "You'll catch your death, standing by the window in that little scrap of linen."

"Dane is going to fight," Gloriana said weakly, allowing herself to be pulled to the table, where Judith poured the wash water into a basin.

"Yes, milady," the girl agreed, without apparent concern.

Gloriana felt sick. All her life, she'd watched men clash on the training field at Hadleigh Castle, seen them wielding swords and daggers and lances, watched them wrestling like bears under the hot sun. Combat had been nothing more to her than a rough game, but the forthcoming skirmish with Merrymont's troops would be real. Men on both sides of the conflict would suffer terrible wounds, and even die.

"Sit down, milady," Judith commanded, "you look green as malachite."

Gloriana dropped into a chair and submitted while Judith brushed her hair and wound it into a plait, chattering as she worked.

Once Gloriana was dressed, in a bright yellow gown with a golden overskirt and a belt set with colored glass, she left the tower room, too restless to stay in and read or stitch. The sky was an ominous charcoal color when she stepped out into the main courtyard, wondering if her pony was in the Kenbrook stables or still at Hadleigh. In the end, she mused, it didn't matter, because if she tried to follow Dane into battle, the results would be humiliating at best and disastrous at worst.

The crooked, ornate stones of the graveyard drew her, perhaps because of her gloomy mood. If she was to be mistress of Kenbrook Hall, she reasoned, she must know every part of it. When Dane returned, she would ask him about his mother and all those who rested with her.

Elaina's warning seemed unreal, in the light of day, however thin it might be—merely the ramblings of an unfortunate but imaginative woman who spent too much time alone, listening to voices.

Gloriana stood among the stone angels, gazing at the marble crypt where Dane's mother's remains rested. A stiff, chilly wind blew off the lake, piercing the warm woolen of her kirtle and the linen of her chemise to sting her flesh. It would have been a comfort to think Lady Aurelia had joined the angels in heaven and could somehow watch over Kenbrook and keep him safe, but Gloriana was afraid to hope for that.

She had come to her senses and was just turning around to go back into the keep—out of the corner of one eye, she saw Judith approaching determinedly—and huddle near a brazier when a headache struck her, as sudden and blinding as the blow of a broadax hard swung. She swayed and reached, groping, for one of the marble angels, lest she fall. Her stomach clenched violently, and she dropped to her knees, no longer able to stand.

Gloriana could see nothing but a roiling darkness, as though she'd been taken up by storm winds, where she spun like a leaf. A thunderous, wailing roar filled her ears, and she clasped her hands to them, bent double on the ground, and screamed.

"Dane!"

The nightmare was timeless, without beginning or end, and Gloriana could not guess how long had passed when her vision slowly returned and the awful noise subsided, bit by bit, to a thrumming hum.

Gloriana raised her head, so dazed that, for one terrible moment, she couldn't remember her name or what she was doing in a rain-swept graveyard.

Slowly, she became aware of voices around her, speaking in a strange, rapid language. She blinked as a rush of awareness came at her, as startling in its own way as the headache, which had now faded to a hollow throb.

People were clustered about, staring at her. It was raining, and brightly colored canopies bobbed above their heads.

Umbrellas, whispered the voice of memory from the back of Gloriana's mind.

They chattered, pointing, and she retreated a step, shaking her head.

"Poor thing," someone said. "She's frightened."

"Look at those weird clothes," said someone else.

The same part of her brain that had recognized the umbrellas translated their odd, clipped words, but with painful slowness. The greater horror, of course, lay in the realization that what she had so dreaded had happened. She had made the transition, whatever it was, from the thirteenth century to some much later year. In this time and place, Dane and all the other people she loved were long dead, mere dust and bones in their graves.

Gloriana gave a loud, piercing cry of pure despair, and a man stepped out of the crowd, extending one arm, speaking very gently.

"Here, now," he said, his words falling heavy and separate upon Gloriana's mind, to be wrestled with, one by one, "don't be afraid. I'm a doctor, you see. I'll help you."

Gloriana closed her eyes and willed herself back to Dane, back to Kenbrook Hall.

"There, there, you're all right now, aren't you?" the doctor fussed, laying a heavy woolen garment over her shoulders— a coat that smelled pleasantly of rain and some muted, vaguely spicy perfume. "Come along with me, and we'll see you're taken care of." Supporting Gloriana with a strong arm, the man pushed his way through the small, fascinated crowd. "What's the matter with you lot?" he demanded. "Haven't you ever seen a sick person before?"

Frantic only moments before, Gloriana now felt numb. She stumbled along beside the man who'd wrapped her in his coat, too bewildered to do more than allow herself to be led.

"My name is Lynford Kirkwood," the man told her, bending his head toward hers. "My car is just here, beyond the gate, and I have a surgery down the way. We'll take you there, get you some hot tea and dry clothes, and after that we'll have a bit of a chat."

Gloriana's head spun with the effort of making sense of what he said. She was depending at the moment on the kindness she sensed in this quiet, slow-speaking man. She nodded mutely, trying to recall what a "car" was, and remembered when she saw the object itself: a fuel-powered vehicle with glass windows. She looked back, toward Kenbrook Hall, as Kirkwood opened the door for her.

The keep lay in random piles of stone, a bleak husk, utterly broken except for one part—the tower in which she and Dane had been imprisoned together.

"Do get into the car, love," the doctor urged, giving her a gentle push. "You're frightfully wet, and it looks as though you've had some sort of nasty shock."

Gloriana sat, staring wordlessly through the rain-speckled window. She did not ask herself how such a thing could happen, nor did she think she'd gone mad, though lots of good people would have said so. On some level, Gloriana realized, she had always expected something like this.

All that mattered to her now was finding a way to get back to Dane.

Mrs. Bond, the housekeeper, rushed out of the kitchen door the moment Kirkwood brought his elderly Packard to a stop in front of the house. No doubt, somebody up at the keep had telephoned ahead to say he was bringing home another bird with a broken wing.

"Oh, here, now," the old woman stewed, holding a copy of the London *Times* over her frizzy gray head in a vain effort to keep off the rain. "She's fair blue with cold, and see how she trembles!"

Lyn Kirkwood did not respond, but came round to the passenger side and lifted the poor thing out, just as if she were an invalid. She looked like an actress in some authentic pageant, with her strange, simple clothes and single thick plait of hair, braided through with ribbons. She hadn't spoken in the car really, except to murmur something unintelligible, over and over.

He brought her into the small library, since there was a fire burning on the grate, and sent Mrs. Bond for blankets, hot tea, and a robe. While the housekeeper was off attending to these requests, he poured a dose of brandy into a snifter and held it out to his visitor, who was shivering violently— too violently, for someone caught in a warm summer rain.

She gazed at the brandy for a moment, then took it in both hands and sipped, cautiously at first, then with a thirst.

When she gave back the snifter, he could have sworn she said, "Thank you, my lord."

Lyn set the glass aside and sat on the hassock. He was a good doctor, in his mid-thirties, and he loved his home, his work, and his life in general, except that he would have liked to have a wife and children.

"What is your name?" he asked quietly.

She frowned prettily, as though working out what he'd said. When she answered, he did not comprehend the name she gave, it sounded so garbled, but he'd made a study of languages, and he recognized the shape and inflection of her words.

Medieval English, he thought. Impressive.

He made another attempt to communicate. "Lyn Kirkwood," he said, laying a hand to his chest. She was still wearing his overcoat, and he realized his shirt was wet through from the rain.

Mrs. Bond returned then with the blanket and robe, chattering that the tea would soon follow. "You'll want to leave her alone a moment, Doctor," the old meddler said, almost clucking. "So she can get into the robe and all. Don't you worry, though, I'll see she's bundled up proper."

Lyn scowled a little as he got to his feet and started toward the door. There was no need to shoo him out of his own library, he reflected irritably. He was a physician, wasn't he, and had seen his share of naked women. "I'll get the tea," he said, and wondered if he was becoming one of those easily managed sorts—the kind of man he'd always pitied.

"Well, hurry up about it," replied Mrs. Bond. "We'll have a case of the pneumonia on our hands, if we're not careful. My niece Ellen looked just this way when—"

Lyn hurried through the house toward the kitchen, there to find that Mrs. Bond, the soul of efficiency, had already lit the stove and set the kettle on to boil. The crockery pot had been filled with hot water from the tap to prepare the china, and a tin of Ceylon tea waited on the tabletop. He prided himself on the steadiness of his hands, though he wasn't a surgeon, but there was a slight tremor in them now, and he nearly spilled everything.

His mind, of course, was on the hauntingly beautiful crea-

ture he'd found in the graveyard at the ruins of Kenbrook
Hall, looking as terrified as an angel dragged over the
threshold of hell. Moreover, he'd have sworn she'd appeared
out of thin air, though that was impossible, of course.

He brewed the tea, put some biscuits on a plate, and arranged everything none too carefully on a tray. The dishes
rattled when he lifted it, and some of the tea, hot and fragrant, spilled out of the pot's slender spout. He would have
noticed someone like her, he insisted to himself, wandering
about in those strange, wonderful flowing robes. He went
often to the ruins of Kenbrook Hall, even when it rained,
because—well, because all his life he'd been expecting to
find something there, he realized now, with such a start
that he hardly trusted himself to get the tea tray safely from
the kitchen to the library.

Mrs. Bond had done her work when Lyn reached the room
where he spent most of his free time.

"Hasn't said a word," the housekeeper confided in a stage
whisper that would have reached the rear balcony of any theater. "Not a single word, poor creature. Just stares into the
fire, looking as though she's lost her soul. I don't know that
she shouldn't be in hospital."

Lyn studied his damsel in distress. "I'll have a look at
her. You'd better go and ring up Marge." That was his nurse,
who hadn't come in to work that day, since his surgery was
closed. "Ask her to please stop by."

Mrs. Bond made a little huffing sound, as though she
thought Lyn might do something improper if she didn't keep
watch, then padded out.

His bag was on the desk, where he'd left it after rounds
that morning. He opened it, got out his stethoscope, a
tongue depressor, and one of those new digital thermome-
ters. A routine examination proved what he'd already
guessed: his patient was not physically ill, merely agitated,
confused, and afraid.

He offered a cup of tea, and she took it carefully, staring
at the cup and saucer as though she had never seen anything
quite like them—or as if she had, but couldn't remember
what to call them.

Her attention had been fixed on the fire burning low in
the grate, but as she sipped the hot, bracing tea, liberally

sweetened, she began to take in her surroundings. As she did so, her eyes widened, narrowed, and widened again, over and over.

Lyn could almost hear her mind working, silently assigning names to things and deciding upon their uses. If he hadn't known better, Mr. Kirkwood reflected, he would have thought she was a time traveler and not just some poor soul wearing a museum-quality costume.

Chapter

II

Gloriana huddled miserably in the soft chair before Kirk-wood's fire, quite overwhelmed by the magnitude of what had befallen her, stricken mute with shock. That she'd experienced a transition like this before, and that she'd half expected a recurrence, did nothing to settle the roiling tumult in her mind and spirit. She had been a little girl the first time and had often imagined, in her loneliness and neglect, becoming a princess and living in a castle. It was only mildly surprising, therefore, when the dream came true; for so fanciful a child, the boundaries between fantasy and reality are fluid, forever shifting and changing.

She had hoped at first that Kirkwood and his modern world were only illusions, wrought by the crippling headache that had struck her down in the graveyard of Kenbrook Hall on a misty morning in the thirteenth century. Now, however, it was plain from the substance and texture of things and people around her that she had indeed traveled through time, spanning more than six hundred years in a matter of moments.

Gloriana closed her eyes, struggling to hold on to her composure. In this clean but oddly frenzied place where she found herself, Dane was long dead, as were Gareth and Edward, Judith, and Lady Elaina. She was utterly alone, except for the man and woman who had conceived the child Megan and then abandoned her.

In all her confusion and fear, Gloriana could find no desire to search them out. They were, and had ever been, strangers.

An assortment of sounds assaulted her from all sides—faint strains of music, somehow scratchy, the drone of some half-remembered cleaning machine, the tick-tock of the time-keeping device on the mantel, the whoosh of wheels on the rainy street in front of Kirkwood's cottage. Gloriana sighed and opened her eyes again, to find Kirkwood still seated on his padded footstool, regarding her with a pensive and sympathetic expression.

"What's happened to you?" he asked, and this time Gloriana translated what he was saying with much less difficulty. She realized with mingled relief and despair that her mind was adapting to the new surroundings, interpreting, making it possible to communicate. That was vital, of course—but did it mean she was doomed to stay?

She looked about, a little wildly perhaps, her throat still so constricted as to prevent speech, wanting parchment and a quill. Perhaps her rescuer would understand better if she wrote her reply, rather than speaking.

Seeing a desk littered with documents and other items she could not readily name, Gloriana set aside her tea and rose from the chair, shedding Kirkwood's cloak and the coverlet like layers of skin, to cross the room.

She frowned, pondering the strange, gleaming devices that rested on the surface, memories hovering at the frayed edges of her awareness. Her host did not follow but simply turned, watching her with kindly interest.

She pantomimed dipping a quill into a pot of ink and writing.

Kirkwood smiled, though his eyes were yet thoughtful, and came at last to stand beside her. He opened a drawer and brought out a shining cylinder of metal and a pad of paper. Because the tablet, at least, was familiar—she'd drawn endless pictures as the child Megan—Gloriana was encouraged, and a tentative smile rested briefly on her mouth as she nodded. Seating herself in Kirkwood's soft leather chair, she looked around for ink.

Kirkwood took the writing implement from her fingers

and, pressing one end with his thumb, produced a clicking sound. Then, to demonstrate, he made small, squiggling circles on the paper.

Gloriana's eyes widened, and even as she marveled, she also remembered. A pen. As Megan, she had seen adults employ such mechanisms many times, though she herself had most often used bits of brightly colored wax.

Shakily, she took the instrument into her hand and began to write.

I am called Gloriana.

These first words were misshapen and somewhat untidy— her tutor, Friar Cradoc, would not have approved—but as Gloriana got used to wielding the pen, her confidence grew, and she wrote with more certainty.

I do not belong here. I wish to go home.

She glanced back at Kirkwood, who was reading attentively over her shoulder. Although his countenance was somber, he nodded to show understanding, and Gloriana did not feel quite so frightened and alone as before. Perhaps the phenomenon of traveling through time was commonplace in this latter day, and he would be able to help her get back where she belonged.

Kirkwood took up another pen and wrote underneath, *Where is home? Please, tell me where you come from.*

Gloriana pondered the spare, slanted letters for a few moments, her forehead creased with a frown, but gradually their meaning came clear. It was odd and awkward, conversing this way, but their common language had obviously been altered over the centuries, and there was more resemblance between the written versions than the spoken ones.

I am Lady Kenbrook, and I live at Kenbrook Hall, with my lord and husband, Dane St. Gregory. Upon my leavetaking, the year was 1254.

Kirkwood read the words carefully, his brows knitted in concentration. "Where is Geoffrey Chaucer when I need him?" he murmured, and Gloriana did not even attempt to comprehend.

You are indeed a time traveler, he wrote, after pondering Gloriana for some time. *That should surprise me mightily, being quite impossible, but somehow it doesn't. The present year, my lady, is 1996.*

Gloriana felt herself go pale. She had been but five when, as Megan, she had stumbled out of one world and into another. Though gifted, already reading and writing, she had never known or cared about the progression of years, and it startled her to learn that time had advanced so far. Surely, by now, humanity was teetering on the very brink of Holy Judgment!

She laid the pen down and, feeling slightly dizzy, bent forward to rest her head on folded arms.

Kirkwood laid a hesitant hand to her shoulder. "It's a lot to take in, all in once," he said gently, then sighed. "For me, as well as for you. What you need now is rest."

Gloriana felt the meaning of what he'd said, without having to translate it. That, at least, was getting easier. She raised her head and nodded. Oblivion was a welcome prospect. Perhaps after a nap she would awaken and find herself in her bed and Dane's, in the tower at Kenbrook Hall, and marvel at how vividly she'd dreamed.

Within minutes, Gloriana had been taken to a small chamber by the servingwoman, Mrs. Bond, to rest. She was tucked up in a warm, clean bed, and almost eagerly, Gloriana gave herself over to emotional exhaustion and collapsed into a deep state of sleep.

Hours later, she awakened with the immediate and heart-seizing awareness that she was still in Kirkwood's house, which meant, of course, that she had not been dreaming. The grief and disappointment she knew in those moments were so crushing, so omnipresent, that she could not move or make the smallest sound.

Gloriana waited helplessly, tears stinging her eyes and trickling over her temples and into her hair. Strange, subtle sounds ebbed and flowed in her ears, like an invisible tide. Gradually, those noises crystallized into the voices of two women—underlain by a more distant and somehow mechanical one, a man discussing peace talks between British authorities and the Irish Republican Army.

The realization crashed like a thunderclap inside Gloriana's mind. *She understood what was being said.*

"Ought to be in hospital, that's what I say," came Mrs. Bond's observation, from somewhere nearby. "Probably on drugs."

Gloriana sat up a little further on the pillows, listening intently. "Drugs"? She did not recognize the word, but it had an ominous sound to it.

Another voice replied, kinder and younger than the house-keeper's. "She looks too healthy for that." That would be Marge, the nurse Kirkwood had mentioned earlier. "Be-sides, Lyn's a doctor, isn't he, and I should think he'd have known immediately if that were the case."

"I don't like the shape of it," grumbled Mrs. Bond. "Imag-ine someone just appearing that way, practically out of no-where, and in a graveyard, mind you. And you saw her clothes—right out of a museum, except that the cloth is as new and sturdy as the wool in my own good winter coat."

Gloriana would have preferred to cower beneath the warm covers, rather than face the inevitable questions and curious looks getting up would bring her way, but her bladder was filled to bursting. She arose, as awkward and shaky as an invalid, and bent to look under the bed.

There was no chamber pot.

She stood again, confused, searching Megan's memories and coming up with an image of a privy equipped with gleaming porcelain fixtures. It would be indoors and proba-bly at one end of the hallway just outside her bedchamber. She crept across the tiny room, Kirkwood's shirt covering her to her knees, and peered cautiously around the door panel.

The light was so bright that it blinded her, and for a few moments, she simply stood there, blinking and disoriented. Then her vision cleared again, and she saw Mrs. Bond at a table in a cheerful room, with a red-haired woman seated across from her. A pot of tea steamed between them, and everything around seemed to shine.

"She wants the loo," Mrs. Bond's companion said pleas-antly, then added, with a gesture of one hand, "It's that way, lovie. End of the hall."

Gloriana got the sense of the words, if not the literal meaning, and found the privy. She used it, with some trepidation.

It was a bit longer before she recalled how to flush the commode and work the spigots on the basin in order to wash her hands. When she reached the hall again, the nurse, Marge, was waiting for her, smiling and plump and benign.

"Don't you mind Elsa Bond," the woman counseled, in a confidential whisper, bending close and taking both of Gloriana's hands into her own. "She's not really a bad sort. Just has a gruff way about her, that's all."

Gloriana nodded. Again, though she could not have defined the individual words, she caught their essence.

"Would you be wanting a nibble, dear? You slept straight through tea, but I think I can come up with a few things."

Gloriana's stomach translated for her and rumbled softly. Marge was offering food, and the prospect was a welcome one. Once more, she nodded.

Marge smiled and pulled her into the bright room—a kitchen. It was certainly different, Gloriana reflected, from its thirteenth-century counterpart, which would have been much bigger and darker, filled with heat and bustling servants and hounds snoring on the hearth. On one end of a low cabinet sat a box with a flickering screen.

A television set, Gloriana recalled. The man's voice she'd heard earlier, talking about the Irish Republican Army, had come from this machine.

She stared at it in curious fascination as she took the chair Marge offered at the table. Mrs. Bond, muttering that it had been a long day, took her leave, disappearing into the hallway.

Marge, in the meantime, was busily putting together a meal and chatting the whole while. "I'll switch that off if it bothers you," she said. "Bond loves her telly, so it's always yammering away, day and night. If you're wondering where Mr. Kirkwood's gotten off to, he's gone to make his evening rounds. He'll be back in a little while, though."

The name Kirkwood caught Gloriana's attention, and reluctantly, she tore her gaze from the colored images on the television set. She wanted to respond verbally, but she was afraid to make the attempt.

"Poor dear," said Marge, with a cluck of her tongue and a shake of her head. Her hair was short, a mass of springy curls surrounding a ruddy, cheerful face. "Heaven knows what's happened to you. That look in your eyes fair breaks my heart, it does." She gave a great sigh. "Well, then. Never you mind, lovie. We'll look after you, the doctor and I, and make matters right if we can."

Moved by the woman's kindness, Gloriana felt fresh tears spring to her eyes, while her throat constricted painfully. Still unwilling to speak and reveal just how different she really was, she shifted her gaze back to the "telly."

The incessant words and images and strains of music were confusing, but in an odd way they made a bridge between the modern world and the one she had left only that morning. If she but watched and listened, she concluded, she would soon learn how to communicate with those around her.

Marge set a plate on the table before her, and Gloriana recognized the offering as a sandwich, a layer of yellow cheese melted between two slices of cooked bread. She ate ravenously, her gaze never straying from the television set, listening, absorbing, remembering.

The images on the television screen brought the outside world into focus for Gloriana, at least partially. The words were harder to grasp, since many terms were unfamiliar and all were uttered so swiftly as to be nearly abbreviated.

Everyone, it seemed to her, was in a hurry.

"Seeing how you put that first bit of food away," Marge said, sliding a second sandwich onto Gloriana's empty plate, "I thought you might be wanting more."

"Thank you," Gloriana ventured to say, forming the words carefully and pushing them slowly past her lips.

Marge beamed, bright as the room itself, with all its light and shimmering surface. "You're most welcome," she said.

Soon after that, weariness overcame Gloriana again, and she returned to the little room off the hallway, there to tumble into a fitful sleep. Her dreams were vivid, and in them she saw Dane walking the passages of Kenbrook Hall like a specter, calling her name.

Mist shivered down from the leaves of the oaks as the small, weary band rode past Hadleigh Castle and the abbey, progressing slowly but steadily through the twilight toward Kenbrook Hall. Their swords were nicked and bloody, their clothes stained crimson and stiff with sweat and dirt. They were seasoned soldiers to a man, but the battle with Merrymont's forces had raged for more than two hours, with only brief respites. Each had been taxed to the limits of his skills and endurance.

Dane kept his gaze fixed on the looming bulk of his ancestral home, where his heart rested in the hands of a beautiful woman with witchery in her eyes. The invisible chord stretching between them was all that drew him forward, for he had lost his taste for war, and the formidable personal strength that had sustained him for so long was all but spent. He wanted only to kneel at Gloriana's feet, to lay his head in her lap and feel her fingers soothing his temples, threading lightly through his hair.

Maxen, wounded and filthy, his tunic soaked through with blood and rainwater, drew up beside Dane. He was leading a second horse behind his own, with a dead man sprawled across its back. "He's the devil's own spawn, is Merrymont," the Welshman said. "Did you see him up there on that hilltop, watching his men set that crop ablaze with their torches? Kept a safe distance between himself and us, didn't he?"

Dane nodded mutely, remembering. He and Maxen and the others had joined Gareth and his men an hour after the sun's rising, beside the lake. They had not had to search out Merrymont, for the smoke of a burning field had filled the western sky, black and acrid.

Reaching a little huddle of crofters' huts, they found acres of wheat reduced to smoldering rubble. Swine and fowl had been slaughtered, and the thatched roofs of the cottages set afire as well. The villagers had fled to the woods in terror, and some had been pursued and run down for the sport of it.

Dane closed his eyes briefly at the memory. They had fought, his men and Gareth's and Merrymont's, on that smoking field, retreated in their turns, regrouped, and skirmished again. He could still hear the ringing clash of steel against steel, see the showers of blue sparks thrown by the blades.

He had wanted to go after Merrymont, safe on his perch, but that would have meant leaving his own men—leaving Edward, who this day had truly been initiated as a soldier and been baptized in the blood of friends and enemies alike. So Dane had stayed, wielding his sword until he could no longer feel his right arm, then using his left. Always, he had done his best to keep his young brother at the edge of his vision, but there had been times, of course, when that was impossible, because of the dust and the rigors of the fray itself. Finally, at some signal, Merrymont's men had given up the battle and raced into the hills after their leader, abandoning their fallen comrades to their fate.

Both the quick and the dead were gathered and taken from the field on litters and in carts, some to Hadleigh Castle, some to Kenbrook Hall.

Hooves clattered on the ancient stones of the courtyard as Dane and Maxen led the way beneath the great arched gateway.

Dane had envisioned Gloriana rushing to greet him, hair flying, eyes alert for any indication that he'd been injured, but there was no sign of her. The disappointment—it had been her image that sustained him through the awful day—was like a blow, but he did not bow to it. He did not have that luxury.

The dead men, four of them, were laid out on the chapel floor, to be prayed over and buried in the morning. The wounded, seven of whom were Kenbrook men, had been taken to the abbey to be looked after by Sister Margaret and her flock of gentle minions.

Only when Dane had groomed, fed, and watered his horse did he permit himself to enter the keep, in search of his wife.

Her handmaiden, Judith, awaited him in the hall, looking like a small, garish ghost in the flickering light from the fire pits. She was wringing her hands and trembling a little.

"Where is your mistress?" Dane asked quietly. He knew, of course, that something was wrong, had known it when Gloriana did not come out into the courtyard to greet him.

The girl was thin and small, and looked so fragile that a harsh word might break her. A tear slipped down her cheek and her lips trembled. "She was taken from us, milord."

Dane stood rigid, resisting the urge to grasp the chit and shake a more sensible answer out of her. "What the devil do you mean?" he rasped, but he knew. God help him, he knew.

"She was in the churchyard, milord," the servant babbled, bobbing once or twice, as though a curtsy would make what she had to say more credible. "It was raining a little, and I was worried she'd catch a chill, so I found a cloak to take to her—" Judith paused again, and a violent shudder moved through her. "I saw her slip to her knees, as if she was in terrible pain, and I started to run. Before I got to her, milord, she—she vanished." The girl's eyes were enormous, and there was no color to her flesh. "Some of the others, they say—they say the devil came and took her to"—her voice fell to a hushed whisper—"to hell—"

Dane quelled the impatient rage rising within him and thrust a bloody hand through his hair. "Tell them," he said calmly, "that anyone heard passing on such nonsense will be turned out."

Judith nodded, her eyes brimming again, her hands so tightly clasped that the knuckles stood out, white, from their sockets. "You'll find her, won't you, milord? You'll bring her back?"

Kenbrook was possessed of a despair so deep, so inconsolable, that it caused him to sway slightly on his feet. The force that had taken Gloriana from him was one he could not begin to comprehend, let alone combat. And yet he must not only grasp the mystery, but find a way to prevail over it.

Gloriana was his soul; without her, he was not a man, but a living husk.

"There's been some sort of mistake," he said, at long last, disbelieving the words even as he uttered them, taking no comfort from the lie and, by her face, giving none to the girl. "Such things cannot happen. People do not disappear like ghosts."

Judith started to speak—surely to protest—then stopped herself, visibly swallowing whatever she'd meant to say and nodding her head. Her sorrow at the loss of Gloriana was palpable, and Dane wondered if his own feelings were so plain.

In the end, he did not care.

"My men are hungry and tired," he said. "See that food is brought to the hall, and more wood for the fires."

Judith nodded again and hurried away. Dane stood for a moment, stricken to stillness, then took himself to the tower room, where a single oil lamp burned, keeping its flickering vigil.

He lit the other lamps, driving the greedy shadows into temporary retreat, searching, as he moved about the chamber, for some sign, some promise, some trace of Gloriana. Her clothes were there, and the chess pieces were neatly aligned on the board, in anticipation of a new game. He sensed a vague charge in the air, as though she might burst through the doorway at any moment, full of questions.

"Gloriana," he whispered.

Then he shed his sword belt and stripped off his bloody clothes. He washed at a basin and then dressed himself again, in simple woolen leggings, a tunic, and soft boots. Taking up an oil lamp, heedless of the aching exhaustion numbing his body, Dane searched the whole of Kenbrook Hall, from the uppermost chamber of the tower to the Roman baths, calling to Gloriana, willing her to come back.

Gloriana awakened to a sunny morning and the knowledge that she was still in the latter part of the twentieth century. Her first impulse was to wail with despair, but because she knew it would do no good, she bit her lower lip and waited until the worst of the urge had passed.

Someone had left a stack of clothing on the cushioned seat beneath the window, modern things borrowed from some neighbor or relation, no doubt.

It was not courage that finally drove Gloriana out of bed, but a desperate need to use the privy. As she passed along the hallway she caught a glimpse of Kirkwood, seated at the kitchen table. He must have known she was there, but he did not look up or speak, perhaps sensing that she didn't want to be noticed, wearing only his shirt.

Upon returning to her room, she went straight for the stack of clothes—blue denim pants, comfortably worn, modern undergarments, still in their packages, a green short-sleeved shirt with the word "Oxford" printed on the front in large white letters.

After donning the skimpy, legless breeches—she remembered them from her childhood—Gloriana pondered the other item, a very odd bandeau, plainly meant to support her breasts. She could not recall ever seeing one before, and some time had passed before she figured out how to put it on. She was a little breathless with frustration, in fact, when she came out of the bedchamber, wearing the Oxford shirt and the leggings—"jeans," her memory called them.

Kirkwood acknowledged her this time, smiling and rising from his chair. "Good morning," he said.

Gloriana hesitated in the doorway, feeling self-conscious again. She glanced behind him, hoping to see the friendly Marge, or even Mrs. Bond, but there was no one else in the room.

"Good morning," she replied, almost inaudibly and with great care.

He looked pleased and gestured toward the chair opposite his own. "Come in and sit down. There are some sausages and eggs if you want them. Not a very healthy breakfast, I admit, but we all have our little deceits."

She frowned, taking the offered place at the table, confused. The food looked uncommonly good to her. Surely there could be no fault in eating it.

Kirkwood chuckled at her consternation. "My God," he breathed, "I am getting caught up in this little fantasy of ours. If Mrs. Bond and Marge and all those gawkers at the ruins of Kenbrook hadn't seen you, I'd think I made you up. Tell me—are you truly a damsel in distress?"

Gloriana filled her plate with painstaking care. Where she came from, people used their fingers at the table and occasionally a knife for cutting or spearing, but here there were all manner of utensils to contend with. She sorted Kirkwood's words one by one, extracting every nuance of meaning before attempting a reply.

"I want to go home," she said firmly. "To Kenbrook Hall."

Kirkwood sighed. "Yes," he replied, taking the spoon from Gloriana's fingers, when she would have eaten her sausage, and replacing it with a pronged instrument. "That may be a problem—going home, I mean. Kenbrook is a ruin, you see. Except for the tower, of course. The government's made a museum out of that."

Gloriana ached, and her sorrow came out in her voice, even though she was trying hard to be brave. "You don't know how to send me back?"

He flinched, as though he'd felt her pain. "My dear, I can't explain how you got here, let alone get you back. In fact, I'm still trying to figure out why I believe this is anything but a hoax or a grand delusion on your part."

She laid down the utensil and pushed away her plate, all

appetite gone. Her face must have showed the depth of her anguish, for Kirkwood reached across the table and took her hand, his grasp warm and strong.

"If there is a way to help you, Gloriana," he said gravely, "I shall find it. But you must be patient."

Gloriana nodded. A silent, frantic sob caught in her throat, and she swallowed it. She could not, *would not* spend the rest of her life in this gleaming, clamorous place, separated from Dane. She must find a way to return, and she would begin her quest by returning to Kenbrook.

She got out of her chair and started for the door. It could not be far. Perhaps if she simply stood where she'd been standing before in the churchyard . . .

Kirkwood reached her while she was still considering the knob and took her arm in a gentle hold. His next words made it clear that he had guessed her intention.

"I'll take you there in the car," he said. "Can't have you out wandering about on your own—the world is a dangerous place."

Five mintues later, they were driving along a lane that edged the lake. They passed the abbey, reduced by time to a few low walls, and when Gloriana looked for Hadleigh Castle, she saw no visible trace of it. Kenbrook, as she had seen for herself the day before, was naught but a tower now, surrounded by piles of dark gray stone.

Kirkwood paid a toll, as though they were crossing a stranger's bridge, and they were admitted to the grounds. Except for the attendant, there was no one else about.

Gloriana scrambled over the shallow wall surrounding the graveyard and hurried to the place where Aurelia St. Gregory had been buried. The sentinel angels had fallen to dust long ago, but the crypt itself was there yet.

Standing very still, closing her eyes and holding her breath, Gloriana willed herself back to the century she knew, back to Dane.

Nothing happened. When she looked again, after an interval of very hard wishing, Kirkwood was standing before her, hands in the pockets of his trousers, head tipped to one side, expression sympathetic.

"Why?" she whispered. "Why did this happen?"

"I don't know," Kirkwood replied gently.

Gloriana started resolutely toward the tower; it was that or dissolve into tears of defeat and sorrow. Once, while she and Dane were prisoners there, she had been flung from that world into this one, though the effect had lasted only a few moments. Perhaps she could find a passage into the past after all.

Kirkwood, to his credit, did not try to stop Gloriana, but simply followed her into the tower and up the inner staircase. The place had changed greatly, of course, but she knew her way to the high chamber and climbed steadily toward it. All the while, she was going over the first transition in her mind.

There was a gate.

Gloriana had wandered through it as five-year-old Megan when summoned by the lady Elaina, who had soon brought her to Edwenna. But where, exactly, had this gate been? The memory stayed just out of reach, like a mischievous child playing a hiding game.

The upper room was lined with tapestries, none of which had existed in Gloriana's time, and there were glass cases all around, filled with relics of Kenbrook Hall's glorious past. Bits of tile from the Roman baths. A jade chess piece, once held in the warm curve of Dane's fingers while he pondered his next move. A dagger with a jeweled hilt, originally a gift to Edward, to commemorate his knighthood.

Gloriana stood with her hands resting on the glass, her heart pounding, and said her husband's name, once, softly, like a prayer.

Kirkwood put his hands on her shoulders and turned her around to face him. "Tell me what's happening inside you, Gloriana," he said.

She was trembling. How could she say what it felt like to see such things displayed as artifacts of another time in history? There were no words to explain.

"Please help me," she said.

Kirkwood drew her into a brotherly embrace, and she clung to him and let her head rest against his shoulder.

"I shall try," he promised, but he sounded uncertain, and little wonder. What Gloriana was asking might very well prove impossible, and they both knew it.

Chapter

12

*I*n his heart, Dane had known all along that he would not find Gloriana, but the knowledge did nothing to relieve him of the desperate need to search for her. When at last he fell into the bed in the tower room, half blind with fatigue and sorrow, he sought her still in the dark, misty twists and turns of his dreams.

She was elusive, his Gloriana, and yet somehow near enough that he could almost catch the special, spicy scent of her skin, almost hear her voice. He awakened when the first light of dawn touched his face, as weary as if he had never slept at all.

For a time, Dane sat on the edge of the marriage bed, staring at the table where Gloriana had been sitting on that curious occasion when she had vanished before his very eyes. He sighed and shoved a hand through his hair, baffled. He did not wonder, as other men might have done, if he'd been hallucinating on that occasion, or fallen victim to some clever artifice. During his career as a soldier, Dane had learned to trust his own senses and perceptions implicitly, and he did not doubt them now.

He stood and crossed the room to brush his fingertips lightly over the back of the chair where Gloriana had sat to eat, to play chess, to work her special and singular magic. She'd gone back, he was certain, to that other world that had spawned her in the first place.

For a moment, Dane's grief was so profound, so soul-shattering, that he could not even breathe. His vision blurred, and his throat closed as painfully as if a strangler's fingers had shut tight around his windpipe.

A rap at the door startled him into a semblance of composure. The hinges creaked.

"Dane?" It was Gareth's voice, gruff with worry and impatience, and he carried a lamp, for light spilled into the shadow-ridden chamber, creeping slowly across the floor. "Where is your wife? God's blood, man, you would not believe the rumors—"

Dane turned slowly to face his brother, regarding him in silence. Here was a peril he had not considered in his anguish and confusion. Of course the handmaiden, Judith, would have given her account of Gloriana's abrupt disappearance—it had happened among the gravestones of Kenbrook Hall, to make matters worse—to everyone who paused to listen. Any hint of sorcery was deadly among these people, who ascribed all out-of-the-ordinary events to the provenance of Satan.

"Damn you," Gareth rasped, "will you speak?"

Dane sighed. "If you've heard that Gloriana vanished, I suppose it's true."

"You *suppose* it's true?" Gareth echoed, rousing exasperation in Dane, where only misery had been before. "God's breath, Kenbrook, human beings do not simply dissolve into the air!"

Dane found wine and, despite the early hour, poured himself a portion. Gareth, who would have to serve himself if he wanted refreshment, must have risen before cock's crow in order to reach Kenbrook Hall so quickly. Or, perhaps, he had not gone to bed in the first place.

"No," Dane agreed, at his leisure, after a sip or two, which did nothing to brace him up. He set the goblet aside, with a murmur of disgust. "They do not. But Gloriana is no ordinary mortal."

Gareth glanced nervously toward the great doors of the tower room, which stood slightly ajar. "What is she, then, if not a flesh and blood woman?" he asked, in a troubled whisper.

Dane might have laughed at his brother's tragic expression had the situation not been so grave. "Gloriana *is* a woman, Gareth. You may rest assured of that." He could not help lifting his gaze to the bed he had shared with his wife and recalling, with bittersweet longing, the brief, tempestuous pleasures they had known there. "She is no witch, no sorceress, no minion of the devil, if that's what your precious vassals and peasants are saying."

"They are simple people," Gareth pointed out, sounding mildly defensive and still taking care to keep his voice low. "And what *should* they think, when one of their own is witness to something like that?"

"Gloriana is not evil," Dane said. He paced as he spoke, because he was too restless to sit. "And I cannot explain what occurred, because I do not understand it myself. I will tell you—and may the Holy Virgin preserve you if I find you've uttered a word of this to another living soul—that I once saw Gloriana fade like so much smoke. It happened in this room where we now stand—she was here, and then, in the next instant, she was gone." Dane paused to sigh again, tilting his head back to flex the aching muscles in his neck, and when he met his brother's gaze, he knew he was revealing a great deal. "The difference being, of course, that she reappeared almost immediately."

Gareth at last succumbed and raised Dane's discarded wine goblet to drain its contents in a single swallow. Then he went to the threshold, checked the passageway for eavesdroppers—a belated effort, it seemed to Dane—and closed the heavy doors. While he pondered his younger brother's words, Gareth refilled the goblet from the ewer on a table at the edge of the room.

"Hearing such a tale from the others—well, one allows for the fancies of common folk. They have their legends and stories and the like. But to hear it from you, Kenbrook, is another matter entirely. I don't believe you have, or have ever had, a whimsical bone in your body. God help me, if you swear you saw such a thing, I have no recourse but to believe you."

Dane's smile was humorless, his soul a hollow ache within

him. "Thank you for your confidence—however reluctant you might have been to give it."

Gareth awknowledged Dane's remark with a lift of the appropriated goblet, a slighter motion than before. His brows were knit together in a deep frown as he pondered the matter at hand. "What in the name of all that's holy are we to do about this?" he muttered. "Even if the poor lass manages to find her way back to us—and I pray she does—she'll be in the worst sort of danger."

Dane, who had slept in leggings and a shirt, took fresh clothing from a chest near the bed and began, without self-consciousness, to change. "Yes," he allowed, "there will be those who want to see Gloriana burned for a witch." A shudder moved through him at the images that came to mind; he had seen a similar execution in Europe, and it had been hideous. He strapped on his sword belt and, once again, met Gareth's eyes. "She will return—she must. And I will kill anyone who tries to lay a hand on her. You may tell Friar Cradoc I said so, and please urge him to pass that vow along to the sheep of his flock."

Gareth flushed slightly. "Cradoc is a devout man and a wise one. He will not urge the body of Christ to violence. In fact, I think we should tell him the whole truth, insofar as we know it, and ask for his aid and counsel."

Dane's hand came to rest upon the hilt of his sword by reflex rather than will. "No one is to be told," he said evenly. "*No one,* Gareth."

"Impossible. We cannot manage this situation alone." Gareth spoke earnestly, then paused to take a breath. He proceeded with caution, as though trying to soothe a snarling hound, lest it make a lunge for his throat. "Elaina must be consulted. She has an understanding of these matters. In any event, she'll have heard the tale by now."

Dane lowered his head and, with the thumb and forefinger of his left hand, rubbed his eyes. "Have you forgotten that Elaina is counted mad?" he asked.

Gareth approached, laid a strong, swordsman's hand on Dane's shoulder. "She may be the sanest of us all," he replied. "Come—let us ride to the abbey together, seeking the lady's advice."

"There is something else I must do first," Dane answered. "I'll meet you at the stables within the hour."

His elder brother hesitated a moment, then nodded and, bearing his lamp, took his leave. Dane went to a small chest where Gloriana kept her fripperies and took out one of the narrow golden ribbons she sometimes wove through her hair. After tying the strand around his left wrist and pulling the sleeve of his shirt down to cover it, he, too, left the tower chamber.

He made his way to the chapel. According to legend, the sanctuary was built on the sight of an altar where the ancients had worshipped their goddess. Now, of course, the place was a bastion of Christianity.

Dane, never particularly religious, hesitated on the threshold. There were no candles burning here, as at Hadleigh Castle, where Friar Cradoc was probably offering the mass. He moved by memory down the narrow aisle, passing between the cold stone benches.

At the front, he knelt, his head bowed, and silently prayed.

He did not petition heaven for Gloriana's return, although he wanted that more than anything else. His prayer was a simple one: he begged that his wife be kept safe from all that might do her harm.

The weather was chilly and cold, and the now painfully familiar sight of Kenbrook Hall reduced to a single tower deepened Gloriana's despair. After a short struggle with the door handle, she got out of Lyn's car and moved slowly over the rough ground toward the ancient, tilting stones that marked the graves of Dane's mother's people.

Lyn stayed behind her, obviously trying not to intrude, yet ready to offer his help if she needed him. The borrowed clothes, jeans and a shirt, were soft and supple, allowing her to move easily. She wore an oversized jacket, one of Lyn's, and shoes that were slightly too large for her feet.

Gloriana found the crypt where Aurelia St. Gregory lay and rested her forehead and both hands against the cold marble, willing whatever force had taken her away to send her back.

Nothing happened, except that a chill crept into Gloriana's

bones, and Lyn finally came, took her arm, and led her silently back to the waiting car.

She wept and was grateful that Kirkwood did not speak, but simply drove.

He took her to an eating establishment, located roughly where the tavern of Hadleigh Village should have been. The rain was coming down harder than before, and smoke curled from the brick chimneys at either end of the structure, offering the heartening prospects of light and warmth.

Gloriana glanced at her rescuer, who remained in the driver's seat, his hands resting on the wheel. With every passing day, the twentieth century seemed more familiar, more substantial, more *permanent*. Would she never find her way back home?

"I think something nice and hot to eat might be just the thing," Lyn suggested gently. "Shall we go in?"

Gloriana glanced once more at the smoking chimneys and nodded. She had no appetite, but she was fairly sure she was breeding, and she knew she had to put aside her own feelings and tend to the needs of her unborn child. Dane's child.

The inside of the tavern, which Lyn referred to as a pub, delivered on its promise to raise Gloriana's spirits. There were fireplaces at either end of the long, wide room, with bright blazes kindled on their hearths, and the trestle tables, with their benches, were similar to those at Hadleigh Castle. The lanterns, suspended from the ceiling on long, rusted chains, though powered by that twentieth-century phenomenon electricity, were fashioned to resemble the old oil lamps Gloriana remembered so fondly.

She felt a bittersweet twinge, made up of both longing and relief, as she took in her surroundings. The pub was nearly empty, and a servingwoman in a scandalously short dress ushered them to a table next to one of the fireplaces.

Lyn ordered fish and something called chips for both of them, and the servant went away, humming cheerfully.

The food, when it arrived, was hot and fragrant. Gloriana recalled the potatoes as french fries, and said so.

"Ah," Lyn confirmed, with a smile. "A Yank."

"What's that?"

"An American."

Gloriana thought of her squabbling parents again, the airplane ride to England, and the turbulent, unhappy days that had preceded it. Her shudder was involuntary.

Mr. Kirkwood's eyes widened a little at this, but he did not offer comment. Instead, he raised another subject. "You must think of your future, Gloriana," he said quietly, reaching over to cover one of her hands lightly with his own. "There is, of course, a possibility that you might never return to—wherever you came from."

"You believe my tale, don't you?" Gloriana shaped the question slowly and carefully, but the ability to speak as Lyn and the others did, and to comprehend their words, had by now come to the forefront of her mind.

Lyn helped himself to another morsel of the delicious fried fish. "I don't have the first idea what to believe," he confessed good-naturedly. "But I know a princess in the jaws of a dragon when I see one."

"Some people would say I'm mad," Gloriana ventured, wondering if there were indeed dragons in this modern world, as there were said to be in her own. She was warmer than she had ever been in such weather in the thirteenth century, and now that her stomach was full, she felt sleepy.

Kirkwood's aristocratic jaw tightened slightly at the inference. "I am a physician, after all, and while you may be suffering from a delusion of some sort, you are otherwise quite sane."

Gloriana felt such relief at this pronouncement that she nearly started to weep again. There had been moments, of course, when she had questioned the veracity of her own mind. "Thank you," she said in a near whisper, but she withdrew her hand from his.

As it happened, that day was to set the tone of those that followed. Lyn made his rounds, then he and Gloriana drove to Kenbrook Hall and spent at least an hour prowling the grounds. Gloriana was searching for a passageway back to the thirteenth century, and Lyn, though he never said so, was there to lend support and, probably, protection.

After these thorough and always fruitless sojourns, they usually went to the pub for a midday meal. In the afternoons and evenings, when Lyn was working in his surgery or at the hospital in the next village, Gloriana read voraciously and watched the television set. She was trying desperately to make sense of a new and strange environment, but her yearning to return to Dane was unrelenting.

Lyn's kindness was a comfort, and practically every night Gloriana dreamed she was back in the bed in the tower chamber at Kenbrook Hall, curled against her husband's side. These visions were so real that she felt wounding disappointment upon wakening to find herself alone, enduring the loss of Dane over and over again.

Finally, when she had been at Lyn's house for a fortnight— Marge had gotten her more clothes and taught her to use the washing machine and other latter-day devices—Mr. Kirkwood's sister, Janet, appeared one morning. A welldressed woman in her middle years, Janet owned a shop in the next village specializing in antique books and manuscripts. Lyn had told her about Gloriana, she said, and since she was going abroad for a few months, she needed someone to mind her business. A small salary and a flat above the shop would accompany the position.

Gloriana might have protested, quite rightly, that she knew nothing about managing such an enterprise, but she was independent by nature and thus very anxious to make her own way in the world. Although Lyn had never said so, she knew she was imposing on him by staying. Besides, she suspected that despite the more permissive customs of the twentieth century, it was still not quite proper for a woman to live under the same roof with a man who was not her husband, father, uncle, or duly appointed guardian.

"I should like to work for you," Gloriana told Janet, who smiled and tossed a look to her younger brother that might have meant *I told you so.*

Lyn stood beside the fireplace, one arm braced against the mantelpiece. He had not spoken during the brief interview, but there was something watchful in his manner all the same. And something sad.

"There is no need for you to hurry off," he said at last, his eyes on Gloriana's face.

Before she could speak, Janet offered a brisk, "This is a small village, Lynford, and you are a doctor. You must consider your reputation and Miss—and Gloriana's, as well." She turned shrewd but kindly dark eyes on Gloriana. "What is your surname?" she asked. "I don't believe I've heard you say it."

"St. Gregory," Gloriana replied. She met Lyn's gaze. "I am very grateful for your help," she told him gently, "but your sister is right. I mustn't go on living here."

"Nonsense," Lyn said quickly, and Gloriana noticed that his skin was flushed along his jawline. He was looking at Janet now, and there was an angry glint in his eyes. His next words were cryptic to Gloriana, though Janet seemed to understand them perfectly. "The rules of society have changed since Victoria's time," he said in a tight voice.

Janet squirmed a little, sitting there on the leather chair next to the desk in Lyn's study, but her expression was a stubborn one. Gloriana liked her, though she was intimidating.

"Perhaps they have," she allowed. "But this is not Los Angeles or Paris or even London. Our neighbors and friends and clients—*your* patients, Lyn—are not sophisticated people. You mustn't shake their confidence in you."

Lyn, still flushed, opened his mouth to protest, but Gloriana raised one hand in a bid for silence.

"I do not wish to stay," she said quietly.

Hurt flickered in his eyes and was subdued. "Very well, then," he murmured, after some moments of awkward silence. "It is your decision, of course."

Barely half an hour later, Gloriana was riding through a gloomy drizzle in the passenger seat of Janet Kirkwood's small, nondescript car. The weather was much as it had been on the day she'd left behind all that was dear and familiar to be thrust into this strange, frenetic time.

"There is something very different about you," Janet remarked in her quiet and forthright way, as she drove, squinting through the fogged glass Lyn called a windscreen. Little rods worked rhythmically, splashing away the rain, and Gloriana was fascinated for a second or two before she blinked to break the spell. "My brother is quite mysterious where you're concerned," Janet went on. "And Lyn is *never* mysterious—the man is as uncomplicated as a teakettle."

Gloriana sighed and closed her eyes, pretending to be sleepy. In truth, her senses were wildly alert, since there

were so many sights and sounds and impressions to stimu-
late them.

Janet wasn't about to let her captive evade conversation.
"It will take several days, I suppose, to teach you how to
run the shop properly. Of course, you needn't do anything
much beyond greeting customers, answering the telephone,
and making sure the doors are locked promptly at six. I'll
take care of any bookkeeping or messages when I get back
from France."

Gloriana nodded, but did not open her eyes. "I hope you
do not come to regret your choice. I know little or nothing
of trade, as I told you before." Through her lashes, she saw
Janet adjust the buttons on the radio, filling the car with
soft, magnificent music.

" 'Trade,' " Janet reflected. "What a quaint word, in this
context at least. Where do you come from, Gloriana St.
Gregory?"

Plainly, there was no hope that a companionable silence
might be allowed to settle between them. Gloriana had
hoped to listen to the invisible orchestra in peace. "I'm an
American," she said. It was the truth, after all. It just wasn't
the *complete* truth. "I was born there, I mean. I've spent
most of my life here, in England."

Janet steered the car into a wide turn, and Gloriana,
caught off balance, sat up straight in her seat, eyes wide.
"Hmmm," Janet said, and though there was a note of doubt
in her tone, she did not refute Gloriana's claim.

The shop was housed in a tidy two-story building with
gables and a shingled roof. Gloriana felt an affinity for the
place, despite the terrible homesickness that never quite
left her.

"How wonderful," she said, admiring the shopwindow,
with its display of leather-bound volumes.

Janet smiled, pushed open her door, got out of the car,
and unfurled an umbrella, all in nearly the same motion.
"Thank you," she cried happily, rushing for the shop's entrance and turning a key in the lock.

Gloriana hurried after her, and in a moment, they were
inside a cozy chamber bursting with books. There were

shelves full, reaching from floor to ceiling, while others were stacked on chairs and tables, counters and desks.

"It *is* lovely, isn't it?" Janet enthused, shrugging out of her raincoat and hanging it from a peg beside the door. She left the umbrella open on the tiled floor, well away from the books, to dry. "Of course, if Lyn and I hadn't both been born into money, I wouldn't be able to keep the shop open. My stock is expensive, and folks who can afford illuminated manuscripts and old diaries are a bit thin on the ground these days."

Gloriana frowned, confused. She removed her jacket while working out what Janet had actually said and hung it up in the proper place.

Janet gestured toward the rear of the establishment. "Come along, and I'll show you where you'll be staying. As I said, I've a cozy little flat just upstairs."

Gloriana followed, casting looks of longing over the massive collection of books. "Aren't you afraid to trust a stranger with such—such wealth?"

Janet smiled over one shoulder. "Lyn trusts you," she said. "That's quite enough for me. He has good instincts about people, and besides, if I don't get away, I'll go berserk. Can't bear this weather, you know."

The upstairs flat was indeed pleasant, with a small brick fireplace, comfortable chairs whose like did not exist in the harsher, simpler world Gloriana knew, a television set, and lots of bookshelves. The smaller of two bedchambers was an alcove with high windows, and there was a bathroom, too, with a big bathtub, a commode, and a basin. The kitchen was part of the main living area.

"Do sit down," Janet commanded cheerfully, "and I'll brew tea." She bustled to a cabinet and took out several pieces of bright crockery. "I appreciate this—your looking after the shop on such short notice, I mean. We'll have to ring Lyn soon, though. He'll be worried until I let him know that you're all right, not overwhelmed or anything."

Gloriana couldn't help smiling as she lowered herself into one of the deliciously soft chairs. Surely it was a sin to enjoy such creature comforts as much as she did. Like Lyn's cottage, Janet's flat was fragrant and warm and almost impossibly clean.

If "overwhelmed" meant what Gloriana thought it did, she certainly qualified. She was learning so many new things, so quickly, that sometimes she thought her head might burst from the pressure. Oh, she was intelligent, and she had been a scholar under Friar Cradoc's tutelage, but Latin and Greek and mathematics had been easy in comparison to learning to function in the modern world.

They had sandwiches and tea, and then Gloriana watched in fascination as Janet pushed buttons on the telephone. Although Janet and the others seemed to take such ease of communication for granted, it was miraculous to Gloriana.

Her heartbeat quickened with excitement when Janet handed her the receiver. Gloriana had never spoken over a telephone before, and when she heard Lyn's voice, she was startled.

"Hello, Gloriana," he said gently.

"H-hello," Gloriana responded, somewhat breathlessly. If only there were a device that would allow her to hear Dane speak, as she was hearing Lyn.

"Is my sister treating you well?"

Gloriana nodded, then remembered herself and said, "Yes. Janet is very kind—like you." It was a little unnerving, speaking to someone she couldn't see—rather like carrying on a conversation with a ghost.

Lyn assured her that she could ring him whenever she wanted and gave her the number. After that, she surrendered the receiver to Janet again and went to the window to look out.

She was among friends, she knew that. And yet the need to see Dane, to touch him and hear his voice, was an all-pervasive ache. Would she never find her way back to him? Must she resign herself to spending the rest of her life in the latter part of the twentieth century, where she simply did not belong?

The rain continued through the afternoon, the perfect backdrop for Gloriana's solemn mood. Sorrow notwithstanding, she paid attention while Janet showed her the basics of running the shop—answering the telephone, when to lock up and when to open for business, how to summon help in case of emergency.

Gloriana was amazed that Janet was willing to trust her,

a virtual stranger, with so much responsibility. The shop was full of precious things.

"When in doubt," Janet summarized, much later, when the two women were seated near the shop's little stove, sipping tea, "just turn the lock, pull the blinds, and take yourself out for a walk or upstairs to watch the telly. It's mostly a matter of convenience to my customers, my keeping the place open. Some of them get very edgy if I'm away and they've developed a penchant for some dusty old tome—they hate to wait, poor dears."

"What if I make a mistake?" Gloriana ventured quietly. At Hadleigh Castle, before Dane's return from the Continent, she had been learning to monitor the household accounts, and she had always followed the investment of her personal fortune. The things Janet had shown her, though quite complicated, made sense.

Janet shrugged. "Everyone does, at one time or another. If anything concerning a transaction troubles you, simply ask the client to wait until I come home."

After that, the subject of business was closed. Gloriana retired to her room, bathed, and went to bed early. She had declined supper and immediately tumbled into a dream so vivid that for a few breathless moments she actually thought she had returned to Kenbrook Hall, and to Dane.

It seemed she stood in the tower room, beside the bed she had shared with her husband. He lay sleeping, the covers tangled at his waist from much tossing and turning, his fair hair glimmering in the feeble flicker of an oil lamp's wick.

Gloriana whispered his name as she touched his forehead with the lightest brush of her fingertips. He stirred and murmured something, and she bent over him, realizing by then that she was only dreaming, that in truth they were as far apart as ever. She kissed his mouth, and her tears fell, shimmering, upon his face.

He opened his eyes. "Gloriana," he said, on a ragged breath. "Thank God—"

She felt herself begin to fade and reached for him, but it was too late. She awakened, face wet, heart breaking, in the spare room of Janet's flat. Dane was as far from her as ever, and yet she sensed that he was near too. The special wind-

and-rain scent of him was in her nostrils, and the texture and warmth of his lips were etched into her own.

Gloriana lay back on her pillows, making no effort to wipe away her tears or to stem their flow. As she mourned, she also wondered. Had she dreamed of Dane or, for however few precious moments, had she actually visited him?

Dane lay trembling upon his bed, the room dark except for the dying light of the single lamp he had left burning on a nearby table. He had seen her, had seen Gloriana. She had touched her mouth to his, in the sweetest and briefest of kisses, and he'd seen the love glowing in her beautiful eyes as she looked at him.

A dream? No. Dane had no doubt that she'd been real. Somehow, for the merest fraction of a moment, Gloriana had managed to slip through the veil of time and mystery that separated them. While he was despondent that she was once more lost to him, he was also encouraged. By the grace of God, or some benevolent angel, he would find her again.

He rose, went to the window, and stared out at the moonlight shimmering on the waters of the lake. Had Gloriana been kidnapped or simply gotten lost, he would have been able to bring her home, even if it meant battling every brigand in England, searching every loft and hidden glen. Instead, she had stepped over some mystic threshold, and he did not know how to follow.

The morning after her dream-visit to Dane, Gloriana awakened with a bruised heart, an aching head, and puffy eyes. She splashed her face with cold water in the little bathroom, brushed her hair and teeth, and put on slacks, a sweater, and loafers.

Janet was having tea and toasted bread in the kitchen area when Gloriana joined her.

"Good heavens," Janet said with spirit, rising from her chair and hurrying over to Gloriana, "you look as though you've wept the night away. Are you ill? Shall I ring Lyn?"

Gloriana shook her head, trying to smile because she wanted to reassure her worried friend. "No," she said quickly, miserably. "Don't bother him, please. I'm just—missing someone."

Janet gestured an invitation for Gloriana to sit down at the table, and she did so. Soon, there was a cup of tea steaming in front of her. With a hand that trembled slightly, she added sugar and milk.

"A lost love, is it?" Janet pursued the subject cautiously, taking her own seat again and spreading marmalade onto a slice of bread.

Gloriana nodded and forced herself to follow suit. She must eat, if she wanted to keep up her strength and protect her baby. "I can't explain—not now, at least."

Janet waved one hand. "No need," she said. She frowned, tilting her head to one side and studying Gloriana thoughtfully. "You have the loveliest hair," she mused. "But it must be troublesome to wash and brush."

Gloriana was grateful for a change of subject, and she had noticed from watching the television set at Lyn's cottage and studying passersby whenever they went into the village to shop that modern women wore their tresses in shorter styles. Ladies of the thirteenth century never sheared their hair, though most wore wimples whenever they left the privacy of their bedchambers.

"I should like a change," Gloriana confessed. She suspected Dane would be annoyed if she had her hair cut and say she looked more like a boy than a woman, but as much as she loved and missed her husband, it wasn't his decision to make.

"There's a shop just across the way," Janet said. "I'll ring for an appointment, and you can go over there this afternoon. Just close up the shop and put the 'Back Soon' sign in the window."

Gloriana smiled. It was an outrageous thing to do, cutting one's hair, and yet the more she thought about the prospect, the better she liked it.

Once breakfast was over, Janet went over a few last-minute instructions, then took up her traveling case and left the shop in Gloriana's charge. Gloriana was both exhilarated and terrified, but since no one came in all morning, she had plenty of time to get used to her new position.

At noon, she went upstairs and made herself a sandwich— a trick Marge had taught her—then returned to the shop. Because there were still no customers and no telephone calls, Gloriana contented herself with examining the stock on hand. Some of the volumes were so beautiful, with their heavy parchment pages, artful lettering, and brilliant illustrations, that Gloriana became absorbed in them.

At three—she had had considerable trouble learning to read clockfaces and still went mostly by the number of chimes—Gloriana gathered the notes Janet had left for her, put on her jacket, closed the shop, and crossed the street to an establishment called Cuts and Curls.

It was an exciting adventure in its own right, visiting a twentieth-century barbering place. When Gloriana returned, some two hours later, her hair brushed her shoulders, and even though her heart was still heavy, her step was light.

She paused for a moment to admire her reflection in the window of Janet's shop, then unlocked the door and hurried inside, out of the sharp and chilly wind.

Chapter

13

It was half past six that evening when the telephone in Janet's apartment jangled suddenly, startling Gloriana so much that she almost dropped her tea. She prided herself on the fact that she was functioning uncommonly well in this odd corner of the universe. Still, there were some things that seemed beyond getting used to, and that noisome apparatus was certainly among them.

"Gloriana?" The voice was dearly familiar, though there was one she would rather have heard. "It's Lyn. How are you getting on, now that Janet's gone off to the south of France?"

Gloriana smiled. Her newly shortened hair felt deliciously light as she gave her head a slight toss. "I'm doing well enough, thank you," she replied. "Though I confess I am more than passing lonely."

"I have the perfect solution to that," Lyn replied. "I rang to see if it would be all right for me to pay you a call tonight. I'd like to introduce you to a friend of mine, someone who wants very much to meet you."

Gloriana barely hesitated. "I should enjoy a visit," she said. "It's very quiet here, with Janet away." She paused, frowning, as a glance at the window reminded her that the supper hour was upon her. "Shall I prepare something to eat?"

"Heavens, no," Lyn responded quickly, with a warm chuckle. "I'll bring along some of those fish-and-chips you like so much, from the Village Tavern."

Gloriana was pleased and not only because she was about to have company and sup on some of her favorite fare. She could ride, wield a bow and arrow, read Greek and Latin, and do sums in her head, but cooking was not her forte. In fact, all she knew how to make were sandwiches and tea. "That would be lovely," she said, making no effort to disguise the relief in her voice.

By the time Lyn arrived, mayhap half an hour later, bearing greasy paper bags that emitted succulent smells, Gloriana had built up the fire on the small grate and switched on several lamps. Accompanying Lyn was an older man, very handsome, with white hair and steel gray eyes. He wore an expensive suit and carried a thick portfolio of battered leather under one arm.

"Gloriana," Lyn said, shrugging out of his well-cut tweed overcoat after planting a brotherly kiss on her cheek, "meet my good friend, Arthur Steinbeth. He's a professor at an American university."

Gloriana greeted the other visitor with a tenative smile and a nod. Although she was not afraid of the professor, she sensed that he was scrutinizing her, indeed attempting to see inside her very soul, and she began to wonder if Lyn had told him her strange tale.

"Won't you come in?" she said, because she had heard people on television say just those words when they had visitors.

Professor Steinbeth's smile reassured her a little. "Thank you," he replied, with a courtly inclination of his head. He surrendered his own rain-dampened coat to Lyn, who hung it up, but the portfolio remained within his grasp.

In the kitchen area, Gloriana got out plates and forks in case the professor did not wish to eat with his fingers, and Lyn poured the contents of the fragrant bags onto a large platter. With malt vinegar from the cupboard, the meal was complete.

Only then did Steinbeth lay aside the leather folder, setting it carefully on the floor beneath his chair. Although the older man said little and was unfailingly polite, Gloriana knew he was as aware of her as he was of the portfolio. She glanced uneasily at Lyn once or twice, but did not ask questions.

Finally, when they'd eaten, and Lyn had purloined a bottle of wine from Janet's refrigerator, the three of them repaired to the hearth. Lyn stood with an arm braced upon the mantel, as was his habit, while Gloriana took Janet's leather chair. The professor arranged himself, the reclaimed portfolio on his lap, upon the chesterfield.

"Professor Steinbeth is an expert on medieval literature," Lyn explained. A smile, faintly sad, touched his mouth. "By the way, I like what you've done with your hair, Gloriana. I suppose it was Janet's idea?"

The two subjects, so unrelated yet uttered in virtually the same breath, gave Gloriana pause. She took a few seconds to translate. "Yes," she said at length, lowering her eyes. "Janet suggested that I have my hair cut." She turned her attention to the scholar seated on the chesterfield, again wondering if Lyn had betrayed her secret. "I know a little about medieval literature," she confessed in modest tones.

The professor smiled. His gray eyes twinkled, and a flush of pleasure rose in his cheeks. "So I am told," he said.

Gloriana stole another look at Lyn, who made a face calculated to fend off any annoyance that might be directed his way. Then she returned Steinbeth's smile. "Oh?" she replied. "What exactly have you been told about me, Professor?"

"Please," the teacher said. "Call me Authur."

"Arthur, then," Gloriana conceded. The people of the twentieth century were much more familiar with each other, it seemed to her, than those she had known in the thirteenth. "Please—tell me what Lyn—Mr. Kirkwood—has said."

Arthur blushed again and loosened his collar in a gesture Gloriana suspected was wholly unconscious. His gaze strayed briefly to Lyn's face, as if to seek permission.

"He says you are a time traveler," he replied.

Gloriana stiffened slightly, her fingers interlocked in her lap, and shot a look in Lyn's direction. Her friend was careful not to meet her gaze.

"I see," Gloriana said. "And you believe him?"

Arthur hesitated, let out a long breath. "I suppose I do," he admitted.

"I took the liberty of sending Professor Steinbeth your gown," Lyn interjected, with hasty good cheer. "The one you were wearing when I found you at Kenbrook Hall that day, I mean. He was up at Oxford, working on a paper, you see, for an American journal."

The professor cleared his throat, looking embarrassed. "I examined the garment," he said. "It was seamless, and the weave is antiquated, even by historical standards."

Gloriana merely nodded, refusing to let either the professor or Lyn off the proverbial hook by speaking.

"What Arthur means to say," Lyn put in, pacing the length of the hearth now, his hands clasped behind his back in good English fashion, "what he's *been* saying, until now, and hardly taking a breath the whole while, is that wool is not dyed or spun or woven in that way anywhere on earth. And has not been in three centuries."

Gloriana raised her eyebrows slightly, bidding her friend to continue.

"How did you acquire that gown, Miss St. Gregory?" the professor burst out. He did not sound impatient, but eager.

"It was woven and dyed for me at Hadleigh Castle, from the wool of Gareth St. Gregory's own sheep."

There was a brief silence, during which the only sounds were the crackling of the logs on the fire, the ticking of Janet's mantel clock, and the mournful sigh of the wind, pleading at the windowpanes.

The professor's hands trembled a little as he opened the portfolio, resting until then upon his knees. For a long moment, he stared at Lyn again, almost imploringly, before facing Gloriana. His voice was low, reverent, and somehow broken. "Will you look at this, please?"

With that, he removed a fragile parchment manuscript from the leather portfolio and extended it to Gloriana.

She took it carefully and felt an odd shiver of anticipation move through her as the weight of the pages came to rest in her hands.

"Experts the world over have examined this volume," Arthur Steinbeth told her in a tone of respect and awe. "We believe it is medieval in origin, and yet we cannot be certain.

Some of us feel that it is simply a very good copy, and, well, I should like your opinion."

Gloriana lifted the cover page, which was illuminated with delicate paintings of angels, still beautiful though much-faded. Tears filled her eyes as she read the first sentence, which was penned in a mixture of French, Latin, and Old English.

The manuscript was most definitely genuine.

This being an accounting of the household of St. Gregory . .

She took a moment to gather her wits before attempting to speak. She could not explain why Steinbeth and his colleagues had not been able to make out the lettering, for the words were as clear to her as if she'd composed them herself.

"It is a family history," she said, bracing herself as wave after wave of emotion crashed over her. *It is all here,* she thought with frantic joy and the profoundest sorrow. *Dane's fate, and thus my own. Edward's and Gareth's. Elaina's.*

Lyn came to stand behind her chair, resting his hands on her shoulders. He always knew when she needed comfort and was quick to provide it. "Arthur was hoping you might authenticate the manuscript for him," he said very gently.

Gloriana merely nodded, biting her lower lip, clutching to her breast the heavy clothlike pages, which might very well tell of her future, along with her past. She would have agreed to anything for the chance to read those carefully inked words, now faded to dim, ghostlike shadows upon the parchment.

Lyn cleared the table and washed it with a sponge. When it had dried, he laid a cloth over the surface. From the pocket of his coat, he produced a small, square device, which he identified as a tape recorder, and explained its use. Gloriana was so anxious to begin reading that she could barely concentrate while he demonstrated how to load fresh tape cartridges, also brought from his pocket, into the machine.

Finally, reluctantly, Lyn and the professor said their farewells, put on their overcoats, and left the flat.

Gloriana did not bestir herself to lock the door behind them, for in truth she was so weak with expectation and dread that she could not have trusted her watery knees to support her weight. After pressing the proper button on the recording apparatus, Gloriana began to read, her voice tremulous at first and then rapt.

The manuscript had been written by one of Dane's direct descendants. She put her right hand to her abdomen as she pondered this, wondering again if she would yet find her way home to the thirteenth century and if the child within her would form a link between Kenbrook himself and the author of the history unfolding before her.

Throughout the night, Gloriana read, pausing at intervals to turn the tapes over or to replace them, or the batteries, as Lyn had instructed her. Later, when she heard her recorded voice, she would be surprised at the steadiness of it, for while she was deciphering that ornate script, she ofttimes wept or laughed, or both together.

She reached the account of her disappearance and held her emotions in check as she read it, and she was not surprised to find herself named a sorceress and thereafter referred to as the Kenbrook Witch. But as the events that followed her departure played themselves out before her, as vividly as if she were watching them occur in a scrying glass, Gloriana became distraught. She had to force herself to read on as she learned how Edward provoked Dane, time after time, accusing him of murdering the lady Gloriana, that he might have Mariette de Troyes after all. Finally, Edward had attacked Dane, and thinking he'd been set upon by an outlaw, Dane had killed the youth with a blade.

Gloriana clicked off the recorder at that point and hurried, sobbing, into the bathroom, where she fell to her knees before the commode and was violently ill.

She could bear no more, she told herself, and yet she could not stay away from Professor Steinbeth's damnable, cursed manuscript. She brushed her teeth, splashed her face with cold water, and went back to Janet's kitchen table. There, she settled herself on the same hard chair, dutifully switched on the recorder, and began to read again.

Following that tragic incident, though no one else found cause to blame him for what had happened, Dane had gone half mad with remorse and grief, and he'd been heard to shout blasphemies at God and seen shaking his fist at the heavens.

Kenbrook had, thereafter, apparently divided his time between swilling endless mugs of grog at the village tavern and
harrying Merrymont, a neighboring baron, long past the time
when the man and all his soldiers had been brought to heel.
When Edward had been but a year in the grave, both the
lady Elaina and Gareth, her husband, had fallen prey to a
vile fever and perished.

Again, at this news, Gloriana paused to deal with an overwhelming sense of loss. She had passed the night reading;
her exhaustion was bone-deep, her emotions stretched taut,
her eyes heavy and hot from crying. She had no choice but
to switch off the little machine, stagger into the bedroom,
and collapse on top of the covers.

She did not open the shop that day or answer the telephone when it rang.

Twilight had turned the world to pale purple before she
awakened, roused at last by an insistent pounding at the
door of the flat.

Dazed, Gloriana thrust herself off the bed and made her
way through the dim, chilly rooms to the entrance.

"Who goes there?" she asked rummily, her hand on the
doorknob.

The reply was a masculine chuckle. "Lyn Kirkwood here.
Who's that?"

She opened the door and stared at her friend, sleep-
fuddled and confused.

He laughed, but there was a caress in his eyes. "You're
all right after all. Thank God for that, then. I've been ringing
you all day, both here and in the shop."

"I'm sorry," Gloriana said, stepping back to admit him.
"I was very tired—"

Lyn went past her to the table, where the tape player and
manuscript waited, removing a packet of fresh tapes from
his overcoat pocket. "You didn't have to do it all at once,"
he said, tossing his coat over the back of a chair and moving
to the stove, there to collect the teakettle. He was filling it
at the sink a moment later, voice raised to be heard over
the rush of running water. "Though I must say old
Steinbeth's as anxious as a cat in a room full of mousetraps."

Gloriana looked with sorrow toward the manuscript. She
was half finished with it, and there had been no mention of

her return. Which probably meant, of course, that she would never manage to escape the twentieth century. "I'm not sure I understand why he wants a recording made," she confessed. "But I can tell you this much—it is a genuine artifact."

"The logic behind the tapes is simply this: you, presumably being a thirteenth-century person, will give the words their proper meter. Who else could do that?"

As he spoke, he sat her down at the table, then carefully moved the manuscript and other things to a safe surface on Janet's writing desk. After that, he took pots and pans from the cupboards with a great and comforting clatter. Soon, there was tea to drink and bacon sizzled in a skillet.

Gloriana had sat in something of a stupor the whole time, just watching him. "Time traveling," she sighed. "It is certainly impossible, and yet here I am. Mayhap, what we perceive as magic is really just a natural law we have yet to understand."

"That is a remarkably *un*-medieval way to think," Lyn commented, cracking eggs into a bowl and beating them to a foam with a wire whisk. "But I believe you are right. Which means that traveling from one century to another, as you apparently have done, may simply be an undiscovered faculty of the human mind."

Gloriana bit her lower lip for a moment, frowning as she considered the theory Lyn had just advanced. "It *did* seem to begin within, rather than without—the transition, I mean. There was a peculiar sense that here was something I had done myself, however inadvertently, instead of something that simply happened on its own."

"Fascinating," Lyn said, putting two slices of bread into a shiny metal box to toast. "Do you mean to say that you willed yourself from there to here—or more properly from then to now?"

"Yes," Gloriana replied, marveling that she had not been aware of this before.

"Any other symptoms?" asked Lyn, ever the physician.

"There was a headache," Gloriana recalled. Just the memory of that terrible, ferocious anguish caused her to put the fingers of her right hand to her temple. "It was awful— I thought I would die of the pain."

Lyn turned back to his cooking. His mood was thoughtful as he scrambled the eggs with a little milk and forked the bacon onto a napkin-covered plate. Gloriana reflected that if she ever went back to the thirteenth century, she would sorely miss the wholesome, savory, and very plentiful food of the twentieth. "Some involuntary shift of consciousness, then," he mused, speaking more to himself, it seemed, than his companion. "How extraordinary a thing is the human mind."

Gloriana could not disagree. She shoved the fingers of her right hand through her rumpled hair, then braced her elbow on the table edge and cupped her chin in her palm. "If I did this deliberately, why can't I go back? I want to more than anything else in the world."

As he set a plate of toasted bread on the table, Lyn made a visible effort to hide his sadness and failed miserably. "Is it so wonderful, that turbulent century? I should think it a grim place, rife with disease, full of war and hunger and crime."

Gloriana regarded him steadily. She had watched a lot of television news programs since Lyn had taken her under his wing some three weeks before and read her share of newspapers and magazines as well. "I might say the same of your time, mightn't I? You have plagues, too, and all the rest."

Lyn's shoulders sagged a little as he served the eggs and bacon, got himself a plate and utensils, and sat down to join her at the meal. "Can't argue that. But it's cleaner here, at least, and people have more rights under the law."

"Yes," Gloriana allowed, somewhat uncertainly, taking generous portions of eggs and bacon. She especially enjoyed the latter, not only for its crispiness and flavor, but because she could eat it with her fingers, a method that was very familiar. "Perhaps you're right."

"I hear an unspoken 'but' at the end of that sentence."

Gloriana smiled. "What good ears you have," she said, recalling a children's story read to her by a nanny long before her first sojourn through time, when she was only five.

Lyn regarded her solemnly. "It's Kenbrook," he guessed aloud.

"My husband," Gloriana reminded him gently. They had

discussed Dane on several occasions, and she had always made it clear that she regarded him as her mate, now and forever.

"Yes," Lyn said, at length. "Your husband."

They did not speak of Kenbrook again.

Lyn departed soon after they'd washed the supper dishes, leaving Gloriana to her manuscript. She faced the remaining pages with mingled eagerness and trepidation. Before tackling what remained of the task, she took a bracing shower, put on fresh clothes, and brushed her hair.

Then, when all that was done, Gloriana arranged the fragile parchments upon the table once again, with a clean cloth beneath, to protect them. She put a fresh tape in the recorder—Lyn had taken the ones she'd already made—and began to read aloud. Her voice was low and hoarse with both emotion and overuse as she continued.

The report of Dane's death, when Gloriana reached it, was so brief as to seem almost cursory. He had left his wife, Mariette, and their two young sons to return to the Continent as a mercenary and perished in a shipwreck off the coast of Normandy. According to the author, Kenbrook's family did not miss him overmuch, for he had been a bitter and unhappy man this long while and thought to be under an enchantment cast by the Kenbrook Witch.

Gloriana was not surprised that Dane's life had turned out so, nor did she mind the fact that history blamed her for his suffering. Still, she'd hoped Kenbrook would find peace and solace, if not love, in the arms of his second wife, and it was a fierce disappointment to learn that he had not.

The image of Dane drowning in a frigid and unmerciful sea was so vivid, so shattering, that Gloriana could not go on reading—could barely breathe, in fact.

She switched off the recording machine with a groping gesture of one hand, and went off to bed.

She slept soundly, despite the fact that she'd spent much of that day lost in slumber. It was nearly dawn when, at last, Gloriana dreamt.

She stood on the broken tiles of the Roman bath, there in the depths of Kenbrook Hall, felt their roughness against the soles of her bare feet. Two candles burned, blobs of smelly tallow set in scarred wooden bowls, casting their uncertain glow over the sulfurous waters. Dane sat in the steaming pool, his eyes closed, his face bleak and gaunt in the fragile light.

He was full of sorrow.

Gloriana said his name clearly, but if he heard, he did not respond.

She saw gray in his fair hair and fresh scars on the flesh of his chest, the marks of a dagger or sword. He was still soldiering, then, still making war.

Alarmed, she took a step toward him, but her feet carried her no closer than she had been before. She saw Kenbrook now as if through a shifting curtain of fog and called to him again, more desperately than before.

He turned his head toward her, and she saw a terrible solitude in his eyes and disbelief, as though he were looking upon a specter or an illusion. In the last moment before she was wrenched into wakefulness, leaving Dane behind again, Gloriana suffered a shattering realization.

Dane had been much older in this vision. And that might mean that time was not passing at the same rate on his side of the veil as it was on hers. If somehow she managed to return, she might find that Dane was already dead or a mere babe in arms.

She did not eat breakfast that morning or go near the manuscript and tape recorder, both of which taunted her silently from the dining table. Instead, Gloriana showered and dressed and went downstairs to the shop, where she passed the morning dusting, peering through the rain-speckled windows overlooking the empty street, and praying for a customer.

Janet rang her up in the middle of the afternoon to ask how things were going. Gloriana, glad to hear a familiar voice, confessed that she hadn't opened the shop at all the day before. She said that Lyn had visited, bearing fish-and-chips, but did not mention that he'd brought along Professor Steinbeth and a medieval manuscript.

She feared she could not broach the subject without breaking down.

"I've cut my hair," she said, instead. It was an inane statement, but Gloriana didn't care. She was still very shaken, and even making simple conversation was difficult.

"Have you?" Janet replied, sounding pleased. "I'll bet you look wonderful. But you do sound a bit weary yet, dear. Why don't you close up the shop and go to the cinema or something? I'm sure Lyn would be happy to escort you if he hasn't got any emergencies on his hands."

Gloriana rested her forehead against her palm. Sometimes it was very hard work just comprehending what Janet said, and she was not at her best. She should know what a "cinema" was, for instance, but she couldn't quite recall. "I wouldn't want to trouble Lyn," she said. "He's done enough for me as it is."

Janet sighed. "I feel so wicked—here I am, having a good time, absolutely *saturated* with sunshine, while all my friends and relations are stuck in that endless drizzle." She paused, very briefly, to take a breath. "Well," she went on, in a philosophical tone, "it's not as if you can't get out if you want. There are still coaches—you Americans call them 'buses,' don't you—not to mention trains and taxis."

Gloriana agreed hastily, searching her memory for buses, trains, and taxis. She had just located the correct images when Janet wished her a good night and rang off.

No more than five minutes after she'd hung up the shop telephone, as if directed by the hand of Providence, a bus splashed to a stop outside, emitting a flock of passengers huddled into coats, their umbrellas unfurling in brisk bursts of color as they stepped down onto the sidewalk.

Gloriana was possessed of a sudden and irresistible yearning to ride a bus and dashed upstairs for her money, a jacket, and one of three shabby umbrellas Janet kept in a big urn next to the door. Then she stood peering out of the shopwindow until the big vehicle appeared again, almost an hour later. Quickly, before she could lose her courage, Gloriana locked up the store and sped across the flooded sidewalk to get on board.

The driver took the pound coin she offered and made change, while two women squeezed past to make their way down the steps to the street. Gloriana took an empty seat and gazed out the window, wondering where the great, lumbering coach would take her. They stopped often, with a great screeching sound, to take on new passengers and let off old ones, and Gloriana listened to the conversations around her with interest, though she pretended not to hear.

The bus traveled from one village to another, and the late afternoon gave way to twilight and then to evening. Only when Kenbrook Hall loomed up ahead did Gloriana realize how far she had traveled and that she had intended to go there all along.

"Place is closed for the day, love," the driver said when Gloriana came down the aisle and stood waiting for the doors to open with the now-familiar whooshing sound, as she had seen a dozen other people do. He shivered, squinting through the broad windscreen at the front of the bus. "Nothing but a gloomy pile of rocks, if you ask me. Even on a sunny day."

Gloriana refrained from pointing out that she had *not* asked him and simply waited on the lowest step. With a muttered imprecation, the driver pulled on a lever, and the doors folded back, letting in the wet, icy wind.

"The last coach leaves Hadleigh in an hour, from just there, in front of the chemist's shop," the man warned, as Gloriana stood on the road, gazing resolutely toward the ruins of her home and her most cherished dreams. "Mind you don't miss it, or you might be in for a cold night."

Gloriana raised a hand to indicate that she'd heard, but then launched herself toward the ancient keep, and her steps didn't slow as she wended her way between puddles. A metal fence surrounded the property now, for the stone walls had long since fallen of course, and the gate was locked.

Gloriana was undaunted. Clad in blue jeans, one of the twentieth century's better inventions, by her standards, Gloriana climbed over the barrier and landed on both feet in the old graveyard.

There were lights on in the tower itself, and one burned in the tiny gatehouse too. Gloriana paid no attention whatsoever to either place, but instead moved between the ancient markers like a ghost, heedless of the cold and the incessant, misty rain. Perhaps if she simply sat down in the exact place where she'd been when the transition occurred, she would be taken back.

The mist turned to a downpour, by degrees, but Gloriana

barely noticed. At the foot of Aurelia St. Gregory's crumbling crypt, she sank into the wet grass, her legs crossed, and raised the collar of her jacket against the cold. She had only to wait, that was all. Just wait.

The air turned colder and the night darker, and Gloriana retreated further and further into her own thoughts. After a long time, she heard voices around her, but none of them were Dane's, so she shut them out.

Gradually, the cold turned in upon itself and became warmth, soothing at first, but then oppressive and smothering. The texture of the darkness changed too, exploding in bright crimson flashes that hurt her eyes, and there were more voices and hands touching her.

"Leave her alone." That was Lyn speaking. Even in her distraught state, Gloriana recognized his firm, kindly tones.

How had he found her?

He scooped her up into his arms, and she felt a jostling motion as he carried her through the night. There were people around, but they were only shapes in the hot, blood-colored light, and Gloriana turned her face into Lyn's shoulder.

"You're safe now," he said. "I've got you."

Gloriana might have wept, but the fever burning within her had dried up all her tears. She did not wish to be saved, wanted only the refuge of her dreams, where Dane still lived and laughed.

She drifted in and out of consciousness after that, finding herself in Lyn's car, then in a building of some sort. The dazzle of the place blinded her, and she shrank from the glare. There was pain in her chest; her clothes were removed, and needles pricked her flesh. She was too cold and then too warm, and through it all, she heard Lyn's voice, comforting, cajoling, pleading, commanding.

Nightmares rose up around Gloriana, like the mud of a stagnant marsh, and sucked her under. She did not find Dane in that terrible darkness, though she searched and struggled and flailed.

When she awakened, she found herself in a plain room, and the shades were partially drawn against the watery light of a rainy day. Lyn was with her, his face beard-stubbled and etched with worry.

"There you are, back again," he said, his fingers clasped tightly around hers, as though to hold her here, in his world.

A needle, connected to a tube, pierced the back of Gloriana's other hand, but oddly there was no pain. "You should have left me there," she told him. Her voice sounded raspy, and her throat was raw and dry.

Lyn shook his head, and his eyes, for a moment, were overly bright. He lifted her hand to his face, and she felt the roughness of his beard against her flesh. "All I want is to take care of you," he said. "Won't you let me do that?"

Gloriana turned her face aside, letting his question pass, countering with one of her own. "How did you find me?" she asked, closing her eyes. She knew now that Lyn loved her, and she didn't want him to care, didn't want him to be hurt.

"The caretaker remembered you from before," Lyn answered after a long time. "He recalled that I'd taken you away then, and rang me up at the cottage."

"Please, Lyn," she whispered. "Leave me alone, for your sake, as well as mine."

Lyn made no promises. Nor did he release Gloriana's hand.

Chapter
14

*W*hen she'd gathered her wits about her again, later
that same day, Gloriana was filled with chagrin. She had
been surpassing foolish, going to the ruins of Kenbrook Hall
in the rain, letting her emotions run away with her, sub-
jecting herself and her unborn child to danger. In the future,
she must be far more prudent and consider her actions thoroughly before plunging ahead. An impulsive nature had ever
been her plague.

Gloriana had just decided, quite sensibly in her opinion,
to put the mistake behind her and proceed accordingly,
when Lyn appeared in the doorway of her hospital room. He
looked tired, rumpled, not at all his usual clean-shaven and
chipper self.

"You're pregnant," he remarked, holding her medical
chart in one hand. Lyn was not Gloriana's attending physician, but he was a member of the hospital staff and thus
had access any record he might wish to see. She had
learned much about the workings of medical institutions by
watching Marge and Mrs. Bond's melodramatic "programs"
on the television set, before moving to Janet's flat.

Gloriana shifted restlessly against her bank of pillows.
She ached in every bone and fiber of her being, and she'd

caught a dreadful cold, but she wasn't sick unto death or anything near it. She had been admitted to this bustling, sterile place for observation, according to Marge, who had appointed herself as Gloriana's private nurse.

The diagnosis was simple exhaustion.

She replied to Lyn's statement, at length, with a quiet, "Yes." While Gloriana had not told anyone except Dane that she was carrying a child, it certainly wasn't a shameful secret. She was duly married to the infant's sire, after all—even if the man *had* been dead for some seven hundred years.

"How long have you known?" Lyn remained in the doorway. His manner, while not unfriendly, was cool and a bit distant, injured, somehow.

"From the first," Gloriana replied forthrightly, smoothing her covers. This was no exaggeration, as far as she was concerned. She and Dane had conceived the babe in the Roman baths beneath Kenbrook Hall; in some strange wise, she had felt the beginning of that new life.

"Well, you should have told me," came the crisp reply. Her friend entered the room then and drew up a chair to sit beside her bed. "Great Scot, Gloriana, a pregnant woman needs quiet surroundings and plenty of rest. And vitamins."

Gloriana had no idea what "vitamins" were and didn't ask, for fear Lyn would explain, in detail and at length.

Lyn gazed at her in silence then continued. "The father—?"

"Dane St. Gregory, fifth baron of Kenbrook, and none other," Gloriana answered in a soft but unwavering voice. Her chin might have protruded, just a little way, and her arms were folded.

"Of course," Lyn said, after a deep sigh. "But he's nowhere about to look after you, our Dane St. Gregory, fifth baron of Kenbrook, now is he?"

Dane's absence was a central fact of Gloriana's present life, and her very spirit thrummed with the hopeless pain of being separated from him. Perhaps that was why she grasped so desperately at the last illusory shreds of her independence. "I am neither idiot nor invalid, Lyn," she snapped. "I can look after myself!"

Lyn's expression was one of infinite weariness. He sagged back in his chair and sighed again. "I did not set out to insult you," he said, in a tone of grim and hard-won patience. "I am merely concerned—"

"Well, *stop* being concerned!" Gloriana broke in. "They're discharging me from the hospital this afternoon, and I'm going back to the bookshop. Provided Janet hasn't given me the sack by now."

"You know she hasn't. Gloriana, *will* you listen to reason? You are not in fit condition to engage in commerce—even in an establishment as casually managed as Janet's. You need to rest, and eat well, and live in a peaceful environment—"

"God's blood," Gloriana erupted, "you make me sound like a sparrow hatched without its wings!"

"I give up!" Lyn growled in return, bounding out of his chair to turn away.

"It's about time," commented Marge from the doorway.

Lyn started to say something, stopped himself, and stormed out.

"It's just because he cares, you know," Marge confided, bustling about in her usual efficient manner. She'd brought along a small satchel, and from it she took a beige cable-knit "jumper," which Gloriana recalled from her earliest life in America as a "sweater," a pair of corduroy slacks, stockings, underwear, and shoes. The clothes Gloriana had been wearing on her fateful bus-and-graveyard odyssey were no doubt in the laundry, if not entirely ruined.

"Well, Lyn ought to *quit* caring," Gloriana muttered, folding her arms and closing her eyes tightly for a moment, in an effort to hold back tears of sheer frustration. "He's a good man. He doesn't deserve to have his heart broken."

"But it's his heart to worry over, though, isn't it?" Marge said. "You can't protect people from their feelings, Gloriana. Mustn't even try, for it's bad for all concerned. Come along, now—we'll get you dressed, and I'll drive you back to Janet's shop." She patted the pocket of her medical smock, worn over a pair of matching white slacks. "I've a script here, to fill at the chemist's on the way. Vitamins, and some medicine to make sure that cold of yours doesn't turn into something worse."

Gloriana gave herself up to Marge's bustling charge, and soon she was dressed and being wheeled out of the hospital in a special chair. Her legs were a bit on the shaky side, but she *could* have walked under her own power and been the happier for it. All this fuss and ceremony was very wearing indeed.

After a brief stop at the chemist's shop—Gloriana waited in the car while Marge dashed inside—they arrived at Janet's establishment. Gloriana was relieved; if she couldn't be at Kenbrook Hall, with Dane and their household of servants and soldiers, this place would do quite well. Here, at least, she could imagine that she was taking care of herself.

She thanked Marge profusely for her help and was more than grateful when, after tucking Gloriana into an overstuffed chair, building a fire in the grate and brewing a pot of strong, savory tea, the kindly woman took her leave.

Gloriana swallowed her medicine, the foul-tasting vitamin capsules as well as the antibiotics, and nodded off into a restorative, dreamless sleep. When she awakened, Lyn was crouching by the fire, adding sticks of wood. The scent of something delicious filled the air, and Kirkwood looked so forlorn and so vulnerable that Gloriana forgot her earlier annoyance and greeted him in a cordial tone.

"Do you always come into people's homes wihtout announcing yourself first?"

He looked back at her over one shoulder and smiled his sad, solemn smile. "Not unless I've rung the bell a hundred times already and gotten no answer. How do you feel, Gloriana?"

"Tired, but a bit better. And you?"

He gave a throaty, rueful chuckle. "I feel, as the Yanks say, like I've been dragged backwards through a knothole."

Gloriana couldn't help laughing at the mental picture his remark produced. Watching Lyn, though, and seeing the pain he was trying so hard to hide, she grew somber again. "You've been kind," she said, very carefully and very softly. "And I am more grateful than you will ever know. But for your own sake, Lyn, you must stop spending your time looking after me. I'm not your responsibility."

"But someone must take care of you—"

"Someone is doing that, Lyn," Gloriana interrupted. "*I* am."

He turned his back on her to stare into the fire, hands plunged into the pockets of his trousers, but not before Gloriana saw the flush of annoyed conviction rise along his jaw-line. "And you're having one hell of a go at it, aren't you?" he retorted. "Wandering among the stones of an ancient ruin, in the rain—"

Gloriana closed her eyes for a moment and drew a deep breath. She resolved, once again, to hold her temper, for misguided as his efforts were, Lyn was only trying to help. "I admit that was a blunder," she said. "A very serious one. That doesn't mean I need—or want—a keeper."

Lyn's shoulders sagged slightly as her words, however gently aimed, struck him with an obvious impact. "Glo-riana," he said raggedly, after a very long time, "the past is dead. Please—let me give you a future."

Tears brimmed along Gloriana's lashes, but she dashed them away with the back of one hand before Lyn could turn and see them. "I have a future," she said. "What I need, ever so badly, is a friend."

He was looking at her then, his face hidden in shadow. "I shall always be that," he vowed hoarsely.

"I hope so," Gloriana replied. "For I don't know what I should have done without your help."

With that, there seemed a new, if tentative, understanding between the two of them. Lyn did not mention his personal feelings again, but instead served up some of Mrs. Bond's succulent mutton stew, brought from his cottage and re-heated on Janet's stove.

As Gloriana ate, still ensconced in the chair in front of the fire, Lyn began gathering up Professor Steinbeth's manuscript.

"I'll send word to Arthur that you're not up to finishing this," he said.

Gloriana was exasperated. "You're taking charge again," she warned. "It just so happens, Mr. Kirkwood, that I wish to finish the task set before me. For reasons of my own."

Lyn left off what he'd been doing, holding both hands up high for a moment in comical acquiescence. "Very well," he said. "I'll tell Arthur you're progressing nicely."

"Thank you," Gloriana replied, and smiled.

Lyn glanced at his watch. "I'd better be getting along," he said. "Rounds, you know." He bent to kiss the top of Gloriana's head. "Good night, love."

She answered by squeezing his hand, and he put on his coat and left.

Strengthened by the medicine, several hours of rest, and a hearty meal, Gloriana found herself inexorably drawn toward Professor Steinbeth's manuscript. Setting aside her supper tray and the soft blanket Marge had tucked around her earlier, Gloriana rose and walked steadily to the table.

Within minutes, the small tape player was whirring again and she was completely absorbed in the words penned so long ago by one of Dane's own progeny. The account had moved past Kenbrook's life and death into the tempestuous generations to follow, and Gloriana was better able to detach from the details—which were sometimes dull, sometimes fascinating, and very often tragic.

She finished reading in the early morning and, still feeling uncommonly vigorous, made herself breakfast, took a shower, and went downstairs to work in the shop. She was eager to redeem herself as an employee and prove that Janet had not misplaced the confidence and trust she had put in her.

Several customers came in, breaking the usual monotony, and Gloriana even made a sizable sale to an American tourist.

She was alone in the shop, perched high on the sliding shelf-ladder, replacing a rejected volume, when another headache careened into her, like a runaway bus, and slammed her hard against a wall of darkness. A cold sweat sprang out all over her body, and Gloriana clung to the rungs of her ladder, afraid to let go or even attempt descent.

Her vision was naught but an ebony fog, peppered with bursts of light, and she felt her consciousness seeping down some inner drain, disappearing into nowhere.

And then she was falling.

She fell and fell, end over end, like the fair-haired Alice she'd heard of long ago, when she was still called Megan, tumbling down the rabbit hole. She braced herself to strike the hardwood floor, but the dreaded moment of impact never came. . . .

Someone was poking her with a stick or a broom handle.

"Get yourself up from there, boy," a male voice commanded roughly, "and be on your way. This is no almshouse, nor no tavern, neither."

Gloriana opened her eyes to see a man in a shoddy woolen tunic and leggings standing over her, grasping a shepherd's staff—the object he'd jabbed her with, no doubt. She was leaning against the outer wall of a crude daub-and-wattle hut, and an upward glance showed a thatched roof overhead.

Cautious joy flooded her soul. Was she dreaming?

Or was she back in her own corner of history, and Dane's?

Gloriana scrambled to her feet. "What year is this, pray, and what realm?"

The man simply stared at her, as if dumbfounded. His gaze moved over her twentieth-century clothes with mingled wonder and disapproval, and he took a step backward, as though expecting fire to shoot from her fingertips.

Gloriana held her tongue a moment and concentrated, hoping thereby to make the inner shift back to the manner of speaking proper to the thirteenth century. If indeed that was where she was.

She repeated her question, slowly and carefully.

"Why, 'tis the year of our Lord twelve hundred and fifty-six," the man said. "And this be Britain. Seems you ought to know such things as those, lad. Where do you come from?"

Two years, she thought, stricken. Two years had passed since she'd vanished from the Kenbrook Hall she knew, while hardly more than a month had gone by for her in the twentieth century.

A great deal might have happened in so much time, and Gloriana's soaring gladness was suddenly tempered by dread. Professor Steinbeth's manuscript had not been specific enough for her to know whether she'd arrived in time to avert certain tragedies, but if she hadn't, unbearable sorrow might well await her.

Her next thought was that the man was mistaking her for a male—probably because of her slacks and shorter hair.

He took her arm in a bruising grip. "I asked where you hail from, boy, and you'll tell or feel my boot amongst your ribs."

Gloriana thought quickly and was still not sure, even after the fact, that she'd spoken wisely. "Kenbrook Hall," she said.

The fellow squinted into her face. His breath was foul, and the smell of his unwashed body worse still. "Kenbrook Hall, you say? That be a lie, for certain—for no one lives in that place now but for ghosts. It's but a shell."

Gloriana's heart sank. "How can that be?"

"The master's at Hadleigh Castle these days." He paused to spit, showing his contempt, and Gloriana felt her stomach roll ominously. "That way, he's closer to the tavern."

She wrenched free of the peasant's grasp and rather handily evaded his attempts to get hold of her again. Looking frantically around, she recognized the landscape, knew she was near one of Hadleigh's neighboring villages. It was a distance of several difficult miles to Gareth's castle from there.

Purposefully, ignoring the impatient inquiries and imprecations that were flung after her like stones, Gloriana set out at a fast pace for the cluster of huts round the next bend, hoping to beg, borrow, or, if necessary, steal a gown of some sort. Her latter-day garments would attract too much attention, and questions might be put to her that she dared not answer.

She passed hay-laden carts on the path to Calway and drew her share of stares, but when she reached the village, she was pleased to see a mummer's troupe at its center. There were acrobats and jesters and dancing women, along with a small menagerie of tattered animals in rickety wheeled cages.

Giving a mangy bear on a leash a wide berth, Gloriana approached a gray-haired man, mostly because he was the tallest of the band of players and thus projected a certain air of authority. He was clad in a grand, flowing cloak of azure silk, patterned with shimmering golden stars.

"Excuse me," she said, coming near to touching one of the cloak's great, loose sleeves, but stopping just short.

He turned to look down into her eyes, and a smile touched his lips, as though he found her familiar. Perhaps he and the others had performed at Hadleigh Castle before, while she yet lived there as Gareth's ward. Or mayhap they had been part of the celebration when Edward was knighted.

Gloriana had just concluded that the tall man was a magician when he uttered three unsettling words.

"*There* you are," the merlin said, in the tones of a man finding something that has long been lost and most anxiously and vigorously sought in the interim.

Gloriana blinked, taken aback by his words and mien, but in the end she was so wholly focused on reaching Dane that she did not pursue an explanation of either his remark or his manner. "Where are you bound?" she asked.

"Hadleigh Castle," was the reply, and it was accompanied by a deep and somber sigh. "Spirits are sore sorrowing in that place, and happiness is not found within those walls."

The knowledge that there was such suffering in the midst of her family pierced Gloriana's heart like an icy lance, but she would not give in to emotion again. She had made that mistake before in Lyn's world, wandering in the rain among the ruins of Kenbrook Hall, and she would not willingly repeat it.

"I should like to join your mummer's band," she announced. In this way, she would be given a costume to cover her odd, modern clothes, and perhaps even a mask to hide her face. As eager as Gloriana was to see Dane again, she remembered from Arthur Steinbeth's manuscript that from the day of her disappearance hence, she had been known as the Kenbrook Witch. Presenting herself openly, without assessing the situation first, might bring her to the stake.

"What can you do?" asked the master of the troupe. There was a smile in his eyes. "Be you a dancer—a magician—a fire-eater, mayhap?"

Gloriana swallowed. "I suppose I could dance," she said doubtfully. Then she brightened, recalling all she had seen and heard during her sojourn in the twentieth century. "And I have tales to tell."

"A storyteller, then." He touched her hair, curiously, but not in an objectionable manner. "Be you lad or lady?" he asked.

Gloriana looked down at the very loose sweater she was wearing over her slacks. Her bustline, never very robust in the first place, was modestly disguised. "Which is it more fortuitous to be?" she countered, upon meeting the merlin's twinkling gaze again.

The master threw back his bushy head and let out a great bellow of laughter. "You are privileged to choose? God's breath, but you are a mummer's mummer, if you can be either!"

"I am a lady," Gloriana said quietly, hoping she would not be called upon to explain her sheared hair. Brushing her shoulders, it was still quite long by twentieth-century standards, but this was the thirteenth, where women let their tresses grow throughout their lives.

"Ah" was the gentle reply. A hand of greeting and agreement was extended. "And I am called Romulus. You shall journey with our troupe to Hadleigh Castle, milady, and thereafter—who knows?"

Gloriana narrowed her eyes a moment, wondering. It almost seemed that Romulus knew who she was and that, indeed, he had been expecting her. But when a bright red robe, hooded and embroidered with golden thread, was thrust at her by one of the other players, Gloriana did not hesitate to accept it.

She donned the gown over her clothes and raised the hood. When no one was watching, she scooped up a handful of dirt and applied it liberally to her face and hands, thus assuring a greater resemblance to the other members of the group.

After Romulus had made a few ringing announcements and the single cart had been loaded with various props and hitched to a small gray donkey—which obviously served also as a menagerie attraction—they set out along the rutted, winding road to Hadleigh.

Gloriana did not try to strike up a conversation with any of her fellow travelers, for she was lost in her own thoughts. Part of her wanted to bolt ahead at a dead run and reach Dane as soon as possible. Another part counseled immediate flight in the opposite direction.

She simply walked, hands loosely clasped in front of her, head down, face hidden by the generous hood.

A slender girl in a tawdry brown kirtle, her hair hidden beneath a dingy wimple, fell into step beside her. Like the others, except for Romulus, she was unwashed and seemed blissfully unaware of the fact.

Gloriana, though ever inclined toward cleanliness herself, might not have noticed the contrast if it hadn't been for her recent visit to a later and far more hygienic point in time. She resisted an urge to wrinkle her nose and looked at her companion out of the corner of her eye.

"I am called Corliss," the girl imparted, with such a mingling of reticence and eager affability that Gloriana hadn't the heart to rebuff her. "I dance and cast runes."

Gloriana knew her own smile was probably a trifle sad, but there was no help for it. Corliss couldn't have lived more than two and ten summers, yet she was clearly on her own, dancing for strangers and making up stories about an uncertain future. Heaven only knew what else the child had to do to survive in that harsh world. "Mayhap I shall ask you to tell my fortune," Gloriana said, before offering her name. She made no mention of the St. Gregorys, of course, or her connection to Dane.

Corliss turned wide, guileless eyes on Gloriana's face. "But I know your future, milady, even without the help of the runes."

Gloriana felt a chill of fear. She was not sure she truly wanted to hear what lay ahead, for it might be terrible indeed. And Corliss was the second person to address her as a woman of noble birth since her return. "Why do you call me by such a title?" she asked, in a hushed voice, drawing a little nearer to the girl as they walked, that they might not be overheard. "I am but a poor player, and a wanderer, like you."

Corliss's smile was indulgent. "There is only one in all the kingdom called by the wondrous name of Gloriana. You are the Kenbrook Witch, are you not?"

Gloriana was horrified and linked her arm with Corliss's, giving her companion a little jerk of reprimand. Her response came in a whisper. "Pray, do not utter such blasphemy again. Would you see me accused of sorcery and burned at the stake for a servant of Satan?"

Some of the exuberance faded from Corliss's smudged face, to be replaced by a disconcerted expression. Mummers, usually regarded as outcasts themselves, tended to be more tolerant than the average citizen, and the child had plainly forgotten that any association with magic could be deadly in that society. Even performers like Romulus had to be very careful to evoke only merriment, never fear or even awe.

"But you *are* Lady Kenbrook, come back from the Other World, aren't you?" Corliss pressed, in a breathy whisper. Her assessment was so close to the fact that Gloriana was stunned for a moment.

She considered lying, so desperate were her straits, but she suspected the girl would recognize her answer for an untruth. "What do you know of Kenbrook and the doings at Hadleigh Castle?" she countered. "Tell me!"

Corliss bit her lower lip, not considering whether or not to tell, Gloriana suspected, but simply sorting through scraps of information tucked away in her head. " 'Tis said that Kenbrook killed his own brother, young Sir Edward, in a brawl with knives and fists."

Gloriana closed her eyes at this, the worst possible news, and forced back the bile that surged into her throat, burning there like acid. "Holy Mary," she whispered, as a prayer and not a curse, "Mother of God—"

Corliss shivered with a youthful mixture of horror and anticipation, hugging herself. "They're cursed, the lot of them. Why, Hadleigh himself perished of a sweating fever, and his wife, the lady Elaina, hasn't said a word since. Just stares off into the air, she does, and won't even give a look when someone speaks or touches her."

Grief twisted Gloriana's heart. She was too late to prevent the battle with Edward—her darling, chivalrous Edward— to thank Gareth for his guardianship and bid him a fond farewell, to sit with Elaina and attend her as one attends a sister and a cherished friend in times of bitter despair.

But there was still Dane. Gloriana knew she must go to him, now more than ever, must offer all her love and whatever help and comfort she had to give. Not for one moment did she regret her unceasing prayers that she might be returned to her home and her husband. She would venture into hell itself, if that was what the situation called for.

"Surely such tales are exaggerated, passed from one to another the way they are," she observed to Corliss, when at last she found the words within herself and could trust them to come off her tongue in a steady and sensible fashion.

"You'll see," said Corliss, with a prim little nod.

It was sunset when the troupe, hungry and footsore, finally reached the gates of Hadleigh Castle.

For all her sorrow, Gloriana's heart leapt at the sight of the place, for somewhere within those familiar walls, she would find the man she loved, the man whose soul was an extension of her own.

Gloriana considered her marriage vows as she waited with Romulus and Corliss and the others for the great, creaking portcullis to be raised. Her impatience was such that she feared she would cast off the protection of her disguise and run to Dane when first she glimpsed him and hurl herself into his embrace.

There were pitch torches blazing, noisy and fragrant, at the guardhouse, but the outer bailey, used for gaming and tournaments, was deserted. The lights of the village flickered beyond, modest and dim compared to their electrical counterparts in the twentieth century, yet somehow warmer and more welcoming.

Gloriana's spirits lifted a little as she proceeded with the mummer's troupe along the ancient Roman paving stones that formed a path. The donkey brayed, and at this, villagers came out of their huts to see who approached at such an hour.

Inside the village tavern, Dane St. Gregory set his pewter mug down with such suddenness and force that some of the sour swill within spilled over onto the rough-hewn tabletop. A strange, wrenching sensation, part joy and part alarm, was uncurling in the pit of his stomach.

She is near, he thought, though he was not a man given to illusions.

" 'Tis but a mummer's band," announced the kettle-maker, who had been among the first to rush outside and hail whatever sojourners had set the dogs to barking by their approach.

Dane rose unsteadily to his feet, staring at the door, confounded by the sudden certainty that Gloriana had come back to him. He felt her presence and her love, as tangibly as he had in the most vivid of his dreams, but there was an obvious difference.

He was awake.

And sober, for all that he'd earned a reputation for drunkenness. Not to mention sloth.

He looked down at his clothes, which were rank by his former standards. He lifted a trembling hand to rub his jaw, bearded now, and wondered if the riot of anticipation he was feeling was merely another cruel trick of his own mind. He did not think he could endure the disappointment, should he hurry out and find that Gloriana was not there after all.

"What is it?" Maxen asked from his seat on the opposite side of the table. The Welshman looked worse, if possible, than Dane himself. Two years passed harrying poor, thwarted Merrymont and tossing back bad English ale had not been good for his character. "God's breath, man, you look as though you've seen a vision."

Dane took one stumbling step across the packed-dirt floor, then another, ignoring his friend, drawn toward the door as surely as if a cord had been entwined round his insides.

The mummers, a tattered and pathetic troupe if Dane had ever seen one, were lumbering past as he left the tavern. They would be given scraps from the castle's kitchens to sup upon and assigned places in the stables to lie down for the night, for that was the custom.

He followed them a few steps, then shouted, "Hold!"

Only one of the mummers paused, a player in a hooded crimson cloak—a stranger, and yet there was something in the way the person stood . . .

Dane felt his heart rise into his throat and thunder there, fair choking him, as a mixture of torchlight and thin moon-glow illuminated the familiar features of his lost wife. He had not laid eyes on Gloriana in twice a twelve-month, and every moment of that time had been passed in the most agonizing and largely private of griefs, but when he would have called to her, she raised a finger to her lips and shook her head.

He started toward her, and she waited.

"Pray," Gloriana said softly, "do not embrace me now, or say my name, lest I be accused of witchery. I shall come to you, when it is safe, in the Roman baths where we made our child."

Dane stared at her, desolate and rapturous, aching to touch her, to grasp her close against his chest and never let her go—afraid, even then, that she was not real. Perhaps he was dreaming, after all, upon his pallet in his old chamber at Hadleigh Castle, or mayhap he had consumed too much ale, again.

She smiled at him, softly, as if she'd read his troubled thoughts and wanted to offer reassurance. Then, with the greatest dignity and reluctance, Gloriana turned and fol-lowed her fellow mummers toward the stables.

Chapter
15

$\mathcal{D}$ane had reached Kenbrook Hall before Gloriana and was already up to his waist in the waters of the Roman bath, surrounded by the gentle light of half a dozen smoking tallow candles, when she rushed in, carrying a single lamp to light her path over the broken stones. She had made haste from Hadleigh Castle, following a dark, familiar course around the lake and through the forest of oak, afraid to pass along the road, lest she be seen and recognized.

She paused, her heart thundering in her throat, her breathing shallow and quick. She had dreamed of this moment, both waking and sleeping, this precious time-out-of-time, when she and Dane would be together again and alone, and now she hardly dared believe it was really happening.

As if to echo her thoughts, Dane said in a hoarse, quiet voice, "If you are another illusion, then be gone with you. I can bear no more false hopes."

Gloriana took a step toward him. "Nor can I," she agreed, shedding the red mummer's cloak and laying it upon one of the benches. Slowly, with an awkwardness that was uncommon between them, she removed the garments beneath—the sweater, the shoes with their strange, flexible soles, the corduroy slacks and underthings.

Dane watched her with ravenous eyes, but made no move to leave the bath and approach her. Gloriana returned his gaze just as hungrily. When she was naked, she stood still for a moment, allowing him to feast upon the sight of her, proud of her womanly shape and the small protrusion of her belly, where their child flourished.

Finally, Dane raised a hand, beckoning to her, as he had once done in a dream, and Gloriana hesitated, terrified that if she took another step toward him, he might vanish. Or she might be thrust back into the modern world.

"Come to me," Dane said, and though he phrased the words as a command, they had the low, pulsing timbre of a plea.

Gloriana's paralysis was broken. She moved to the side of the pool, descended the ancient, uneven steps, felt the warmth of the water even as an inner heat of another sort suffused her, making smoke of her bones and mist of her muscles, setting her blood to racing through her veins. When she was within arm's reach of Dane, Gloriana tripped on a raised stone and stumbled, and he caught her, his hands gripping her shoulders.

Just being near Kenbrook was all but overwhelming, mayhap because Gloriana had yearned for him with such unrelenting desperation that she couldn't quite credit the granting of her deepest wish. Now her senses rioted at his proximity, and she might have been drunk on stout wine, so light-headed was she and so unsteady on her feet.

She raised trembling hands to his shoulders as he linked his arms loosely about her waist and looked down into her upturned, tear-misted eyes.

"There is much we must speak of," he said. "But those things will wait, wife, for if I do not have you, I shall die of the wanting."

Gloriana's smile was bittersweet. There were indeed matters to discuss—Edward's death, and Gareth's, to name only two—but Dane was right. There would, if God was merciful, be time for such sorrowful topics later. Because she could not manage even a word, Gloriana nodded her agreement.

Dane bent his head and kissed her, cautiously at first, as though he feared that too much pressure would cause her to vanish again. When he found Gloriana's mouth warm and resilient beneath his, however, and ready to open for him like a spring flower expanding to receive the sunlight, a primitive groan escaped Kenbrook and his kiss deepened rapidly.

Gloriana clung to him, transported and yet returning Dane's fierce desire in full measure. He lifted her, and she clasped her legs round his hips, embracing him now with all her limbs. She tilted her head back, making a sound that was part grief, part triumph, as he planted greedy kisses along the length of her neck.

Finally, Dane put himself inside Gloriana, as he had done on that other occasion, when they had conceived their babe in that very pool. The frustrating difference was that now he was teasing her with just the tip of his staff, withholding the utter possession she craved. Hands clasping her buttocks beneath the steaming water, Kenbrook looked deep into her eyes as he spoke.

"Later, milady, in our bed in the tower room, I will have you at leisure and give you such pleasure as you have not yet imagined. But for now, I simply haven't the strength to go slowly."

Gloriana kissed his mouth, his eyelids, his temples and cheeks, and strained upon him, urging him to plunge deep. "Do not make me wait, milord, I pray you," she whispered breathlessly, in between attempts to consume him whole. "Have me, and spare me nothing of your passion or your power—"

With a great cry and a powerful thrust of his warrior's hips, Dane sheathed himself in her to the hilt. Gloriana flung back her head in the most elemental of ecstasies, lost from the first in a maze of exploding lights and sensations so intense that she did not expect to survive them. Kenbrook held her firmly as she spasmed around him, his face buried in her neck, and did not slacken his thrusts, but instead drove her to greater and greater pleasure, until she was mindless, sightless, and no longer bound to the earth.

She arched as the pinnacle was at last attained, her legs spread wide in surrender, her fingers buried in his hair. She heard him groan, felt him stiffen and spill sweet warmth into her core.

Afterward, they clung together, each somehow supporting

the other, since neither could have stood on his or her own, there in the center of the pool. They were no longer two separate entities, but a single soul, forever fused into one.

Gradually, passion-scattered thoughts found their way home again, settling into one brain or the other, like bright-winged birds. Voices returned, breathing slowed, hearts beat at their normal rate.

Dane was the first to speak. Cupping his hand under Gloriana's chin and raising her face to look through her eyes to her spirit, he whispered, "I love you. Now and beyond eternity."

With a fingertip, she traced his lips—swollen, they were, like her own, from frantic kisses. Her body was weak with satiation, but the details of Professor Steinbeth's manuscript were clear in her mind.

"Have you married Mariette de Troyes?" she asked without rancor or judgment. Men like Dane needed heirs, and in the thirteenth century marriage usually had more to do with expediency than love. If he had taken another woman to wife, it would not be a repudiation of what he felt for Gloriana, but simply the next logical step along a difficult path.

"No," he said. His gaze was steady upon hers; he did not try to avert his eyes. "But she is betrothed to me. Our vows were to be offered in a fortnight."

"Then I have not made you an adulterer," Gloriana teased. Her relief was acute, and there were fresh tears in her eyes, despite her frivolous words. When next she spoke, her tone was soft and her expression serious. "Do you love her, Dane?"

His embrace tightened slightly. "You know the answer to that, Gloriana—I care for no woman but you." He paused, and the faintest of smiles touched his lips, just at one corner. "If it makes you feel any better, the lady bears no special fondness for me, either. She has made it plain enough that she would prefer to pass the remainder of her days in the nunnery."

Gloriana lifted an eyebrow. "Where you once wanted to send me," she reminded him.

Dane chuckled and kissed her neck. "Yes, fool that I was," he replied. "Come, milady, and I will attend you properly, in our marriage bed. But first you need a wash."

She allowed him to lift her into his arms and carry her to the side of the pool, where he set her gently on the steps and began to cleanse the smudges of dirt from her face. Gloriana was embarrassed, for she had forgotten that aspect of her disguise, but soon, as he bathed other parts of her with light, splashing caresses, she forgot everything but her beloved.

He had brought a gown for her, from one of the chests upstairs no doubt, and when they had dried themselves with bits of worn cloth, he dressed her. The mummer's cloak and Gloriana's modern clothes were left behind, along with the sputtering candles, as the lovers made their way through familiar passageways to the tower steps.

Their bedchamber, when they stepped over the threshold, seemed a damp, deserted place, like the rest of the hall, and was illuminated only by the thin, eerie glow of a faltering moon. Plainly, Dane had not slept within those curved walls in a long time, though the furnishings remained as they had been, except that now the chairs and tables were draped in cobwebs and layered in dust.

After setting their one lamp in the center of the table, Dane went to the bed, wrenched off the covers, and gave them a great shake. Gloriana watched, from her vantage point in the center of the room, devoutly hoping no mice would be found nesting in the straw mattress and at the same time knowing that nothing would keep her from sharing that thick ticking with her husband. Nothing, of course, except another abrupt shift between centuries.

Gloriana trembled slightly at the prospect, and Dane, perceptive where she was concerned, caught the motion and turned his head to look at her.

"What is it?" he asked.

She looked around, somewhat nervously, before answering. "What if it has something to do with this room—my vanishing, I mean? It happened here once—"

Dane ceased his efforts to freshen their bed and came to her, taking both her hands into his. "If you want, we shall find another chamber, or return to Hadleigh."

But Gloriana shook her head at that suggestion. The tower room was almost sacred to her, for it had been here that Dane had first made love to her, here that they had laughed and argued and bested each other at chess. "I wish to stay," she replied.

He caressed her cheek with the callused edge of one index finger. "I fear there is no safe place where we might hide from this bumbling magic of yours, milady. But whether we are together for an hour or a hundred years, let us make good use of every moment."

"You are very practical, my lord," Gloriana replied, slipping her arms around his neck once more. Her smile was fragile, tentative, because she knew they could be wrenched apart at any given moment, perhaps never to see each other again. The knowledge frightened her and, at the same time, made every second precious. "We must live only for the present. But there are things that need saying."

Dane sighed and propped his chin lightly on the crown of her head. With his strong, swordsman's hands, he massaged the muscles in her lower back, which were already tightening as tension, both physical and emotional, returned. He thrust out a second ragged breath before speaking.

"Many sorrows have visited the St. Gregorys, Gloriana." Dane drew back to look into her searching eyes. "There is no gentle way to put it—Edward has died, by my own hand. And Gareth, too, is lost, to a fever."

Gloriana had known of these tragedies, of course, but she did not say so, nor did she show surprise. She simply listened.

"There can be no grace granted to a man who would kill his own brother," Dane said, in a raspy voice. "But before God, Gloriana, I did not mean to do this deed."

"What happened?"

Dane left her then, went to one of the great, open windows, and braced his foot against the low sill, gazing out toward the lake. His broad shoulders looked stiff, even in the faint light. "Edward plagued me unceasingly after you left. He thought I'd done murder and searched everywhere for some sign to prove me guilty. He lost interest in everything else but my supposed crime, and no one, including Gareth, could reason with him. Edward challenged me, again and again, and I always turned and walked in the other direction. One night, though, he sprang at me from atop a low wall—I was full of wine and so cannot be held blameless." He paused, shoved one hand through his beautiful, unbarbered hair. "I did not guess that this was Edward until too late. I had already put my dagger through his throat, thinking him a brigand or one of my own soldiers seeking vengeance for some slight."

Gloriana did not wipe away her tears, was not even fully aware of them. Before, Edward's death had been naught but a tale told in a musty old volume of history, but now it was painfully real. And so was the all-encompassing sorrow of the man who had brought it about.

"I am so very sorry," she said.

Dane turned to look at her, his face and indeed most of his body hidden in shadow. Gloriana sensed his feelings, instead of reading them in his countenance or expression. "Then there was Gareth," he said brokenly, after standing still and silent for a long time. "He fell ill with a fever, and might have recovered, but for his grief over Edward's passing. The loss left Hadleigh weak in spirit, for the lad was more son than brother to him."

Gloriana nodded. The terrible task was not yet finished; Dane must still speak of Elaina, for his own sake if no one else's.

"Elaina lives, but barely," he told Gloriana.

"She has long been ill, Dane."

"Yes," he agreed hoarsely. "But now she utters not a single word from one sunrise to the next. She would die, if the nuns did not spoon broth and gruel into her mouth and force her to swallow. She sees nothing, and yet never closes her eyes."

Gloriana swallowed, full of sorrow. Elaina had been a good friend to her, Gareth a wise and generous guardian, Edward the dearest companion of her youth. "The fault is not yours alone," she said softly, grievously, "but mine also. If I had not gone—"

He was before her again in an instant, his hands grasping her shoulders. "It was a mishap, your going from here—you cannot be blamed."

Gloriana touched his face. "Nor can you," she reasoned quietly. "Edward would not have rested until he'd goaded you into some sort of fight; surely you understood him well enough to know that. And if Gareth chose not to prevail over the fever, he alone is accountable."

Dane let his forehead rest against Gloriana's, and a great shudder of despair went through his body. "Hold me close to you," he whispered, putting his arms around her. "'Cause me to forget, for the space of one night at least, all the burdens that are mine to bear."

She wanted to weep for Kenbrook, for in his way he, too, had been among the lost, along with Gareth and her poor, sweet, foolish Edward. But now he was found, and in her arms, where she would give him solace.

Gloriana took Dane's hand and led him in silence to their bed, long abandoned and smelling faintly of mildew. She spread the coverlet over the mattress, then turned back to her husband and began raising his tunic over his head. After that, she took his breeches away, then slipped the soft leather boots from his feet and, kneeling before him on the cold floor, rolled his leggings down.

When he stood before her, naked and magnificent, she did not rise, but brushed the hard musculature of his thighs with her lips.

Dane trembled, utterly vulnerable, completely hers. His manhood towered against his hard belly, in a sort of arrogant surrender, and when Gloriana closed a hand around it, he gasped and murmured some exclamation.

She brought him to her mouth, nibbled at him, and teased him with a few light flicks of her tongue, wringing a long, low moan from his throat. This was his punishment for withholding himself earlier, in the Roman bath, however briefly he had done so.

Despite the chill of the evening air, Dane broke out in a sweat. His skin, everywhere that Gloriana touched him with a free and roving hand, was slick with moisture. While she enjoyed him, he began to rock slightly on his heels in an effort to be taken more thoroughly. But when she took him full in her mouth and suckled hard, it was only to add to his torment, for the instant before Dane would have been satisfied, she always drew back.

He endured the game as long as he could, but finally raised her by her upper arms and gently pressed her backward onto the bed. The straw within the mattress rustled as Dane pushed Gloriana's gown up and braced her heels against the broad frame. He knelt, and she shivered as he parted her knees, his hands gliding slowly, slowly, over the flesh of her inner thighs.

"Now, milady wench," he said, and she felt his breath against the warm, moist nest of curls that sheltered the nubbin of flesh he meant to feast upon, "I shall have recompense for what I have just endured."

Gloriana groaned and arched her back, offering herself to him. When it came to Dane, and the pleasures he gave her, she was utterly without inhibition or shame.

He laughed, putting the pad of his thumb to the place that wanted his tongue and making slow circles. "It is only the beginning, wife. I will have you wailing and thrashing upon this bed when the sun rises, and long after."

Gloriana was bucking under his words and caresses by then. She dragged her kirtle the rest of the way off, over her head, and lay bare in the moonlight, a tigress, flexed and eager for the attentions of her mate.

He tongued her in one long, lapping stroke, and she uttered a lusty shout, setting her heels into his shoulders and raising herself to him, a chalice of flesh.

Dane chuckled, the sound reverberating through her from her most sensitive center, and caused her to cry out again, this time in furious frustration, with the lightest, swiftest of nibbles.

He raised his head from her, and over her own soft whimpering, she heard his amusement. "What is this? Does the morsel tell the mouth how to savor it?"

A deep shudder moved through Gloriana, culminating in a sob of passion. "I must have you," she pleaded. "Pray, do not tease me anymore—"

Dane drew on her in one long, mind-splintering pull of his lips. "I have heard your petition, milady," he said, when she lay trembling on the mattress, every inch of her flesh shimmering with perspiration, every nerve screaming for satisfaction, "but I must deny it for now. I am enjoying you too much, you see, to stop. And I have not forgotten, alas, how you brought me to the brink of ecstasy in these minutes just past, but granted no quarter."

Gloriana began to toss her head from side to side on the

ticking. Her hands clawed the coverlet and every muscle in her thighs and belly quivered as she awaited his attentions.

He allowed her no shred of mercy in the hours of frenzied delight that followed, and she sought none. At dawn, they slept, limbs entangled, too exhausted to move or even to dream, and awakened when the sun was past its zenith.

Dane, as ever, was the first to rise. During the night, some faithful servant—no doubt instructed ahead of time by the master of Kenbrook Hall—had brought a large ewer of water and a basket of food. There was cheese inside, a cold joint of venison, and two small fowls, crisply roasted.

The succulent scents roused Gloriana, at least partially, from a floating daze of contentment, and she lifted herself on her elbows. "I'm starved," she said.

Dane laughed. "Considering your exertions of the night just past, madame," he said, "that is not surprising." He brought the basket to the bed and they sat facing each other, naked and cross-legged, in the middle of the mattress, to partake of their meal.

Gloriana made a wry face at his comment, but withheld a reply until she'd consumed the better part of a guinea hen. Then, because the chamber was chilly, she donned the kirtle she had discarded the night before.

"I am quite certain," she said, when she was seated again, and gesticulating with a drumstick, "that it is not good manners for a gentleman to offer comment on the degree of a lady's passion."

Dane chuckled. "Were I a gentleman rather than a brigand, or you a lady, rather then a lovely and spirited wench, civilities might be a consideration." He took a bit of cheese from the basket and nibbled at it in a way that heated Gloriana's blood. "I would not have you otherwise."

Gloriana felt color in her cheeks and, indeed, in the rest of her body. She was glad she had put on her kirtle. "Nor would I change you, my lord," she said in a tone of unwillingness. "But now we must speak of serious matters."

Dane arched an eyebrow. He had put on his breeches, but had not bothered with a tunic or leggings. "What matters are these? I have told you of Edward's death, and of Gareth's—"

Gloriana suppressed an urge to touch her husband, lest

they end up making love again and accomplish nothing else. "We will mourn them together," she said quietly, blinking back tears. "I would tell you what I know of the future." She touched her abdomen with one hand, lightly, in an unconscious caress. "While but a few weeks passed where I was, in the latter part of the 1990s, two years have gone by here, in your world."

He said nothing, but simply watched her and waited.

She prayed he would understand what that time difference meant in terms of her pregnancy—had she stayed in the thirteenth century, she would have borne the child more than a year before. "We conceived a babe, you and I," she said.

Dane nodded. "I know," he answered.

Gloriana put down the drumstick, her appetite gone. "It is all so confusing—so impossible—"

He took her hand, running the rough pad of his thumb gently over her knuckles. "Yes," he agreed. "What are you getting at, Gloriana?"

"The babe," she said miserably. "I couldn't bear it if you thought I'd deceived you."

Dane smiled. "There is no comprehending what has happened to us, but this much I know—the heart beating beneath that lovely breast is a true one, and pure. I do not think, sweet Gloriana, that you can lie, nay, not even when it would be the most prudent course."

She curved her fingers around his and squeezed tightly. "But I must live all my life in secret, my lord—have you forgotten that I am called the Kenbrook Witch? Do you not see that I will be hanged, or burned, if the servants and villagers learn that I have come back?" She looked down at the food basket, now empty but for scraps and crumbs, and felt herself go pale. "I do not want to die," she finished.

Dane pushed aside the obstacle between them, sending the basket tumbling to the floor, and, kneeling, drew her into his arms. "Before all the saints, Gloriana," he whispered hoarsely, into her hair, "before the Holy Virgin, the Christ, and Jehovah Himself, I will allow no man or woman to do you harm!"

She clung to him, resting her cheek against his bare shoulder. The muscles beneath that smooth, warm flesh were hard and unyielding, and yet she could have asked for no better pillow. "You cannot fight the whole of Christendom," she answered. "You are but one man, though the finest and strongest anywhere, and they are many."

He cupped her face in his hands and thrust her head back a little way that he might look into her eyes. "We will say you were kidnapped and returned to us in secret, after a great ransom was paid. Maxen will help to spread the tale."

"But Judith saw—"

"The handmaid's grief at your passing was nearly as terrible as my own. She can be made to swear that you were dragged away by outlaws and that her fear was so great that only now does she recall what really happened."

Gloriana was eager to believe Dane's plan would work, although it seemed far-fetched. On the other hand, these were simple people, and if the tale was well and colorfully told, they might accept it. Surely an abduction by bandits was easier to credit than the idea of a flesh and blood woman melting into nothingness like steam from a kettle!

"Bring Judith to me," she said, after a long moment. "Friar Cradoc, too, and Eigg. We will try your scheme, Kenbrook, but you must make me a promise first."

"Anything," Dane agreed, smoothing her love-tangled hair back from her face with one hand.

"Do not be so quick to pledge yourself, my lord," Gloriana warned, in all seriousness. "You have not heard my petition." She paused and drew a deep, tremulous breath, then let it out slowly. "If fate goes against us, and I am accused of witchery, you must swear, for my sake and that of our unborn child, to send an arrow through my heart before they burn me."

Dane went gray as a corpse at this injunction. "I pray it will not come to that," he said, holding her hands now, so tightly that they ached. "But you have my word, Gloriana— you will die mercifully, by my hand, but you shall never feel the flames."

"It is agreed, then," Gloriana said gravely, searching Dane's eyes and thus his soul for any sign that his was a spurious oath, and finding none.

Having reached their grim agreement, Gloriana and Dane made love again, slowly and solemnly this time. The culmination was no less splendid, no less shattering, for all that it was the seal upon a deadly bargain.

When it was over, Dane poured water from the ewer that had been brought with the basket, and they washed. Then he dressed, strapping on his sword belt, and left the tower room, enjoining Gloriana brusquely to lock the doors behind him.

She did as she was bidden, though it chafed her pride to obey. A command, however sensible, was still a command.

She busied herself, through what remained of that long afternoon, by going through her chests, shaking out various gowns and kirtles and capes, draping them over chair backs and tabletops to air. She read from some of the books that had been left to molder there in that damp chamber, but mostly, she paced and haunted the high, narrow windows, watching and listening for some indication of Dane's return.

He came at twilight with the friar and the Welshman, Maxen, as well as Judith and Hamilton Eigg, the steward. Gloriana, having seen them below in the courtyard, was waiting with the doors of the tower room flung wide long before they reached the top of the winding staircase.

Judith, at first sight of her mistress, let out a wretched, joyous sob and flung herself down at Gloriana's feet. "Milady!" she cried. "Oh, milady, it is as I have so often prayed—the Holy Mother has wrested you from the hands of Lucifer and given you back to us!"

Gloriana touched Judith's hair with a tender hand. The girl had always been faithful and industrious, expecting nothing but food and a robe and a place to sleep, aspiring to nothing beyond the approval of those she served.

"Your prayers have indeed saved me," Gloriana said softly. "Now rise. Please."

Dane stood watching, his arms folded, while Eigg struck a flint to light the oil lamp, driving back some of the shadows. Maxen guarded the door, sword drawn, and Friar Cradoc came and took Judith's thin arm, lifting her to her feet.

"Poor child," he said, and though he was speaking of Judith, his gaze was fixed on Gloriana's face. His eyes were wide with amazement, but there was nothing unusual in his tone or countenance. "She was so frightened on that dreadful day that she cannot be sure what she saw."

Judith was still weeping, and the sound was pitiful to hear.

"There were outlaws in the churchyard," Dane said evenly, like a necromancer imparting a trance. "They hid behind the gravestones, didn't they, Judith? And caught your lady unattended?"

Judith's lower lip trembled, and her tear-filled eyes never left Gloriana's face. "Tell me what I saw, milady," she whispered, "and I will give that account, and never stray from it, on earth or in heaven."

Gloriana knew this was true, and she was moved, once again, by the astounding depths of her handmaiden's loyalty. "I am unworthy of your devotion," she said, "but I must depend upon it, and upon you, for my very life." Tenderly, Gloriana took Judith's hand and led her to the table, and sat her down as an equal. Then she drew up a chair and sat facing her servant. "Listen carefully, Judith, and remember all that I tell you. On that day two years ago, there was a light fall of rain, barely more than mist, and you saw me wandering amongst the gravestones of Kenbrook Hall. You were coming to fetch me"—that much, at least, was true— "when you glimpsed men hiding there, lying in wait for me. You were powerless to come to my aid, being only one small girl, after all, and there was no one to call upon for help, because my husband and his soldiers were away fighting."

Judith seemed spellbound, clutching Gloriana's fingers, staring off into space as if the scene were being played out for her on some celestial stage. "You cried out, milady, you were that afraid, and it fair broke my heart to see you handled so roughly—you, the finest lady in all the realm."

Gloriana swallowed. "These were highwaymen you saw," she went on evenly. "Strangers." No one could be left to speculate that Merrymont might have been behind this crime, or there would surely be more bloodshed. "I screamed and struggled, but they took me away with them, and you did not see me again, from that day until this. I escaped and made my way back to Hadleigh Castle in the company of a mummers' troupe."

"Yes," Judith agreed eagerly, her tearstained face transfixed. "It is so, milady. Just as you have said."

Over and over, throughout that evening, Judith was

coached in the telling of the tale, quizzed in their turns by Dane and then Eigg, Friar Cradoc and even Maxen, who might have been an outlaw himself, so wild and unkempt was his appearance. By the time they'd finished, Gloriana was sure the poor creature truly believed the story that had been implanted in her mind.

"Tomorrow," Dane announced, when Judith had crept into a corner and curled up on a pallet of musty blankets to sleep, "we shall announce the return of Lady Kenbrook to her home and her people. There will, of course, be a grand celebration."

"God knows, the place could use one," Eigg commented gruffly, and received a glare from Friar Cradoc. No doubt the friar deemed the remark unseemly, though he uttered no word of reprimand.

Dane held out his arm to Gloriana and drew her close against his side. For that brief and shining interval, she allowed herself to believe that things could be set aright, that she and her beloved husband might live happily ever after.

Chapter
16

*W*hen Maxen and Eigg and Friar Cradoc left the tower room at last, Gloriana turned to gaze upon the sleeping Judith. "Look at her, lying there like a dog," she said. " 'Tis not fitting for human beings to live in such wise."

Dane stood behind Gloriana, his hands resting lightly on her shoulders, offering strength and comfort. "Methinks we seem a primitive lot, when held up to those enlightened souls you've known in the future. Do you long for that time, that place?"

Gloriana turned and looked up into her husband's eyes. His words had been easily spoken, but even in the dim glow of the oil lamp she could see that he was genuinely troubled. "No," she answered, as certain of this as she had ever been of anything. "All I want, now or ever, is to be with you."

He traced the length of her cheek with the tip of one finger. "But things are better there, are they not?" he pressed, albeit gently.

She sighed. "The twentieth century has plagues and perils all its own, and it seemed to me that people had not changed all that much, not inside, where it counts."

"You met a man there—one who loved you," Dane in-

231

sisted. There was no accusation in his voice, no bitterness or censure.

Lyn Kirkwood, Gloriana thought, and felt a little pinch in one corner of her heart. Though she hadn't and would never return Lyn's tender sentiments, she missed him, and Janet and Marge too. Friends the likes of those three were exceeding rare, in any time or place. "But I did not love him in return," Gloriana replied, her gaze steadfast upon Dane's face. She held her breath for a moment, before asking. "How did you know?"

"You called to someone, while we were yet abed. You were dreaming."

Gloriana slipped her arms around Dane's lean waist and rested her cheek upon his shoulder. "No doubt it was you I was calling, for I have sought you, waking and sleeping, from the moment we were parted."

He embraced her, and she marveled that so simple a caress could nurture her on such deep levels. His words, however, were gravely spoken.

"A little while ago, my lady, you caused me to promise that I would make yours a merciful death before I let you burn for a sorceress. Now, I must ask a boon in return."

She raised her head to search his face. Her heart fluttered behind her ribs, like a small bird startled into flight, only to find itself caged. "What is it?"

"If we cannot be together, Gloriana—if, God forbid, you are taken from me once again—you must accept the love this man offers, and give yourself to him." She started to protest, but Dane silenced her by resting a fingertip on her mouth. "Hush," he went on. "You will need someone to help you if you are thrust into a foreign world, and so will our babe. It would give me some peace, knowing that you and our child had a protector."

Gloriana swallowed the tears that had gathered in her throat, blinked back those burning behind her eyes. There was no point in explaining to Dane that women of the twentieth century did not commonly marry for such reasons; as intelligent as he was, Kenbrook couldn't be expected to understand the mores and manners of a culture so alien to his own.

"If you would ask this of me," she said when she could

manage to speak, "you must first tell me—how I am to bear the touch of another man's lips and hands, the weight of his body on mine, the sound of his voice in my ears? For it is you I love, and you I *shall* love, whether we are together or apart, for all there is of time."

Kenbrook bent his head and kissed her. The contact was soft and brief. "I can tell you only this, madam," he said, his breath warm upon her lips. "To imagine you as someone else's wife is agony. But to think of you alone, in want, or in danger, with no way to provide for our child, is far worse. By what name is he called, this man who shelters you in his heart?"

"Lyn Kirkwood," Gloriana replied, feeling bereaved, as though her fate had somehow been sealed. It seemed a betrayal, just to say the name in her husband's presence, though she had never been unfaithful to Dane, even in her thoughts. "But I do not wish to—"

He silenced her again, with a second kiss, longer and deeper than the one preceding, then demanded, "Swear it, Gloriana—by your immortal soul. If something happens, and we are parted, you will turn to Kirkwood and pledge yourself to him."

How could she make such an outrageous promise when she loved Dane St. Gregory with the very essence of her being? How could she *not* give her most solemn word when he was looking at her with such tension, such fretful adoration in his eyes?

Such an oath upon one's soul was no small matter, even to Gloriana, who was hardly a conventional woman of her time. She had still lived most of her life in the thirteenth century, and she took such matters as souls and vows very seriously. To do otherwise was to court eternal damnation, with all its pitchforks and fiery horrors.

But as she looked into Dane's face, Gloriana knew he would not rest until he had her word. She sighed and gave a quick, unwilling nod. "It will be as you say," she said.

He chuckled, and the sound held suffering as well as mirth. "I am pleased, wife—because you make this vow, and because you so clearly wished to refuse."

Gloriana's gaze strayed to the window and found it filled with stars. In Lyn's world, so near and yet so far away, the lights of the cities were so bright that it was hard to see the splendors of the night sky at all, and one could barely hear the songs of birds or the whisper of the wind over the din of everyday life.

"I must see Elaina," she said. "Will you take me to her? Now?"

"Yes," Dane replied after a moment's hesitation. "For if I said no, you would surely set out on your own."

Gloriana offered her husband a feeble smile. She was in the tower room with Kenbrook standing before her, solid and real. She could kiss him if she wanted, touch him whenever she chose, pick an argument just to hear his voice. How foolish to waste even a moment dreading things that might never occur.

"You are right, my lord," she said, mocking him in dulcet tones, making a little curtsy. "I shall visit the lady Elaina whether you attend me or not. How discerning of you to know that without prompting."

Dane rolled his eyes and gestured toward the doors, which Maxen and the others had left agape. Grabbing up a cloak, Gloriana led the way over the threshold.

Kenbrook's horse, Peleus, was tethered in the courtyard. Dane saddled the beast, while Gloriana watched, then he mounted and bent to hand her up behind him. A moment later, they were clattering over the cobblestones toward the gate.

Clinging to Dane, Gloriana assessed the landscape or what she could see of it in the light of the trifling moon. How odd it was to think that there was not just one Kenbrook Hall, or one Hadleigh Castle, but many—perhaps an uncountable number—laid one on top of the other like layers of parchment. Perhaps each new moment was a world in its own right, separate and whole.

It was past comprehending.

Full darkness had fallen by the time they reached the abbey wall, and there were few lamps burning inside, for the good sisters retired early and rose before the birds to make their prayers. Still, when Dane called out, the hinges of the great gate creaked, and they were admitted.

Sister Margaret stood in the courtyard, clad as always in

a rough gown and plain slippers. Her hair was covered by a
wimple, her face upturned in curiosity.

"Where is Elaina?" Dane asked, dismounting and lifting
Gloriana down after him. Although the mistress of Kenbrook
Hall had worn a hooded cloak on the short journey, she
made no effort to disguise her identity from the abbess. The
woman was shrewd, and any attempt to deceive her would
surely prove fruitless.

Sister Margaret's hands were folded modestly in front of
her, and she inclined her head to acknowledge Gloriana before replying to Dane's question. "She lies abed, and dying."

Gloriana had visited Elaina many times over the years, of
course, and she needed no direction. She simply set off for
the walled garden, for Elaina's tiny cell of a chamber opened
onto it. Dane, leaving Peleus with his reins dangling, followed her.

They found the lady Elaina lying on a narrow cot beneath
an uncovered window. One candle flickered on a table, sending shards of moving light over her unbound hair, which
trailed over the blankets to her feet. She stared forlornly at
the ceiling, her hands folded upon her chest as if she'd been
laid out for burial.

One nun kept a vigil, seated on a three-legged stool beside
the bed and offering a litany for the salvation of her ladyship's soul. At a nod from Sister Margaret, the younger
woman rose and slipped out.

"And yet I was not summoned!" Dane charged, moving to
Elaina's side, crouching on the cold stone to look into that
still face. "This woman is my brother's widow and thus
my charge."

"What could you have done?" the elderly nun responded
calmly.

Dane's eyes were fierce as he looked back at the abbess,
the fingers of his right hand intertwined with Elaina's limp
ones. "I might have made my peace, madam." He turned
his attention again to the unmoving form upon the bed—an
aging but still beautiful fairy-tale princess under an evil
spell. "I might have told my lady sister I was sorry for so
very many things I did and did not do."

"I trust my lady knows that yours is a repentant heart,"

Sister Margaret said peacefully, and turned to leave Dane and Gloriana alone with Elaina in that humblest of cells.

Gloriana took the stool, drawing it up close, laying a gentle hand to Elaina's forehead. Her flesh felt cool, like wax. "Oh, Elaina," she whispered. "Must you leave this life so soon?"

Dane got to his feet and went to stand at the window. He did not speak, but there was no need of that, for Gloriana knew perfectly well what he was thinking—he blamed himself, however indirect his guilt might be, for this decline of Elaina's. If not for Edward's death and the grief that had weakened Gareth in the face of an illness . . .

Elaina stirred slightly and then opened her eyes. Gloriana leaned close, but she was not heartened, for she knew too well that the dying often rally briefly just before they pass over. She had seen the phenomenon before when dear Edwenna had succumbed to the fever.

"Dane!" Gloriana whispered.

An almost translucent light shone in Elaina's exquisite face. She groped for Gloriana's hand, and her fingers tightened around it with surprising strength. "Gareth—is dead," she said.

Gloriana nodded, willing herself not to weep. "Yes, dearest, I know."

"You—could change everything—bring my husband back—and poor Edward—"

A chill spun itself along the length of Gloriana's spine. She did not say such things weren't possible, did not dare to look at Dane. It still stung, the knowledge that she had not been able to return to the thirteenth century in time to avert Edward's death, if not Gareth's.

Elaina's strange, bright gaze groped for and finally grasped Kenbrook, who had moved away from the window. He stood just behind Gloriana now, so close that she could feel the warmth and substance of him.

"Dane," Elaina said softly, slowly, measuring her words out one precious breath at a time. "Did Gareth tell you the truth, before—before he died? That you are indeed the rightful heir to Hadleigh Castle, despite your bastardy?"

Gloriana was stunned, but Dane's voice was quiet and even when he responded. "Yes, milady—he told me long ago, on the day I was knighted."

Elaina lay silent for a while and very still. Her thin eyelids fluttered against her cheeks, and it was plain that she was gathering her strength.

"Forgive me," Dane said. He bent and placed the lightest of kisses upon the lady's alabaster forehead.

"There is naught to acquit you of," Elaina said, without opening her eyes. "Go now, in peace, I pray you, that I might bid Gloriana a private farewell."

Gloriana held tightly to her friend's hand, raised it to her face, and rested her forehead against those fragile knuckles, no longer able to hold her tears in check. Dane touched Gloriana's shoulder, then moved away, closing the door of the minuscule chamber softly behind him.

Elaina immediately opened her eyes, and her voice, while reedy and thin, was at the same time steadfast. "Hear me well, Gloriana," she said. "It is vital that you heed what I tell you now."

Gloriana raised her tear-streaked face in surprise and waited, speechless, for the other woman to go on.

Lady Hadleigh echoed Dane's plea of a few minutes before. "Forgive me," she said, with effort. "I might have shared your burden—I never told you—" When she paused, Gloriana gave her a sip of water from the wooden cup on the windowsill above the cot. "I knew the truth of what happened to you, Gloriana, though I think you forgot over the years that I was there when you crossed over. It was I who summoned you here."

Gloriana was nearly as dry-throated as Elaina had been, so great was her shock. It was not the fact of Elaina's presence that surprised her, for she vaguely recalled that, despite Edwenna's assiduous efforts to make her forget. No, it was the lady's confession that she had not only led Gloriana through the fated gate, but beckoned her to it in the first place.

"How could this be?"

Elaina's smile was fleeting and ethereal. "I practiced the old religion," she said. "Ah—you are my witness! Lightning did not strike me for my blasphemous words—nor did the roof crumble over our heads. I have always had powers, Gloriana, far beyond those people spoke of, and I took up the practice of magic when I was but a child." She stopped and took a few more sips of water from the cup Gloriana held to her lips. "Good magic—it was always good magic—but of course it had to be a secret."

"Did Gareth know?"

Sadness moved like a shadow in Elaina's gleaming eyes. "It was one of the reasons why he put me from him. He never understood."

"You said you summoned me here. What did you mean?"

"I saw your world, as if through a thin curtain. I always have. Then I began to see you, specifically, in my dreams. You were such an unhappy child, yet so beautiful and so brilliant. Then, one day, there you were, on the other side of the gate, apart from the other children and clutching your little doll as though it were your only friend. You seemed too full of sorrows, for one so small. So I called to you and held out my hand. When you heard me, saw me, I knew you were capable of crossing over. You were so wretchedly sad in that other place, so alone. I wanted you for my own—I had never given Gareth a child—but I knew even then that I could not keep you. My husband had already spread the word that I was mad, to keep me from those who claimed I was the mistress of Satan."

Gloriana shivered. She remembered that sunny twentieth-century afternoon, remembered it clearly. She had come to Kenbrook Hall with a group of other children, from Briar-wood School, where her battling parents had left her, and she had known Mommy and Daddy weren't coming back for her ever, that they neither loved nor wanted her.

"So you gave me to Edwenna to raise."

Elaina nodded. "Yes. She was a good woman, the wool merchant's wife, with the means to care for you properly. I knew she would love you without reservation."

Gloriana bit her lower lip. She still grieved for her foster mother, longing for Edwenna's humor and uncomplicated affection, her unwavering devotion and infinite patience. "I do not wish to go back to that other world, ever," she said.

"But you must," Elaina said. "It is fated."

After suppressing an urge to put her hands over her ears, Gloriana shook her head. "I cannot—will not leave my husband—my heart's home is with him. Besides, I am with child."

"More is required of you, Gloriana."

"No," Gloriana protested, rising awkwardly, upsetting the stool in her distress. "No—I can do nothing more—"

"It is decided," Elaina said, and it seemed to Gloriana that Lady Hadleigh had grown smaller somehow in those few minutes since Sister Margaret had ushered them to the door of this room. "You returned too late. You must go back, and try again."

Gloriana was not only upset, she was baffled. It wasn't as if she could travel back and forth through time at will, after all. Not consciously, at least. She had been desperate to come home to Dane and the thirteenth century, but in the end it had happened accidentally. Before she could voice any further misgivings, Elaina sighed, like a child settling into a warm bed to sleep.

"You will be called back to your own time," she said, her eyes closing, her voice dreamlike, growing fainter, more whispery, with every word.

Gloriana went to the door and called softly to Dane, and when he came in with Sister Margaret and the three of them had stationed themselves about Elaina's bed, Lady Hadleigh sighed again, very deeply, and died.

Sister Margaret covered the white, peaceful face with a thin coverlet, then slipped out of the room. Gloriana turned and flung herself into Dane's arms, and he held her until her trembling had ceased. Then, grimly, they went out.

After services that would be held in the private chapel at Hadleigh Castle on the morrow or that of the day to follow, Elaina would be buried beside her husband. In the meantime, she belonged there in the abbey, where she had lived out the last days of her life.

Dane led Gloriana to Peleus, who waited patiently in the main courtyard, and lifted her into the saddle before mounting behind her. The ride to Kenbrook Hall was passed in a daze, and when they reached the tower room, Dane awakened Judith and sent her out to sleep in the passage.

She went without protest—indeed it would not have occurred to her to argue—carrying her bundle of woolen blankets with her.

When she was gone, Dane and Gloriana lay down on the

bed together in all their clothes and held each other close. They were silent for a long time, and then Gloriana spoke.

"You are truly the heir to Hadleigh Castle, as well as Kenbrook Hall?"

Dane let out a long, raspy breath and tightened his arm around her, as if he feared she might slip away. "Yes," he said.

"And Gareth was your father, not your brother?"

Dane sounded weary. "Yes," he repeated. "My mother was fifteen, and a delicate girl. She perished in childbirth, as many women do." He held Gloriana a little closer, no doubt thinking of their own babe, nestled within her, and all the perils inherent in bearing a child.

"But why was it a secret—that Gareth sired you?"

"My mother, Jillian, was Merrymont's youngest sister," Dane explained, after considering the matter in silence for a while. "She met Gareth by accident one day, when she was out riding and had escaped her retinue of attendants. They were taken with each other, were Gareth and Jillian, but their sires were sworn enemies and both knew a marriage between them would be impossible. In fact, I doubt that either of them ever expected to be together longer than the length of a summer. I was conceived, and a great furor was raised, of course. Gareth claimed to be the father of Jillian's babe, but the lady herself denied even the merest acquaintance with him. When I was born, and my mother died, Merrymont, Jillian's guardian as well as her brother, was wild with grief. He threatened to kill me in retribution for the girl's untimely death. A nurse bore me away in the night and brought me to Gareth, at Hadleigh Castle. My grandfather declared me to be his second son, and my grandmother evidently supported his claim."

"Why didn't you tell me?" Gloriana asked.

"Because it didn't matter," he replied. He brushed her temples with his lips. "Sleep now, sweeting—tomorrow will be a difficult day."

Gloriana was grateful for Dane's embrace, even though it was nearly bone-crushing, because she needed to be close to him. She grieved for Elaina, but she was also haunted by what Lady Hadleigh had predicted.

She was to go back to the twentieth century.

"No," she whispered.

"Hmm?" Dane asked, barely awake.

Gloriana made no answer, for she knew she could not utter the smallest sound without weeping, and he did not press her for one.

She awakened with the dawn and, as usual, found that Dane had already risen. He had also fetched her red mummer's cape from the Roman baths or perhaps sent Judith for it, for the garment lay neatly draped over the back of a chair. There was no sign of the handmaiden, but several lamps were lit and there was water for washing.

Gloriana rose and splashed her face at the basin.

"What happened to your hair?" Dane inquired.

She gave him a wry look, despite the pain of knowing that Elaina was gone and that she herself might have to leave Dane again—mayhap forever. "It took you long enough to ask, my lord," she said. "I had it cut. Women in the twentieth century wear their hair at all lengths."

Dane pondered her, his expression solemn. "It makes you look rather like a page at court." Gloriana flushed with indignation, even as a broad and brilliant smile broke over Kenbrook's magnificent face like a sunrise. "The resemblance ends there, of course," he finished.

"I should hope so," Gloriana replied coolly.

He crossed the room and kissed her. "Gloriana?"

"What?" She still felt pettish, though his kiss had soothed her somewhat.

"I spoke in jest. You are as confoundingly beautiful as ever."

"I am not amused, sir," she said, but she was smiling a little.

He kissed her again, without haste, and then curved one hand over her cheek. "There can be no celebration, of course—not so soon after Elaina's passing."

"No," Gloriana agreed sadly.

"All the same," Dane went on, raising her chin with one finger when she would have lowered her head, "there will probably never be a better time for you to return. With the villages and all of Hadleigh Castle in mourning, people might not ask so many questions."

"It doesn't seem right that Elaina's death should be—well—convenient."

"No," Dane said. "It doesn't. But surely you have already discerned, beloved wife, that ours is not a just or reasonable world." At Gloriana's despondent nod, he put his arms around her and held her for a long moment before pulling back a little, to search her eyes. "Are you ready to be mistress of Hadleigh Castle, as well as Kenbrook Hall?" he asked.

"I don't think it matters," Gloriana replied pragmatically. "Whether I'm ready or not, I mean."

Dane kissed her forehead in wordless agreement.

Dinner was being served in the great hall when Gloriana, wearing the red cape, entered with the mummer's troupe. Corliss had painted her face by the light of the kitchen fire, adding great blue tears to her cheeks and giving her a red, down-turned mouth. The occasion was a sad one, and the players would perform accordingly, mirroring the grief of their audience.

Somber as the mood was in the hall that night, Gloriana suspected that only she and Dane and the inhabitants of the abbey truly mourned Elaina. Lady Hadleigh had been a stranger, a figure of mystery, to the villagers and probably even to many of the servants within the keep itself. It had been years, after all, since Gareth's wife had actually lived inside these walls.

As the minstrels played haunting, dirgelike tunes, Gloriana followed the others further into the hall, moving in a slow, graceful, and wholly instinctive dance that expressed the depths of her sorrow.

Dane, seated at the head table, stood when he saw her. He had not expected her to wear the cape or the paint, but simply to walk in and announce that she had gotten free of her kidnappers and come home. Gloriana had lost her courage as the hour of revelation drew near, however, and felt a need for the anonymity of disguise. Now she went still in the center of the hall, her gaze locked with Kenbrook's, as he moved away from the table, descended nimbly from the dais upon which it stood, and strode toward her.

For a long interval, they faced each other, neither one speaking.

Then, at some nearly imperceptible sign from Dane, Gloriana raised both hands and pushed the hood of her cloak back onto her shoulders. Her hair, though sheared, was a distinctive shade of reddish gold and had oft been seen, due to her old habit of shunning wimples and other modest headdresses.

Someone gasped, and then a lower murmur arose from the small assembly.

Dane took Gloriana's shoulders in his hands, and still he did not utter a word, but simply gazed deeply into her eyes, as though reading her very soul. She was supposed to tell the story of her escape at that point, but she was caught up in some private enchantment and could not find her voice.

"Behold," Dane said, at great length, but in a tone both ringing and authoritative, without once looking away, "my true wife has returned at long last."

Gloriana's spell was broken then, but not by Dane's announcement. Over his shoulder, she had glimpsed the fair Mariette, seated at the head table. The other woman turned pale and rose slowly from the bench. The silence in that room was palpable and might never have been broken had not one of the hounds begun scratching himself by the fire, hind leg thumping against the floor in a loud rhythm.

Friar Cradoc, also dining at the master's table, stood quickly, a wondrous smile spilling across his face. He spread his arms in a gesture of overwhelming joy and came quickly to join Dane and Gloriana in the center of that enormous, drafty room.

"May the Holy Mother and all the saints be praised," he exclaimed. "Tell us, child—how do you come to be back here, with your people?"

Gloriana swallowed. She was very much aware of Mariette, still standing as if paralyzed on the dais, and her own heartbeat seemed to thunder through the whole of the chamber. She looked into her husband's eyes again. "I was captured by brigands, lo these two years past," she said, and did not sound, in her own ears at least, at all like herself. "I have been all this while seeking a means to flee—"

It was then that Romulus, the magician, came out from

amongst his now-silent mummers, resplendent in a harle-
quin's costume of black and white velvet. He spoke as one
with authority. "Your lady happened upon our troupe of players, and begged us to take her in. We did so, that she might
be brought safely home to those who mourned her."

Another murmur of speculation rippled down the room.
The people of Hadleigh Castle and its environs had regarded Gloriana as one of their own, and yet they were loath
to part with the splendid horror of her disappearance.

Judith, trembling and small, came out of the shadows
cloaking the walls. " 'Tis purest truth my lady speaks," she
said. "There were outlaws in the graveyard on that cursed
day, lying in wait. I remember it clear, now that I see her
face again." Reaching Gloriana's side, the girl dropped to
her knees and, with a great, soul-chilling wail, pressed her
forehead to her mistress's feet. "I feared they'd kilt you!"
she sobbed.

Gloriana raised the servant to stand upright, uncomfortable with such obeisance. "Here, now," she said gently, and
made no effort to be heard by the others, since her words
were not part of the performance. "I stand before you, safe
and well. There is no profit in such grief."

Tears streaked Judith's thin, dirt-smudged face, and looking into her reddened, overbright eyes, Gloriana knew the
girl truly had made herself to believe the tale they'd con-
cocted in the tower room, remembered the events as if they
had actually happened.

She touched Judith's arm. "Go and have your supper,"
she commanded gently.

Dane, standing near Gloriana, was looking thoughtfully at
Romulus. The magician stared back, unperturbed, but at the
same time, he gave the new mistress of Hadleigh Castle a
slight push toward her husband.

When Dane instinctively put his arms around Gloriana to
steady her, the ominous, pulsing silence suddenly ruptured
into an earsplitting cheer.

Kenbrook, now Lord Hadleigh as well, smiled solemnly
and executed a deep, formal bow. Then, in the next moment,
he swept Gloriana off the floor and into his arms.

"You will pardon me," he enjoined the clamorous throng,
"if I tender my beloved a private welcome?"

On the dais, Mariette sat down upon the bench drawn up to the master's table, and her servant, Fabrienne, rushed to her side. Gloriana linked an arm round Dane's neck, her gladness tempered by the other woman's obvious distress.

She allowed Dane to carry her out of the great hall, up the stairs, and into the chamber that had been Gareth's before offering comment.

"You told me that Mariette would be relieved not to marry," she said, when Dane set her on her feet. "But I was watching the girl, just now when we played out our scene in great hall, and she looked distraught."

Dane reached for a ewer of wine resting on a nearby table, alongside an oil lamp, and there was no guile in his countenance as he met his wife's penetrating stare. "I assure you, Gloriana, Mariette is anything but 'distraught.' When I broke our betrothal, in fact, she threw her arms about my neck and kissed me, so delighted was she."

Gloriana arched an eyebrow and set her hands on her hips. "You had best be telling me true, my lord, for if you play me false, I shall have a vengeance quite unlike the kind you and I generally employ."

He laughed and poured wine, though only a scant portion, Gloriana noticed. He knew better than to offer any to her, on account of their unborn babe, and tossed back the draft before setting both ewer and cup aside. "I shall summon the lady to this very chamber, if you wish, that you may hear the words from her own lips."

Gloriana bit her lower lip, thinking. She believed Dane, and besides, he was her husband, and she would not give him up simply because some other woman wanted him. Doubtless, there were any number of females, within and without the castle, who dreamed of sharing his life.

"I do not question your word, my lord," she said. "I believe you would tell me outright if you wished to dally with some other woman, for you are just arrogant enough to consider it your right as lord and master of two great holdings. But I saw Mariette's expression clearly, and she looked as white as death. Indeed, I thought sure she would swoon."

Dane stood before Gloriana, his eyes reverent as he reached out to stroke her modern hair with one hand and loosed the tie at the throat of her mummer's cloak with the other. " 'Twas relief, and naught more," he said. "No doubt the lady feared that I would change my mind and take her to wife after all."

The cloak drifted, with a crisp rustle, to the floor, and Gloriana stood before her husband in a simple blue kirtle with a brown woolen tunic over it. With a half-smile, he took her hand then and led her to a basin on a side table, where he dipped a cloth and began to wash her face.

She'd forgotten the paint Corliss had applied earlier, with a liberal hand, and she blushed at the reminder, feeling foolish.

"I can understand," she said when Dane laid the cloth aside at last and slipped his arms around her waist, "why a woman might be afraid to give herself to you."

Dane frowned, but there was a wry light in his eyes. "Oh? Am I so fearsome an ogre as that?"

Gloriana touched his wonderful golden hair, his strong jawline and high cheekbones, all in their turn, memorizing his features with the tips of her fingers, as a blind woman might do. "No," she said. "You are not half so ferocious as you would like the world to believe."

"Then why be afraid of me?"

She kissed his mouth lightly before replying. "Once a lady's heart has been given into your charge, my lord, there is no retrieving it, now or ever."

Chapter

17

*T*hat night, spent alone with Dane in his chamber at Hadleigh Castle, was an idyllic one for Gloriana, despite the encompassing sorrow of Elaina's death—or perhaps because of it. Each of the lovers took sanctuary in the warmest regions of the other's heart, and when at last they fell to slumber, their bodies were yet joined.

Dane awakened Gloriana with a kiss come the dawn and gathered her close against his chest. Although they had parted in sleep, their spirits were yet fused, one to the other, and Gloriana doubted that even seven hundred years could truly part them.

Still, she could not help shuddering slightly at the prospect of being wrenched away from Dane, whether for a day or all that was left of her life.

Having felt her trembling, Dane cupped her cheek in his hand and gazed into her eyes. "What causes you to be afraid, my lady?" he asked, and though the tone of his voice was gentle, its timbre low, it was plain that he would not allow her to sidestep his question.

"I thought of—of being lost from you."

Dane's thumb, though callused, coursed tenderly over her cheekbone, down to her chin, a silken caress. There was no jealousy in his words. "But surely your Lyn Kirkwood would rejoice at your return." He frowned. "Unless he is unworthy—"

"Would you hold me to my promise if he was?" Gloriana asked quickly, hoping for the dissolution of her vow to put herself and the child in Lyn's care if she indeed found herself in the twentieth century once again. "Unworthy, I mean?"

"He is not," Dane decreed, with solemn conviction. "No dishonorable man could win your friendship, let alone your love."

"I do not love Lyn," Gloriana insisted. It was important for Dane to understand that, no matter what happened in the moments and days and weeks to come.

"Tell me about him."

Gloriana moistened her lips with her tongue, stalling. Finally, though, the silence grew uncomfortable, and she said in a grudging tone, "Kirkwood is a physician, and very kind."

"A leech?" Dane asked, his frown deepening.

"Not exactly," Gloriana replied, almost as unwilling to speak as she had been before. "Latter-day healers do not practice the letting of blood, nor do they treat wounds with dung or even herbal poultices. The practice of medicine is a true science in the future, and an art."

Dane pondered this briefly, before responding. "Tell me, wife—can we here in this time hope for justice? Can you say what lies ahead for the realm?"

Gloriana sighed and laid her head on Dane's shoulder. "I do not know overmuch about the twentieth century, my lord—I was there such a short time. But I did see many marvels and splendid inventions."

"You did not answer my question." He could be intractable, could Kenbrook, when the spirit so moved him.

"In parts of the world," Gloriana relented with deliberate, breathy reluctance, "there is significant personal freedom for some, and England is one of the great nations of the earth. But many people are yet enslaved."

Dane moved downward, until his face was even with hers on the pillow. "What else?"

Gloriana was beginning to warm to the subject, and being

human, she couldn't resist taking modest pride in knowing things even the most brilliant thinkers of the century, or even the ages, could not have imagined. "Well, for one thing, the world is not flat," she said, recalling an educational program she had watched on television while staying at Lyn Kirkwood's cottage. "Nor does the sun revolve around it."

"Heresy," Dane said, but he sounded intrigued.

"The planet is suspended in an endless void, called space," Gloriana went on, grateful for the distraction from darker thoughts. "It's cold and black out there, beyond the sky, but not empty, for there are many other heavenly bodies—so many that no one has yet been able to count them all. The stars we see on clear nights are actually suns, like our own, but of all sizes. And some are so far away that even though they've long since burned out, the light still reaches us many thousands, even millions, of years later."

"What says the Church in regards to this?"

Gloriana smiled against Dane's shoulder. "Nothing much, my lord. It is accepted fact, and men have even traveled to the moon and back."

At this, Kenbrook thrust himself upward again, looming over Gloriana, braced on one elbow and searching her face. "You do not jest," he murmured in surprise, after a few seconds has passed.

She shook her head. "It is a most interesting place, the future. Though not without its own perils, of course."

"What dangers are these?"

"I have told you. There are plagues, and they have devised horrible weapons that are capable of destroying everything that walks upon the earth or swims in the sea."

Dane absorbed this news grimly, then turned the subject in another direction. "How are babies born?"

Gloriana laughed. "In the usual manner, my lord." She slipped her arms around her husband's neck. "And they are made in the same way too."

He settled himself between her warm and pliant thighs, and she drew her knees up to accommodate him, for as always his nearness rendered her wanton. "Like this?" he asked, and entered her, in a smooth, powerful stroke that made her arch her neck and close her eyes, gasping softly as pleasure flooded through her in warm waves charged with electricity.

"Yes, my lord," she crooned, wriggling a little to tease him and thus take some small vengeance for his conquest. "Exactly like that."

Gloriana was almost afraid to enter the graveyard, given what had happened at Kenbrook Hall on that gloomy day not so long past, when she had been taken from her husband and her home and thrust into another world. Still, she could not refuse to attend Lady Elaina's burial, for her personal rules did not allow it, and neither did those of her station in life.

So Gloriana moved with the funeral procession, cloaked in black, her arm linked with Dane's, out of the chapel to stand among the cold, tilting stones that marked the resting places of generations of St. Gregorys. Elaina's coffin, hastily fashioned of raw, still-fragrant wood, was lowered into the yawning pit beside Gareth's grave and covered.

Friar Cradoc offered a final prayer, and the mourners straggled away, some to the castle, some to the village. Dane lingered, seemingly unaware of the rain, and Gloriana stayed with him, although she longed to bolt.

It was the good friar who broke Dane's revery, laying a hand to his shoulder and speaking in a quiet but firm voice. "Go inside and warm yourself by the fire, my lord," he said. "The lady would not wish to see you, or your noble wife, mourning her in the rain."

Gloriana felt Dane start beside her, and when he turned and looked down into her face, she saw that he had forgotten her presence until Friar Cradoc reminded him. Tenderly, she drew him toward the shelter of Hadleigh Castle, now his home and her own.

The great hall was drafty, as always, but there were fires roaring on the hearths at both ends of the room, and the oil lamps had been lighted early in order to dispel some of the gloom of that sad, rainy morning. Seeing Maxen warming himself before one of the blazes, a mug of ale in hand, Gloriana urged her husband toward his friend and went to speak to Romulus, who sat alone at the table farthest from the dais.

At her approach, the old man raised his head and offered a smile properly tempered by the solemnity of the occasion.

"You are a comfort to your good husband, my lady," he said, inclining his head in deference to her rank. He did not rise, however, or unfold his loosely clasped hands, and Gloriana, caring little for such customs, had not expected him to do so.

She regarded the magician curiously for a long interval, then spoke in a voice carefully calculated not to carry through the hall or even beyond that one table, empty except for Romulus.

"Who are you?" she asked bluntly.

He raised a bushy white eyebrow. "I have told you. I am Romulus, a humble player."

"Nonsense," Gloriana whispered, somewhat sharply, glancing uneasily toward her husband. "You are something more. You were not startled by the oddness of my garments when I approached you in that other village, before we came to Hadleigh. In fact, it seemed you were expecting me."

Romulus shrugged, but his eyes danced with knowledge he evidently did not choose to share. "You tell me your tale, and I shall tell you mine," he said.

Gloriana looked at Dane, saw him shake his head when a mug was offered by a servant. Then she met the magician's gaze again and knew somehow that it had not wavered, even while she was watching her husband. "I am a traveler in time," she said almost spitefully.

He smiled. "I know," he replied. "I had seen you in the scrying glass, even before you asked to join our troupe." The old magician's smile faded to a solemn expression. "You must not lose courage, my lady, before your quest is through. So much depends on your steadfastness."

"What—?"

"Mademoiselle de Troyes draws nigh," Romulus interrupted, without looking either to the left or the right, but straight into Gloriana's heart. "You must not mention your magic in her hearing. While the girl means well enough, she is weak by nature, and with such as she, superstition oft eclipses reason."

Gloriana was slightly flushed as she turned to face the young woman her husband had intended to marry, and out of the corner of her eye she saw Romulus hasten out of the great hall, clutching his thin cloak close about him.

Mariette did not speak to Gloriana, but simply inclined her head in greeting. She was yet pale and seemed smaller than ever in her plain mourning garb.

Gloriana returned Mariette's nod. "I should have hoped to see you again under happier circumstances," she said.

Mariette's eyes had a feverish glint to them, and her gaze darted to Dane, who was watching them now, before coming back to Gloriana's face. "I would have made Kenbrook a good and obedient wife," she said, "though 'tis true I never loved him as you do."

Gloriana willed Dane not to come to her before she and Mariette had made some sort of peace, however strained. "I am told that you were happy to be spared the duties of marriage," she said.

A blush burned in Mariette's otherwise pale cheeks. " 'Tis true," she confessed, in a scant whisper. "I was content at the abbey, and wanted only to stay there until the end of my days." She paused, and the bright color ebbed slowly from her face. "But Fabrienne, my maidservant, had a vision, and an angel came to her and told her I must give myself to Lord Kenbrook, so that a child could be born."

Resisting an urge to find the meddling maid and throttle her, Gloriana reached out to take Mariette's hand in a gentle grasp. The girl's flesh felt hot over the fragile bones of her fingers, as though she suffered from a fever. "I am sorry," she said.

Mariette's embrace was brief, sudden, and almost desperate. "No," she replied, shaking her head as she drew back, poised as if to flee. "Do not entertain remorse on my behalf. I loved Edward and—and though I should not, I cannot keep myself from hating Kenbrook for his death. I—I meant to plunge a knife into the master's throat, as he lay upon our marriage bed." She was ready to bolt by that point and did not seem to notice Gloriana's look of horror. "Mayhap the Holy Mother has intervened, by sending you back, and you have saved me from the fires of hell—mayhap, I shall be forgiven—"

With that, the girl pulled her hand from Gloriana's and

fled, with her handmaiden, Fabrienne, in determined pursuit.

"What was that about?" Dane inquired.

Gloriana had not heard or sensed him there and was startled. With a hand to her breast, she turned to her husband and looked up into his haggard face. Should she tell him what fate his erstwhile bride had planned for him on the occasion of their marriage?

In hardly the space of a heartbeat, Gloriana decided against the idea. Dane was a reasonable man, but these were barbaric times, and he might banish Mariette de Troyes from the castle and village alike if advised of her treachery. The girl was pale and hot with the beginnings of some malaise, and thus unfit to undertake such a journey.

"You spake true, my lord husband," Gloriana said, with a smile, the tenderness of which was not feigned. "The mademoiselle is glad to return to the abbey in peace."

Dane attempted a smile, but did not quite succeed. His affection for his late sister-in-law and his grief over her untimely death ran too deep to permit it. "You doubted me?" he challenged, his words meant only for her and pitched accordingly.

"No," Gloriana answered, in all truth. "But I am concerned by the lady's dismal countenance, as I have already said."

"No doubt she mourns the lady Elaina, as we all do," Dane reasoned wearily, thrusting a hand through his golden hair. "God's blood, Gloriana, I can't bear it. First Edward, then Gareth, and now—now—"

She touched his face. The scent of rain mingled with the still more common smells of smoke and stale food and the unwashed bodies of the servants and soldiers and villagers crowding the hall. "This tragedy is not of your making," she said. Then, dropping her hand, she clasped his fingers in her own. "Come—let us fetch Peleus from the stables, and a mare for me. We'll ride and perhaps outrun our grief, if only for a little while."

"You are breeding," Kenbrook pointed out, quite unnecessarily, "and thus in a delicate state. 'Twould not be prudent."

"I shall go without you, then," Gloriana said, and started

toward the nearest door. She had removed her woolen cloak when they entered, but now she snatched the garment up again as she passed the bench where she had left it.

Dane caught up to her just as she was lifting the hood, preparing to step out into the courtyard, where the stones glimmered, smooth with age and rain. He took her elbow in his hand and held on. "You are the most contrary of women," he said, but there was a light in his eyes, and she knew the thought of a ride in the fresh air and open country appealed to him and would give him comfort.

"Fortunately for you," Gloriana agreed. "Were it not for my contentious nature, serving as it does to spend the worst of your unruly temper, my lord, you would surely be known far and wide for a tyrant and a brute."

He managed a fleeting grin and arranged the cloak more closely about her shoulders. "Arrogant chit. Do you take credit for the rising and setting of the moon, as well? The ebb and flow of the tide, mayhap?"

Gloriana gave him a sidelong look, linked her arm with his, and dragged him out into the soft, warm fall of rain. "On occasion," she confided mischievously, "I believe I have caused the earth to tremble."

Dane might have laughed under other circumstances. As it was, he simply strapped on the sword belt brought to him by one of his soldiers and acknowledged her statement with an inclination of his head. "There can be no denying that, my lady wife," he replied when his man-at-arms had gone and they were crossing the courtyard together. "When you receive me, peace becomes the tempest."

In the stables, where assorted grooms and men-at-arms gossiped, gambled, and snored in the straw-filled lofts and stalls, Gloriana and Dane did not converse, for they knew their every utterance would be heard, remembered, and recounted.

Peleus was saddled, as was a small, prancing gray mare Gloriana did not recall seeing before. Outside, in the mild drizzle, they mounted, Gloriana first, with her husband's unneeded assistance, and then Dane. They rode out of the courtyard together, through the baileys and the village to the great gates, which stood hospitably agape now that Merrymont had been put in his place.

No one questioned their passing into the countryside on such a wet and dreary day—no one would have presumed to do so—but there were inquiring looks.

Once they had gained the road beyond the drawbridge and moat, Dane turned his mount toward the abbey and Kenbrook Hall, setting an easy pace. No doubt this was out of deference to Gloriana's "delicate" condition, and she was touched by the tenderness of the gesture.

They passed the abbey without stopping, and the hall as well, riding through the woods to the high meadow behind the old keep. There, under the shelter of a canopy of intermingled oak and pine trees, Dane got down from his horse and stood looking over his holdings from that natural vantage point. Gloriana did not follow suit, but sat sidesaddle on the mare's back, patting the creature's neck as it fitgeted.

"Sometimes," Dane said, after a long time had passed and without looking back at Gloriana, "I wish I had never come back to England. It seems I've brought only death and sorrow."

Gloriana struggled not to cry; the situation called for strength, not weakness. "Methinks you pity yourself overmuch, Dane St. Gregory," she said. "You are the master here, and much needed by your people."

He turned then and gazed into her face, his mouth curved into a sad smile. "What shall I give them?" he asked.

"A brave and just liege lord, to begin with," Gloriana replied without hesitation. She rested one hand on her abdomen, while the other gripped the mare's bridle reins. "And stalwart sons and daughters to follow when you and I are gone."

Dane came and stood looking up at Gloriana, with one hand resting lightly on her thigh. "I pray you, my lady— never leave me. I am naught without your counsel and your love."

Gloriana leaned down and rested her hands on his shoulders, but before she could speak, a terrible blackness rose up from the earth, swamping and smothering her. Her head ached as though pressed between two great, shifting timbers, and although she heard Dane call out to her, felt him lift her down from the horse's back, she could not answer him.

In the next moments, east and west, north and south, up and down, and left and right seemed to compress, then converge into a meaningless, throbbing void. There was no light, and the pain was everything, reaching into every corner of the universe, permeating Gloriana's marrow and flowing in her blood.

Gloriana struggled to resist the phenomenon, for even in her almost unbearable suffering she knew what was happening, but it was all for naught. Her fate had been decided; she was being wrenched yet again from Dane's side, and that knowledge was the worst anguish of all.

She was kneeling on soft, moist ground when the horrific inner tempest subsided at last, her fingers digging deep into sweet meadow grass. As her vision cleared, she saw a man crouched beside her, and for a moment, she knew a wild and desperate hope that she had not been taken from the thirteenth century after all. He wore leggings and a tunic, soft boots, and a sword belt, and his hair was overlong, even by latter-day standards.

Then, with crushing disappointment, Gloriana realized that the garments were not authentic, but merely a clever costume. The way he framed his words, in the twentieth-century fashion, confirmed her suspicions.

"Are you all right, then?" he asked, in the quick, lilting tones of modern English.

Gloriana managed a nod, not caring that the gesture was an untruth in and of itself, and looked warily about. Brightly colored silk pavilions were scattered over the long meadow like exotic flowers, and crowds of people in medieval costume moved between them, talking and smiling and generally making merry together.

"That's a splendid outfit you've got on," the man said, taking Gloriana's elbow and raising her carefully to her feet. She was briefly, insanely, grateful that she had not been sick on the ground—or her gown.

"Th-thank you," Gloriana said, after shifting mental gears from the old way of speaking to the new. "I-I'm fine—just a little tired, I think."

He brought her to the stump of a tree and seated her there. "I could ring someone, if you'd like."

Gloriana ran her tongue over her lips, wondering what

year it was, exactly, but unable to make herself ask. She recognized the meadow, at least, and the grim, looming profile of Kenbrook Hall, but she could not be sure what part of the twentieth century she was in. She was not about to confide her dilemma to a stranger, however kind he might seem. "If you would ring Lyn Kirkwood, please—in Hadleigh Village?"

She held her breath while her young knight received her question. Judging by his calm and jovial manner, he had not seen her appear out of the past.

"Oh, there's no need for that," he said, with a delighted grin. "Lyn's here at the fair somewhere—sit tight, and I'll bring him to you straightaway."

Gloriana was half sick with relief—until it occurred to her that she might have arrived *before* her last visit to modern times, in which case Lyn would not recognize her. If there were rules governing these shifts between one century and the other, she had not been able to guess what they were.

"Yes," she said. "Please get Mr. Kirkwood."

When Lyn came rushing out of the milling crowd, clad in the grander garb of a duke or an earl, Gloriana saw in his eyes that he knew her. He looked no older or younger than before and clasped both her hands in his as he knelt to gaze up into her face. "God in heaven, Gloriana," he whispered, "I thought I'd never see you again."

Gloriana did not speak until the man who had brought Lyn to her returned to the merriment surrounding them.

"What is this place?" she whispered.

Lyn summoned up a smile. "This is a medieval fair, Gloriana. There are those of us who like to pretend, for a little while at least, that we live in your time instead of our own."

Gloriana buried her face in both hands, trembling and overwhelmed. The words of Job echoed in her mind. . . . *the thing I have most feared has come upon me. . . .*

Lyn left her for a few moments and returned with a cup of cold water, which she accepted with unsteady hands and swallowed in hasty gulps.

"You are not well, Gloriana," he said kindly, when she had finished.

She shook her head, her vision blurred by the tears of

panic and sorrow she could not restrain. "Take me away from here—please."

Lyn put an arm around her waist and gently helped her to her feet. "My car is close by," he said. "I'll drive you to the cottage and ring Janet and Marge from there."

"How much time has passed since I left?" Gloriana asked, keeping her voice low as they made their way slowly through the costumed revelers toward a parking area. Now that her mind had cleared a little, she could tell that these leggings and tunics, kirtles and wimples and cloaks, were all much too fine to be real.

Lyn looked at her in surprise, but did not slow his pace as he ushered her along. "It's been four months, Gloriana—and in all that time, I was never quite sure what had happened. I thought perhaps you'd had some sort of spell and wandered away from Janet's shop, perhaps gotten into a passing car with some maniac—Gloriana, I was frantic!"

Gloriana glared at her friend as he opened the passenger door of his vintage automobile and waited for her to get in. "You think me so moonstruck as to trust myself to a villain?"

"Never mind," he said, giving her a gentle shove into the seat. As soon as she was settled, he closed the door and came round to get behind the wheel. "Tell me what happened—*exactly.*" He started the engine and shifted the gears. "Don't leave anything out."

Gloriana meant to leave plenty out, since a good bit of her time in the thirteenth century had been spent making love with her husband. "I was working in Janet's shop when it happened," she murmured miserably, squinting in the glare of a midsummer sun. She touched the skirts of her gown and found that it was still moist with rain that had fallen seven hundred years before. "I'd climbed one of the ladders, to place a volume on a high shelf, and suddenly I had this terrible headache, as if someone had struck me with a cudgel. I was blinded, and I fell. When I came round again, I was on the ground, leaning against some crofter's hut."

Lyn muttered an exclamation, then waited for her to go on.

As they drove, Gloriana related those parts of her story that were fitting for another person to hear.

*　　*　　*

Dane stood with his forehead resting on the shuddering withers of Gloriana's mare, one hand grasping the pommel of her empty saddle, the fingers of the other entangled in the coarse hair of the horse's mane. He wept silently for a long time before drawing back and dragging one arm across his face in an effort to recover his dignity.

Gloriana was gone.

One moment, she had been fine, seated on her mare's back, chiding him for feeling sorry for himself, reminding him of his responsibilities, as he looked up at her. Then she had cried out, as if in pain, and he had been terrified by the sudden waxen color of her flesh. Her head had lolled back, and she had slipped into his arms, unconscious.

He shouted her name, in his fear, but she did not hear him.

She lay convulsing on the ground for a few moments, but then, in a trice, she'd vanished, leaving no trace besides her spicy scent and the imprint of her slender body in the soft, dew-beaded grass. Dane had thrust back his head then and given a piercing, anguished shriek of protest and fury, like a wild creature snared in some cruel trap.

The mare had been startled by his cry and began prancing and nickering and tossing her head. He'd gotten hold of her just when she would have bolted, but then he'd thought again of Gloriana, mayhap gone from him forever, and lost control.

When he'd done with weeping and searched the whole of the meadow and much of the surrounding woods, hoping in vain to find her, he mounted Peleus at last, and rode back to Hadleigh Castle in a state of mute despair.

Gloriana was not ill, nor was she injured, but she was overwrought. For that reason, she allowed Marge and Mrs. Bond to strip away her gown and tuck her into her familiar bed in the spare room. Lyn gave her a superficial examination and ordered complete rest, then went out, taking the others with him.

Elaina had warned Gloriana that this would happen, that she would be taken from Dane and brought back to her own century, and so, in his cryptic way, had Romulus, the magician. Still, she had hoped not to drink from this cup, and

now she was fair crushed by heartache. Had it not been for
the babe, she might not even have wanted to survive, but
with that little life growing inside her, giving up was not
a possibility.

All the same, Gloriana ached with despondent yearning,
and she curled into a tight ball in the middle of the bed,
sheltering her babe and the broken heart that sustained
them both. She was too stricken to weep, too angry and
afraid to pray, so she just lay there, groping her way from
one breath to the next, awaiting the return of reason.

Lyn came first, bringing a syringe and a cotton ball soaked
in alcohol.

"Just a little something to make you sleep," he said with
tears in his voice, if not his eyes, as he gave Gloriana an
injection in the fleshy part of her arm. "Nothing that will
harm you or the child, so don't resist it, love. Just let go
and try to rest."

"Oh, please, Lyn," Gloriana whispered brokenly, "you
must help me—say you'll help me—"

He bent and kissed her temple. "You know you can depend on me, sweetheart."

She nodded. She *did* know that. Lyn was her friend, the
only person in the modern world who really understood her
plight, and he would never leave her. She gave herself up
to sleep and tumbled into the deepest recesses of her mind,
where half-formed dreams swam to and fro like blind fish.

When Gloriana was awakened, many hours later, by the
grinding hunger in her belly and the taxing of her bladder,
Professor Steinbeth was sitting in her room, next to the fire,
an open book on his lap.

Gloriana dashed to the bathroom to relieve herself, returning, still bundled in Lyn's toweling-cloth robe, in which
she'd slept, to collapse onto the bed again and draw the
covers up. She hoped she would not be required to enter
into conversation, for her emotional state was still very fragile indeed.

Steinbeth was having none of that. With a benign smile,
he drew his chair close to the bed and settled himself in it.
"Open your eyes, Gloriana. I know full well that you haven't
drifted off—for one thing, you are ravenous. I can hear your
stomach rumbling from here."

Having no choice, Gloriana obeyed his injunction and looked at him.

"Mrs. Bond left a plate warming for you in the oven," the old man said. "I'll get it for you, if you like."

Gloriana shook her head. She was as starved as a wild creature foraging in winter, but she feared she wouldn't be able to keep anything down. "Why are you here?" she asked.

"Because of you," the professor answered kindly. "I believe I've found something that might be of help."

She felt her heartbeat quicken with a hope that was probably unfounded. "What?" she asked.

Arthur Steinbeth produced a small, tattered book from the pocket of his suit coat and extended it to her. "Herein," he said gravely, "is an account of another's experience—one much like your own, I suspect."

Gloriana turned the volume in her hands and peered at the title, which was pressed in golden letters all but worn away by time, but she could still read it: TALES OF A WITCH'S TRAVELS THROUGH TIME.

Chapter
18

Gloriana's heartbeat tripped into a peculiar, lopsided rhythm as she held the old book close against her chest and stared at the professor in perplexity. "What is this?" she finally managed to ask in the most tremulous of voices.

Arthur Steinbeth smiled in a fatherly way. "I believe, my dear, that it might be your ticket back to that beloved husband of yours, and that bloody century you seem to hold so dear." He paused, while Gloriana squirmed to sit further up on the bed, still clutching the witch's memoirs. "That isn't the original volume, of course—I found that particular copy in 1929, I believe it was. Fascinating stuff, though difficult for most people to grasp."

Gloriana looked at the title again—she had read it easily—but on a second examination she saw that the spellings were archaic by twentieth-century standards. With her mouth dry and her heart thundering in her ears, she turned to the first page, but the words blurred so that she could not make them out.

"This is a book of spells?" she asked with what she hoped was a subtle sniffle.

"It is the story of one woman, who lived in the latter part of the fourteenth century, as nearly as I can tell." The old man expelled a heavy sigh and slapped his hands to his thighs in a gesture of resolution. "Read the tale for yourself, Gloriana—it is beyond my powers to explain."

"But I am no witch," Gloriana said, in case such things mattered as much in this time as they had in her own.

Steinbeth stood, making ready to take his leave. "No, my dear, but you are quite the enchantress." He sighed, adjusting the lapels of his tweed suitcoat. "Be careful of Lyn's feelings, will you please? He's a good sort, and he's met a woman. They're just beginning to find their way."

Gloriana was heartened by this news, for she wanted Lyn to be happy and to find the love he deserved, but she was a little fearful too. Though she was an independent woman and planned to remain so, whether in that century or any other, she was in the twentieth now, perhaps for the remainder of her life, and she needed Kirkwood's friendship.

"I shall not interfere with Lyn's romance," she said, at long last, and a bit stiffly. A new thought occurred to her, and she looked down at the precious book, which she still clasped. "Did he knew about this volume?"

The professor cleared his throat. "I have no idea," he said. "Lyn is a scholar, as well as a physician. Doubtless he has read many books in his time, as I have, and thus cannot readily remember them all."

Gloriana said nothing. She did not allow herself to believe for a moment that Lyn would have withheld information that might be vital.

Arthur executed a little bow. "Before I go, I must thank you for verifying and recording that history for me. I wrote a check—drawn on an American bank and made out to both you and Kirkwood. I believe Lyn's sister, Janet, has kept it, with the things you left behind."

"Thank you," Gloriana said. Of course she would need money, for herself and the babe, if she could not find her way back to Dane once and for all. How ironic it was that she held a vast fortune of her own in the medieval world and was all but indigent in this one.

"Farewell, then," the professor said, and went out.

Gloriana was half wild to read the book and discover the secrets it contained, but she knew she would not be able to concentrate until she'd calmed down a little. Another irony, she thought, rising and putting on the clothes Marge or Mrs. Bond had left for her. She went out to the kitchen after that, to forage in the oven for the dinner Arthur had mentioned, and quickly realized that the cottage was empty, except for her.

She sat down at the table to eat and found the food tasty and quite wholesome, if a little on the dry side. It was certainly an improvement over the crude and ofttimes unsanitary fare of her own century, and she knew she would miss it—along with the ready and seemingly endless supply of hot water and the miracles of modern medicine.

After finishing her meal, Gloriana washed the plate and utensils and put them in their proper places in the cupboard, then went back to her room and curled up in the chair in front of the hearth to read the book Professor Steinbeth had given her.

It was a short volume and crystal clear to Gloriana. She devoured it whole, in great, wide-eyed mental gulps, before turning back to the first page and beginning all over again.

The author never gave her name, but that was of no moment to Gloriana, who felt a kinship with the long-dead woman because their experiences were so similar.

The "witch" had been born in the fourteenth century, just as Professor Steinbeth had said earlier. As a child, she was sent to the abbey near Hadleigh Castle to study, and while wandering the grounds one day, she had passed through a gate and immediately suffered a headache so crippling that she had fallen to her knees, retching and blinded by the pain.

When her vision cleared, the little girl found herself in the same and yet a very different place, a world pulsing with sound and fury. She had been taken to an orphanage by the authorities, where she was well cared for and soon adopted by a middle-aged couple, who were devoted to her.

Gloriana felt a pang reading that part, for the story was so like her own, except that the time periods were reversed. When dear Edwenna became her mother, she had known the first true happiness of her life. Whatever befell her, she would always be grateful to a kind Fate for delivering her into the hands of that gentle woman to raise.

At no time had Gloriana missed her true parents, and

even now she felt no curiosity about them, no desire to establish contact, though she sometimes wondered what they'd made of her initial disappearance, so long before. Had they mourned her, or worried—or, more likely, simply been relieved that she was no longer their responsibility, even indirectly?

Gloriana laid a hand to her abdomen, just beginning to swell in accommodation of the child, and silently vowed that her son or daughter would never have to question her love, even for a moment. But a new fear presented itself in the wake of that silent promise: there was a possibility that, once this babe was born, the two of them could be separated, just as she had been torn from Dane's side.

She closed her eyes, feeling sick, and then forcibly turned her thoughts back to the book before her. The woman had grown up in the twentieth century, married, and moved to America, where she pursued a career as a teacher and poet. On occasion, she had returned to England and stood near the ruins of the abbey gate, working up her courage to pass over into an earlier time. Although she had been happy in her new identity, she had yearned for a glimpse of the friends she had known within the sacred walls.

In this enterprise, however, she was unsuccessful; on the first visit, she found only primeval forest where the nunnery should have been. On the second expedition, she arrived in the year 1720.

The woman had returned to the twentieth century and resumed her life, never to make the transfer again. Her conclusion was that, having found its rightful place in the universe, her spirit had chosen to settle itself there.

A little disappointed that there was no talisman mentioned, no magic potion that would carry her back to Dane, never to be parted from him again, Gloriana was nonetheless certain that she had found a way to go home.

She was tired, but could not rest, for her mind was abuzz with reckless schemes. She would put on her own gown, she decided, so as not to stand out unduly when she reached her destination. She had only to find that star-crossed gate again, in whatever state of ruin it might be, and step over the threshold.

There was, of course, no guarantee that she would not

arrive at the wrong time in history, as the woman in the book had done. Still, she had to try—something inside pressed her toward that end, something separate from her love for Dane, but just as deeply rooted in her soul. She felt a new urgency to return, sensing that she might never have another opportunity.

Leaving behind an oxblood ruby set in a ring of woven gold, the only piece of jewelry she'd been wearing when she'd suffered her last spell and left Dane calling her name in that rain-dampened meadow, Gloriana took various medicines from Lyn's surgery cupboards and the well-stocked medicine cabinet in the bathroom, along with a thick book on first aid, a volume on herbal remedies, and, finally, a small amount of cash from a leather box on his desk in the study.

She left a note for Lyn, apologizing for the necessary thefts and expressing the hope that the gem she'd left would suffice as compensation, along with Professor Steinbeth's check, which he was to keep for himself and use as he saw fit. After thanking Lyn for all his help and bidding him a life of joy, she signed the paper and hurried out of the cottage, carrying the purlioned items in a plastic grocer's bag.

The money covered her cab fare to the ruins of the abbey, which, like Kenbrook Hall and Hadleigh Castle, was little more than rubble now.

The summer sun shone bright on Gloriana as she made her way between the broken walls and uneven paving stones, searching for that one special place—it must have been near Elaina's courtyard—where she had crossed over as the child Megan. She prayed silently all the while that the magic would still work, that she might find her right place in time and never have to leave it again.

When she found what was left of the gate, however, she hesitated, her heart thudding in her throat, for there was a sense of permanence in this undertaking. She could not help glancing back at the world she hoped to depart and never to look upon again. She did not want to live there, and yet she had no doubt that the place would seem very good to her if she missed her mark and wound up in the wrong niche of time.

Then, resolved, clutching her bag of stolen miracles, Gloriana squared her shoulders, raised her chin, and walked through.

Nothing happened.

There was no headache, no darkness, no change at all. The world looked the same as it had before—a jet passed overhead, leaving a stream of white across the azure sky, and out on the paved highway beyond the crumbled outer walls, a car tooted its horn.

Gloriana stood still for a long moment, dealing with her disappointment. Then she recalled the witch's tale, and decided to try again. She would simply go back to where she'd started and pass through the gate once more.

She drew a deep breath and stepped forward.

This time, the world seemed to tilt at a dizzying angle, though only for a moment. There was no pain, no black sickness, only a violent inner shift that made her breath catch and her heart skitter over a few beats.

The walls rose whole and high around Gloriana, and the sky was darkening with twilight. She heard the nuns singing their lovely chants in chapel—vespers—and swallowed a sob of mingled relief and dread. There was no way to know what year or century she was in, and instinct warned her not to make herself known.

Gloriana made her way out of the abbey through a postern gate and immediately turned her gaze toward Kenbrook Hall. It looked much as it had when she and Dane had been imprisoned there and conceived their child in the Roman baths hidden beneath, but that was no indication that she had managed to return during her husband's lifespan. The hall had been a fortress for the legions once and had not changed greatly over a period of nearly eight hundred years.

Biting her lower lip, Gloriana turned to Hadleigh Castle and the lake. There were lights blinking in some of the windows, but it was already eventide and growing darker by the moment.

Carefully, Gloriana tied the plastic bag up under the skirts of her gown, affixing it to the lacework in her chemise.

There was but one way to find out if Dane yet lived, and Gloriana's suspense was too great to put the task off until the morrow. Following the hidden path through the woods and around the lake that she and Edward had blazed as children, she proceeded toward Hadleigh Castle and her destiny.

Moonlight spilled over the waters, but Gloriana did not stop to admire its silvery dance, as she might have on another occasion. Her mind was fixed on finding Dane, and naught else.

Perhaps that was why the rider was almost upon her before she realized she was not alone on the path. With a little cry, Gloriana jumped to one side just before she would have been trampled by a horse.

"Who goes there?" demanded a familiar voice, as the rider reined in and then leaped deftly to the ground to face her. "God's breath, Gloriana—*is that you?*"

Edward! Joyous tears rushed into Gloriana's throat, all but choking her and making it impossible to speak. With a sob, she flung her arms around his neck and planted copious kisses all over his face. *Edward.*

He was alive.

He thrust her back to look at her, his eyes narrowed, his exquisitely drawn features gelded with moonglow. "Have you gone mad, wandering about in the dark like this? And where have you been—we've searched the whole of the countryside for you!"

Gloriana struggled to regain her composure, but there was no succeeding—all she could do was laugh and weep and snuffle ingloriously. Edward stood before her, hale and hearty, which meant that Dane and Gareth and dear, dear Elaina were yet among the living. By the grace of God and His angels, she had managed to return in time to make a difference.

"Well, I'd better get you back to home and hearth," Edward said, sweeping her up onto the horse and mounting deftly behind her. "Dane is certain that Merrymont has kidnapped you, and if Gareth hadn't locked him up in the dungeon, he'd be out tearing the man's holdings apart stone by stone, searching for you."

Gloriana rested her head against Edward's shoulder and laughed insensibly before lapsing into a spate of hiccoughs. "Just—take me—home," she managed to say, and Edward reined his mount back toward Hadleigh Castle and spurred the animal with the soft heels of his boots.

"How long have I been missing?" Gloriana asked, in a small voice, when they were passing over the drawbridge and into the lower bailey, where the tournaments were held.

Edward looked even more worried than he had before. "You don't know where you've been, or what you were doing?"

She hesitated while the sights and sounds of her beloved world entered her through every pore and follicle. "No," she admitted as they progressed through the village at a slower pace.

"You were walking in the graveyard at Kenbrook Hall yesterday morning," Edward said. "Your handmaiden, Judith, was bringing you a wrap, and bent on begging you to come back in and sit beside the fire. Something distracted her— just for a moment, she swears—and when she looked again, you had vanished."

Yesterday morning. For all that had happened, or seemed to happen, in the interim, she had actually been separated from Dane for only about thirty-six hours! He would not remember her last visit, when she had been parted from him in the meadow behind Kenbrook Hall; for him, that had never happened. Neither, of course, had his fatal encounter with Edward. Hadleigh's fever had not come upon him, and Elaina was surely as well as could be expected, given the chronic nature of her illness.

"I—I must have struck my head," she said, for she could not tell Edward or anyone else what had really happened. Even Dane must remain in ignorance, for he would not believe the truth.

"You are safe now," Edward replied with supreme gentleness, "and that is all that matters. Kenbrook will be beside himself with joy."

No doubt apprised by watchful guards that Edward was returning with Lady Kenbrook in tow, Gareth was standing in the private courtyard when they arrived. He was attended by several men-at-arms, who held torches aloft. A servant stood nearby with an oil lamp.

"Where is Kenbrook?" Edward asked. "I have brought his wife."

Gloriana slipped down from the saddle before anyone could help her, even before Edward, himself an expert horseman, had managed to dismount. She gave her elder brother-in-law a greeting similar to Edward's, flinging her arms around his neck and planting a great, smacking kiss on each of his cheeks.

"You're alive!" she crowed.

Gareth gripped his erstwhile ward by the shoulders and held her at arm's length, searching her face. "God's blood, Gloriana—of *course* I am alive! It is you we'd nearly given up for dead. Where in the name of all that's holy have you been?"

"She was wandering and does not remember passing the day and night," Edward said. "I found her in the woods."

"Have you lost the ability to speak for yourself?" Gareth demanded, his fingers tightening a little on Gloriana's shoulders.

"No, my lord," Gloriana answered, suppressing a smile. She must remember, she told herself, that from the viewpoint of those left behind, she had been gone only a short time. "May I see my husband, please? I'm told that you've locked him up to keep him from murdering Merrymont."

"Aye," Gareth said, with no hint of remorse, snatching a lamp from one of the men and dismissing the others with a nod. "He's in the dungeon, my brother. It was that or have him storming the walls of our neighbor's keep and taking an arrow from Merrymont's crossbow for his trouble." With this explanation, Lord Hadleigh put his free hand lightly to the small of Gloriana's back and steered her into the castle and through the great hall. Edward kept pace, walking in silence on her other side.

"I appreciate your efforts to protect my husband," Gloriana said to the lord of Hadleigh Castle, "but I can't imagine that imprisonment has done his character any good. He'll be fit to throttle you for holding him captive in such wise."

Gareth gave his sister-in-law a dour, sidelong look. "No explanation will be required of me," he said, putting a pointed emphasis on the last word. "Duty demands that I warn you, Lady Kenbrook—my brother won't settle for this silly prattle you've given Edward about wandering in the woods, lost and confused, for the better part of two days. He will demand to know what you've been about."

Gloriana felt a certain sweet uneasiness, but she was too eager to see Dane again to waste time worrying. She would deal with his inevitable irritation somehow.

They entered a passage behind the great hall, leading down a steep set of stairs, cut spiral fashion in the stone. The light of several torches made a golden pool at the foot of the steps, and Gloriana heard her husband's voice even before she saw him.

"Gareth, if that's you," Dane called, from somewhere below, "you'd better be bringing the key to these damnable irons, for if you're not, I swear I'll have your liver before cock's crow!"

Gloriana's heart soared, and she hurried down the steps, leaving Gareth and Edward behind, and raced into the dungeon. She had never been in the place before and might have been fascinated if her attention hadn't been fixed on the solitary prisoner.

Dane sat, disheveled and plainly annoyed, in a pile of fresh straw near one of the dank walls, and he was chained to the wall by one ankle and one wrist. At the sight of Gloriana, he started to rise, but she didn't give him a chance. She nearly flattened him with the exuberance of her embrace.

"Gloriana," he said, and the ancient iron chains rattled as he raised his hands to cup her face. He must have felt the odd bundle under her skirts but, mercifully, he said nothing of that. "Oh, God, Gloriana—*where have you been?*"

She kissed his mouth, his eyelids, his cheeks and forehead. "I'll explain later," she said.

Dane's handsome face hardened, though the love in his eyes was not lessened by his anger. "You will indeed, my lady wife," he said. "At length and in great detail."

Gloriana nodded, trying to look meek. "Yes, my lord," she answered, but there was no trace of true humility in her tone or manner, and the fact did not go unnoticed by anyone in that terrible room. She turned a sharp gaze upon her brothers-in-law, who had no earthly idea that they had been, in effect, resurrected from their graves. "Unlock these chains immediately."

"Contentious woman," Gareth grumbled. But he produced a rusted key from the pouch tied at his belt—the dungeons at Hadleigh Castle were seldom used, and torture had been outlawed many years before—then squatted to work the locks, which resisted his awkward efforts for so long that Dane finally took over the task.

Gareth and Edward wisely took their leave before their angry brother had managed to free himself, and thus Gloriana was at last alone with her husband.

She wanted to have her way with him in the straw, she'd missed him so terribly, but for him the separation had not been overlong, and now that he knew she was safe, he was furious.

"I will ask you once again, woman," he said, rising and pulling Gloriana to her feet as he did so. *"Where have you been since yesterday morning?"*

Gloriana wished she'd taken the trouble to think up a viable tale to explain her absence, but she'd been too caught up in the evening's reunions to do so. Besides, until she'd encountered Edward by the lake, she hadn't known what she would find when she reached Hadleigh Castle. Dane's ancestors might have been living there, or even his descendants.

"I could tell you on the morrow," she offered hopefully. "When we've both had a good night's rest."

"You will tell me now," Dane replied, folding his arms. Although he did not say so, Gloriana suspected he had other plans for the hours ahead, and sleep was not among them.

Gloriana was beginning to lose patience. She loved this man enough to cross the very borders of time to live out her days at his side, but if she allowed him to bully her, she would be setting a disastrous precedent. Dane St. Gregory might as well learn, right now, what she would put up with and what she wouldn't.

"Take care, my lord," she told him angrily, "that I don't refuse to speak to you altogether. I am not your dog, your squire, or one of your men-at-arms!"

Dane shoved splayed fingers through his hair, which needed barbering, as always, and was filled with bits of straw that glittered in the shifting light of the torches affixed to the walls. His frustration was nearly palpable, but he was making an admirable effort to restrain his temper.

"Explain," he rasped through his teeth.

"What will you do if I refuse?" Gloriana challenged, putting her hands on her hips and squaring her nose with his. "Give me a good drubbing? Banish me to the nunnery?"

Dane opened his mouth, then closed it again. He was utterly magnificent, Gloriana thought, even in a state of fury. "God's breath," he spat, "you know I would never strike a woman, be she wife or whore or both—and as for banishing you, there probably isn't a convent in the realm deserving of such a fate!"

Gloriana tried to retain a fierce expression but, in the end, she couldn't do it. Dane was being impossible, of course, but she was simply too glad to see him to remain angry. She started to laugh, and when he glared at her, she laughed harder.

Finally, after a muttered curse, Kenbrook wrapped her in his arms, spun her about once in celebration of her return, and then kissed her soundly.

"I'm sorry you were frightened," she said in an unsteady voice, when Dane released her at last. "I didn't mean to leave you."

Dane's look penetrated deep, searching her soul. "I believe that, milady," he said gravely. "I can't think why I should, but I do."

"I love you," Gloriana said with a sniffle. Her vision was blurring again. She wondered if she needed spectacles, then concluded that they probably hadn't been invented yet.

"And I love you," Dane responded, touching the tip of her nose with an index finger. "Are you all right, Gloriana? Were you hurt, or sick?"

She shook her head. "No," she said softly.

He frowned, his hands resting gently on her upper arms. "That day in the tower room, when you vanished for a few moments—was it something like that?"

Gloriana swallowed, then nodded.

"You were in the future, then?"

"Yes."

Dane sighed and clasped her close against his chest, as though fearing that she would be torn right out of his arms.

Gloriana wanted to reassure him and drew back slightly to look up into his face. "It won't happen ever again," she said.

"How can you be sure of that?" Dane demanded.

"This time was different," she answered. It was not the proper moment to tell Dane about her other visit, to what would have been his future, when both Edward and Gareth had been dead and they had been together in Elaina's cell at the abbey, keeping a sorrowful vigil. Even so, Gloriana could not resist showing off a little of the knowledge she had gained on that particular excursion. "I am told you wanted to kill your uncle, thinking he had taken me captive."

"My uncle?" Dane spoke firmly, but he could not hide his surprise.

"Merrymont," she said. "Your mother, Jillian, was his younger sister, wasn't she?"

Dane looked as though she'd struck him. "Did Gareth tell you this?"

"No," she said, in all truth. "I found it out in my travels."

He sighed, rubbing his wrist where the irons had chafed the flesh. "You are past understanding, woman," he said. " 'Tis a good thing I am a patient man."

"You are anything but 'a patient man,' " Gloriana countered, moving toward the stairs and trusting her newly freed husband to follow, which, of course, he did. "I fear your temperament is oft unsavory, and wants a great deal of work."

Behind her, Dane made a contemptous sound. "While yours, my lady," he drawled, "is beyond reproach, a shining example to lesser souls, such as I."

Gloriana looked back at him. "Thank you," she said, as if he'd meant the words as a compliment. "For all your foibles and shortcoming, my lord, you can, with effort, be a charming fellow on occasion."

He gave her bottom a light pinch. "And tonight," he said, "is going to be one of those occasions."

The bag rustled and bulged beneath her gown, at thigh-level.

"What *is* that?" Dane asked, in a baffled rasp.

Gloriana pretended she hadn't heard the question. There was clearly no need to keep secrets from her husband, but if any of the servants or men-at-arms were to become curious, the results could be tragic.

*   *   *

274

In Dane's chamber, the fire had been lighted and the covers turned back on the bed. There was water for washing, and because word of Gloriana's "rescue" by brave Sir Edward had surely reached everyone within the castle's far-reaching walls, one of Lady Kenbrook's favorite dressing gowns had been laid out for her use.

Dane closed the door once they were inside, lest they be interrupted by Judith or some other well-meaning maid, and stood facing his wife with one brow raised. He did not need to speak; his countenance said everything.

Gloriana blushed slightly and brought the bag out of its awkward hiding place, offering it to him, holding it out wordlessly for his inspection.

Kenbrook accepted, his frown deepening as he rubbed the thin plastic back and forth between his thumb and two fingers. After a glance at Gloriana, he took the strange pouch to the bed and upended it upon the mattress, causing the things inside to spill out in a colorful jumble.

One by one, he examined the books, the bottles containing vitamins and various wonder drugs, such as aspirin and mild antibiotics. He examined the tubes of toothpaste, in their bright cardboard boxes, and unstrung a length of the dental floss, his brow still knitted in consternation.

Gloriana laughed softly. "Be careful with that, my lord husband," she teased. "It has to last more than six hundred and fifty years."

Dane put the floss down, still glowering, and took up one of the books. After touching the smooth paper and examining the many-colored pictures inside, he raised his eyes to Gloriana again in frustration and wonder. "I cannot make out these words," he complained. "What language is this?"

She went to him and kissed his cheek. "English," she said, her eyes dancing.

Dane peered at the dark, even print again, then slammed the book closed. For all its violence, the gesture was somehow reverent, too. "Can you read it?" he asked. He did not relinquish the volume, but instead held it tightly in both hands.

Gloriana nodded. "It will come to you plain, my lord, when you've studied the letters a while."

"Tell me about this," he said, shaking a plastic pill bottle.

"Medicine for fevers and infection," Gloriana said. While in Lyn's care and keeping, she had read many of his medical journals and overheard his telephone conversations with patients and the local chemist.

Dane dropped both bottle and book, as if they'd burned his flesh. "God's breath, Gloriana, if anyone hears you talking so, you'll be put to the stake for serving Satan."

"But you won't let that happen, will you, Dane?" Gloriana asked, feeling a little thrill of fear as she stood close to her husband and put her arms about his neck. "You promised to pierce my heart with an arrow, before matters reached such a pass."

He went white. "I made no such vow," he breathed.

And, of course, he was right. The oath had been offered in another time, a tributary of the future that they would now bypass completely.

Gloriana simply looked at him, asking a new pledge by her silence.

"I will not see you suffer," Dane said gravely, after a very long time. "No matter what I have to do to prevent it." He drew her close, and she felt his mood lighten, even as other parts of him grew noticeably heavier, harder. He glanced briefly at the magical items lying on the bed. "I mean to learn what there is to know about your books and medicines," he said. "But just now, my lady wife, I wish to study other things."

Chapter

19

Gareth stood on the dais in the great hall, holding his tankard of ale high in the air. His voice boomed, joyous, through that vast, drafty chamber, from the rush-covered stone floor to the huge oak beams supporting the ceiling.

"Milady Gloriana has returned to hearth and husband," he thundered. "Let us rejoice, one and all, and give thanks to heaven that she was spared from harm."

Gloriana sat at Dane's side, at the head table, her eyes lowered, her breathing shallow and quick. She would have preferred that little be made of her homecoming; too much ado was bound to stir speculation and remind people of her strange disappearance. Their theories concerning the vanishing of Lady Kenbrook could only be dangerous.

There was murmuring among the soldiers and servants, but the company lifted their own tankards in acknowledgment of the celebration, and the evening meal went noisily on.

Music flowed, merry, tinkling stuff, from the minstrels' gallery overhead, and a mummers' troupe moved between the tables, capering, juggling, playfully snatching the occasional boiled turnip or bit of roasted meat from a trencher. Gloriana scanned the painted faces for Romulus or Corliss, but did not find them—these performers were strangers, then, and not members of the company she had met on her last visit.

Said visit having never occurred at all, if one wanted to be precise. It was difficult and confusing, having memories of a time that no one else shared. And how could they remember, when none of those events had actually happened?

"What is it?" Dane asked, startling Gloriana out of her convoluted reflections. He was seated beside her at the head table, but had forsworn the wine everyone else was drinking for plain water.

"I am uneasy, my lord," Gloriana confessed, looking at his cup and frowning. Given the state of thirteenth-century sanitation, she figured he would have been far better off drinking the wine. "Something troubles me, but I cannot account for it."

Kenbrook smiled, speared a roasted carrot from a bowl, and plopped it onto her empty plate. "Little wonder that you are distracted, my lady wife," he said. "You haven't taken a bite."

With a sigh, Gloriana pretended to nibble at the over-cooked vegetable. She felt a strange, almost heady tension thrumming in the air, flowing beneath the surface of the happy music and so vibrant, so charged with portent, as to be nearly audible.

Normally, Gloriana took care to nourish herself properly, whether she wanted food or not, because of the baby. That evening, the first following her return from the twentieth century, she could not force herself take so much as a bite.

Something was going to happen.

She looked down the table, to her left, and saw Edward and Mariette engaged in quiet conversation, their youthful faces translucent with affection. Eigg and Friar Cradoc were at the other end of the board, talking with Gareth, who had by then returned to his seat of honor as lord of the castle. Nothing was amiss, as far as Gloriana could discern, and yet . . .

Suddenly, the music stopped, but only after a great, silent crescendo, which couldn't have lasted more than a moment or two, yet seemed to reverberate through the whole of the keep. This was followed by a whistling hiss, projected from the minstrel's gallery.

With an ominous thump, an arrow lodged itself in the thick wood of Lord Hadleigh's table and quivered there, its thin, pliant shaft still making a faint, resonant sound. It was directly in front of Kenbrook.

A furor erupted; Dane's fighting men, and Gareth's, overturned the benches at the trestle tables, so fast did they rise, arming themselves as they moved. Kenbrook drew his sword and, in virtually the same motion, tried to thrust Gloriana to the floor. She resisted and saw the mummers produce blades of their own from beneath their cloaks and costumes, the angry knights of Hadleigh and Kenbrook in immediate and fierce battle.

The servants screamed and fled, the hounds whined and scattered, and high in the minstrels' gallery, one false musician stood, bow raised, quiver upon his back, ready to send a rain of arrows onto the inhabitants of the great hall.

The man was somehow familiar, though Gloriana was certain she had never seen him before. His hair was the same pale shade of gold as Dane's, his eyes, even from that distance, were plainly the same icy blue.

Gloriana felt a dizzying rush of sheer terror, followed by indigntion. After all she had been through, being taken from her husband to a strange century, struggling to return, this knave thought to end her happiness before it had truly begun.

She wouldn't have it.

"Hold!" shouted the man in the gallery, in a voice of authority. He was finely dressed in a green velvet doublet and hose dyed to match and looked to be about the same age as Gareth.

The clamor of warfare ceased instantly as both sides raised their eyes to him in wonder, in consternation, in awe.

Nobody, including Dane, Gareth, and Edward, was moving. If someone didn't take action soon, all would certainly be lost.

Disgusted, Gloriana clasped her eating knife, the only weapon at her disposal, and moved a little closer to Dane, who was looking up, his face an unreadable mask, his powerful muscles frozen as he readied himself to fight. He did not seem afraid, only alert, but there could be no doubt of his fury. He radiated anger, exuded it from his very pores.

"Who is that?" Gloriana whispered.

"Merrymont," Kenbrook replied, spewing the name from his mouth as if it tasted foul.

Gloriana looked at the invader with renewed fascination. This, then, was the dreaded foe, the mad uncle who had wished to murder Dane in his cradle out of grief for his lost sister, Jillian.

She eased away from the table, drawing no notice from her husband or anyone else.

"What do you want?" she heard Gareth demand as she moved along an inner wall, where the light of the oil lamps did not quite reach. His voice was low and fierce.

"I have come," answered the lord of Merrymont, "to avenge my good name."

Gloriana made her way up a rear staircase and along a secondary passage draped with cobwebs and littered with the bones of mice and birds. She and Edward had played in that seldom-used corridor often as children, pretending that the castle was under siege and they alone could save it. Knowing Gareth would have the hallway sealed off if he learned of its existence, they had kept it as a secret between themselves.

Standing in the shadows, holding her breath and clutching her pitiful blade in one hand, Gloriana assessed the situation. It was not a heartening one.

There were two burly guards outside the gallery, swords drawn, eyeballs gleaming white in the musty gloom. Gloriana sensed their fear and understood it: they were within the walls of an enemy holding, after all, and therefore in obvious peril. They were also superstitious men, as befit their time, and almost surely wondering what vengeful shades and spirits might lurk in the seemingly impenetrable darkness.

Beyond them, inside the gallery, Merrymont was still speaking; Gloriana saw the back of his velvet doublet and the leather quiver filled with arrows and thought, *He's really quite splendid. It's a pity he isn't on our side.*

"You refuse, Kenbrook, to apologize for defaming me all over the realm, calling me a kidnapper and even a murderer?" the man demanded. His arrogance made him resemble Dane even more than his coloring and build.

Gloriana bit her lower lip. Dane would surely be too stubborn to admit remorse, she expected, though for a moment she indulged in the vain hope that the problem might be resolved peacefully.

"Yes," Kenbrook replied, in a clear voice. "I refuse."

Gloriana picked up something from the floor, being careful not to see what it was, and tossed it into the deeper shadows. The guards advanced hesitantly upon the sound, prepared to fight. Before they could turn around, Lady Kenbrook was inside the gallery, with the knife pressed into the small of Merrymont's back.

"Order your men-at-arms to put down their swords and daggers," she said evenly, "or I shall skewer your kidneys like a pair of hens on a spit."

Merrymont stiffened, then chuckled, down low in his chest. But she had not reckoned on his strength or his swiftness. In the length of a heartbeat, he had knocked the blade from her hand with a motion of his elbow and gripped her in both arms, holding her with her back pressed against his chest.

Gloriana's breath stopped in her lungs and throat as the baron swung her out over the stone railing of the gallery, her feet dangling at least thirty feet over the hard floor of the great hall. If he dropped her, she would not survive the fall.

"Your lady wife is indeed brave, Kenbrook, if foolhardy," Merrymont called down to a grim-faced Dane. "Had I known she had such a fiery spirit, nephew, I should surely have been guilty of the crime of which I was accused. Such a luscious morsel begs kidnapping."

"You have your apology," Dane said, not very charitably.

Gloriana was not only scared, but irritated. Couldn't he see that this was no time for truculence?

"Damn you, Merrymont," Gareth put in, from somewhere outside Gloriana's dazed range of vision, "this is an outrage—"

Merrymont's grip was tight, a fact for which Gloriana was eternally grateful, although she of course regretted that she hadn't stabbed the blackguard when the chance afforded itself. "Just moments ago, Kenbrook, you begrudged me that simply courtesy," he said in his loud, melodic voice. "Now, suddenly, you are willing to humble yourself?"

"Yes," Dane answered without hesitation.

Gloriana squeezed her eyes shut. If she hadn't been so afraid of falling, she might have felt some remorse herself, for putting Dane in such a position. He would be required to humiliate himself if he wished to save her.

"Excellent," Merrymont replied, holding Gloriana with just one arm now and brandishing his sword with the other. "I shall have my vengeance on the field of honor," he called to Kenbrook. "When I'm finished with you, you will lower yourself to one knee, lay your blade at my feet, and call me 'my lord.'"

Dane did not reply, though Gloriana knew he was holding back a scorching reply for her sake. She was, after all, still dangling over the great hall like a butchered stag hung from a rafter when the hunt was over.

"There is one more penalty," Merrymont decreed happily, in apparent afterthought. "If you should lose our contest, nephew, the lovely Gloriana will live in my keep and be my ward for as long as I wish to enjoy her company."

Even from that terrible height, Gloriana saw pure wrath move up Dane's neck to pulse in his face. Under the circumstances, he probably would have agreed to anything, but she knew her husband, knew he was aching to get his hands on Merrymont's throat. Furthermore, if by some miracle they both survived this predicament, Kenbrook was sure to be almost as furious with her as he was with his uncle.

"If I lose," Kenbrook said with just the faintest emphasis on the word *if,* "it shall be as you say."

Gloriana began to kick and struggle at this, her terror replaced by ire. Merrymont drew her back over the railing with ease, but did not release his hold on her waist. "Very good," he said to Dane in the most patronizing of tones. "I'm sure you'll understand if I keep milady with me, until I've reached the sanctuary of my own walls and roof. Our little tournament will be held there, on the morrow."

"Leave my wife here," Dane said. The words were uttered clearly, and they made a command, not a plea. "You shall have your contest, on whatever terms you name."

"Ah, but I have already stated my terms," Merrymont answered. "The lady will accompany me. What is it, Kenbrook? Do you dare malign my honor further, even now, by suggesting that this lovely creature would not be safe in my care?"

Gloriana had given up the struggle against the baron; he was too strong, and to resist his hold would be a waste of valuable energy. Looking down at her husband, who stood white-faced in the center of the great hall, his sword still clasped, battle ready, in his right hand, she willed Dane to hold his tongue.

A muscle in Kenbrook's jaw tensed visibly as he fought to maintain control.

It was Gareth was shouted a rash vow. "If you harm that girl, Merrymont," he bellowed, "I'll cut out your organs, while you yet live!"

"Methinks you would do that anyway, if given the chance," Merrymont responded. Then he swept out of the gallery and down the passage, carrying Gloriana in his arms, flanked by the two guards.

"You do realize," she said as he strode down a staircase where more of his men waited, "that what you are doing is hypocritical? You came to Hadleigh Castle to protest being called a kidnapper, and now here you are, living up to the name!"

"If you are quiet," Merrymont told her reasonably, "I won't have to gag you."

Gloriana flushed and resisted speaking until they were outside, though it was difficult. There were men on the parapets, with bows drawn and arrows trained on the invaders, but no one dared shoot for fear of striking Kenbrook's wife.

Horses were waiting in the courtyard; the band of men, led by Merrymont himself, rode through the village and the outermost bailey as boldly as if they'd been invited guests. Gloriana rode sidesaddle, in front of her husband's uncle.

"This is all too much," she said.

Merrymont glared down at her with eyes so like Dane's that Gloriana thought she could have liked the man if he hadn't been abducting her. "You are determined to make conversation," he said. "Perhaps I have made an error in stealing you."

"You most assuredly have," Gloriana said with conviction.

"If you had any idea of what I've gone through to be with Lord Kenbrook, you would give up this nasty enterprise out of sheer sympathy."

She thought she saw a smile hiding in his eyes, but couldn't be sure. "What makes you think I could feel such a noble emotion as pity?"

Gloriana sighed. "We were minding our own affairs. I don't see why you had to start up a whole new feud."

"I assure you, Lady Kenbrook, I have a very good reason. Not that I intend to explain my motives to you, of course."

They rode on in silence, Gloriana gazing back over his shoulder at the lights of Hadleigh Castle and its tiny village.

"He'll come for me, you know," she said, when they had ridden into the forest, heading away from both Kenbrook Hall and Gareth's keep.

"Yes," Merrymont said, "I'm quite sure he will."

"You want to kill him," Gloriana accused, angry and more afraid for Dane than she had ever been for herself. Which wasn't entirely sane, she admitted, though only in the privacy of her own soul.

"You don't have the first idea what I want," the older man corrected easily, "and neither does that hotheaded young knight, so eager to save you."

"Are you planning to hurt me?" It seemed a sensible question, under the circumstances.

"No," Merrymont replied. "But do not provoke me. I can be pushed beyond my limits, like any other man."

"What about my virtue?"

Merrymont chuckled. "What about it?" he countered.

Gloriana blushed hotly. "I should like to know, sir, whether or not it is in peril."

This time, he laughed outright, but it was a sound void of mirth, and he almost immediately turned somber again. "Is that what Hadleigh and Kenbrook say about me—that I am a despoiler of young women? I guess I should not be surprised, or wounded—but strangely, I am."

They were pursued through the gathering night; Gloriana knew it and so, she was certain, did Merrymont. Yet no one dared attack the party of night travelers, for fear that she would be killed or injured in the fray, and after an hour or so, they clattered over a shadowy drawbridge, into what might have been a phantom courtyard, for all she could see of it.

The portcullis crashed resolutely behind them.

Merrymont gave a few brisk orders, and the soldiers vanished into the darkness. Then he swung down from the great horse and lifted Gloriana after him.

"Come along," he said brusquely. "You will want sleep."

Gloriana followed, because she had no other choice. "I am with child," she said as she attempted to keep up with Merrymont's lengthy strides. "If you cause me harm, you will also hurt the babe I carry. And Kenbrook will never rest until he kills you."

"He shall have his opportunity on the morrow, upon the field of battle," Merrymont said wearily, and did not hesitate, except to take Gloriana's elbow in a strong but painless grasp. They entered his keep, small in comparison to either Hadleigh Castle or Kenbrook Hall, and were greeted by female servants, carrying flickering lamps that cast more shadow than light. "This is my niece," Merrymont told them distractedly, as though his mind were already on other things. "Put her somewhere clean and warm."

"Yes, milord," the women said, in chorus. Gloriana squinted, but could not tell how many there were.

In the final analysis, it didn't matter, since even if she managed to overcome them all, she still couldn't escape. The walls were high, the gates were closed, and the place was full of men-at-arms, fierce despite their mummer's faces. Gloriana told herself to be content with the fact that Merrymont wasn't taking her to his own chamber.

Mayhap he had spoken true, at least in saying he was no "despoiler of young women." Unfortunately, only God and the Holy Virgin could know what *else* he might be.

Gloriana was taken to a small chamber, lit by three tallow candles. There was a berth affixed to one wall, with a mattress of rope.

"Do you want sustenance, milady?" one of the servants asked, when Gloriana had been provided with a blanket and a ewer filled with water.

"If I eat anything, I'll vomit," Gloriana responded. She had not meant to be crude; it was just that she was tired and overwrought.

The servants exited, bowing their heads as they went. The door was latched behind them and, alas, from the outside.

Gloriana sat down on her rope bed with a deep sigh. Come the morrow, Kenbrook would arrive, as instructed, delivering himself into what could only be a trap, and there was no way to save him. All their love, all their pain and longing, laughter and tears, had been for naught.

She stretched out upon the narrow berth, her eyes burning with unshed tears. *Don't do it, Dane,* she thought, knowing the hope was futile even as she cherished it in her bruised heart, *don't try to save me. For whatever reason, Merrymont means to kill you.*

Gloriana closed her eyes and yawned. She wouldn't be able to sleep, she was certain of that, even though she was weary to the center of her soul. There was too much at stake.

Her next conscious realization was that the sun was shining hot and bright in her face.

She sat bolt upright, mildly surprised to find herself in a small, strange room, before she remembered that Merrymont had kidnapped her, that today he would kill her beloved husband.

Gloriana had no doubt that even if Dane were to win the contest, whatever it was, Merrymont's men would finish him before he got to the drawbridge. Kenbrook meant to ride into the jaws of the lion, and she was the bait that would draw him to certain death.

She went to the door and hurled herself against it in frustration and fury. "Let me out of here, Merrymont!" she screamed. "Come on, you bloody coward! Are you afraid of a woman?"

The heavy portal opened so swiftly that Gloriana practically tumbled into the passage. She hastily smoothed her ruffled plumage on the threshold.

Merrymont was standing before her, looking handsome and benevolent in the morning light. His tunic was fresh, his fair hair gleamed, still wet from a washing, and his smile was broad and oddly indulgent, for a captor.

"No," he said warmly. "I am not, as it happens, afraid of you or any other woman."

Gloriana glared at him. "That is your mistake, my lord,"

she said. "If you had any sense at all, you would be terrified."

He laughed. "Kenbrook has found a match in you," he said. Then his eyes darkened, and the curve of merriment left his lips. "Would that I had been so fortunate," he said, taking Gloriana's arm, not to lead her anywhere, but to make a point. "Make yourself pretty, milady," he commanded. "Your husband is even now at the gates, with his men-at-arms, prepared to join in battle."

Gloriana wrenched free. "Why are you doing this?" she asked, her head full of horrible, graphic images of Dane suffering, Dane dying, Dane dead. "What can you possibly accomplish by engineering the death of your own sister's son?"

The questions gave Merrymont pause, and he went pale at the mention of the lost Jillian, whom he had apparently adored. He started to speak, then stopped, bracing himself against the heavy framework of the door and lowering his head while he engaged in some violent inner struggle. When at last he met Gloriana's gaze again, she could already hear the clatter of horses' hooves on stone and the raucous shouts of men.

She dashed to the window, hoping for a glimpse of Kenbrook, but all she saw was a dovecote and a fountain, long dry, broken, and etched with grayish green moss.

"Why?" she reiterated, turning to watch Merrymont's wan face as he worked to recover his composure.

"You will know soon enough," he replied, and went out.

Gloriana washed and dressed hastily, and no one barred her way when she entered the outer passageway. Encouraged, breathless with the need to reach Dane's side again, she hurried through corridors and chambers, down stairs and across large, empty rooms, until she was outdoors again.

Dane had left his army outside the walls, an act of madness as far as Gloriana was concerned. It was plain from his gaunt appearance that he had not slept, and the stubble of new beard on his jaw, coupled with the fierce expression in his eyes, made him look more like a Viking than ever. He raked Gloriana with his gaze.

"Has he done you any injury?" he asked.

Gloriana shook her head. "I have not suffered, my lord,"

she said quickly, holding back her tears. She wanted to beg Dane to rein Peleus around and go back to Hadleigh Castle, but she knew it would be useless, that indeed the very request would be an insult to this man she loved above all else.

Merrymont stood behind her, and he laid a hand to her shoulder with surprising gentleness and drew her back. Then he stepped forward, unarmed and yet revealing no evidence of fear.

"You have come alone," he said in an appraising voice, otherwise void of emotion. "I am impressed, Kenbrook. Mayhap your St. Gregory blood has not poisoned you completely."

Dane's right hand rested lightly on the hilt of his sword; Gloriana saw his fingers flex in preparation and was more afraid than ever. If he were killed now, with all they had dreamed of and all they had hoped for still before them, she would not be able to bear it.

And yet she *must* bear whatever was to come, for the sake of their child.

"I love you with the whole of my heart, Dane St. Gregory," she said.

Merrymont gestured grandly toward the open gate in a nearby wall, his gaze fixed, almost fondly, on Dane's face. "Come, Kenbrook," he said. "Let us wage our private battle and have done with it. Leave the horse—you will not need him—but bring the sword."

Dane swung down from the great beast's back, his eyes not on Merrymont's departing figure but on Gloriana's face. None of the men-at-arms who had posed as mummers the night before seemed to be about, nor, of course, were any of Kenbrook's soldiers present. It was very odd.

"And I love you, milady," Dane said.

Merrymont paused in the gateway, smiling benignly, one hand spread over his heart as if to mock the exchange. But the steel blade of his sword glittered in the morning sunlight, and Gloriana had no cause to doubt that he was an expert in its use. He was older than Dane and probably slower, but experience was on his side.

In a small, sunlit courtyard, Gloriana took a seat on a stone bench, not because she wanted to be a spectator, but because her knees refused to support her for another moment.

Kenbrook and Merrymont squared off a few yards away, swords drawn, poised to kill each other. There was a morbid magnificence to the scene, for both men were wondrously made.

Their blades made contact with an echoing clang, the noise exceeded, as Gloriana reckoned the matter, only by the pounding of her own heart. The battle began, and for a long time it was oddly graceful, a stately dance performed by two masters of the art.

With each strike of steel upon steel, Gloriana winced, but she did not look away, much as she longed to do exactly that. If Dane must fight and die, she concluded fitfully, witnessing his sacrifice was the least she could do.

Merrymont's blade struck Dane's upper thigh, leaving a crimson slash in its wake.

Gloriana stood up with a cry, and then sat down again.

The battle grew in intensity after that; soon, both Dane and his opponent were sweating, and both were bloodied. Neither would relent, however; each new wound only served to spur its recipient to a more fierce resolve.

Covering her mouth with one hand, lest she scream or vomit, Gloriana watched and prayed helplessly that Dane might be spared.

When at last the answer came, though whether from heaven or elsewhere she could not have said, Dane swung with the last of his strength and sent his uncle's sword clattering across the stones of the little courtyard. Then, pressing the point of the blade to Merrymont's throat, he rasped, "Would you have me kill you? My own mother's brother?"

Merrymont was breathing hard. His fine clothes, like Dane's, were covered with blood and dirt and sodden with perspiration. He dropped to one knee, in exhaustion rather than humiliation, and when he raised his face, to Gloriana's great amazement and probably her husband's as well, Merrymont was nearly smiling.

"I am sore weary, Kenbrook," he confessed in a composed if still breathless voice. "But I find within myself no desire to perish on the point of your wretched sword. I brought you here because I have need of an heir."

Dane was clearly even more stunned than Gloriana.

"*What?*" he demanded, looking as though he might behead his uncle after all, or at least run him through.

Merrymont rose unsteadily to his feet, and though Dane did not aid him, neither did he attempt to interfere. Gloriana, for her part, sat rigid on her spectator's bench, unable to move, afraid even to blink.

"I have had three wives," he said, "none of whom survived childbed. Nor, alas, did the poor babes they tried to bear me. You, my sister's son, are the only one to whom I might leave my holdings."

Dane sheathed his sword, but said nothing. He looked furious, as though he wanted to pounce on his uncle and throttle him.

Gloriana found her voice and the strength in her legs at last. She bolted to her feet and cried, "Why in blazes did you try to kill my husband if you wanted him for an heir?"

"A reasonable question," Merrymont allowed. A servant appeared, bearing wine, and the defeated but unhumbled baron took the unadorned wooden goblet in both hands and drank deeply. He was looking at Kenbrook when he answered Gloriana's outraged inquiry. "I would have allowed these lands to revert to the King before turning them over to a man who could not hold them. I required proof, Dane St. Gregory, fifth baron of Kenbrook, that you were fit for the task."

Dane scowled at his uncle, gesturing with one hand, when Gloriana would have uttered another angry protest, for her to be silent and stay back. "You are not yet old," he said quite grudgingly, for in its way the remark was a compliment and Dane, understandably, was not anxious to flatter his host. "Why do you need an heir now?"

Merrymont's smile was not without some lingering malice. "Not because I'm about to do you the supreme favor of dying, nephew," he said. "But when that day comes—may it be far in the future—all must be in readiness." He turned his gaze to Gloriana, and this time there was a certain tenderness in his countenance as he bowed his head to her. "You, my lady, are a fit mistress for *any* holding, with your courage and your beauty and your incredible loyalty to the man you love."

Gloriana was not about to say thank you. She glared at Merrymont, flushed, and moved to Dane's side.

He put an arm around her as they walked to where Peleus had been waiting, scanned the parapets for marksmen, and then hoisted Gloriana onto the horse's back before swinging up behind her and taking the reins in one hand. The other rested, once again, on the hilt of his sword, sheathed though it was.

"Tell me," the uncle said, looking up at his nephew, "what will you call yourself, when Gareth and I are gone and you are master of three of the greatest estates in the realm? Will you be Hadleigh or Merrymont?"

"I will be Kenbrook," Dane replied quietly. Then he reined the great beast toward the gates, and no one tried to stop the master and mistress as they rode out of the keep, together at last, and for all of time.

Epilogue

Kenbrook Hall, several months later ...

The furious squall of young Aric St. Gregory, one day
to become sixth baron of Kenbrook, heir to the estates of
Merrymont and Hadleigh as well, rang through the small
hall outside the tower room, loud with wrath and full of
strength. Dane, who had been pacing the small corridor for
most of the morning, bolted toward the chamber door at the
sound, only to be halted by Merrymont on one side and Gareth on the other. Edward might have been there, too, but
for his recent marriage to Mariette de Troyes; they were off
on a wedding journey to London Town.

"Give the women a few moments to do their work, lad,"
Gareth counseled gently, holding tightly to Dane's arm.
" 'Tis a private matter, and they'll summon you when 'tis
proper."

Dane was all but frantic; he wanted to see the babe, of
course, but more than that, he needed to look upon Gloriana, to know she was unharmed—that she had not given
her very life to deliver a broad-shouldered St. Gregory son,
as his own fair and youthful mother had done.

"Gloriana—?" he rasped.

"—is strong." Merrymont finished for him. In the interval
since their confrontation with swords, Dane and the older

man had become friendly, after a fashion. Dane had yet to address his relative by his Christian name, which was Landry, but he knew that in time such an accord would be reached.

After what seemed the lifetime of one of those distant stars Gloriana had told Dane about, the heavy door swung open and Elaina appeared in the chasm, smiling as she regarded Kenbrook.

"Come in, milord. Your lady wife and a sturdy son await you."

Dane shrugged free of Merrymont and Gareth and might have overset his sister-in-law in his hurry to reach Gloriana and the babe, had Elaina not been quick to step back out of the way.

Gloriana lay in the great bed they had shared so happily, hair trailing, freshly brushed but still moist with her exertions, skin glowing. Her green eyes were bright with pride as she met Dane's suddenly blurred gaze.

In her arms lay the babe, swaddled now, red and ugly and roughly the size of a piglet.

Gloriana laughed at his expression and beamed as her husband bent to kiss her forehead. She had ever been able to read Dane's thoughts, and this time was no exception. "Don't worry, my love," she said. "He'll be as handsome as you are one day, and no one could ask for more than that."

"Did he hurt you?" Dane whispered. They had long since agreed, he and Gloriana, that their child would be a boy, to be called Aric in honor of an especially brave St. Gregory ancestor, but even his worst fears had not prepared Dane for the sheer size of the little brute.

Gently, Gloriana caressed the babe's fair, downy head. "Aric did nothing but get himself born," she said in a soft, weary voice. "The midwife says I'm well built for the bearing of children, and the others will come easier."

As though touching a holy relic or a part of the true Cross, Dane laid a tentative fingertip to his son's plump cheek. "There have been times," Kenbrook said reverently, "when I doubted I would live to see this day."

With her free hand, Gloriana reached up, her graceful fingers threaded through Dane's rumpled hair. "Can you stand the strain of it, milord?" she asked, teasing. "It does appear that fatherhood has already taken its toll on you."

Dane's eyes filled with tears of relief, of joy, of love. "I was never so afraid," he confessed, for Elaina and the servants had gone, and they were alone in the round tower chamber that had once, however briefly, been their prison.

"Did I not tell you I could stand childbed, and much more, Dane St. Gregory?"

"I heard you scream," he said, and shivered at the memory. He had heard other shrieks of pain, in far grimmer circumstances, but none had affected him in quite the same way Gloriana's cries had. He'd hurled himself at the door and had to be restrained.

" 'Tis natural to cry out," she said. "Yes, there's pain. A lot of it. But the screaming served more to let go of tension than anything else."

He took her fingers from his hair and kissed the knuckles, one by one. "All the same, I would sooner take the ordeal on my own shoulders than see you suffer."

She chuckled, and her bright eyes twinkled. "The man hasn't been born who could stand the birthing of a babe. God knew that and, in His wisdom, left the task to women."

There was a gentle rap at the door, and at Gloriana's summons, the Lady Elaina entered. "The wet nurse is here," she said. "Shall I take Aric to her now, before he starts to howl again?"

Gloriana smiled and nodded, though she parted hesitantly with their son, Dane noticed. In a few days, she had explained earlier, her own milk would come in, and she would feed the child herself, having read something in one of her modern, secret books about a process called bonding.

She patted the mattress beside her, and Dane stretched out on the coverlet, taking care not to jostle her, gathering her tenderly into his arms.

"I ofttimes wonder, my lady wife, why God saw fit to favor me with one such as you. Surely I am undeserving."

Gloriana kissed his forehead, much as she had kissed the babe's minutes before, and Dane reveled in her gentleness. Although he would not have admitted the fact, there was in him a little boy who loved to be coddled and caressed and might in some wise be ever so slightly jealous of the son he already adored, were it not for these private times with Gloriana. The man in him preferred her lovemaking, of course, but it would be a while before she was ready to receive him again, and he did not mind.

He felt her frown against his temple, rather than saw it, and raised his head to look into her face. "What troubles you, Gloriana?" he asked.

"Will you take a mistress, now that I have given you an heir?"

Dane hoisted himself onto one elbow, stunned and a little insulted. "What sort of question is that?" he countered. "Have I not told you a thousand, nay a million, times that I love you more than my own life?"

She gazed at him fearlessly, but there were tears in her eyes. "Gareth keeps his Annabel, in the cottage by the lake, and no man ever loved a woman more than he loves Elaina."

"Gareth reveres Elaina the way a saint does God, not as a husband cherishes a wife. I will not be untrue to you, Gloriana. I swear that on the heart of our first child and all those to come."

She sighed and snuggled closer to him, and was soon asleep.

He lay, holding his wife in his arms, until she awakened many hours later, for he did not want her to open her eyes and find him gone.

Gloriana smiled at him, and he kissed her softly on the mouth.

"You didn't leave me," she said.

"I won't," he promised. "Not ever."

Aric was eight weeks old when Gloriana had his cradle moved from the tower room to a nursery, there to be attended by the faithful Judith and the experienced wet nurse from the village, Ilsa.

Dane was out hunting that day, with Merrymont and Edward and some of his men-at-arms, and the weather was sunny and fine. Gloriana meant to use the time well, for her husband would return before vespers, and she wanted eveything to be in readiness when he arrived.

With the help of the kitchen servants, she swept the chamber and covered the floor with fresh, fragrant rushes.

The mattress was emptied and filled with fresh ticking, sprinkled through with herbs, and all the lamps were polished and filled. The bed linens were replaced, and wood was laid for a fire.

Twilight was near when the bathtub was brought up from the kitchen and filled to brimming with hot, scented water. A meal of cold meats and succulent cheeses and fruits was arrayed on the table in the center of the room, where Gloriana and Dane often played chess.

Finally, Gloriana sent all the servants away and stripped to her linen chemise. Her hair, brushed to the brightness of copper, fell free around her shoulders, the way Dane liked it.

She heard his footsteps on the stairs to the tower room and felt the familiar thrill in the center of her heart. Her breath stopped in her throat when he entered and paused on the threshold, instantly guessing the meaning of the many changes in the chamber since morning.

He set his sword aside, then closed the door, gazing at Gloriana in a way that made her feel as beautiful as any of the old goddesses. Beneath the thin cloth of her shift, her nipples hardened in anticipation of nourishing a man instead of an infant.

"I've made a bath for you, milord," she said, with a slight inclination of her head. It was a motion of both obedience and pride, for although no man would ever be her master, she knew great joy in serving this particular one.

"And I am sore in need of one, I fear," Dane said, in a husky voice. "That and much more, milady."

Gloriana crossed the scented rushes to her husband, since he seemed incapable of moving, and unfastened his sword belt. That done, she removed his tunic, pulling it off over his head, and spent a few delicious moments running her hands over his scarred and perfect chest before loosing the ties of his breeches.

"I have missed you," he whispered.

"Here is proof of that," Gloriana said, closing one hand hard around his erection.

Dane groaned as she ran her thumb round and round over the moist tip.

"But first your bath." She spoke lightly, and released him, eliciting another groan.

He was quite docile as they crossed the room, but once he'd stepped over the edge of the copper tub into the water, all that changed. "You will join me, lady wife," he said, and, taking Gloriana by the waist, brought her to stand facing him in the bath.

His kiss sent warm honey flowing through her, followed by wildfire, and she sagged a little against his chest, as starved for him as he was for her. They dropped to their knees simultaneously, the kiss unbroken until Dane drew back to drag the sodden chemise off over Gloriana's head and throw it aside.

He nibbled at her earlobes, her neck, her breasts, making her wet and wringing soft cries from her. All the while, however, Gloriana held her own, washing his pulsing staff with sweet soap, preparing Kenbrook for a conquering.

"I cannot wait for you, my love," he rasped as she rinsed him, making a delightful torment of every motion, every splash.

"But you must," she replied, and bent to her husband, taking him full into her mouth.

Dane gave a low, hoarse cry of mingled protest and pleasure, and Gloriana felt restraint in his hands as they came to rest on either side of her head. Triumph, as well as passion, swept through the mistress of Kenbrook Hall as she pleasured her husband.

She had meant to be relentless, but finally Dane put a halt to her ministerings, gasping for breath before he spoke. Expertly, he touched her in that most private and womanly of places, and found her ready for him.

"I pray you, lady," he pleaded. "Do not make me wait."

"I can wait no longer myself, milord," Gloriana replied.

Dane grasped Gloriana's hips in powerful hands and raised out of the water, impaling her on the tip of his shaft. Their eyes met in unspoken communion before he lowered her onto him, forcefully and yet without haste.

At first, they moved slowly, setting a rhythm, their bodies slick with water, meeting with a soft, smacking sound as Dane sheathed and unsheathed himself within her.

Gloriana was transported; she had yearned for this re-

union with mind and soul as well as body, and as Dane
claimed her, she leaned back in his embrace, in utter sub-
mission. He tongued the hard points of her full breasts, and
their pace increased, by increments, until water splashed
over the sides of the tub and the graceful joining turned
fierce and primitive.

Dane and Gloriana reached the point of ultimate satisfaction at exactly the same moment, and fell into each other's
arms, trembling in its aftermath. When at last she could
speak, Gloriana raised her face to her husband.

"I love you, Dane St. Gregory, in this time and all others."

He kissed her. "And I you," he replied.

And they are together still.